PERSONA NON GRATA

"My name is Nathan Crewe. I'm a Hengeli citizen. I request to see a lawyer."

The corners of her lips curled up sardonically. "A lawyer?"

Alarm prickled the hair on his neck. "Under the human rights directives of the Convention, I am entitled to legal counsel."

Vasant Subah stared at him, and rubbed her forefinger across her chin as if to stifle a laugh. "*What* Convention? Vanar never signed any Convention. You are subject to Vanar laws now. You're suspected of being a saboteur or a terrorist."

"Terrorist!" he blurted in shock. "Don't I even get a trial?"

"You've already had your trial. You've been found guilty of illegal entry."

"Fine, no problem, I admit it. So deport me."

For some reason that made her smile even wider . . .

❧   ❧   ❧

ACCLAIM *FOR*

MASTER of NONE

"Combining the gender mind-bending of Ursula K. Le Guin, the exoticism of Robert E. Howard, and a feel for aliens reminiscent of C.J. Cherryh, MASTER OF NONE offers the reader both food for thought and dessert for delectation. I recommend it to all fans of plenary world-building and absorbing sf adventure."
> **—James Morrow, author of *Only Begotten Daughter* and *Towing Jehovah***

"Of all the great books I have read on the politics, nature, and meaning of gender, this is one of the very best."
> **—Michael Moorcock, author of the Elric Saga**

MASTER of NONE

N. Lee Wood

ASPECT®

WARNER BOOKS

NEW YORK   BOSTON

Aspect
Warner Books

Time Warner Book Group
1271 Avenue of the Americas, New York, NY 10020
Visit our Web site at www.twbookmark.com.

The Aspect name and logo are registered trademarks of Warner Books.

Printed in the United States of America

First Printing: September 2004
10   9   8   7   6   5   4   3   2   1

Library of Congress Cataloging-in-Publication Data
Wood, N. Lee.
    Master of none / N. Lee Wood.
       p. cm.
    ISBN 0-446-69304-9
    1. Power (Social sciences)—Fiction. 2. Man-woman relationships—Fiction. 3. Life on other planets—Fiction. 4. Matriarchy—Fiction. 5. Botanists—Fiction. 6. Sex role—Fiction. I. Title.
    PR6073.O613M37 2004
    823'.914—dc22   2004005840

Book design by H. Roberts Design
Cover design by Don Puckey/Shasti O'Leary Soudant
Cover illustration by Dave Bowers

This one's for Jon.

MASTER of NONE

Prologue

NATHAN FOLLOWED THE *SAHAKHARAE* FROM THE MEN'S GATE INTO THE wide portico surrounding the star-shaped courtyard. Blue shadows cut the sunlight into brilliant shafts through a lace of stone, hurting his eyes. In the center of the garden, water cascaded over layers of rough, black rock into a pool. Koi flashed under the ripples, tiny shivers of striated jewels, ruby, pearl, and gold.

Two young men reclined on the grass, half hidden by the tall heads of flower blossoms nodding in the heat. Obviously infatuated with one another, their hands slipped inside undone clothing to expose smooth brown skin gleaming with sweat. They broke off their embrace and stared in silence as the sahakharae ushered Nathan along the path across the cloisterlike garden.

A dozen or so men occupied the interior courtyard. In the cool arcades around the garden edge, old men lounged against stone pillars in the shade, conversing in quiet voices. All but one were wrapped in milky blue *sati* to protect them from the sun, the gauzy edges of cloth pulled over heads to shade their wrinkled faces. Fans of colored paper warded off insects. The loner wore nothing at all, stretched naked on the lip of stone, his body sun baked to mahogany, his own sati folded neatly for use as a pillow.

As the old men caught sight of Nathan, they hushed, watching him in silence. He tried to keep his attention politely focused on the intricate braid swinging between the sahakharae's shoulders, but couldn't help glancing around the courtyard.

A group of boys sat on the fountain edge, the youngest no older than ten, a thick tumble of black hair screening his face. They laughed as they splashed each other with water, flicking wet fingers and dodging the drops. Alerted by the change in sound, they glanced around, smiles vanishing as they watched with wide, inquisitive eyes.

Nathan found it hard not to stare back. The naked man sat up, one hand shading his eyes as he squinted in the sunlight. The courtyard was so silent Nathan could hear the faint melody of birds overhead. He was acutely aware of his shabby appearance, the ragged edge of his linen sati, his own short braid and dusty bare feet.

The sahakharae extended one hand mutely to direct him to a passage leading into the dark interior. As Nathan passed the old men, he held his hands together in greeting, bowing his head in respect. The old men did not respond, but the naked man nodded a fraction in response. The youngest child by the fountain suddenly giggled, his high laugh cut short as his companions shushed him.

Nathan stumbled after the sahakharae up the curved stairway, his eyes not yet adjusted to the gloom. From outside, the Nga'esha House dominated the hill like a huge fortress, a city in miniature. The interior seemed even larger, a rambling web of arches and corridors connecting numerous wings. The sahakharae halted at a carved doorway of the main wing, pulling one side open and indicating to Nathan to go in with a graceful motion of his hand and a small bow.

Nathan stood alone as the door closed behind him. A thrill of panic shot through his gut before a door opposite opened to admit him. The woman regarding him was young, dark hair pulled back severely from around a narrow, heart-shaped face, brown eyes hard but, he hoped, not hostile. She wore loose *saekah* trousers, the bloodred sheer fabric gathered in cuffs at her ankles, the pleats of her watery blue tunic brushing just below her knees. Dozens of heavy gold bracelets stacked both arms, extending from wrist almost to elbow.

With the palms of his hands together, he pressed his crossed thumbs hard against his sternum, fingertips nearly touching his chin, exactly as he'd been taught. Keeping his spine straight, he let his head fall forward on his neck, eyes down, and stood rigidly in this awkward position.

He heard a faint staccato of breath, and realized she had laughed. When he looked up, she was smiling, her eyes crinkled in amusement. He knew he'd done something incorrect, but not what. To his relief, it didn't seem to matter much as she nodded politely toward him, signaling an invitation to enter.

Inside, she gestured toward a small fountain flowing from the wall, the pipe designed to shape the continual stream of water into a coiling arc splashing into the wide shallow basin. He had learned enough to understand by now what was expected, stepping into the basin to hold his hands under the running water, scrub briefly at his face, and wash the unclean dust of the outside from his feet.

Once ritually cleansed to her satisfaction, he followed her down the hall, her sandals and his wet bare footsteps noiseless against the thick carpet. She led him through a wide stone entry into a huge, sunny room, sunlight pouring in from double rows of arched windows supported by deceptively frail columns. Brilliant white plastered walls reflected prismed rainbows from cut glass. The smell of hot earth and honeysuckle drifting through open windows mixed with the scent of burnt incense. Long streamers of silk hung from the ceiling arched high overhead, rippling in the slight breeze, tiny brass bells sewn to weight their ends. Dark and light grains of wood wove an intricate maze on the inlaid floor, spiraling toward the center of the spacious room, the burnished wood reflecting the raised platform like an island on the surface of a still lake.

Half a dozen other women were scattered around the edges of the room, on low settees or large floor cushions, some dressed in the traditional close-fitting silk *mati* underneath lengths of shimmering blue silk elaborately folded and wrapped around slender bodies. Gold jewelry sparkled on dark skin, long black hair laced with pearls and gems. The rest wore bright saekah trousers and *kirtiya* cinched at the waist with ornate belts. One of them idly fingered a carved staff lying beside her, eying him distrustfully.

An old woman reclined on the dais, dressed only in a loose *tasmai*, her frail body half buried in pillows. One arm stretched over an edge, the tip of a water pipe dangling from her fingers. She blew a stream of smoke from her thin lips, watching him with heavy-lidded reptilian eyes, the sclera as yellowed as her teeth. She reminded him of a hawk: contemptuous, powerful, the hint of steel hidden under velvet feathers.

The younger woman bowed loosely toward her, and seated herself with two other women at a discreet distance. He stood uncertainly, listening to the faint laughter of boys in the garden outside as she nodded. "Be welcome, Nathan Crewe," she said in his native language, her husky voice gentle. The sound carried clearly across the vast room. "A pleasure to see you again."

He had had to petition at the Nga'esha gates for several weeks before he was granted another audience, this time following the correct and complex formalities. Making a spectacle of himself a second time would not be tolerated. Despite her apparent congeniality, he knew his intrusion into the agenda of the Nga'esha *pratha h'máy* had better be of interest to her, rather than merely vital to him. He inhaled a deep breath, more for courage, and strode toward her, stopping exactly three steps away from the dais. Methodically, he swept the edge of his white sati to one side and knelt, knees together, buttocks resting on his heels, right foot crossed against the flat of the left. He put his palms against his thighs, fingers together, and inclined his torso in a slight bow, paying scrupulous attention to the details.

"I pray, *l'amae*, that I find you in good health," he said in Vanar, carefully parroting phonetic sounds he had memorized, words he barely understood, "and wish you continued long life and good fortune." His tongue strained against the complex diphthongs and glottal stops threatening to choke him, the endless nasalized umlauts his surly tutor had literally tried to pound into his skull.

Suppressed laughter whispered around the room. His cheeks burned with a sudden flush. "I said that wrong, didn't I?" he asked the older woman, switching to his native Hengeli.

The old woman squinted in amusement as much as from the smoke curling in her eyes. "Not at all; entirely correct," she assured him in the same language. Her lilting accent would have been sensual in a younger woman. "You are making excellent progress indeed." He settled back on his heels, and stared at her as if for the first time. Compared to the other women in the room, her dress was somber, no jewelry but the bracelets on her forearms, the blue birdsilk tasmai robe pulled around her with the Nga'esha family emblem hand-embroidered against each shoulder. He had been allowed to see her only once after his release from custody, and her health had clearly worsened since that nearly disastrous fiasco. Her skin had paled to a sickly yellow beneath the olive complexion, thinning white hair exposing the bumps of her skull. She seemed brittlely thin, her ankles more like knots on sticks covered with bloodless parchment.

He knew Yaenida was not simply old, but *ancient*, in the way only those who could afford repetitive regenerative treatments were. Yet her dark eyes were still as energetic, as shrewd and hard, as the day he had first met her.

"Pratha Yaenida," he said, trying to keep his pulse down, "I'm not making much real progress at all."

"Nonsense—"

"Please," he interrupted more sharply than he intended. The younger women in the corner glanced up with narrowed eyes, murmuring between themselves. "Please," he repeated, softening his tone. "I am *not*. You don't do me any favors by lying to me, Yaenida."

She frowned, her thin mouth marked by deep fissures in her skin. He sat very still, knowing he was taking a huge risk by speaking to her with such intimacy. Once she had found his naive familiarity with her charming. He remembered how amused she had been by his shock once he realized the depth of his ignorance. Now he had no excuses to forget exactly who and what she was. Or who and what he was now.

Vanar was a closed world with only one major corporate interest: interstellar Worms, the lifeline linking over three hundred systems with Vanar at their core like a tiny spider in a giant web. No one owned the Worms; they were simply a mysterious artifact of space. But only Vanar Pilots were capable of flying ships in and, more importantly, out again at another part of the universe in one piece. Since the secretive Vanar Pilots were the only creatures who could guide the luxury liners and cargo freighters safely across the huge expanse of space, Vanar maintained its monopoly on not just interstellar trade but on *all* travel between solar systems.

Vanar charged a moderate sum for each Worm transfer, affordable to each individual shipper, and service remained cheap and reliable.

But the traffic added up to an enormous fortune for the Nine High Vanar Families who controlled the Worms.

Hundreds of thousands of people outside Vanar were directly employed by her companies; millions more worked for companies servicing other Vanar corporations. The Nga'esha Corporation owned half the stations in the known star systems, which comprised all of the systems under Hengeli sovereignty. The politics of a hundred planets were shaped and moved by Vanar corporate interests. He could almost feel the weight of that enormous wealth around him, channeled through the High Families into the hands of the few great l'amae like the pratha h'máy Yaenida dva Darahanan ek Qarshatha Nga'esha, quite likely the most powerful being in all the inhabited systems. His chest began to ache as he realized he'd been holding his breath.

"All right," she conceded, breaking the tension, and waited for him to speak.

He exhaled and tried to keep his relief off his face. "I asked to see you exactly because I am having a lot of trouble with both your language and your culture. I'm a botanist . . . I was a botanist," he corrected himself. "I was never very good at xenosociology."

She brought the tip of the water pipe to her mouth, sucking it thoughtfully. Turning her head, she blew a thin stream of pungent smoke away from him out the side of her mouth, keeping her eyes on him. They glittered in her cavernous sockets. "I take it you are dissatisfied with your current tutor?"

"No," he said hastily, "absolutely not." At their last meeting, he'd had to abjectly beg for help to get even the sullen elderly woman the Nga'esha family paid to coach him in Vanar language and protocol. He wasn't about to jeopardize even that small benefit by criticizing his tutor to her employer. "Any fault or misunderstanding is entirely mine—"

Yaenida chuckled. "Oh, do stop it, Nathan, and get to the point. What is it you want from me?"

"Be my teacher again, just for a few minutes." He waited, and when she inclined her head, he said, "What does it mean when a woman gives a man three shafts of grain?"

Her eyebrows raised in surprise, making her look owlish. "What kind of grain? What color?"

"Thin yellow stalks, so high." He measured with his hands. "Multiple heads of grain, reddish, definitely nothing native, but not in the *Triticum* or *Oryza* genera, either. Possibly a hybrid variant of some monocotyledonous grass related to the Avena family." He saw her draw on her pipe to hide her mirth. Bubbles sputtered in the pipe through a cloud of thick liquid. The smell of the drugged smoke cloyed the back of his throat. "I think the common name is *muhdgae*. Dark brown color. Seed pods are already open. They're tied together with two pieces of ribbon—one a burgundy color, the other a sort of pale purple."

"Ah," she said, knowingly. "A young lady from the Changriti motherline?"

He nodded.

She looked out the window at the scuttling clouds. "How interesting. Is the young woman's name Kallah, by any chance?"

"Yes," he said, his stomach sour.

"Did she offer it to you personally?"

"Yes."

"Did you take it directly from her hands? Publicly, in front of witnesses? *Female* witnesses?" Yaenida was grinning.

"Yes," he said. He had bumped into Kallah Changriti, quite literally, when she passed him while in the company of another young Changriti woman. She had acknowledged his halting apology and bow with an arrogant nod of her head, but her shy smile completely spoiled the effect. She'd said nothing to him, but when she glanced back, he impulsively winked at her. Her eyes had widened and she'd clamped a hand over her mouth to stop the laugh, then disappeared in the crowd still clutching the arm of her companion. That one friendly gesture had been his fatal mistake. A week later, he had unwittingly accepted her strange gift—a gift that had nearly gotten him killed.

"She just walked up to me with a couple of her friends and shoved it in my face without a word. I didn't know what else to do, so I took it. I didn't want to be impolite."

She laughed, leaning back into the thick cushions. "Impolite!" Her laughter came from deep in her chest, rumbling and wet.

His face prickled with alarm. "But what does it mean, exactly?" he pressed as her laughter subsided.

She laboriously dragged in another lungful of pungent smoke. Smiling broadly, she shook her head in amazed disbelief. "It means, my poor ignorant child, you are both astoundingly lucky and standing nose deep in a large pond of watery pigshit. Or have I confused another of your colloquial expressions?"

"L'amae, please," he persisted. "Have I screwed up again?"

"Not at all. You've been offered a proposal, sweet boy—and may I point out an extraordinary but favorable one—for matrimonial union with a High Family. By taking Kallah's symbolic gift from her own hand, you've accepted. May I have the honor to be the first to offer you my sincere congratulations."

"Oh God," he breathed, his fears confirmed. "Kallah is the daughter of Pratha Eraelin Changriti."

Yaenida reclined even deeper into the pillows, obviously amused by his situation. "Quite so," she admitted.

"The Changriti pratha h'máy hates me," he said, pronouncing the words with the distinctness he would use for a child. "Two days after that, she tried to have me murdered!"

The healing gash in his side twinged with the memory of the frantic struggle in the dark, the choking smell of bitter cinnamon in the cloth clamped over his nose, the blade scraping by his ear to impale the sleeping mat. Only the advantage of his size and strength as well as the skills learned as a boy growing up hard had saved him. The would-be assassin had vaulted through the small half-moon window, vanishing like a cat over the rooftops, leaving him crumpled on the floor and bleeding more from his nose than from the wound along his ribs. The *pahlaqu* guardian where he lived had been summoned by the hospital, and viewed the torn scrap of dark burgundy silk in his fist with zealous indifference, strongly advising him to forget the incident had ever happened. Yaenida echoed that opinion.

"An accusation I should be careful to speak of very discreetly, were I you," she warned him. "If Pratha Eraelin dva Hadatha Changriti wanted you dead, you would *be* dead, and she would not appreciate your slanderous allegations of incompetence."

"Then she was quite competent in scaring the hell out of me. I can't marry her daughter. I would be living in the household of a woman who would make my life nothing *but* a large pond of watery pigshit."

"But, Nathan," she chided, nearly laughing, "you did accept."

"I didn't know what I was doing!" he protested, his hands gestur-

ing for emphasis, breaking strict Vanar convention. The women in the corner looked up sharply. As two stood, Yaenida waved them away impatiently. He forced down his anxiety. Never show anger, *never*. He knew better. "How was I supposed to know what she was offering?" Nathan continued, keeping his voice low and his sweating palms on his thighs. "Isn't there some way of explaining this to her? I can't legally be held to agreements I didn't know were being made, can I?"

She smiled at him pityingly, and he bit his lip to shut up. Ignorance of Vanar law, he'd already been well taught, was no excuse.

"Nate," she said, using the intimate name he hadn't heard from her since his imprisonment. The unexpected familiarity made his throat hurt. "Kallah is a respectable and influential member of a High Family, and you are in no position to be choosy. Believe me, you could do a lot worse."

"I don't have anything against Kallah Changriti, although she's probably more interested in me because I'm 'exotic' rather than from any real affection. Surely it's not my sparkling wit and charm. Come on, Yaenida, I can barely even talk with the girl!"

Yaenida raised one eyebrow, which he took for concurrence.

"Isn't there some way around this without breaking protocol or upsetting her? You're the Nga'esha pratha h'máy, can't you explain to her I didn't understand what life would be like for me in Pratha Eraelin's House?"

"The pratha h'máy of a High Family does not involve herself with the problems of *naekulam*," she said ironically. "That would be too far beneath my dignity."

He stared at her in disbelief.

She sighed. "Nobody cares about how unpleasant your life would be in the Changriti House, and I'm sure Kallah is well aware of what her mother is like. No doubt part of her reason for making such an absurd offer in the first place was to antagonize Eraelin. But *your* feelings are not important, and would not be of interest to anyone."

Nathan closed his eyes for a moment, fighting the impulse to ball his hands into fists.

"It is a remarkable development, however," Yaenida mused thoughtfully, speaking more to herself. "Although on reflection, not that absurd. You wouldn't be any liability to business alliances. Kallah already has two kharvah from favorably positioned Families as well as a houseful of excellent sahakharae."

"But I'm not a kharvah or a sahakharae."

"Ah, but you are the irresistible combination of both!" she said, her eyes lighting up. "What is more tempting and seductive than the unique, especially when it's safe? If she couldn't acquire you as sahakharae, her only other option is marriage. There's certainly nothing wrong with your seed, wonderfully exotic as it is, Nathan, but you are still naekulam, without Family. It is not unheard-of, but rare, for such an offer to be made to someone with so little to bring into a union. You should be delighted."

"What if," he said carefully, "it was explained to Kallah that I am only a stupid foreigner, that not only had I misunderstood but that I was already committed to marrying someone else?"

Her eyes were bird bright, sparkling in the sunlight. "I had forgotten about your sort, Nathan," she said softly. "So very . . . passionate. A flair for the dramatic. Well, well, you have fallen in love with yet another of our fair young maidens, and are now trapped in the timeless predicament of love and rivalry? How entertaining."

He held himself as rigorously erect as possible. "It is not a question of love, l'amae Yaenida. But if I am to 'unite,' if that's the word for it, I would prefer doing so with a different House."

"Tell me, dear boy," she said, smiling broadly. Her teeth were smoke stained, the gums atrophied away from the roots. "Just to satisfy an old woman's curiosity, who is this charming maiden who has warmed your blood and stolen your heart? Who is it you wish to wed?"

He sat back on his heels and hoped his face was unreadable. "You."

It took her a moment to react, then her eyes widened. She started to cough violently, strangling on the smoke and laughter competing for control of her lungs. The younger women stood, distrustful and alarmed, to be waved back by Yaenida's impatient arm, bone-thin wrist snapping in the air, the bracelets jingling. She continued to laugh for a long minute, her eyes streaming, until Nathan flushed and looked down. The three slowly retook their seats, glaring suspiciously at him.

"Oh, Sweet Lady Mother!" Yaenida gasped, setting off another round of laughter, then wiped away the tears from her wizened cheeks. "Thank you, Nathan, I haven't had such a thrill in years."

He kept silent, his jaw clenched. She coughed lengthily, a deep, wet, chronic congestion, still chuckling.

She spoke in rapid Vanar, and one of the younger women left long enough to return with a glass of green-tinted water as another two knelt by her side. One fanned her face anxiously as the other tucked the fingers of one hand around Yaenida's wrist while she studied the medical scanner in her other. Yaenida submitted impassively without even acknowledging her presence as the women loaded a medgun and pressed the muzzle against her upper arm. It hissed as Yaenida gulped the water noisily to ease her cough. He could smell the delicate scent of mint and medicinal bitters. Within a few minutes, her cough had eased and the color returned to her face.

"Come now, my love," she finally rasped out, handing the empty glass back without looking at the women and waving them away imperiously. Her attendants withdrew to the window reluctantly, hovering like flies around a corpse. "Am I supposed to believe you prefer these ancient bones to Kallah's supple young flesh?"

She drew the edge of her embroidered tasmai away from her body, holding the elegant folds of cloth open just far enough to reveal the shadows of her slack breasts, the dry skin hanging in folds from brittle ribs, the glint of gray hair in the bony recess of her groin. The women around her murmured, puzzled. "Tell me you find me irresistible," she said softly. "Tell me your blood runs hot with desire at the sight of this body. Could you really perform your duty as a kharvah on this worn carcass?" Her face was contorted in a smile of scorn and resigned loss.

He swallowed hard, and raised his head to stare unblinkingly into her eyes in clear breach of protocol. "Pratha Yaenida, were you to honor me as a member of your House, I would perform my duty in any manner you required, and would do so with pride and pleasure." He hoped he sounded far more confident than he felt.

Her eyes narrowed as she drew the tasmai wrap back over her skeletal body protectively, her green-veined hands fussing with the intricate folds. "I almost believe you," she said, and looked out of the windows at thin clouds skimming high in the afternoon blue. The younger women stared at them with perplexed expressions. "From anyone else, I would suspect such an audacious scheme was nothing more than brazen ambition and greed. But not from you." She glanced back at him, her look as hard and cool as marble. "Explain yourself."

He looked down at his hands still pressed against his thighs. "I have no one to talk to," he finally answered. His throat hurt, as if trying to swallow against a stone lodged there.

She snorted. "Is that all?"

"For godsake, isn't that enough?" he asked, and heard his own voice catch with repressed anger. "I've been on Vanar over a year, and I'm dying in this isolation! Living in a charity shelter isn't all that much different from prison, Yaenida, and at least in prison I had you to talk to."

"There are no prisons on Vanar."

"I wasn't ill, l'amae," he said, knowing his resentment leaked out, "and the people asking me all those questions weren't doctors."

Her eyes watched him impassively as she worried the stem of the pipe with her teeth, squinting as tendrils of smoke escaped from her nostrils and curled past her face. He felt his frustration rising.

"My life is constant hell here. No one dares talk to me; they're all too nervous even without that Changriti *bich'chú* stopping me in the street to keep me properly terrified." She raised an eyebrow at his use of vulgar slang to refer to the Qsayati Vasant Subah, head of the Vanar security police. "Not that it matters since I can't learn this damned language, with or without my tutor. I'm *naeqili te rhowghá,* and I know exactly what that means, she's managed to teach me that much," he said sharply at her surprise. "I'm in fact worse than the lowest of outcasts: everyone knows who I am, but I'm treated like some dangerous animal set loose by accident. I try and stay out of trouble, sitting around doing nothing until I'm out of my mind, but the instant I go out, I make one mistake after another. I have nowhere else to go, Yaenida, I need your help, *please!*" He was shouting, leaning forward on his knees as he gestured angrily toward her.

From the corner of his eye, he saw one of the younger women rise, snatching up her staff and striding toward them with protective hostility. He only knew one way to respond, and immediately "turtled," elbows against knees, his forehead against the back of his hands pressed against the floor. He cursed inwardly, prepared for the blows, and hoped she'd at least spare his head.

He heard rather than saw the argument: a fast whipping of Vanar,

one voice sharp, the other cracked with age but strong. Yaenida's emaciated fist smacked against the cushions. The only words he caught
were "Get out." A fast padding of feet, the glimpse of satin-clad heels
past his face, and the sudden silence pressed against his ears.

"Vultures," Yaenida muttered. "I'm not dead yet." She grunted as
she shifted awkwardly on the pillows, then said, "Nathan, you look
ridiculous. That position is for small children. Don't be so damned idiotic. Get up off the floor and give me a hand."

He was up instantly and helping her to her feet, her bony talon
cold in his hand, her elbow in the other as frail as a stick. She was star-
tlingly light: a decent puff of wind could have carried her off. He half
carried her, her legs like stilts as she hobbled, to the wide windowsill,
settling her on the ledge overlooking the garden. Crystal and bronze
wind chimes hung from the corners of fluted roofs, their clear sound
blending with trills of songbirds. The sun shone directly on her face,
outlining every crease with unflattering clarity.

"Ah, Nathan," she said gently, and stroked his cheek, her hand as
smooth and dry as parchment. "You do tempt me, you do. Not a kind
thing to do to an old woman in my condition."

He caught her hand and brushed a kiss against her palm before he
released it—a purely Hengeli gesture. She smiled and with a graceful
motion invited him to sit on the ledge opposite her. When he hesitated, she said with mock seduction, "We're alone, no one's watching.
We can do whatever we like."

He wondered just how true that really was but settled his back
against the stone across from her, one leg drawn up casually, hands
laced around his knee. He was more grateful for this private familiarity and breach of propriety than he could have told her.

"Let me give you some advice," she said, gazing away from him to
the garden below. "I have had five husbands in my life, as well as any
number of sahakharae. Sahakharae come and go, as sahakharae do, in-
terchangeable amusing things. All but one of my kharvah have died.
He's old, like me, and we are comfortable with each other. We have
had many children, our children have children, and we have even lived
long enough to see our grandchildren's grandchildren. Many dozens of
them. He would not understand, and it would only upset him if I were
at this late date to take a sixth kharvah, a young and handsome one at

that." She nodded toward the garden. "Genetic maintenance only goes so far, and I am nearing the end of my life. Appealing as I might find your offer, I prefer not to complicate what remains of my time with the sort of disruption and jealousy only the young have the stamina for."

"It could be just a formality," he pressed. "If I were part of your House, I could see you whenever you have the time to teach me to speak better Vanar, be somewhere safe long enough to learn what I need to adjust to this culture. I'd be no worse off when—" He stopped in embarrassment.

"—I die," she finished serenely. "You can say it. Death is too intimate a companion for me to have any false inhibition about it."

"Yaenida, I swear I won't get in your way. I'll stay in the corner of the kitchen, sleep in the attic, anywhere." He hated the desperation in his voice and waved a hand at the edge of jungle stretching forever on the horizon beyond the villa walls. "Send me to one of the Nga'esha estates in Dravyam or Praetah. I'll spend the entire day out there picking flowers and searching for *svapnah* seeds," he joked, the anxiety in his chest straining his voice.

She chuckled, a dry husking sound. "Oh, no you won't! And scandalize my neighbors? Indeed not." Her smile vanished, old face solemn. "Nathan, you have the rare chance to marry with a young woman from a very good House. Take it. There is no future for you here."

His disappointment tasted like acid, but he did his best to resist pleading with her. "I accept your decision," he said, "although I can't understand your reasons."

"They are simple enough: I am an old woman. I will have no more children. Soon, I will die. My kharvah will be taken care of because he has daughters within this House whose duty it is to support him. You will not. Once I am dead, you would be turned out of the House by my daughters before my corpse was even cold."

"And all the other men in your House, those there?" He nodded toward the figures barely visible beyond the screened garden. "What happens to them?"

"Some of them belong to daughters. Some are unmarried sons and grandsons. Some are various cousins and nephews hanging around because it's more pleasant here than with their own Families. Some are friends from different Houses who have *práhsaedam*, boyhood companions they wish to remain with. Some are merely guests from lesser Families hoping to attract the attention of a potential marriage partner. Others are sahakharae, and they will either find new favorites within the House, if they haven't already, or leave for other, better pastures. At the worst, they all have Families of their own. You are none of these."

She pulled the folds of her embroidered cloth over her knees, wincing as she tried to shift her spine into a more comfortable position. "If you turn down this offer, you *would* be worse off, that I can assure you. The Changriti are one of the Nine High Families—don't forget that—and Kallah has already violated custom and defied her own pratha h'máy to offer marriage to a naeqili te rhowghá." She smiled, and her quick scrutiny made him glance away. "Even such a delightful naeqili te rhowghá. Defiance of one's family is not customary Vanar behavior. Kallah is taking an amazing risk for you, and you did accept, in front of witnesses. Spurned now and humiliated, Kallah would not ask you again at some later date.

"Privately, I'm sure Eraelin would be relieved if you refused, but publicly, you will have gravely insulted her Family. A lowly foreigner, without Family, rejecting the heir to the Changriti fortunes?" Yaenida shook her head with feigned dismay. "You will have antagonized a formidable House, and you've already discovered for yourself how extreme Eraelin's ill will can be." He shuddered. "I doubt you will ever be offered much better in the future. Without a union to a good House, without Family to protect you, your options would be limited. It is possible you could find a kaemahjah willing to train you to become sahakharae, of course. . . ." She shrugged as he paled.

"I'm not interested in being a whore," he said stiffly.

She remained silent for a moment, knowing more about his past than he was comfortable with. "Sahakharae are not prostitutes, and the kaemahjah is an honorable institution," she said gently. "You don't have to be sahakharae, though you might find it quite profitable. I can see where you would be popular, even without proper training."

"I can't even *talk* to people," he snapped, irritated. "I don't play music, I can't dance, I don't know any Vanar poetry. I'm hardly going to be capable of dazzling conversation, am I? So what exactly is it I would be popular for, Yaenida?"

She smiled. "True," she conceded. "There are those who enjoy the kaemahjah for less refined reasons. But if not that, Nathan, the only thing left is the temple, and I seriously doubt that would suit you. Then, what will you do when you can no longer attract a wife or make a living in a kaemahjah? Without family, you'll barely exist in some grubby charity shelter, surrounded by all the other unwanted naeku-lam, the mentally disturbed, the terminally ill, the disgraced husbands, all the sad misfits and surly malcontents who've been abandoned or expelled by their families, year after year alone, until you finally die of old age. Or just old."

He remained quiet, looking out over the vast green of the jungle blurring the horizon beyond the neat walls of the House. She re-spected his silence, closing her eyes, and leaned her head back with her face toward the sun, catlike.

"Yaenida, let me go," he said in a low voice, without hope. "Please. I don't belong here. It was a mistake. Let me leave Vanar."

"Poor child," she responded unsympathetically, her eyes still shut. "You can't."

He hadn't expected any different. He nodded, defeated, and stood. "Thank you for your time, *jah'nari l'amae,*" he said formally. She cracked her eyes to watch him, her heavily lidded eyes deceptively sleepy. "I humbly apologize for disturbing your tranquility." He bowed from the waist, then turned away. His back rigid, he had walked halfway across the spacious room before she called out, "Nate . . ."

He stopped without turning, afraid he would weep in front of her.

"There might be one other possibility, should you be interested."

Relief threatened to buckle his knees, and he had to swallow hard to regain his self-control before he faced her. She was smiling: a tiny, fragile creature swathed in bright cloth huddled on the ledge.

"It's true your circumstances are unique and I do feel a certain, well, responsibility for your welfare. And it is quite likely my interest in you piqued Kallah's curiosity in the first place, as much as it may have been to defy her mother. She's a strong-willed girl, if not quite as malicious as Eraelin. The Changriti are not as . . . broad-minded as are the Nga'esha"—Nathan appreciated the understatement—"and this may indeed provide unexpected benefits for the Nga'esha. Yes, this could work . . ."

Her thoughtful expression suddenly focused on him astutely. "I will discuss the peculiarities of your situation with Kallah in private," she said decisively. "You will, of course, marry her, and you will take advantage of whatever time her other jealous kharvah allow you. Once you are married, fuck her every chance you get. Fuck her until her eyebrows fall off, do you understand? Please her if you can, but more importantly, make her pregnant if she'll allow it."

He nodded, unable to speak.

"But until you are married, you will come to stay in my Household. After you are married, Kallah will agree to allow you to continue to spend the majority of your free time here. She will allow this because as you have no House, I offer mine as your adoptive Family. This will no doubt take a little time to arrange, but I will become your . . . mother." She laughed, eyes twinkling. "Eraelin is of course entirely correct; a Changriti heir cannot possibly be allowed to marry naekulam, the indignity is totally outrageous. But once you are Nga' esha, Eraelin can have no objection since it will create a favorable bond between two powerful Houses. It will also provide *you* with a measure of personal security, as it would certainly be very bad manners indeed for anyone to make an attempt on the life of a member of my Family, no matter how minor."

She smiled at his obvious relief. "As you seem to be having communication problems with your current tutor, you will study with me, personally. In return, you will help me in the writing and correcting of my research on early Hengeli art. You will live and work in my House, and you *will* learn Vanar. You will accept your fate with grace, cease this childish sniveling about leaving and how wronged you've been, and learn to behave as a proper, respectable Vanar man. This is the best deal you will ever be offered, Nathan. Is this alternative acceptable to you?"

He walked back with rubbery legs, and stood tentatively until she proffered her hands. He held them both gently. The breath was constricting in his throat. "Thank you," he finally squeezed the words out.

"You made me remember what it was to be young again," she said softly, her eyes distant. "I was more outrageous then, reckless and impulsive. I've since repaid that misspent youth a hundred times over, dedicated my life and energies solely to Nga'esha interests, so staunch and steadfast and stodgy and totally boring." She smiled mischievously, the skin around her eyes wrinkling. "I'd like to think that other part of me hasn't died yet. I can see why Lyris Arjusana was so infatuated with you, foolish girl."

He winced, not willing to reminisce on either the young woman or the botched scheme that had trapped him here.

She raised one eyebrow at him. "I am still gullible enough to want to believe your absurd offer was made because you like me, rather than merely as a tactical strategy."

"I do like you," he said, then admitted, "but it was both."

"Of course." She hesitated, then asked, reluctantly curious, "Could you really have been able to make love to me?"

For an answer, he cupped her chin in his hand to tilt her face upward. Leaning over her, he brought his mouth down on hers, first a gentle press of his lips against hers. Then he parted her mouth with his tongue, and kissed her deeply, ignoring the smell of smoke on her breath, the faint taste of decay and death. He closed his eyes, feeling a sudden tenderness, something beyond passion or carnal desire, a sadness and affection for this dying old woman.

The kiss went on with a growing intensity until, to his own astonishment, he felt a flutter stirring in his gut. Her hands caressed his arms, the brush of bird's wings against his skin. His heart was beating fast before she was the one to finally push him away, two bright spots of color on her wrinkled cheeks.

"You would kill me, Nathan," she said, and laughed. He heard the girl's lighthearted laugh and kissed her again, this time only a chaste touch of his lips to her forehead.

When he stepped out into the sunshine, his body protected from the hot sun by layers of undyed linen, he walked quickly away from the men's gate as it shut behind him and stood at the edge of the road leading away toward the center of the city below. He looked back up at the sprawling estate dominating the hillside, trying to determine which arched window she might be behind. No birdlike figure perched above to see him off, the high walls of the enclosed House as impervious as the formidable *Dhikar* guards watching him with deceptive tranquility.

But he found himself smiling as he walked away, bare head up and enjoying the sunshine before he caught the disapproving scowl of two women passing him on the other side of the road.

He ducked his chin down and covered his head with the edge of the dingy cloth as he walked. Keeping his eyes lowered, he pulled in his natural confident stride to one less assertive, more restrained.

More appropriate for a proper, respectable Vanar man.

PART ONE

I

It had seemed like such a good idea at the time. All he had wanted was enough sketches and notes and field samples for a narrow but formative article on indigenous Vanar botany, enough to make his name within the narrow confines of academics at least. He'd thought it simple enough, choosing a spot as far away from human habitation and any contamination of native flora from terraformed fields as possible to be undetected. Looking back now, it had been utterly preposterous that he could have Lyris drop him in a pod from the *Comptess Dovian* down to the planet, run loose through the jungle undetected, grab up a bunch of plants, and dash back to the *Dovian* before it took off for another cargo flight.

He didn't even last thirty seconds after landfall. In the midst of the densest alien rain forest he'd ever imagined, he'd opened the pod to find an entire contingent of women in their quaint native dress waiting to greet him. He'd been disappointed, but not frightened. Surely the worst that could happen would be immediate deportation on the next ship out, with or without a stiff fine. And these ladies looked harmless enough, until he'd smiled and advanced toward them, hoping to talk his way out of trouble. . . .

The next thing he remembered was waking up in a small cell. He had expected to be interrogated, but instead had been escorted through a series of different buildings and passed from hand to hand until he found himself undergoing a thorough medical examination. He had been stripped, prodded, poked, scraped, scanned, and bled, then abandoned to sit naked on an examining chair in a locked room.

All of the medical personnel had been women, none of whom spoke Hengeli, which was nearly as disconcerting as the brusque treatment. He had never been on any world where, no matter what the native language was, Hengeli hadn't been the most widely used vernacular. Insignificant as his home world might have become, her tongue was spoken on a hundred worlds throughout the star systems. All except, it seemed, on Vanar. The few memorized phrases Lyris had taught him achieved only blank looks and silence.

After several hours, he dozed off, jolted awake when the door hissed open. A lone woman stood in the doorway, studying him curiously. Her face was light bronze, dark eyes over high, sharp cheekbones. Her black hair was pulled back from her face and hung in a thick ornate braid over her shoulder. Her full lips and small delicate nose didn't soften her hard expression in the slightest.

He covered his groin with his hands, both embarrassed and vulnerable, but she didn't appear to notice his absurd gesture of modesty.

"My name is Vasant Subah," she said in accented if fluent Hengeli. She wore the simple blouse and loose-fitting pants he had seen Vanar women on Station wear, hers a luminous white with a deep burgundy border. Although she didn't appear sympathetic, she didn't seem hostile, either. "Who are you?"

"Thank God," he breathed. "My name is Nathan Crewe. I'm a Hengeli citizen. I request to see a lawyer, please."

The corners of her lips curled up sardonically. "A lawyer?"

Alarm prickled the hair on his neck. "Or whatever the Vanar equivalent is. Under the human rights directives of the Convention, I am entitled to legal counsel."

Vasant Subah stared at him, and rubbed her forefinger across her chin as if to stifle a laugh. "*What* Convention? Vanar never signed any Convention; we were never part of your Territories. You are subject to Vanar laws now."

Now he was truly afraid. "Am I under arrest, then?"

"You could call it that. As you've trespassed into Vanar illegally, you're suspected of being a saboteur or a terrorist."

"Terrorist!" he blurted in shock. "I'm no terrorist, I'm a botanist. All I wanted was to take some samples of Vanar flora for scientific examination. Ask Lyris Arjusana, the subcaptain of the *Comptess Dovian*. She'll tell you—"

"We've already spoken with Subcaptain dva Arjusana." Vasant Subah cut him off. "Her story seems a bit too far-fetched to believe."

He swallowed, his anger tempered with fear. "But it's the truth. Don't I even get a trial? You people must have some sort of a justice system, don't you?"

"Of course we do. You've already had your trial. You've been found guilty of illegal entry." The woman's stiff formal attitude had softened, although he wasn't certain the contemptuous humor replacing it was much of an improvement.

"Fine, no problem, I admit it. I'll pay whatever the fine is. So deport me."

For some reason that made her smile even wider. "That almost convinces me," she said. "Who would send a terrorist into Vanar as ignorant as you are?" Her eyes glittered with malicious amusement. "But whatever happens to you isn't my concern. Others will have to decide what to do with you."

"So why are you here?"

Her smile faded as she stepped toward him. "To find the truth."

He glanced down at her arms as she flexed strange muscles, ropy cords writhing under the skin. When she touched him, he understood.

II

HE QUICKLY FOUND HIS DEMAND TO SEE A HENGELI OFFICIAL REPRE-
sentative was not only futile but his daring to even question the Vanar
legal right to hold him prisoner punishable in ways he hadn't dreamed
of. His indignation at this injustice quickly turned to desperate offers
to pay whatever fine or serve whatever time or hard labor they chose
to sentence him to, all attempts at reasoning or pleading with his cap-
tors utterly ignored. He never stopped thinking of escape, but eventually he stopped talking about it, realizing his best defense was to
remain silent and compliant.

After several months of Vasant Subah's agonizing interrogation
whenever she felt he was too slow or unwilling to answer her relentless
questions, he couldn't imagine his torture could have gotten any worse.

He was wrong.

He couldn't remember how he had gotten where he was, wherever that was, dimly aware of being cradled inside a spongy egg-
shaped chamber, a soft white glow all around him. His entire body was
enveloped in blood-warm membrane, and he gagged as he realized he
couldn't breathe, no air in his lungs. He flailed in horror before he realized he wasn't actually suffocating. The membranous fluid enclosed
his face, down his nose and throat into his lungs, keeping him alive. All
he could smell was bitter cinnamon. He could move, but it was like
swimming in jelly. It pressed lightly against his eyes, making even
blinking slow. He ran his fingers over the surface of the smooth, soft
barrier. It felt like living tissue, deceptively fragile, but no amount of
desperate clawing at it had any effect. Although he wasn't hungry, he
couldn't remember when he'd last eaten, his stomach oddly tight.
He'd never been so terrified in his life.

Drugs washed him in and out of unconsciousness, the sticky membrane delivering the chemicals through his skin and lungs. Every time
he managed to fight his way back into waking, *something* knocked him
down again. He fought the dreams, one nestled into the next, like an
infinite set of hollow dolls, prying one open only to find another inside.

He had no idea how long he slept. It might have been hours. It could have been weeks.

It was certainly forever.

Suddenly, he was no longer asleep. Three women, barely visible through the opaque membranous wall, watched him. Two of them he knew now to be Dhikar, the Vanar equivalent of police. The other he recognized. The Qsayati Vasant Subah, head of Vanar security.

"Where am I, what is this?" he struggled to say, heart beating rapidly. His voice sounded strange, muffled in his own ears, and he wondered if she could hear him.

Apparently, she could.

"It's called a whitewomb. These are designed for disturbed patients."

"Patients? I'm not ill."

She smiled wryly, her face distorted through the membrane. "There are no prisons on Vanar. We didn't know where else to put you. It was decided this was the best solution, for your own protection as well as ours."

His anger flared even through the stupefying drugs. "If this is how you treat people, I'd settle for being treated like dirt, that might be an improvement." He watched her idly stroking the implants in her arm, and fought down his panic. He pressed his hands against the pulpy wall to steady himself. "But you *are* going to kill me if you keep me in this thing for too much longer," he said less heatedly. "Or is that what you intend to do to me?"

She stared at him for a long moment. "Your alien physiology does seem incompatible with our whitewomb system. Most patients find it . . . soothing."

He gasped as he felt his palms being pulled into the whitewomb's membrane, and tried to pull away.

"Stop resisting," Vasant Subah advised him. "You'll only hurt yourself."

His hands were sucked through with a wet pop. The gelatinous fluid flowed around his face as the membrane expelled him, his arms waving eagerly like a blind man's in front of him. He felt the odd vibration of her implants as Vasant Subah took his forearm. Without thinking, he tried to jerk away from her.

"If you fight me," she warned, "you'll go back inside."

His fear of the whitewomb barely outweighed his fear of her, but he stopped struggling.

"Don't pull," she said as his head was released, his eyes opening wide as the membrane peeled back with a wet smack. She held him steady as his remaining foot was slowly spat out, her fingers wrapped firmly around his biceps. He shivered in the cold air, his naked skin worm white against the brown of the woman's hands. Trying to inhale, he panicked when his lungs didn't respond. His knees buckled as he vomited, expelling a huge amount of membranous jelly from his lungs and throat. The women allowed him to remain on his hands and knees, coughing hoarsely until he could breathe again, before helping him to his feet.

He glanced at the whitewomb behind him. It had sealed up without a seam, and now resembled a partly deflated oversized beachball someone had forgotten to add air into. A dozen more squatted in neat rows, a few as pale as mist, others with their shadowy contents moving sluggishly inside, hidden from view. He looked away, shuddering.

The women took him to a place where he could shower the sticky white coating off his skin. Once he was clean, one of the impassive Dhikar silently handed him a paper jumpsuit. He pulled it on with trembling fingers. As he fastened the disposable suit, the second Dhikar produced a pair of gold bracelets decoratively incised and set with small gems. She clipped one around each of his wrists, their function made clear when she locked them together quite functionally as handcuffs.

No one spoke as the two slender Dhikar held him casually between them, following the Qsayati through the long corridors. His damp bare feet stuck to the hard floor. Although he stood a good head and shoulders taller than either of the Dhikar, by now he knew better than to even think of resisting them. Their slightest touch was enough to inspire his wholehearted obedience.

A stocky woman waited as they approached, a large door at her back. Like Vasant Subah, she wore a loose shirt and pants, but of a pale blue shimmering silk, intricately embroidered, pleated, and immaculately pressed. She had one thumb hooked on an ornate belt around her waist, standing with her legs apart and her chin arrogantly high.

She examined him with undisguised contempt as they stopped in front of her.

Vasant Subah nodded toward the Dhikar. They bowed slightly to the Qsayati and left without a word. The woman in blue held a quick conversation with Vasant Subah while he watched expectantly, his starved senses jittery.

"Personally," Vasant Subah said finally as she turned to Nathan, "were it up to me, you would remain permanently in the whitewomb. I don't care if it killed you or not. However, others higher in authority have taken an interest in your welfare."

She stepped close to tighten the elaborate handcuffs, the metal grinding into the bones of his wrists. He stifled a small grunt of pain.

"You will not speak unless requested to do so," Vasant Subah said quietly, close enough to breathe the words in his face. "You will do exactly as you are told without resistance. You will answer any questions put to you promptly and courteously. You will offer no opinions, make no demands, and ask no questions. You are to be respectful and cooperative." He felt the hum of her implants through the metal on his wrists, and shivered. She didn't blink as she watched him struggle for self-control. "Do you understand?"

He nodded, doing his best to prove himself very respectful and cooperative.

She glanced away from him toward the woman in blue, then back, her dark eyes hard. And nervous, he realized with surprise. The woman in blue grunted, frowning, and turned to pull the door to one side. It slid open on silent tracks. He followed them into a large room, his damp feet sticking to the cold floor.

They stopped three paces away from an immense mountain of embroidered cushions where a small, ancient woman reclined. She wore a bright silk tunic underneath shimmering blue cloth ornately folded and wrapped around her gaunt figure. Gold bracelets sparkled against her dark skin, tiny beads of lapis lazuli woven into her intricately braided silver hair. He gazed back at her with interest, his eyes hungry for color.

Gracefully, the Qsayati Vasant Subah bowed and knelt, sitting back on her heels on the floor, her palms against her thighs. "Do as I did, Nathan Crewe," she said softly, without looking at him.

Awkwardly, he bowed and lowered himself to the floor, heels tucked under him, his shackled hands in his lap. The old woman studied him curiously, dark eyes glittering in amusement. Unsettled, he lowered his gaze to the ornate manacles on his wrists, his knuckles whitened as his fingers laced together tightly. He was shaking uncontrollably.

"My name is Yaenida Nga'esha. You may address me as Pratha Yaenida," the old woman finally said, her voice hoarse but her Hengeli fluent and nearly unaccented. She chuckled at his surprise, a dry rasp of humorless sound. "I will be your teacher."

III

SIX MONTHS LATER, NATHAN HAD BEEN RELEASED, THE TRANSITION DISconcertingly abrupt. He had awoken in his locked cell one morning like any other, dressed in his white prison trousers and tunic, and now that it had grown long enough, combed his hair back from his face and tied it into a short queue at the nape of his neck. Then he waited patiently for the Dhikar to arrive.

They appeared exactly on time. By now, he knew most of the Dhikar who came to escort him to Pratha Yaenida. Although none of them were malicious, courtesy was critical: the slightest show of defiance would be instantly punished. He stood as soon as he heard the door begin to slide back. Feet together, spine straight, his palms together with his thumbs pressed against his chest, he greeted his guards with a slight bow and a murmured, *"Tah byáti, bahd'hyinae."* Good health, elder sisters.

When he had begun to speak to his guards, the Dhikar had stared at him blankly and treated him with indifference, polite but impersonal. The first time one of his guards hesitated and recognized him with a nod and a soft, *"Tah byát bah'chae,"* he'd been unable to re-press his laugh of pure delight with his success. She glanced at her companion, then back at him before she shrugged.

What exactly his "lessons" with Pratha Yaenida were supposed to encompass were, at first, difficult to understand. His lack of ability to master even the fundamentals of the Vanar language obviously disap-pointed her, and his explanation that he was a botanist, not a linguist, had irritated her. Eventually, she began to tire of him, often days pass-ing before he saw her. Her disinterest spurred him to try even harder, as she had made it clear his aptitude toward Vanar protocol and lan-guage was crucial if he hoped to attain any measure of freedom ever again.

This day, like any other day, he exchanged this small greeting with the Dhikar before they marched him silently down the long, empty corridors. But instead of turning toward the teaching rooms, they escorted him to a large office. Behind the low table that served as her desk, the Dhikar police chief, Vasant Subah, examined a reader, its faint light reflecting in her dark eyes. He hadn't seen her since the arrival of Pratha Yaenida, and had fervently hoped never to see her again. His heart dropped, but he bowed politely, exactly as he'd been taught, and steeled himself for another round of grim tor-ture.

The Qsayati's gaze flicked up to him briefly, but she didn't ac-knowledge his greeting.

Like the Dhikar, she wore her hair pulled back tightly in a plain braid down her back. But she was smaller, more delicate than the usual caste of big-boned, muscular Dhikar, and the subtle burgundy edging along her shimmering white kirtiya declaration enough of her higher lineage allying her to what he now knew was the Changriti Family. In the hollow between her clavicles, a tiny subvo-cal transmitter gleamed black like a necklace suspended without a chain. Her only other ornamentation was the soundpearl nestled in her ear.

She closed the reader and rose from the table. He flinched invol-untarily as she took his arm, her fingers cool. Even dormant, he imag-ined he could feel the implants under her skin vibrate. But he'd simply been given a new white linen sati, a box with his few possessions in it, a blank datacard in a pouch hung around his neck, and a slip of paper with an address written in corkscrew Vanar script. Vasant Subah had unceremoniously escorted him up through the underground levels out into the open street, hailed a passing taxi, and told the driver where to take him.

"I'm free?" he had asked, disbelieving.

Her smile was devoid of warmth. "You've been released," she said in her lightly accented voice. He was sure it was not at all the same thing.

"But . . . Pratha Yaenida?"

"Has no further interest in you."

"I don't understand. What do I do now?"

"The best you can," she said derisively, and left him alone with the driver. The taxi had abandoned him at the foot of the charity shelter, apparently paid in advance as Nathan had no money, no idea what Vanar money even looked like. He had managed to find the apartment simply by holding up the slip of paper to passersby with a hopeful expression on his face. After several attempts resulting only in irritated scowls from women, a small elderly man dressed in white like himself emerged from the shelter and pointed a shaking finger up the narrow stairway before scuttling hurriedly away. Nathan climbed up one flight after another, stopping for several more confused queries before someone grudgingly led him to a tiny room at the top of the complex.

He sat for several hours in the room trying to mentally adjust to the change before the panic began to creep in. Despite all his lessons with Yaenida Nga'esha, all the information he'd wheedled from Lyris on the *Comptess Dovian*, he knew next to nothing about the society he had just been dumped into. He couldn't speak the language, knowing only a handful of Vanar phrases he'd memorized by rote. He didn't know where he was, or what was expected of him.

Barely wide enough to take five paces in any direction, his new room was not all that much bigger than the locked hospital cell, if more colorful. The walls flowed one into the other, rough plastered and shaped by hand. Previous occupants had decorated the walls with a riot of odd animals and flowering plants, strange huge-eyed lizards hiding in the leaves. The paintings ranged from the crudely amateur to exquisite artwork, abstract designs and symbols or the twisted Vanar script scrawled over dozens of drawings of highly explicit sexual acts, many with a faceless woman of monumental proportions. Some of these fantastic women had more arms or legs than normal, some with strange-colored skin, some in ritualized poses as if frozen middance. But always, the woman was naked and her blank visage wreathed with waving lines Nathan assumed to represent blazing light. He found the chaos of images unsettling.

Quarried natural stone on the floor had been polished by many generations of bare feet. An alcove recessed in the far wall included a lumpy sleeping mat and several well-worn pillows. Above that was a half-moon-shaped open window with no curtains or shutters, only an overhanging screen on the outside wall to keep the rain out. A narrow ledge ran along the two side walls, neither of them square, and neither with a sharp edge. The fourth wall was barely more than an open doorway, an arched opening into the hall with no door. Other than the sleeping alcove, he had no furniture, not even a rug thrown down on the floor to relieve the emptiness.

At one end of the room, a miniature kitchen was built into the ledge: a tiny refrigerator, a kettle for hot water, one microburner for cooking, and a flash sink to clean the few pots stored in the cabinets under the ledge. By midafternoon, he was hungry and had no idea how even to feed himself. A quick examination of the kitchen revealed only a small supply of smoky dark tea and a small earthenware pot of old damp sugar probably left behind by the previous tenant, but nothing else.

At twilight, the odor of cooking and the murmur of voices began to fill the halls. But when he went in search of a possible meal, he met only with hostile stares and eloquently turned backs. He drank heavily sugared tea that night to fill his stomach. He slept badly, unfamiliar noises waking him several times from hazy, disturbing dreams he forgot instantly. In the morning, he wrapped his sati around himself clumsily before beginning the journey down twenty flights of stairs in search of food.

He explored the broad main pedestrian street lined with tiny shops and filled with people, the vast majority of them women. After so many months in prison, seeing only his guards and his teacher, the sudden presence of so many people was almost overwhelming. It also became quickly apparent his appearance made him the object of open curiosity. People stopped at the sight of him and turned to stare as he walked by. He had never considered himself a big man, but in the midst of a crowd of slender, dark-skinned Vanar, he felt huge and awkwardly conspicuous.

He kept on walking doggedly, smiling and bowing and observing everything around him with desperate determination. He paused several feet away from one shop, the entire front wall folding down to convert into an accordion of shelves displaying vegetables in artful arrangements. A plump woman wearing a garishly bright sati stood behind the rows of fresh vegetables and chatted with another woman examining her goods, even white teeth flashing in their dark faces. He watched carefully as the customer handed her a datacard the seller then brushed a finger across. His hand went to his chest, feeling for the datacard in its pouch.

But when he tentatively approached the vegetable seller, her smile turned down into a scowl. She spoke rapidly, her speech incomprehensible to him, but her surly expression and shaking finger clear enough.

He had had nothing for more than a day, his stomach empty and his head light. *"Vahdaemih be mát Vanarha ko,"* he said insistently, *I don't speak Vanar*, and pointed at the vegetables with one hand while holding out his card hopefully with the other.

As soon as she heard him speak, her own harangue cut off midsentence. She stared at him in almost comical surprise, stepping back to look him up and down in a broad theatrical gesture, eyes protruding in obvious alarm. Then she started again: a fast shrill of gibberish and a clear gesture for him to leave, clear off, go away.

He swallowed, too hungry to give in, and said again, "Vahdaemih be mát Vanarha ko, l'amae." He offered her his card, pointing toward the vegetables, smiling so hard his face ached. *"Bhukh'tsit."* Hungry.

Her diatribe increased in loudness, drawing a curious audience. Her feet spread apart and fists planted firmly on her hips, she complained to the neighboring merchants drawn out of their shops to watch. At any moment, he expected her outburst to draw the unwelcome notice of the Dhikar police.

"Okay, okay," he said in Hengeli and backed away with hands held up appeasingly. "Just forget it . . . ," and started when he felt someone grasp his forearm. He stared down at a young woman, her head tilted as she squinted in the sunlight. She wore a pale green saekah under a tunic of the same color, the rich birdsilk shot through with intricate silver embroidery. The sheer layers of cloth seemed to float around her slender body, hinting at the shape underneath. When she spoke, he understood nothing. His shoulders slumped. "Vahdaemih be mát Vanarha ko, l'amae," he repeated miserably.

Her lips opened in a slow, knowing smile, teeth bright. No more than fifteen or sixteen, she was slender, with the softly contoured face of adolescence. She examined him with the same frank curiosity mingled with fear as the merchant had, then, to his astonishment, reached up tentatively to touch his hair. Barely long enough to pull back and tie with a short piece of string, stray curls were always escaping. He forced himself to remain motionless, acutely aware he was becoming the focus of unwanted attention by the small crowd.

Her arm dropped, several layers of gold bracelets jingling. She turned and spoke arrogantly to the merchant, who, still glowering, tossed a selection of vegetables onto a broad green leaf, rolled it expertly into a package, and handed it her. The girl spoke again, her tone reproachful. The merchant's scowl deepened, but she reached under the counter and produced a small bundle to slap on top of the package. When the girl attempted to offer her card, the merchant refused with melodramatic wounded pride.

The girl bowed before she turned and gave the packages to Nathan. With his arms full, he bowed to her as best he could, but she had apparently not finished with him. Taking him possessively by the arm, she led him away from the bad-tempered vegetable vendor to another small shop along the boulevard. People gaped as they passed, whispering and pointing and nudging one another. She seemed oblivious to it.

She stopped and spoke to him, gesturing to indicate he should wait outside. He nodded, watching her through the window as she selected a few objects from the shopkeeper, paying for them with her own card. She emerged to add these to his load, chatting with animated gaiety, clearly enjoying herself. He had no idea why she had elected herself his benefactress, but he was in no position to discourage her.

After two more stops, she asked him a question he did his best to decipher. Belatedly, he realized she was asking where he lived, it was easier to juggle his goods and give her the folded paper he kept sandwiched inside his datacard than attempt explaining that he knew his way back. Taking his arm again, she strode briskly in the direction of the charity shelter. She kept up the stream of conversation, indifferent to his inability to understand her, but he noticed she kept scanning the route around them, searching for something.

A few blocks from the shelter, she tugged on his arm, urging him into the shadow of a narrow alley. It curved and opened onto a cul-de-sac, a small, barren courtyard used for storage. Wooden crates weathered gray with age were stacked to one side. She pushed him around the corner, against the wall, then held him in place with one hand pressed against his chest while she scanned the passageway to be sure they were alone.

One lesson he had learned well in his unpleasant war-torn childhood was that the kindness of strangers most often came at a price. Although he outweighed his newfound friend by several kilos and could have easily shoved her out of his way to escape, he remained passive, waiting.

Once she was sure they were hidden from view, she leaned toward him intimately, her eyes sparkling with mischief. She pointed to herself. "Namasi dva Ushahayam ek Sahmudrah," she pronounced slowly, then pointed at him questioningly.

He had to clear his throat before he could answer. "Nathan Crewe."

She nodded knowingly, as if he had given her an answer she already knew. "Aadmae Hengelianha?" *You're the Hengeli man?*

"Hae'm, l'amae."

She giggled suddenly, excited, and glanced again down the empty alleyway cautiously before she leaned back toward him. She pressed light fingers on top of the bundle in his arms meaningfully. "Chúp

raho, hae'm?" she said softly. It took him a moment before he understood. *Be quiet.*

"Hae'm, *l'amae."* His voice sounded strange, thick.

She reached up to slide the string from his small ponytail. Freed, his pale hair tumbled loosely around his shoulders, and he held himself still as she fondled it, marveling. She gave him another significant look before her fingers slid to the edge of his sati, exploring the folds at his hip. Her hands were shaking. He leaned back, his shoulder blades pressed against the hard wall as she spread the cloth aside to fumble for the hem of his mati. She glanced at him warningly as she lifted it, then stooped to examine his naked groin. He stared down at the top of her head, her black hair parted into zigzags and intricately plaited with silver beads.

The air chilled his exposed thighs. His breath came shallowly, the strange mixture of his fear and excitement quickening his blood. She jumped, startled, as his erection squirmed upright, dumbly expectant. For several seconds, she simply stared, then dropped his clothing.

When she stepped back from him, she blushed furiously, embarrassed. Pressing her hands together, she bowed, giggling, before she darted down the narrow alleyway, sandals slapping, and vanished around the corner.

Amazed, he stood alone for several minutes, his legs rubbery and, although the air was cool, his face uncomfortably sweaty. Clutching his goods, he walked back to the shelter and climbed the stairs, stopping to catch his breath halfway up.

When he unpacked his goods, he found that besides the vegetables, the girl had given him bread, soft-shelled eggs, a bottle of clear yellow oil, a sack of honey-colored short grain, several small jars of unfamiliar condiments. Not a bad bargain for a clandestine peek at his pubic hair, he decided. The second bundle turned out to be a selection of spices, equally strange. He recognized few of the vegetables, experimentally cutting and sniffing, touching them to his tongue before electing to cook it up as a soup. The result was not delicious, but at least edible.

He did not go hungry that evening.

IV

HE DREAMT OF SOMETHING VAGUE AND FRIGHTENING, OF BEING trapped inside a ruined house, occupation military police searching outside. A huge hand smelling of smoke clamped across his mouth, threatening to suffocate him; a heavy body crushed him facedown into the rubble-strewn floor. Labored breath whispered beside his ear in time with the constant thump of artillery in the distance. Pressure rather than pain hammered into him, familiar, sour. The dream shattered, and he struggled bolt upright, heart pounding, queasy with momentary disorientation. It took him several seconds before he remembered where he was and wondered what had awakened him.

That: the sound of urgent voices in the hail. His feet had barely swung over the edge of the sleeping shelf before a woman appeared at the archway of his room and strode directly inside. She wore a voluminous saekah of bright rainbowed geometrical pattern cuffed at the ankles, her kirtiya blouse a shimmering purple. On someone slightly taller and slightly younger, it might have been attractive, but on her it only seemed garish. "Tah byat, bahd'hyin," he said quickly, bowed and straightened to comb his fingers through sleep-disheveled hair falling over his face.

She merely grunted in reply and stared at him: a middle-aged woman with an unsympathetic square face, before inspecting the flat-reader she held cradled in the crook of her elbow. "Nay-teen Kah-roo."

He wasn't sure it was a question, but answered anyway. "Hae'm l'amae."

She studied the screen and said in an oddly syncopated Hengeli, "My name is Dronsanu Harinyua. I am pahlaqu, guardian to this place." She looked up at him critically. He realized she was reading from a phonetical text without any idea of the meaning of the words, gauging by his reaction if he understood.

"Hae'm l'amae."

She nodded, satisfied, then consulted her reader again. "I be financial manager of you." Her words were chopped into ponderous syllables. "I to come one times every month, same times. You obligatory here. No here, very bad trouble."

She glanced up again, eyes narrowed, and stabbed one finger at the floor emphatically. Behind her, a few of his new neighbors hovered by the archway, watching curiously but ready to jerk back out of sight should she suddenly turn around.

"Hae'm, l'amae," he repeated.

He would repeat it several times before she struggled all the way through her prewritten text, and he wondered if she'd done her own translation. This charity shelter, he managed to work out, was one of several in the city for naekulam, men without families. It was one of the better ones, she informed him, reserved for the elderly, the disabled, and other nonviolent residents. Any infraction and he'd quickly find himself in less pleasant accommodations where his independence would be severely restricted. No violence, she warned with an insistent edge. She glared at him, and he realized her arrogance wasn't skillful enough to cover her fear of him. He wondered if she knew where he had just spent the last six months of his life.

"Hae'm, l'amae," he said with heartfelt sincerity.

The pahlaqu would come to observe him, see that he had enough to eat, make sure he got medical treatment if he was unwell. No one was homeless on Vanar. No one starved. Although no one would much care if he committed suicide or not, as he would discover later. There were usually one or two a month, with the resulting mayhem as tenants scrambled to swap their own rooms for one better, a noisy, heated restructuring of the social hierarchy.

She demanded his datacard, flipped it open, and painstakingly showed him how to use it. Even as a naekulam, Nathan would have a nominal government subsidy to draw from. It was enough to cover food and small luxuries such as tea and coffee, soap and bath fees. In the meantime, his limited funds precluded anything much more expensive than wandering the streets for entertainment. Her lecture finished, she smiled scornfully at him. "Do you have beings to asking of no questions?"

He smiled back. "Máat, l'amae."

She snapped her reader shut and left. He heard her speaking with several other men, tones of entreaty or admonishment more eloquent than the words.

Even armed now with food and a few guidelines from his pahlaqu, he was abandoned to his own devices. He had no more lessons with Pratha Yaenida. Other than the pahlaqu, no one ever came to see him, no one questioned him. But he knew that if he had any hope of ever escaping, he would have to learn as much as he could about his prison, find the chinks in the walls, learn the rules before he could break them. Not an easy job when you couldn't even ask directions to the nearest airport.

His new life, although better than prison, was not that less Spartan. A small crate made of thin woven reeds held what few possessions he owned: his spare mati and two worn hand towels, his toiletries, the handful of bookcubes Yaenida had given him along with a secondhand reader. He'd found a discarded pot and planted a hydrangea cutting he'd furtively taken from a public garden, the plant just now sending out roots from its place on his windowsill.

He spent much of his time struggling to learn Vanar from simple bilingual children's stories translated into painstakingly correct Hengeli. Obviously translated by someone whose Hengeli was slightly less than fluent, sometimes the mistakes were amusing, sometimes simply puzzling. A woman's voice read the stories in the most basic audio Vanar: "The girl has a ball. The ball is red. See the red ball." He tried to decipher the ornate squiggles matching the sounds before giving up and simply listening to the stories, repeating the words. More than a few nights, he would end up with the reader propped on his chest and an empty cup on the floor beside him, sound asleep despite the strong tea.

The charity shelter had been built wedged into a rock cleft running down the side of the far west bank of the river. Twenty layers of boxlike rooms balanced one atop the other, latticed with haphazard staircases. Roofing overshot narrow porches barely wide enough to allow space for a single man. Passing another habitant along the balconies often meant squeezing by while avoiding looking over at the sheer drop below. His was one of the less-desirable rooms, a tiny cell at the top of the complex accessible only by plodding up several steep stairways. There was a service elevator, he eventually realized, but that was locked, restricted for use only by the police authorities or emergency medical teams. The winding stairs served to keep the inhabitants either physically fit or indoors.

He spent the next few months watching his neighbors, listening, wandering the streets for clues. He learned where to buy his food from following other white-garbed naekulam, how to pick up extra money on his card by leaving the complex before dawn with an eye out for shopkeepers willing to pay naeqili te rhowghá, the ostracized class of familyless outcasts, for such odd jobs as sweeping the storefront or hauling away the previous day's rubbish. Hiring a human being for such manual labor, before the computerized cleaning machines keeping the city scoured and pristine arrived and automatically totaled the charges, was not only cheaper, the Vanar considered it a charity to recognize the men's existence at all. The little money he earned with such menial labor supplied a bit more luxury than the state stipend allowed. He was grateful for any such jobs, his size and strength and cheapness occasionally winning out over the shopkeeper's wariness of him.

While the other residents had no objection to his trailing them, so long as he maintained a safe distance, his first few attempts at friendly gestures were utterly rebuffed. Offers of a shared meal or simple company earned him only nervous, hostile silence. After his initial tentative approaches failed, his personal contact with his fellow naekulam was reduced to wary nods in passing. While he had no friends in the complex, at least he had made no enemies, either. But the sound of laughter made him even lonelier.

He tried to ignore other sounds, the soft, urgent moans in the night. He listened with passive incomprehension to quarrels usually conducted with muted hostility, not knowing how to cross the isolation even enough to enjoy arguing with his neighbors. He watched as they passed by in the hall, pretending not to see him. Despite his long isolation, he craved the illusion of privacy and used his spare linen sati to hang across the doorless entrance to the room, another feature of Vanar architecture he could not get used to. Then, instead of his fellow residents ignoring him, he was subjected to having his makeshift screen twitched aside at any moment, curious eyes peering in to see what he could possibly be hiding. He finally took it down.

He practiced folding the long sati into intricate patterns in his hands and tying the pleats he'd made from it around his body, as Pratha Yaenida had taught him. Eventually, Nathan's technique improved so that the knots didn't unravel to leave him standing in the one-piece mati with a pile of cloth tangled around his ankles. In the confined privacy of his small room, he walked in circles and trained himself to balance on one leg while hooking his foot around the edge of the sati to move it from around his knees before he knelt, just the edge of the mati showing over his knees. Too little and the cloth would be trapped under his legs and jerked out of its intricate folds. Too far, and his thighs would be bared, the mati hitched up indecently.

Other simple things—the nuances of gestures and body language, the unspoken minutiae understood by everyone but himself—continued to elude him. Or blindside him. Razors, for example, were not a common item. Vanar men were as smooth-faced as the women, keeping their face and bodies denuded by using the various depilatories supplied at public baths in the complex. He had watched one afternoon in amazement as one resident subjected himself to having all his body hair removed, the hair on his chest, back, legs, and groin ripped away with a gluey paste embedded in cloth. The man had not made a single sound, his bored expression one of habitual practice. Nathan chose to shave in private, as the public baths tended to want to also strip the hair from areas of his body young Namasi had found so fascinating.

He had thought about her since then, and once believed he'd spotted her on the streets. But when the woman had turned around, her ivy green sati over a wine-colored mati, he was both relieved and disappointed to see it was someone else. The woman had stared at him, and touched her companion on the arm, nodding her head in his direction. Embarrassed, he'd pretended to be unaware of their scrutiny, and had walked by with the end of his sati drawn up over his head to shadow his face.

Although he was lonely, he was rarely alone. Everything about Vanar life tended to be conducted in the company of others. The Vanar men spent a good deal of their waking hours in the shelter's community baths, more, he suspected, out of boredom than an obsession with personal hygiene. Nathan's flash sink doubled as a toilet, but for anything more than a simple piss in the night, he had to use the community baths on the ground floor.

He found the baths a necessity, but didn't enjoy the curious stares or the silence that fell whenever he walked in, the empty circle that formed around him as people backed away in distrust. Whenever he disrobed and fed his clothing into the bath's cleaner, standing naked and impatient for it to reemerge, he endured the open examination of men marveling at his freckled pale skin, the whispers and indiscreet pointing at the blond hair at his groin, the glint of gold curling across his chest. Only their obvious fear kept him from being physically touched.

He finally learned to use the baths at night, by silent agreement with the other residents. Alone, he exercised nude in the shelter's gymnasium and swam to exhaustion in the long, shallow pools, his muscles slack from long disuse in prison. As his body hardened, he felt his mood improve, his spirit reviving. He had survived growing up in Westcastle. He could survive Vanar. Eventually, just as he had Westcastle, he would escape Vanar as well. He would never give up hope.

Although he was still treated with wary distrust, he was often stopped in the streets, usually by a Vanar woman either scolding or curious. His halting apologies and incomprehension usually discouraged any lengthy conversation. He learned which areas to avoid, not for fear of crime, but because naekulam were discouraged from invading areas reserved for more privileged classes, particularly women from the Nine Families.

Curiously, one place that was not off limits to him, or any Vanar regardless of family, sex, or rank, was the Assembly of Families, the heart of Vanar justice. The Assembly was the largest building in the city.

A long, undulating staircase led up to the columned porch of the semicircular building, and an assortment of Vanar citizens usually could be found scattered across the steps, a colorful spectrum of sati. Anyone could petition to be heard by the Assembly, even the white-robed naekulam generally huddled protectively at the far end of the shadowed colonnade, with expressions of either hope or dejection as they waited for their hearing.

He spent several weeks sitting on the floor in the men's public balcony watching the proceedings on the multiple layers below, not understanding a damned thing, but entranced by the mystery. It became the highlight of his day, hours spent enjoying the choreographed chaos, the multitude of discussions flowing around him like atonal music. Here was the key, he knew, to the soul of Vanar. He knew there was some kind of pattern, just outside his comprehension. The gestures and faces were curiously relaxed, like a family reunion of a thousand contentious relatives, everyone at ease with the familiarity and the arguments.

He watched as an elderly naekulam gestured eloquently with his hands as he talked to two Vanar women, serious expressions on their young faces. Whatever point the old man had to make, it convinced the women to lead him off across the vast hall, swallowed up by masses of other discussions. Nathan saw the three later when he descended from the balcony, the old man and two women now kneeling beside an older woman seated against the marble wall, the naekulam silent and immobile as the younger women discussed his plight, their hands moving with the same grace as they spoke. He wondered if the old man had won his case, wondered what his case might have been. Wondered if he would ever be able to understand Vanar well enough to plead his own causes.

Occasionally, he would see a face he'd seen elsewhere in the city in the swirl of figures in the vast open hall and feel the strange shock of recognition without actually knowing who she was. Once he had seen young Namasi dva Ushahayam ek Sahmudrah, sitting on a ledge with a woman in an identical shimmering green sati who could have been her sister. He observed how they spoke, their hands flitting like butterflies in rhythm with their speech. It made him again deeply lonely and intensely aware of how naturally the Vanar touched each other with casual ease, all but him. Namasi threw back her head and laughed, her round face smooth, delicate, her companion's arm around her shoulders. He felt his face flush hot, a bittersweet tension in his gut, watching from his hidden vantage until they left.

Once he saw the Dhikar police Qsayati, Vasant Subah, walk by below him, unaware of his presence. His skin prickled with a strange fascination. She strode confidently across the marble floor, kneeling gracefully before two other women seated along the curved ledge. The Qsayati bowed and sat back on her heels. As she spoke, she gestured languidly with one arm. Even from this distance, Nathan knew which arm it was. Her mouth moved, words drowned in the chorus of voices echoing through the hall.

And once, he had seen a high-level meeting of the nine *prathae h'máyah* of the High Families, all but two in the flesh. Of the two being sent in remote, he recognized only Yaenida Nga'esha, the other transmitted image of a woman far younger and, he assumed, far from Vanar. The nine matriarchs of the High Families sat with the female members of their families in a circle around the center of the hall, listening as several women took their turn to speak. The audience was larger than usual, tension in the air, but he understood no more of this discussion than he had the old naekulam's. One pratha h'may had spotted him in the crowd, a woman with a face like chiseled stone, wearing the Changriti burgundy. Even separated by the mass of bodies milling between them, he felt the hatred in her eyes like an unpleasant intimate touch. Not all Vanar found him an entertaining novelty.

Vanar was a warm planet with a shallow axis, the seasonal difference between winter and summer measured in rainfall. Even in the dead of winter, it was infrequently cold but rained constantly. He found a discarded umbrella in a rubbish pile in the early morning while wandering the streets looking for odd jobs before the automated cleaners arrived. Half a dozen of its intricate spokes were broken, the fragile silk torn. He sat cross-legged on the floor of his room with tiny bottles of varnish and glue, scavenged scraps of cloth and pieces of wood shims he carved himself, carefully repairing the umbrella while rain fell in gray sheets outside his window.

His nearest neighbor across the hall, an elderly man with a ratty white-streaked braid reaching nearly to his knees, sometimes halted just beside the archway, watching him while pretending not to. Nathan learned to ignore him, surprised one dismal afternoon as the man leaned in the doorway and placed a bright red umbrella against the wall then brushed away an imaginary insect from his face to avoid looking at Nathan. When the man left without a word, Nathan examined his umbrella, opening it to find a long rent in the silk.

He studied it thoughtfully, then shrugged. Basting the torn edges together, he glued a long strip of discarded silk across the tear and let it dry before he painted on a layer of thin varnish to waterproof the surface. He left it balanced against the open doorway before he went to sleep, and found it gone in the morning.

Two days later, the old man walked straight into his room, and without a glance in his direction began to cook a meal using Nathan's own food supply. He watched carefully as the old man expertly chopped his vegetables, adding pinches or handfuls of different spices, and stirred it into a hot oiled pan. The old man served one platter for Nathan, one for himself, and they ate together in total silence. It was certainly the best meal he had had since his release. When they had finished, the old man cleaned up their dishes before he left without a word or glance.

If Nathan had any hope he might start up a friendship, it was quickly dashed, the old man ignoring him as studiously as before. He tried to reciprocate, walking into the old man's room with food to prepare another meal, but had been firmly and all but physically ejected. A debt had been paid, that was that.

Nathan spent a good deal of his time sitting on the lumpy sleeping mat in the alcove, his chin resting on arms crossed on the window ledge, gazing out the moon-shaped window. This was the only truly pleasant aspect of his apartment, the view overlooking the city all that kept the room from being claustrophobic. He still had trouble with bad dreams. When he couldn't sleep, he sat in the dark and stared out into the night.

The city, which he later learned was called Sabtú, extended out in the valley below him, bisected by the river. The lights of the old town glittered in the dark like gems of necklaces thrown down carelessly. The rest of the city fanned out from the narrow hills at the mouth of the valley and spilled into the basin for thirty miles. Streets branched off to looped clusters of residential villages, each quarter populated by its own extended family network, complete with small markets and cafes and entertainment. A cluster of bridges roped across the river, and on the other side of the river, a compact mix of tall spires towered at the core of the city, gleaming white spikes and turrets blended together like fused crystals. The lights of taxis and long public trains lit the roadways. Long boulevards trailed from the center like crooked spokes of a half wheel, and at their far ends, the roads ended at the walls of sprawling private villas of the High Families, the palatial estates tiny cities in their own right on the hillsides. He eventually determined which of them belonged to the Nga'esha, the massive fortresslike walls snaking their way across the hillside, nestling where the river forked on the edge of the city.

Most days, the haze of mist obscured the horizon around the city. On a clear morning, Nathan could see as far as the agricultural fields, rolling land cleared of the massive native trees. All he had wanted to do was to walk out into the fields to examine the drones trundling along the rows of crops, sunlight glinting from their metallic beetle backs as they searched out what few bugs had managed to elude Vanar importation screens. There had been no fences, no gates that he could see, but he'd only reached the edge of the fields before he'd been stopped politely but firmly on the road by solidly built women in drab green coveralls. Sitting between them, sweating and terrified, he'd been taken back to the city in their maintenance patrol hoverfloat and dropped off at the first street they came to. He didn't attempt it a second time.

Sometimes, if the clouds had lifted far enough, he could even just make out the black band of indigenous forest in the distance that surrounded the edges of the city like a lake of darkness. The Vanar cared surprisingly little about the native rain forest, their efforts concentrating on terraforming an ever-increasing expanse of land. Vanar or Hengeli, human beings needed food evolved from the same genetic foundations, native Vanar flora too primitive and too alien for human physiology. Narcotics the Vanar derived from the native svapnah were not as strong or as effective as those of other off-world sources, nor could Vanar hardwoods compete with the giant forests of other long-established timber companies.

Occasionally, he saw a convoy wandering through the jungle toward Dravyam to the south, or the high-speed train to Praetah in the northeast, lights winking briefly before it disappeared, burrowing its way through the dark. Far behind him, hidden on the other side of the mountain, cargo lifters launched from a remote airfield, bright specks of light like shooting stars in reverse, arrowed at an angle into the night sky.

But as elegant as it was, Sabtú was small for a capital city and an unimposing center for the planet's government. Compared to the glittering cities of other planets in the settled systems, Sabtú appeared almost naively provincial. But appearances, Nathan knew, were deceiving. To his eyes, Vanar houses most resembled half-melted wedding cakes, built from natural materials and decorated with colored glass windows, copper tiled roofs, open atriums, and fountains and breezy verandas drenched in flowers and climbing ivy. Its rustic ambience was careflully crafted, with all of Vanar's sophisticated technology deep underground, hidden under a veneer of simplicity. Nathan tried not to think too much about their technological capability he had already experienced at firsthand.

It was as much an act of minor defiance as boredom to grow a mustache. He'd only once let the hair on his lip grow as a teenaged boy, curious to see how it would change his face. The spotty growth had made him look even more an ungainly adolescent. After a few months, it was a relief to finally shave it off. Now it grew in with an adult luxuriance, a thick red gold he enjoyed stroking with his fingertips. He kept it immaculately trimmed with a pair of tiny scissors, every hair clipped neatly in a line just meeting his upper up. He smiled whenever it was stared at in the streets, with a strange perverse pride.

When the rains let up, he escaped the monotony and loneliness of the charity shelter by walking through the parks of Sabtú. Taking advantage of a sunny day, he was grateful to have the freedom to wander, open air on his skin. The trailing edge of his sati hung limp from one shoulder, the heat of the sunlight against his bare head as he wandered through the wooded park. He stopped to admire a dense mass of purple linaria growing along the winding path, then crouched on one knee to let his fingers trail through the rich earth under a carefully pruned ginkgo. When he stood, he plucked one of the ginkgo's rounded leaves, rubbing his thumb across its surface as he studied the splotches of yellow against the dark, vibrant green. He absently wondered what the pH of the endless rainfall was, missing his portable analysis lab kit, and was trying to diagnose what might be causing the discoloration when a light touch on his arm made him jump.

As he turned his head to look at the woman standing beside him, someone grasped him by his other arm. He caught the glint of a bead inserted within the woman's right ear. Each of them had a tiny button of black protruding from the hollow of the throat where a subvocal transmitter had been surgically embedded. The rest of the implant was barely detectable, the spidery threads of a subcutaneous parasite wrapped around the windpipe just visible under smooth skin. He recognized a couple of the devices clipped to their more functional than decorative belts, as well as the emblems pinned to their shoulders. White kirtiyas over white saekah, theirs was not the unbleached drab colorlessness of his linen sati but pearl white, iridescent, luminous white. The color of power and authority.

The color of police.

The two Dhikar smiled at him, professional cold smiles as each of them kept one hand on his arms while the other remained casually loose, palm open and ready. His mouth suddenly dry, for a wild moment he was convinced he was being arrested for picking leaves. As they pulled at him gently, urging him down the gravel path, he tried to explain, unable to think of the Vanar words to protest his innocence. He was physically stronger than either of the women, but before he could object further, one of them had almost lazily grasped his wrist. The implants under her skin vibrated, and sharp agony shot through his entire body, bringing him gasping to his knees. The humming stopped, but the pain lingered. Even so, he knew from previous experience he'd gotten off lightly. They led him stumbling down the pathway, incapacitated, murmuring to him encouragingly, but warily cordial.

Another woman in a white kirtiya sat on one of the carved stone slabs Nathan had never been sure was meant to be sculpture or bench. Her face was dappled in the shadows of a tree, bent over an open reader balanced on her thigh, one leg tucked under her, deceptively benign. Light winked from her sati clip, the polished stones a deep wine color. The women stopped him a few paces from her, the three of them lined up side by side with their hands firmly gripping him between them.

As she looked up, Nathan recognized her, even expecting her. He would have been surprised had it not been her. Vasant Subah. He knew what the words meant now in Vanar: *spring morning.* Her dark eyes would have been pretty had their expression not been ice cold.

The two women did not relinquish their grasp on him, his arm still numbed to the shoulder, preventing him from greeting her with anything more than a small bow of his head. At the same time, he remembered he still held the ginkgo leaf in his other hand, the one not numbed. His fingers closed over it, crushing the tender evidence in his sweating fist.

She didn't return his salutation, simply staring at him impassively for a long moment before snapping the flatscreen shut and placing it on the bench beside her. She stroked light fingers along her forearm absently, as if unaware of her habitual action, the implant pushing up the skin of her wrist into knotted ridges. He glanced at it, then forced himself to look away, his heart twisting hollowly in his chest.

"The public exposure of male pubic hair is considered indecent," she said finally. She spoke in Hengeli, her accented voice mild. It was the complete lack of anger or hostility that frightened him more than had she shouted. He felt suddenly sick, wondering how they had found out about Namasi.

She waited, and when he didn't respond, she said, "Complaints have been made. To continue to intentionally exhibit your sexual hair is not only obscene, but deeply offensive." Now he was confused, and that frightened him even more. *Sexual hair?* Then he understood, almost laughing with the tension. He reached up despite the grip on his arm to touch the edge of his mustache incredulously.

She smiled, a thin, polite grimace. "Get rid of it," she said. "You won't be warned again, *ajah ae malinam.*" The insult was spoken in such an amiable tone, he didn't realize until he'd translated it in his head: *worthless shit from a goat.* She waited until she was sure he'd understood. Then she stood, and the two women on either side released him and followed her at a languid pace. His hands trembled badly as he pulled the edge of his sati over his head to conceal his face.

The attendant at the baths was an old man, bad tempered and sullen, and Nathan was sure it gave him a certain malicious delight to strip the offending hair from the face of the foreigner. Without his mustache, his upper lip felt oddly sensitive. That night, he swam by himself in the baths, trying to exorcise his fear by sheer physical exertion, but it left him feeling sick and depressed.

He sat staring out of the tiny window, his wet hair cold against his back, while his fingers constantly brushed the denuded skin of his upper lip. Fear wore out to a numb rage, memories of the months of interrogation obscuring the view of the city below.

"It's just a goddamned mustache," he murmured to himself, trying unsuccessfully to convince himself.

That night, he dreamed again. A dozen blue-robed women silently watched his futile efforts to dress himself in an endlessly long length of linen that seemed to grow out of the cracked floor. His wrists were weighted down with heavy gold bracelets studded with jewels, locked together like manacles, making it impossible to drape the cloth around his hips. The folds frustratingly slipped from his nerveless fingers. The cloth crumbled into dust in his hands. He looked up at his silent judges as Vasant Subah stepped over their cardboard figures.

She glared at him with undisguised distaste, dark eyes over high, sharp cheekbones. The skin of her forearm writhed, drawing his unwilling attention. He stared in helpless fascination as the implant came alive, metamorphed into a black insect slowly waving long stick legs as it oozed out from under her skin and crept around her wrist, intimate in its wiry knowing embrace. His own skin crawled. He would do anything, he knew, say anything, submit to *anything* to escape that creature's touch.

"Answer the question," she said, but her voice was Yaenida's. He was startled; he couldn't remember being asked any questions, but suddenly wanted desperately to answer them, wanting to make this woman believe him.

The sati in his hands vanished, as if sucked back into the center of the earth. Vasant Subah pointed over his shoulder. "It is for your own good." He looked behind him at the whitewomb in dread. Thousands more squatted in long rows, so many they vanished into the dream-darkened horizon. He tried to run.

Without knowing how he had gotten there, he was abruptly inside it, the whitewomb skin sealed up behind him without a seam, jelly crawling down into his throat, filling his lungs.

"Mer'iv báat sunoh," he called to the obscure forms moving outside the whitewomb wall. He pressed his fingers against the pulpy skin, begging. "Listen to me, please . . ." The shadows continued on, ghost figures, unconcerned. He woke to more rain, clawing his way

into consciousness and gasping, the air too thick and humid in his lungs. His head pounded with a vicious headache.

It rained for four days, a constant lukewarm drizzle too tenuous to be anything more than annoying. At night, the lights of the city were obscured in the glitter of the crystal drops of water running from the edge of the roof jutting over his window. Nathan's window faced west, and in the morning, the light poured in on his face, golden on clear days, the color of molten lead on cloudy days. At sunrise and sunset, he was high enough to look down on sharp-winged black swallows, the patch of white between their shoulders, sweeping and tumbling close to the building. Higher above him, the specks of dark purple martins spiraled, trilling as they rode the air currents to feast on insects driven up by the rain. By midmorning, both martins and insects vanished, seeking shelter from the humid afternoon heat to wait for evening.

The humid heat slowly turned his tiny room in the public residence into a sauna. After four days of confinement in his microscopic apartment, the constant noise of his neighbors echoing down the hallways, not even the heat, the rain, or insects could keep him inside.

Fear locked him in, loneliness drove him out, enough to risk another encounter with Vasant Subah.

He left his apartment, beginning the slow climb down from the complex to the narrow street emptying out into the city below. The streets, at least, were swept clean if not dry, and by pulling the end of his sheer sati over his face as a screen, he could discourage the worst of the tiny gnats still hovering in clouds.

While the white sati marked him as an outcast, it also gave him a certain luxury of isolation, free to roam the wide, sculpted boulevards with tiny oases of parks, winding streets lined with shops and tall Vanar houses, all curves and melting shapes. Steel gray clouds hovered close to the ground, the rumble of thunder in the distance, and when the rain began its slow drizzle, he ignored it, as did most Vanar habituated to the endless wet. Within minutes, his clothes were soaked, and he held his well-patched umbrella up more to keep the water from running into his eyes than for any hope of staying dry.

He was not the only one on the streets, but he was one of the few men outside, and the only one unaccompanied. Naekulam were supposed to be socially invisible and politely ignored, but he knew he wasn't an ordinary naekulam. Whenever the curious stares became too uncomfortable, he stood in front of shop windows, pretending to examine merchandise he could never even hope to afford.

As he turned away from one of these shops, he caught sight of her, at first not recognizing the tall woman in the red sati. It was more her gait, the roll of her walk that jogged his memory. Then he saw the flash of dark auburn hair.

"Lyris," he said to himself, a blaze of hope singing in his blood. Then, louder, "Hey, Lyris, it's me!" The woman didn't turn her head as she walked away from him. Here it was, his chance to get off this goddamned planet, escape from this nightmare. He broke into a run after her, hobbled by the wet cloth adhering to his legs. "Lyris!"

When she didn't respond, he thought he might have made a mistake, but when she turned a corner, she glanced back at him, the glimpse of her face enough. *"Lyris!"* He jerked up the edges of the sati, freeing his legs to run. If he saw it, he didn't understand until later that she had sped up her pace, trying to avoid him. "Lyris, wait . . ."

He grasped her arm lightly as he reached her, forcing her to stop. She swiveled her head to one side, then the other, as if she wasn't sure which way to turn to look at him. "Lyris, it's me, Nate."

He wasn't prepared for the hostility as she spun around and glared at him. "I know who it is," she said harshly. *"Everybody* knows who you are. Leave me alone, Nathan, okay?"

"Lyris, you have to help me, please. . . ."

"Let go of me!" She shook off his hand fiercely. "I want nothing to do with you, Nathan. Don't bother me, or I'll call the Dhikar, do you understand? Just leave me the hell alone!"

He stared after her, too shocked to feel hurt as she walked swiftly away. Disbelieving, he mouthed her name. A sudden flurry of motion out of the corner of his eye made him turn his head just in time for a stinging slap to his face. He staggered, then nearly fell as a short, furious woman jabbed stiff fingers hard against his chest. He was taller than she, outweighing her by nearly half, and he stared at her as she berated him loudly, jerking at his sati, shaking an indignant finger in his face, shouting at him angrily. A small crowd formed as women stopped to watch, a few grinning. They laughed as she pushed his chest again.

All the repressed fury and resentment suddenly boiled up in him.

He took a single step toward her, his fists clenched, teeth bared, shaking with anger and even eager for a fight. She froze, her eyes round, her mouth an O of astonishment as she jerked back from him. He stopped, glancing at the expressions of alarm and outrage from the gathering witnesses. Several others from the crowd stepped up protectively beside the short woman. It took all his self-control to unclench his fists and bow his head meekly.

Emboldened by the reinforcements, she resumed her harangue with more belligerence. The mood of the crowd had changed, the amusement replaced by a grim hostility as he was pummeled. Ringed in by the women slapping and pushing him several more times, he stumbled and tried to pull his wet sati to cover his legs and arms before he gave up. Although the blows were more annoying than actually painful, the ominous quiet frightened him. The women finally left him huddled with his face pressed against a building, fingers clutching at the damp stone wall.

When he turned, the spectators had gone but for a lone woman standing quietly, the rain tapping against her umbrella. His own lay torn on the street. He shot her a glare of pure hatred as he adjusted the edge of his soaked sati over his head with shaking fingers and picked up his broken umbrella. She watched him, her eyes impersonal, then *tsk*ed before she turned away. It wasn't sympathy, he realized, but the disapproval a benign mother might give an ill-behaved child.

He knew he could not take much more. Not even Vasant Subah had been able to crush him as thoroughly as this place was doing now. His dream of escape had shattered. But if he was going to at least survive here, he knew he had to find help.

It took him the rest of the day to walk the long boulevard leading to the Nga'esha Estate. Slogging through the rain and mud, ignoring the traffic speeding by him, he hiked up the wandering hillside toward the walled villa. The road ended at a large gatehouse. Two Dhikar women who could have been clones of those with Vasant Subah but for the blue and gold edging embroidered on their white kirtiya and saekah, watched him approach with wary curiosity. They emerged, right hands flexing the cords of the implants under the skin of their forearms in warning.

He stopped in front of them, his body trembling from fatigue. His drenched sati clung to him, slovenly and mud-stained. Miserable, his head hung, the rain pouring from the ends of his wet hair like a veil of beads over his face.

"My name is Nathan Crewe," he said in stumbling Vanar, praying they could understand him. "I want to see Yaenida Nga'esha."

He suddenly covered his face with his hands, appalled at himself but unable to keep from weeping. Slowly he went to his knees in the wet road, no longer caring, unaware of the gentle hands on his shoulders and the women's surprised and uncertain concern.

V

AFTER HIS SECOND AUDIENCE WITH YAENIDA, SHE HAD GIVEN HIM NO idea of exactly when he would be summoned back to the Nga'esha House, leaving him waiting a lot longer than he ever expected or hoped before she sent for him. While he waited, whenever he couldn't stand the cramped closeness of the shelter, he worked off his nervous energy by walking. From one end of the city to the other, wandering the streets aimlessly. He learned to walk with his eyes down, diffidently polite, his shoulders hunched to try to make himself appear as small and nonthreatening as he could manage, not easy when he stood a good foot taller than everyone else.

Once, in the center of the city, he had seen a gathering of women on the streets suddenly stop and bow low, hands pressed palms together and raised against their foreheads. Five people appeared clad in voluminous black sati, the ends drawn up over their faces. They walked slowly, their own hands pressed together and bowing slightly in response to the crowd with each step. With a shock, Nathan realized they were men. He stood gaping in surprise as they passed. One of the five stopped in front of him, staring back with mild green eyes in puzzled curiosity. He was nearly as tall as Nathan, his freckled skin light, his hair dark red.

"*Bhraetae*," the man said, his voice questioning. *Brother.*

Nathan shook his head, speechless. Still puzzled, the man smiled, and walked on with his companions. Nathan watched them pass through the respectful crowd.

"*Bhaqdah,*" a woman's quiet voice said beside him. He jumped, glancing down at her. She grinned at him in a manner that made him uncomfortable. He had no idea what the word meant. "Bhaqdah," she repeated, nodding toward the figures disappearing in the crowd, and laughed. He bowed to her quickly and escaped.

When his tutor arrived, it took a bit of complicated explanation before he realized the men were devotees of the Goddess, in the service of the temple. She wasn't able to clarify why one of them had been a tall, green-eyed redhead.

Whereas the city's lone temple was secreted behind high walls, a high-security fortress heavily guarded by Dhikar, nearly every neighborhood had its own kaemahjah, most of them unassuming buildings surrounded by modest gardens. He'd watched the men and women who frequented them, heard the faint music and laughter behind the screened windows. While it was not generally encouraged, not even naekulam were forbidden inside its walls. Once or twice, strange women recognized him, smiled and beckoned to him, their implication clear. He had bowed and smiled politely in return, pretending not to understand, and moved on.

He remembered too much of his childhood in an occupied country, and the succession of men in the enemy military police who'd adopted him as their unofficial mascot, perched him on their desks like a pet, his baby legs bouncing against their knees. They'd laughed and pampered him and given him sweets, most of them simply fathers missing their own children far away. But one or two had given him money in exchange for a few minutes of privacy in the shadows behind the barracks. It had seemed natural; they were nice to him, and he had *wanted* to make them happy in return. Although he hadn't enjoyed it, none of them had ever done anything to hurt him.

Except once, the one who had smelled of sweat and had wanted something different, something Nathan's small body wasn't yet able to

accommodate. When he'd been found, bloody and crying, his other friends had promised him they would make sure that man never hurt anyone again. True to their word, the bad-smelling man disappeared, although Nathan never questioned what might have happened to him.

It took several more years before his own sexual feelings fully developed, mixed up with feelings of guilt and anger and a desperate need to survive. Now that past seemed unreal, as if it had happened to someone else far away. But he was deeply, viscerally lonely.

He didn't want to go back to the shelter, even though the day had been hot, his sati sticking to his sweating skin. He had reached the road turning toward the charity shelter, and stood looking toward its rooftops, unable to face another evening listening to conversation and laughter he was excluded from. He veered off and half an hour later found himself standing uncertainly outside a local kaemahjah.

A woman emerged from the cool shadows under the archway, eying him curiously. He adjusted the sati over his head, more to reveal his light hair and distinctly un-Vanar face, and felt as exposed as a street whore opening her coat to display what was on offer, both aroused and disgusted with himself.

As he expected, she recognized him, smiled broadly, and beckoned to him encouragingly. There were very few in the city by now who didn't recognize the tall, blue-eyed naekulam with light hair and pale skin. He'd even seen pictures of himself in the media, shown to him by an astonished woman who had looked up from browsing the news on her reader to find him standing in front of her in the flesh. He couldn't read the corkscrew script, wondering what it said about him, wondering when and how anyone had been able to record him in the first place. He was famous, and felt anything but.

Now that the Nga'esha had extended a nominal patronage, giving him a certain amount of protection, the uncertain hostility toward the alien in their midst had diminished. More often than not his novelty made him the object of fascination, but his ignorance still left him surrounded in a bubble of isolation. The woman spoke to him, and raised one eyebrow questioningly. He caught the word *thirsty*.

"Yes." His voice was hoarse. "I am thirsty."

"Come inside, and have a cool drink."

The door opened into a dark, cool interior, the woman's hand

pressed genially against his back. He felt dizzy, as if he were falling inside, pulled into the dark, lost and oddly excited.

Whatever he might have imagined it to be like before, the reality was disappointing. The woman at the gate led him into a small office, plain in its furnishings. Like most Vanar buildings, the walls were curved, with no sharp angles anywhere, and textured with a light earth-colored plaster spread on by hand. Dilapidated pillows had been scattered along the low ridge running the length of the wall. Dappled sunlight from the carved screens of half-oval windows placed well above his head threw sharp patterns on the plain flecked granite floor, buffed and polished. No paintings or other decorations lessened the room's austerity. A low desk of dark red wood dominated the room, littered with papers and cubes, the reader left powered down and silenced.

A younger woman in a plain saekah and kirtiya entered just long enough to hand him a cold glass of an infusion with a scent of saffron, and after wading through the usual confusion of garbled words and gestures, he gave her his datacard. She left him alone, seated on the uncomfortable ledge.

Already he regretted the impulse, trapped in an isolated office without his card, his nervousness building. He had finished the drink, and was debating whether or not to go in search of his card, when she returned in the company of a heavyset woman. He didn't need the gold trim on her Middle Family sati to know she was an important official, her bearing itself enough. She held up an imperious hand to keep him from jumping to his feet. "Tah byát, bah'chae," she said.

He greeted her with pressed palms and bobbed his head jerkily. "Large health, l'amae, and long fortune," he blurted, knowing his mistake as he made it. Too late he remembered his knees were apart, and jerked his legs together. The heat on his face told him his skin had reddened with embarrassment. All he wanted now was his card back and to leave as quickly as possible.

She returned his pathetic salutation with grave dignity, her right hand held over her heart, and a slight bow. "Good health to you, young brother, and . . . long fortune," she returned with an amicable smile. She spoke to him in rapid Vanar, a question from the upward inflection.

"My Vanar is very bad," he said, one of the few phrases he knew correctly. "I apologize, please speak slowly."

"Ah." She settled herself behind the low desk and shook back the heavy gold bracelets on her arms before she laced her fingers together across the polished surface. "I am Mitaeb dva Shukvhar," she said, pronouncing each syllable with exaggerated care. "Would you like another drink?"

He flushed as he recognized her use of the pronoun; she had placed him in lowest possible rank, the *you* usually employed for young children. "No, thank you, l'amae," he said with as much self-respect as he could, and was careful to use the highest pronoun he knew, although he wasn't sure of the proper verb form that went with it. The corners of her mouth twitched in what he hoped was amusement.

Mitaeb opened his card, examining it briefly before she slid it into the reader. The geometric patterns vanished, replaced by lines of data in the corkscrew script he couldn't read. She spoke, and the younger woman bent to gaze at the screen, the two conferring as he waited, feeling invisible. They discussed his card at length, pointing to this item and that, Mitaeb doing most of the talking while the younger woman punctuated the conversation with occasional grunts of assent.

Mitaeb glanced up once at him, and asked skeptically, "Sahakharae?"

He gulped. "No," he said quickly, and wished he knew how to explain the misunderstanding, he had changed his mind, he would just like to go now. She frowned as she tried to comprehend his mangled grammar. Then she leaned back, rubbing the fingernails of one hand under her chin before she finally shrugged, uncomprehending.

There was more discussion he couldn't follow, except for words here and there that left him feeling more apprehensive. He caught the name *Nga'esha* and watched her associate lift one shoulder eloquently, perplexed.

Mitaeb popped his card out of the reader, tapping it against one palm as she studied him silently, then nodded to her associate. The younger woman indicated he was to follow her, and he stood. Hesitating, he held out his hand toward Mitaeb for his datacard, and received a look of amused surprise. When she made no move to give it back to him, he dropped his arm and allowed himself to be propelled out.

He became quickly lost in the maze, shuffled from one room to the next, the incomprehensible gibberish battering him. Dazed, he found himself in a small chilly room with two people, a man and a woman. The woman spoke cordially to him, then stepped out as the man began to remove Nathan's clothing. Resigned, Nathan held his arms up as the man unwound his sati, then gestured for Nathan to strip off his short mati. His naked flesh goosepimpled, Nathan watched him fold them all neatly. The woman returned as the man stood in one corner, and she examined Nathan's body with a brusque thoroughness he had not been subjected to since prison. She probed every surface and orifice of his nude body with complete indifference. Once done, she patted his arm as if he were a child, and left.

The man handed him a small paper cup, and after a few gestures, it was clear what was next expected of him before he was left alone. Nathan stared at the closed door numbly for a minute, stepped to it, and cracked it open to peer out. The man's back was to the door, and he glanced over his shoulder as the door opened, smiling and nodding at him encouragingly. Nathan quietly closed the door.

There was nowhere to sit down in the tiny room, not even the usual built-in ledge, and he found himself leaning against the cold wall, his face cradled in the crook of his arm with his eyes squeezed shut, the chill air raising gooseflesh as he struggled to get an erection. *What a world*, he thought, massaging his slack penis. *I can get it up for a dying old woman, and now I'm trying to make love to a paper cup . . .*

He tried to think of something erotic, trying not to remember the back alleys of Westcastle, floundering for nebulous images. His hand tired of pumping. "Come on, you son of a bitch," he muttered, glaring down. His penis thickened slightly, and he pumped harder as it swelled. "Yes, that's it, let's do it . . ." And he suddenly remembered there was a strange man standing a few feet away, waiting for him to finish. His penis sagged.

After several more minutes of concentration and steady rhythm, he felt a tiny shiver in his legs and stomach. He watched the semen dribble into the cup, feeling more relief than pleasure. His hand ached, his penis was ruddy and sore, and he felt his back twinge from the awkward position. He hadn't enjoyed sex less than this in a long time. He wasn't sure if a glorified sperm bank was much better than straightforward prostitution.

He opened the door, and the man took the cup from him, snapping a transparent lid on it deftly, disinterested with the contents, then pointed to a small washbasin and took the cup away down the hall. The woman returned after he had replaced his clothes, and he found himself in a large, sunny room with a half dozen other men, most of them the oddly androgynous sahakharae. The others lounged on low settees, conversing in hushed monotones. Another man sat removed from them, also a naekulam but dressed in a white sati in considerably better shape than Nathan's own. He sat absorbed in a religious book, judging by the way he silently mouthed the words while rocking slightly.

All but the pious naekulam gaped at him as he was left standing in the room, his alien blue eyes and light skin, his sati bundled clumsily around himself. One man leaned over and murmured something to his companion, who smirked maliciously.

Ignoring them, he sat cross-legged on a well-worn floor pillow, staring at his hands in his lap. Once in a while, a woman would appear, call out a name, and one of them would stand lethargically and plod after her. After what felt like hours, she stood in the doorway and said dubiously, "Nay-teen Kah-roo?"

"Close enough," he muttered, and followed her back out into the maze, past rooms that looked somehow familiar now, and ended back in Mitaeb's offices. He walked through dust motes floating in the shafts of sun through the carved screen, his white sati momentarily splashed with golden motifs. Mitaeb looked up as he entered, and they each went through the ritual greetings before he sat down. She came out from behind the desk to sit next to him, her thigh almost touching his, with the reader in her lap. Picking up his hand, she pressed it to the screen against an idealized swirl to record his fingerprints.

"This is your registration," she said slowly. "Genetic registration. Understand?"

"Yes," he said. He would have said yes even if he had not, anything to get it over with and be allowed to leave.

"Good anywhere. When you want, you come. If you don't want, you don't. No . . ." she said a word he didn't know, but guessed it meant responsibilities. Or maybe problems. Or limitations. Or maybe something completely different. "Understand?"

"Yes."

She then handed him back his datacard, the square of blank white plastic seemingly unchanged, along with a thin booklet written in the incomprehensible Vanar script, and delivered a small lecture he couldn't follow, finishing with *"Pasyáthme?" Understand?*

"Hae'm, l'amae."

She stared at him, her eyes shifting back and forth as she studied his face. He looked away, embarrassed as he saw she knew he did not. She tapped the card in his hand, and spoke to him slowly, simple words a child could follow. "You come. We pay. You are only naekulam, not kharvah, not sahakharae. Not big money. Little money. Okay? Now you understand?"

"Hae'm, l'amae. Pasyáthsi."

She nodded, satisfied, then tapped the booklet. "Read it," she ordered, and stood up, finally allowing him to go.

He clutched his card and the booklet, thanking her as he bowed and walked backward, impatient to leave. It was already near sundown by the time he was ushered back out onto the street.

The same woman was at the gate, and she pressed a small coin into his hand. It was not money, but a Family token, presumably hers, for what he had no idea. He thanked her hurriedly, stuffing it in the sleeve of his mati.

"Come again soon, young bhraetae," she called after him.

Not bloody likely, he thought determinedly as he walked quickly away.

VI

JUST WHEN HE WAS BEGINNING TO DESPAIR THAT YAENIDA HAD FORGOTten her promise, his pahlaqu arrived with a stout middle-aged woman in Nga'esha watered-blue saekah and kirtiya. He had not even the tiniest regret to be leaving the lifeless room in the charity shelter, and it took him less than two minutes to pack. The Nga'esha woman stood in the doorway, arms crossed across her robust chest, and glared ominously as he quickly threw his possessions into the wicker box: his spare sati, his few toilet articles, the battered reader and collection of bookcubes, the patched umbrella, the small potted plant just beginning to bud into flower, the few odds and ends he had collected since he had been released.

His heart thumped as he added a small box he'd scrounged from the rubbish, worn and stained with berry juice, expecting her to make him open it. It contained the dried leaves and seeds of what few unknown plants he had been able to collect for study. She didn't, and when he closed the lid, she merely grunted and turned away. He carried the wicker box down the stairway and out into the bright sunlight. She had kept a taxi waiting. The driver took his luggage from him, tossing it carelessly in the open back before she indicated Nathan should follow suit. The pahlaqu and Nga'esha woman sat next to the driver inside the protected cab, their backs to him. He was only grateful he wasn't expected to carry the damned box all the way on foot.

They drove through the massive gates of the Nga'esha Estate, the pahlaqu disappearing into the women's quarters while the heavyset woman indicated for him to follow her before striding off without a backward glance. He picked up his luggage and trotted after her through the men's gate. The star-shaped courtyard was deserted, the koi in the fountain sluggish under the rain-gray clouds.

He was shown to a large room in the House littered with large, embroidered pillows. A low, narrow bench ran both lengths of the long room, holding both a collection of rolled-up sleeping mats and wicker boxes much like his own. She led him to an unoccupied mound of heavy cushions, the farthest from the window. He stood in front of it, the wicker box still in his arms. After a moment's hesitation, the woman muttered to herself, took the box from him, and dropped it unceremoniously on the shelf behind the rolled bedding.

When she left, boy's faces materialized as if by magic, bright eyes watching him. None of them were over ten, which explained the bed's minuscule surface area. He unrolled the sleeping mat and settled into his small space, arranging pillows under his back against the wall. Trying to ignore the giggles and whispers, he studiously reread one of the few books he had in Hengeli for a few hours before Yaenida finally sent for him.

Vanar medical genetics and submolecular technology matched or surpassed any of that of other modern worlds, the preservation and manipulation of bloodstock common for producing such utilitarian castes as the Dhikar. But that was as far as Vanar doctrines took genetically designing their offspring. Although mothers were quite capable of controlling the sex of their children, most chose not to, at least not those in the Nine Families. Vanar kinship expanded into complicated networks, the individual subsumed into the huge community of relatives. Child swapping and adoption were common and children raised with little attention to their genetic parentage. Daughters were needed to continue running the family business. Sons were valued for the profitable alliances the family could make with other business families. Those families with no daughters, rather than resort to a medical remedy, often arranged with another to adopt a younger infant from one blessed with too many in order to carry on the adoptive family's financial interests. It was always better to be the only adopted daughter than the one competing with two or three other natural-born sisters.

Neither castes nor position within the family were rigid. Competition in the Common and Middle Families was fierce, as a woman of outstanding talent from the lower classes could always hope for marriage or even adoption into the High Families, supplanting a less-talented natural daughter. Business was paramount to blood. The households of the Nine Families were well supplied with such *tae-morae*, unmarried professional women hoping to find either patronage or high-caste men who would make advantageous marriage partners.

For him, his adoption was far less complicated than the marriage would be. Only the peculiar circumstances entangled what was normally a relatively simple matter. As Nathan was neither an infant nor daughter and with Yaenida blessed by an abundance of family, including several sons as well, there had been a heated dispute over the necessity of adoption. He had had no family to negotiate for his side, or even to sign the legal papers. The argument continued, up to the last minute. After much vociferous haggling, he was made a temporary ward of the state for the two minutes it took his pahlaqu to sign the adoption consent papers, and Yaenida paid the token sum determined to be his fair childprice.

Nathan watched from the sidelines, along with dozens of Yaenida's family and friends who gathered, he suspected, more out of curiosity than for the celebration. He understood little of the heated debate, despite Yaenida's running commentary to him in Hengeli, although he felt vaguely affronted by this haggling over his childprice value and his lack of any legal rights. But neither would an infant have much say about the proceedings, and the contortions the Vanar Court found itself having to perform in order to satisfy its own laws amused him.

Yaenida asked for his datacard, and he pulled it out of the little holder around his neck he kept tucked inside his sati. The chief legal clerk slipped it into her reader to transfer the data to his new card, this one a pale blue ringed with High Family gold. Anyone could wear a blue sati, but it was harder to forge an identity card, his DNA encoded in the strip making it useless except to the one person whose genetic prints matched the card. The new card was adjusted to reflect his new family alliance and suddenly elevated status. There was some confusion and argument, which Nathan understood once he was brought over to the reader. The space allowed on the form to record an infant's handprint was far too small to accommodate his adult-sized hand. Finally, they were satisfied with his thumbprints only. No one seemed particularly interested in the fact that he was literate enough, even in Vanar, to have signed his own name.

Her hand had to be supported on the reader, but Yaenida signed with a bold if shaky signature, then turned toward him with a brash smile. "Welcome, my son," she said with a touch of irony. "Come and kiss your mother with the respect she is due."

He kissed her brow, then the palms of her hands, before he knelt on the floor beside her chair, receiving congratulations and gifts from friends and family. Some were traditional: cloth and foodstuffs for the new mother, and an herb to lessen teething pain for him. The young woman who offered it stiffly was nearly vermilion with embarrassment, obviously unaware of the nature of the "child" when she had received the invitation. She couldn't know how much Nathan valued it:

he would examine the herb later, his botanical interest kindled by its medicinal properties.

Some gifts were practical: a full sati and matching mati for him in pale Nga'esha blue that would identify him thereafter as an unmarried member of Yaenida's family. When he married, the mati would be changed to Changriti burgundy. Yaenida's daughter, Yronae, laid it in his lap smiling at him arrogantly, her expression both chilly and faintly amused. Yronae may have been his new sister, but she was also Yaenida's heir, the next pratha h'máy of the formidable Nga'esha Family. He also knew she had not approved of her mother's odd arrangement. He thanked her in carefully deferential if stilted Vanar.

The amount of jewelry he received surprised him, until he later understood it was useless as none of it actually belonged to him. It was a sort of dowry, adding to his personal value as a spouse. Although he would keep it the rest of his life, he would be expected to wear it only at certain times, family ceremonies and spiritual holidays, as an advertisement of his quality for his wife's benefit. The rest of the time, it would remain in Yaenida's coffers until his marriage, when it would be transferred to Kallah's. If he was lucky enough to father a daughter, most would be given to her first husband on her marriage day.

Two of her granddaughters supported Yaenida's surviving kharvah as he tottered toward him, a man even more aged and frail than Yaenida herself, and one not in full control of his mental capabilities. "This is your new son, Grandpapa," one of the women said gently, and placed the old man's hand on Nathan's face. It was dry and cold, feeling Nathan's features with a tentative lightness, like the brush of insect wings.

"Welcome, my son," the old man quavered, a bewildered look on his blind face.

Nathan kissed his brow and hands. "Thank you, Father," he said, and the old man looked even more confused by his new son's strange accent as he was steered away toward his own seat surrounded by his male relatives.

The afternoon's feast, he later knew, was not as sumptuous as it might have been, but then, he was not really a child. Nor was he a girl, thus the celebration might have been unseemly were it too lavish. But Yaenida was the matriarch of one of the most important Families on

Vanar, and, bizarre or not, it was necessary to congratulate her for the new addition to her family.

It would also have been an unforgivable insult to Yaenida had Eraelin Changriti not showed up, but the hostility was palpable as she stepped in turn to praise Yaenida's new progeny. Nathan had the brief impression of the evil fairy hovering over Sleeping Beauty's cradle, predicting horrible death by spinning needle, as the Changriti pratha h'máy recited her formal admiration of Yaenida's "infant" in a cold monotone. When she finally turned away, he shivered, reluctant to admit even to himself just how badly the woman unnerved him, still shaken by the murderous attempt on his life.

Her daughter, his future bride, smiled apologetically. Kallah dva Ushahayam Changriti, heir to one of the wealthiest and most powerful women on Vanar, who would someday become pratha h'máy of the Changriti branch of the Nine Families in her turn, was slightly overweight and more than a little plain. She pressed a small box into his hands, her own trembling, before moving on. That touched him until he remembered he would be her third kharvah, lowest man on the totem pole. As they had not been included in the day's ceremony, he had yet to discover their feelings about her marrying him.

He opened the box surreptitiously, and glanced inside. A small gold brooch in the shape of a fat beetlelike creature nested in the colored paper. Its body was a polished dark red stone, its middle legs designed as a clasp to hold the folds of his sati secure. It looked old, and very expensive.

"How nice," Yaenida said quietly from her vantage point above him, and he shut the box quickly in reflex. "It's yours, by the way," Yaenida added in the same hushed stage voice. "You can keep it. It's not part of your marriage value."

He slipped it into the folds of his sati.

The feasting went on until late into the night. Yaenida had dozed off, snoring gently, cocooned in her chair with her fingers curled around the stem of a cold water pipe. His new father had been led away hours before by his small entourage. Nathan remained where he was, seated cross-legged on the overlarge cushion by Yaenida's chair, adrift on his life raft in a sea of women.

They kept his glass full, and his head buzzed, pleasantly inebriated. His facial muscles began to hurt, and he realized he had been grinning rigidly for too long. He drained his glass, and rested it on his knee while he watched a group of women dance together at one end of the room, arms linked, feet weaving enthusiastically if somewhat erratically in a complicated pattern to the music. When one stumbled, and at that stage of intoxication it happened frequently, the line rippled like dominoes on a string, the dancers laughing as they flailed for balance. It was fun to watch. He nearly dropped his glass when someone filled it. Startled, his head jerked around. It was Kallah. She nodded to him stiffly and sat down beside him.

"Hello," she said in hesitant Hengeli.

That surprised him. "Hello," he returned.

After a few moments, she said, "How are you?" with the cadence of someone who has memorized phonemes by rote with no understanding of their meaning.

"Fine, thank you. And you?"

She looked around, obviously at a loss, before she smiled, her eyes squeezed by the flesh of her cheeks, and shrugged. "That's all I know," she said in Vanar. That she had bothered to make the effort surprised him.

"Good," he said in his own primitive Vanar. "Good you Hengeli very much to say." He was distantly aware of how drunken his voice sounded, and he struggled to remember the words at all.

Then they sat together awkwardly, isolated by his lack of vocabulary and her stiff reserve. *And I'm going to be married to this woman for what might end up being the rest of my life?* he thought dryly, and wished she hadn't sat down beside him.

A dancer tottered, then her feet slid out from under her, dragging down the line on either side. Her companions laughed as she crawled drunkenly on hands and knees out of the dance toward the cushions piled around the pillars. Kallah watched them, slapping her palm against one thigh in time with the music, ignoring him as completely as if she had forgotten his existence.

"You," he said, gesturing with his hand toward Kallah, then at the dancers, "*nartamasi*, dance, no?"

She glanced at him, intrigued, before he remembered it was bad manners for a man to initiate a conversation. Then she shook her head, and said something he didn't understand. He nodded knowingly, as if he did, while fervently hoping she asked him no questions that would reveal his pretense. After a few more strained moments, Kallah patted his hand and rejoined her friends, to his relief.

He finished his glass, and watched it magically refill as one of his new "sisters" passed by. Almost as a game, he drained one after another, just to see how long it took before it was replenished. Soon the room spun and his ears burned. The skin on his face felt like it was all trying to crawl into a point on the bridge of his nose. He knew he was very drunk, and didn't care. He hadn't been drunk in a long time. It was satisfying. He polished off another.

Another dancer went down, and he laughed with the rest, clapping his hands loudly in rhythm to the music. A few of the women turned toward him, faces flushed with the dance and wine. On impulse, he pointed to himself, then toward them questioningly. They laughed, and beckoned playfully for him to join them.

He lurched to his feet, his stomach rebelling at the sudden shift of gravity. Men did not dance with women, he knew, but the astonished delight on the women's faces told him that the violation of etiquette would be allowed this once. He was drunk, he was the evening's celebrity, and most important, he was a foreigner. He knew he could be forgiven a good deal for his alienness, and would get away with much more than a native. He pushed the sleeves of his mati up his arms as one of the women slipped the end of his sati between his knees and tied it firmly around his waist to keep him from tripping over it. Gripping the forearms of the women on either side of him, he slowly bounced on the balls of his bare feet in imitation as they linked into the circle, coordinating their steps with the music. The line abruptly jerked, and he felt himself nearly lifted off the floor as the circle moved. Sheer cloth billowed as they kicked and whirled, dozens of feet jingling with gold ankle bracelets, stamping a complex rhythm against the floor.

The shorter woman on his left took up the responsibility of teaching him steps, and the rest rewarded his efforts with cheers and laughter. The musicians played slowly, then gradually faster, accelerating the pace until he felt as if he had somehow become a disembodied part, caught up with the pulse of the dance, his feet remembering steps without his conscious effort. He felt the sweat on his palms making his grasp slippery, and he held on tighter, feeling his partners' fingers dig into his own arms. The tempo sped up, dancers whirling faster and faster, reaching the limits of their abilities. He concentrated on the movement, not feeling the ache in his shoulders as he was pulled along, the burning in his calves as he pushed himself to dance as fast as he could.

A dancer two down from him missed her step, and he found himself yanked off balance, not realizing he had fallen into a near dream state until it had been broken. He tumbled to the floor, sitting down heavily, exhilarated and exhausted. His wet face suddenly hot and uncomfortable, he laughed with the rest, tangled into a pile of arms and legs and sati. His heightened senses became aware of the smell of sweat and perfume, his rapid heartbeat echoing in his ears, the rainbows of colors through a lingering haze of sweet smoke, and most of all, the touch of women's hands as they helped him off the floor, their arms around his waist, the heat of their bodies as they balanced him against their hips, half guiding, half carrying him back to his place by Yaenida's now empty chair.

His excitement subsided as he caught sight of Kallah, frowning disapprovingly in his spinning vision. Music vibrated in the pit of his stomach. An aftertaste of wine with a hint of bile rose at the back of his mouth. He pretended he hadn't seen her.

He didn't remember falling asleep, but remembered waking once, knowing it was far late in the night. He lay curled on his side, fists tucked under his chin, his head resting on the firm thigh of a young sahakharae. His neck hurt from being in one position for too long, his cheek damp with sweat. The boy smiled at him, stroking Nathan's hair from his forehead. He rolled onto his back, distantly aware of his dislike of sahakharae but unwilling to give up his pillow, and glanced around the room through an infant hangover.

Most of the women had gone, and those left were mostly Yaenida's family. They lounged around on cushions scattered haphazardly across the wide floor in various stages of consciousness, a few sprawled comatose, but most smoking water pipes and talking quietly between themselves. The musicians still played, but the dancers now were men dressed in ornate costumes leaving their young, lithe bodies half naked as they swayed seductively in a complicated spiral, taut muscles undulating. A boy child about two years old, still diapered, imitated the dancers, potbelly bared, chubby hands held splay-fingered above his head as he spun around and around in an erratic circle. A few of the women cheered him on, to the baby's unmistakable pleasure.

Nathan rolled his head to one side far enough to see his new sister Yronae leaning back against one of her kharvah, Baelam, a rather unattractive, serious-faced young man who kneaded her shoulders with studious attention. Her eyes half closed, she watched two sahakharae, the couple he had seen caressing in the garden, as they wrestled naked but for a single strip of cloth between their legs bound up around their waists. Their hands groped over their smooth, oiled bodies in an almost stylistic ritual, feet shuffling as each sought to overturn the other. Straining muscles stood out in sharp relief.

One slipped, their bodies slapping together, limbs twisting together like snakes mating. The other swung his hip into his opponent, tossing him onto his back. As he fell, he clutched the cloth around the other's waist, taking him down to the floor with him, their braided hair swung like whips. After a moment's struggle, he was pinned to the floor, his opponent's body pressed down on his like a lover. They panted, chests heaving, their open mouths nearly touching. Nathan could clearly see the frustrated desire in their faces as they stared at each other.

Yronae nodded, and they disentangled, bowed, and began again. She glanced at him, her dark eyes glittering with too much alcohol and arousal. When she smiled, it was definitely not a sisterly expression. He smiled back weakly and let his eyes close.

When he woke the second time, he was alone, the room empty and silent. Sunlight through the screens spackled the room with brilliant coins of gold. He groaned. His head pounded with a full-grown hangover, and he badly needed to piss.

"Home sweet home," he muttered to himself. "I wonder where the toilet is?"

VII

HE SLEPT FITFULLY PART OF THE MORNING ON THE SMALL SLEEPING mat he had been relegated to in the boy's communal room, his head bludgeoned by a now monster hangover and his stomach in serious rebellion. By midmorning, the headache had lessened to a point where he could stagger toward the men's baths to vomit.

He still felt bad enough that he didn't mind the sahakharae's eager hands caressing his body with curiosity, almost grateful to let them carry him as though he had no will of his own. They soaked him in a huge pool of near scalding water, scrubbing his head and body like a baby. It took all his effort to concentrate on not throwing up rather than on the language, their conversation no more to him than nonsense sounds. He hadn't even objected when they lingered over his genitals, inspecting the gold hair of his groin with more curiosity than titillation.

When they lifted him weak-kneed from the bath and stretched him belly down on the thin mattress on the floor, one of them pressed a cup of dark, syrupy liquid into his hands with an encouraging smile and a few gestures. Nathan grimaced at the bitter taste, but within minutes the pain lessened noticeably and the nausea was gone.

A soft warmth spread through his body as one of the naked sahakharae, an older man with bulging arms and strong fingers, settled himself onto Nathan's buttocks, kneeling with one leg on either side, and began massaging his back and shoulders. He felt the man's weight pressing the bones of his pelvis into the thin mat.

Nathan's mind drifted, and he realized with a dull start he had been thoroughly drugged. He twisted his head to glance over his shoulder at the man kneading the aches from his body, distantly admiring the way the sahakharae's muscles rippled all the way up his arms and across his smooth chest. Beside him, a younger sahakharae sat with slender arms balanced across his knees. The naked sahakharae smiled, even teeth shockingly white, a knowing expression in his dark eyes. Remotely, Nathan realized the sahakharae could do anything at all with him and not only was he incapable of stopping them, he couldn't even work up enough energy to care. He sighed dreamily, rolling his head back on his arms, and closed his eyes.

By the time Yaenida sent for him in the late afternoon, he had been dressed, his new blue sati properly folded, wrapped, and tied around his body. His nails were cleaned and trimmed, and now that it had grown out long enough, his hair was braided into a short queue reaching nearly to his shoulder blades. He had eaten a full meal, and both the hangover and the drug had long vanished, leaving a feeling of well-being in their wake. He walked down the long corridor, the weight of a solid gold bangle one of the sahakharae insisted he wear around his left ankle making him hyperaware of the way the folds of his sati kicked out in front of him. He didn't feel quite as good when Yronae slid open the doors.

The Dhikar chief Vasant Subah turned as he entered, her hands clasped casually behind her back, and merely raised an eyebrow as he flinched away from her reflexively. He wondered, not for the first time, if she had been the would-be assassin in the night. She smiled at him coldly, then bowed slightly to the two women sitting cross-legged on pillows arranged on a low raised dais in front of the massive low table. One of them was Yaenida Nga'esha.

The other was Eraelin dva Hadatha Changriti.

Yaenida's daughter politely directed Qsayati Subah from the room and closed the door behind them, leaving him alone with only the two women.

He stopped three paces away from the two women, hands together, crossed thumbs to his chest, and mumbled his greetings. "Tah byáti, l'amaée." Managing to wobble only slightly as he brushed the folds of his sati apart with his foot, he knelt with his legs tucked under him, palms against his thighs, and bowed from the waist.

When he straightened, he looked up at the slender Changriti pratha h'máy sitting rigidly erect next to the old woman. Wearing a dark burgundy kirtiya and saekah trimmed with gold thread, Eraelin Changriti had one leg curled under her, her hand resting on the knee of the other in a position Nathan could now recognize as one used only by higher-ranked women. She glared at him with narrowed eyes, her face with flattened cheekbones making her expression harsh. He could see the unflattering similarity between her and her daughter.

Her scowl reminded him eye contact was another of those Vanar hierarchical formulae he had yet to master. But he dared not avert his gaze abruptly enough to risk being considered tactless. Nuances were all-important. He turned back to Yaenida, looked slightly past her at an angle just enough to be polite, trying to appear attentive without looking directly at either of them.

The younger woman spoke to Yaenida in rapid Vanar, her caustic voice unpleasant. Yaenida listened politely as she puffed on her water pipe. When she had finished, the old woman turned to Nathan.

"My *tulyah*, l'amae Eraelin dva Hadatha ek Ushahayam Changriti, would like to impress upon you the fact that she is the pratha h'máy of the Changriti Family, one of the great Nine Houses." Yaenida regarded him with a bland expression he couldn't read.

"I already know that, Pratha Yaenida."

Her smile barely twitched the ends of her thin mouth. "I believe the point she wishes to make is that even though you are now Nga'e-sha, you still do not and will never have sufficient status to sully her personal name with your barbaric accent. When you are required to speak to her at all, you will address her as *jah'nari l'amae*."

He glanced at the younger woman watching him closely. "Hae'm, jah'nari l'amae," he said, doing his best to inject a note of earnestness into his struggle with the subtle pronunciation.

His effort went unappreciated. Eraelin frowned, replying in a swift rush of words. Yaenida nodded gravely, listening until the woman was finished. As Yaenida spoke to her quietly, the younger woman's face grew darker with anger. She snorted when Yaenida had finished, then glared at Nathan as she replied. He caught only a scattering of words, not enough to understand but sufficient for the sense of alarm in his gut to increase. Yaenida sighed as the younger woman concluded her tirade.

"I've explained that while you are currently studying Vanar, you are not yet capable of conversing in our language. Although I've assured her you will be competent enough soon, she has expressed doubt you will ever be sufficiently fluent. She feels this proof you might inject an undesirable genetic trait into the Changriti line. But even if you do have the intelligence to learn our language, she considers you too old and too foreign to genuinely adapt to Vanar customs, and are thus unfit for marriage to her heir."

Underneath her mild tone, Nathan sensed the edge in Yaenida's voice. "She has suggested it might be better for all concerned if you were to become sahakharae, and has offered you a modest place as such within the Changriti House." Before he could object, she continued in the same, mild voice, "I have already pointed out that this is not a fitting option for the son of the Nga'esha pratha h'máy."

Nathan sat back on his heels. Warily, he glanced at Eraelin. *"Jah'-nari l'amae, may'm Vanarha sihtay hmah,"* he said firmly. *I will learn Vanar.* The woman scowled, irritated as Yaenida smiled faintly.

He kept his eyes meticulously averted as the two women argued in heated, clipped Vanar too fast for him to follow, trying to read from their gestures and expressions what he couldn't understand. His legs began to cramp, but any shifting to ease his position would be a sign of boredom. The argument seesawed back and forth for several minutes, their rising voices punctuated with several slaps against the table, palm cupped for the maximum effect. Each time it happened, he jumped, unable to keep his nerves steady. They stopped speaking as if switched off. In the sudden quiet, he looked up.

"Remove your clothes, please, Nathan," Yaenida said.

Taken aback, he stared at her. "Excuse me?"

"Remove your clothes, please," she repeated.

Slowly, he stood and pulled the length of cloth from where it draped over his head, and unclipped it to let it unwind from his shoulders and torso. As he loosened the sati from his waist, the intricate folds around his legs came apart, spilling into a pile at his feet. He stood in only the short mati, and glanced at her questioningly, uncomfortable.

She nodded, and he pulled the mati over his head, leaving him nude but for his ridiculous gold anklet. As his flush spread down his face and reddened his chest, he glared up at the two women defiantly.

But neither Eraelin nor Yaenida seemed to be enjoying his humiliation. Yaenida had her cheek propped up on one hand, not even looking at him as she traced her finger in an idle pattern on the tabletop finish. Eraelin was gazing at him with the same detached indifference as the medical crew at public service. Her gaze lingered for a moment on the still-healing jagged gash down his left side, a permanent memento of Changriti displeasure. He resisted the urge to hide the scar protectively, then straightened to display it to her with perverse defiance. Her eyes narrowed, flicking briefly to his face in anger. Then she spoke, and he understood what she wanted by the motion of her hand before Yaenida translated.

"Turn around, Nathan."

He did, and the lack of any erotic interest, or even any evidence they meant to degrade him, made him feel all the more naked and objectified. And infuriated.

"Thank you," Yaenida said. "You may dress now."

He turned around, unable to hide his resentment. "Don't you want to examine my teeth?" he said sarcastically.

Eraelin could not understand what he said, but surprise shot across her face before she glared at Yaenida and asked an annoyed question. Obviously he was objecting to something considered perfectly normal and reasonable, his reaction out of place. His hands shook as he snatched the sati from the floor, winding it sloppily around himself before looping the bulk of it over his shoulder.

Yaenida did not change expression. "That won't be necessary," she said in a carefully neutral tone. "Your medical files cover that area. Aesthetics, however, is a subjective judgment." She waved a hand at him, shooing him off. "You may go now."

Stunned, he left without a word. As soon as the door closed behind him, several sahakharae grabbed his arms to hustle him into the men's quarters. He knew he was in trouble by their nervous looks at each other as they rearranged his sati in silence. He removed the gold anklet and handed it firmly back to its owner.

This time, Yaenida did not make him wait long.

Eraelin was gone, and Yaenida had been moved to the mountain of pillows, her water pipe already stoked and bubbling. He bowed and knelt patiently. Yaenida let him sit for several minutes, scowling moodily. Yronae and her eldest daughter watched him skeptically from the side, no doubt expecting him to screw up and breach protocol. He wondered sourly if they'd placed bets on him.

"If you have any questions, you have permission to ask them now," Yaenida said brittlely.

"Thank you," he said with exaggerated politeness. "May I ask what that was all about?"

"*That*—" she leaned forward, her eyes glittering with restrained anger—"was a financial negotiation, and none of your damned business."

It would have been easy to let his anger explode, regardless of the cost. It would have been equally as easy to curl up into a ball, back down, and crawl away. He forced himself to do neither, desperately balancing his reaction. "It is my business when you drag me in front of someone who would like nothing better than to see me dead and force me to strip so she can look me over like a slab of meat. I'm only asking you to explain why."

She brought the tip of the pipe to her mouth. To his amazement, her hand was shaking. She drew in a long breath of smoke, watching him silently past heavy-lidded eyes clouded behind the haze.

"Nathan, you get away with a lot more than you should simply because you're Hengeli, not Vanar. I've allowed it because you amuse me. But it isn't wise to push your luck." She leaned back, coughing gently, a deep wet sound. "Defiance is not only unseemly, it will also get you nothing but into trouble. You can't afford it with the Changriti."

Blowing a stream of smoke into the air, she jabbed the pipe in his direction for emphasis, her voice dangerously flat. "And I assure you, you truly *don't* want to jack too far with me."

He swallowed his anger and lowered his eyes. "Humblest of apologies, jah'nari Pratha Yaenida," he said in formalistic Vanar. He hoped it sounded as sincere as he could make it.

She coughed again, a long, rumbling sound that gradually died away, leaving her slightly flushed and a sheen of sweat on her forehead. "But as you are unfamiliar with our customs, I suppose you are owed some explanation," she said, not the least fooled by his act of contrition.

He kept his mouth shut and waited.

"You are now my son. You might consider that just strategy in some complicated game, but in Vanar eyes, you are legally and factually Nga'esha, the youngest son of Pratha Yaenida. That does more than simply protect you, it also makes you highly valuable."

"Despite my genetic defects," he couldn't help saying, then bit his lip. To his relief, she chuckled. The danger was not yet past, but it had lessened palpably.

"That was only the usual barter nonsense, Nathan. She may detest you personally, but she wants this marriage, very much so. She has not been the Changriti pratha h'máy that long, and her authority is still somewhat uncertain. She has many sisters and cousins quite willing to replace her if the opportunity arises. She needs this alliance with the Nga'esha. I am old, and all of my first-rank sons were married off long ago. We will need time and a good tutor to train you properly before you are fit to marry anyone, but as a new Nga'esha *umdhae putrah*, you have gone overnight from being naeqili to the most eligible bachelor on all of Vanar." She laughed at his astonishment. "If this marriage falls through, there will be hundreds more suitors who suddenly find you irresistible, properly educated or not. I'll have to place guards on you to prevent you from being kidnapped."

He hadn't expected that, nor did he much like the prospect.

"The Changriti are strict isolationists: they believe not a single foreigner should ever be tolerated on our sacred soil." She snorted her contempt. "That such stringent restrictions would make it near impossible for the Nga'esha to negotiate contracts with many of our off-Station clients is not a valid objection, naturally. What is the loss of Nga'esha revenues when compared to the Changriti ideal of cultural purity?" Her mocking tone evaporated. "But involving myself in your personal troubles has provoked substantial controversy within other Families. It's even been suggested that the so-called attempt on your life as well as her daughter's proposal was a deliberate maneuver, using my personal interest in you as a weakness to force my hand, hoping I would bow to pressure and get rid of you one way or the other."

"But that's not true. Is it?" He couldn't believe the assassin in the night had deliberately spared him. Or that Kallah's proposal had been her mother's idea.

She shrugged eloquently. "I am not quite so naive, nor is Eraelin quite so cunning. But I'll neither confirm nor deny it. Adopting you as my son was a countermove no one expected, least of all Eraelin. The Changriti are no friends of the Nga'esha, but instead of forcing me to dispose of you, she's now in a position where she has no choice but to accept you into her Family." She smiled coldly. "The irony does amuse me."

He felt less like her son than a pawn in a chess game, and wondered how she treated her own children.

"My reputation is secure, so it makes little difference to me what story the Changriti put forward to save face." Her glacial smile widened. "As long as they pay well enough for the privilege. With Kallah married to you, it contractually joins her Family and mine. There are considerable legal and financial obligations involved. These terms must be negotiated, and she will do what she can to get the best deal for the Changriti. How many shares against my Family is she entitled to, how many of hers can we demand liens on, termination clauses and quit claims in case of death, dissolution of the marriage contract or amount of damages if you should prove sterile, and so on."

"How romantic. I'm flattered," he said, deadpan. His mouth might get him into trouble, but he knew Yaenida well enough to know it often could get him out of trouble as well. It was the tightrope walk between the two fraying his nerves.

She tried unsuccessfully to hide her mirth. "We are a business people. Families are everything. There is no business without Family, and there are no Families without business. You either marry or are born into it. It's a closed union, Nathan. And I have brought you into my Family and made you Nga'esha. Yes, it might have been the whim of an eccentric old woman." She waved a careless hand as if brushing away gnats. "Because I'm bored and you amuse me. Because I enjoy injecting a bit of farce to irritate my overly dignified daughters. Because I'm dying and I don't give a damn. It doesn't matter what my reasons are."

Her humor faded. "But my whims are not trivial, not for you. Do try to keep that small fact in mind," she said quietly. "Here, without Family, you have nothing. You are nothing. You are *naekulam*, an outsider, unimportant, without value or rights or future. It is the worst thing that can happen to you, to lose your Family."

A bad morning, scorched bread for breakfast or spilled tea, a snap of her fingers and the lives and fortunes of billions on a hundred planets would feel the aftershocks. A world cut off from the rest of civilization would be economically ruined and left to wither, all on the caprice of a fragile, eccentric old woman. He felt light-headed.

"Remember you are Vanar now as well, not Hengeli. That part of your life is over. You are entitled to all the rights of a member of any other Vanar family. And as my son, all the responsibility of a High Family. Don't *ever* make me feel I've made a mistake."

"*Ahsmee qhinnah,*" he said softly. *I am sorry.* He meant it.

She inclined her head and looked away, indicating the talk was over. He numbly bowed and got to his feet, following Yronae toward the door. As she slid it open, Yaenida spoke, and he paused to look back at her.

"I have to admit I was pleasantly surprised at the terms of your marriage contract I finally managed to squeeze out of that stingy Changriti bich'chú," she said with a sly smile. "I'm lucky you have such remarkably attractive legs, Nate."

VIII

A TIGHT BAND OF PRESSURE SNEAKING AROUND THE BACKSIDE OF HIS eyeballs threatened to squeeze his brain into yet another bad headache. But this had nothing to do with too much to drink, no such pleasure before the pain.

Articles had been hard enough to memorize, nouns with their three genders divided into four categories of usage depending on social ranking, then everything shifted one more place to the left depending on singular, diplic, or plural forms. Then, of course, each form had its own multitude of declensions to memorize.

"Knife," for example, *churiqa,* was masculine, while "spoon," *qa'archa,* was feminine. That was easy enough to remember, even making a bizarre kind of sense, while "plate," *thaeli*, was neuter. But anything more complicated than "the plate is blue" became a nightmare.

Something as simple as "Please give me your spoons" was loaded with hidden traps. First, there were three different variations of "please," depending on who the speaker was and to whom he was speaking. There were two verbs for "to give," one employed for concrete objects, and the other for abstract ideas.

Then "give me" presumed who was doing the giving, which modified the verb "to give," depending on who exactly was the person being requested to perform the action, and further modified by the status of the "me" who would be the receiver of this action. Also, the verb tense had to be considered, and he had already lost more sleep than he could afford worrying over the various permutations of present tense, imperfect tense, past and future and subjective tenses, and his personal favorite, the ever-popular immediate-conditional-future-first-common-person-second-formal-polite tense.

Once this part of the sentence was properly assembled, "your" and "spoons" amplified his growing headache. The proper form of "your" depended not only on the number of people being addressed—one person, two people, or more than two—but on their relative social positions and what kind of noun the possessive pronoun was being glued on to. He calculated there were approximately seventy-three different ways this sentence could be constructed, and he knew seventy-two of them would be wrong.

Then, of course, pronunciation only added to the fun. Along with all the usual tangled diphthongs and umlauts, certain tonal words differing only by whether they rose or fell on the accent, the Vanar could make at least a half a dozen sounds with their throats and nose Nathan hadn't a prayer of ever being able to imitate.

"*Think*, Nathan," Yaenida scolded. Her reader was open, the Vanar script oversized for her failing eyesight. He sat with his own reader in his lap, taking notes in Hengeli. "If the inflection of the relative pronoun is in question, then in what cases can the passive participle be substituted?"

His headache blooming rapidly into a full-flowered migraine, he rubbed his palms into his eyes. He gave up trying to think, it had all become gibberish. "I don't have any goddamned idea," he grated between clenched teeth.

"When relative clauses are not indicated by a nominalizing particle," she answered, then snapped her reader shut. "You are going to have to learn to speak better Vanar than this before we can even think of tutoring you for your marriage. The Changriti are not happy with your progress as it is, nor am I. Really, you're making it harder on yourself than it needs to be. It's easier for you to learn Vanar than it would be for a woman. You only have to learn to whom you are speaking. As a male, you only need to remember one personal form, and that is far easier than it is for women."

"When you're on the bottom, every way is up," he said sourly.

"Exactly," she said, missing his sarcasm. Or, more likely, choosing to ignore it. "Pay more attention to the way children speak, Nathan. It would be useful for you."

Two days previously he had seen a seven-year-old girl slap a five-year-old boy in the face for daring to call her *mitratam*. Normally, it simply meant "friend," but the boy had not only unintentionally insulted the girl by addressing her in far too low a status, he had had the temerity of using a form exclusively reserved for one girl to address another. The boy had learned a valuable lesson: some children were allowed to grow up to become adults. He would not be one of them.

One of the children's stories he had been given to teach himself to read had been about a wicked frog and a colony of virtuous ants. Although the frog was bigger and stronger than the ants, he ended up fleeing in terror because he knew that to protect their colony, the righteous ants would swarm over him and tear the living flesh from his bones, an inexorable force he could not resist. The underlying moral to that particular tale, Nathan understood, was that the individual would always lose to the community, no matter how strong he was, and that the individual with the strength of the community behind her would always crush the one without it.

"Poor little bastard," he muttered to himself

"Who?"

"Me. This is giving me a headache," he said, recovering.

"Learning is sometimes painful," Yaenida admitted.

Nathan rubbed his forehead. "I've learned enough Vanar history by now to know this language was invented hundreds of years ago," he complained. "But why did you people have to make it so unbelievably complicated?"

"If that is a serious question, I will give you a serious answer." She waited.

He sighed. "All right, it's a serious question." Anything to get out of endless recitations of verb tenses.

Yaenida stared at him and closed her reader, grimacing with pain as she leaned back into her chair. "Language reflects a culture, and re-inforces it. The original language of our ancestors was created by and for men, just as Hengeli was. The original word for 'husband,' for ex-ample, translated literally as 'master,' while the word for 'wife' was 'an invisible or worthless servant.'"

"I thought the first Vanar didn't need a word for 'husband' any-way," he said without smiling.

She took it as humor anyway. "Quite so. Without men, the colonists no longer needed men's language. It wasn't invented out of thin air, that would have been far too tedious as well as unnecessary. The first Vanar simply reshaped their language as they reshaped them-selves."

He kept his expression neutral.

"Families are the basis of our economy, so our language developed over time to conduct complicated business transactions. The authority to speak for one's House depends not only on what status you have, but the changing flow of positions and ability to adapt. That is the na-ture of negotiating: give and take, balancing compromises. We even have several more private dialects used within Families that keep non-Vanar from understanding us too easily. When off-world companies are negotiating between different Houses, it works to our advantage when we can fall back into a tongue they can't comprehend and work out our subarrangements on the spot."

"How does anyone manage to ever learn it all?"

"You must be born into it. If it is any consolation to you, Nathan, you will never be fluent in Vanar. Never."

He stared at her for a moment before he snapped his own reader shut, cutting off his endless notes. "Then what the hell am I doing?"

he demanded. "Why are you putting me through this if you think I'm incapable of learning it?"

"I didn't say you are incapable of learning it. I said it's not possible for anyone to learn Vanar entirely fluently this late in life. If I had been able to say it in Vanar, that nuance would have been quite clear, and there would have been no misunderstanding." He sat in silence for a moment before she went on in a more indifferent voice, this one more dangerous.

"So don't take it personally."

She snapped her fingers arrogantly and pointed her chin toward the water pipe in the corner. He kept his resentment off his face, pushing away from the large table to retrieve her pipe. As he set it up in front of her, she stopped him, one hand on his wrist. Her eyes were narrowed, annoyed. "Get used to it, Nathan," she said, and he wasn't sure if she meant being ordered around or resigned to his language limitation. Or both.

No doubt, had he been able to speak Vanar, he would have been able to discern the nuances.

He sat down and waited as she filled the pipe and lit it, sucking blue smoke through the silty water. "You're trying too hard. It's only important that you are able to speak basic Vanar and understand what is said to you," she continued, more relaxed as the drug infused her bloodstream. "You will not be involved in any business, so that part of the language is unnecessary for you to learn. You have only one personal pronoun inflection to learn, that cuts your study even more. You won't be expected to debate philosophical theory or current politics or any particularly deep speculation on the nature of the universe. As a respectable Vanar man and husband, you are merely required to be a polite conversationalist and make the proper noises of an attentive listener. In fact, you are expected to be silent most of the time, which I should have thought might come as some relief."

He tried to unclench his hands from the fists they had curled into hidden under the table.

"Besides," she said softly, trying to take the sting out, "many people consider your accent and mistakes to be rather charming."

"I don't want to be 'charming,' " he snapped. "Being 'charming' is just one more way of keeping me a prisoner here."

She squinted at him speculatively as she blew out a fine stream of smoke. It hung in thin gauzy layers in the still air of the room. "Nathan, when you have few assets, it's wise to protect the ones you do have with great care."

"Easy for you to say."

She laughed. "But it is. Believe it or not, I was once considered 'charming' by your people. Worse than that: 'cute.' " She batted her eyes at him with a coquettish smile, the affectation made grotesque not only by her ancient features, but by the sharp-edged sarcasm beneath. "But I never made the mistake of thinking it proof I was stupid or naive. Many of those who couldn't see past my charming accent learned that lesson to their financial ruin."

"Is everything like this?"

"Like what?"

"All business? Is friendship based on honesty and respect so impossible without a monetary value attached to it? Don't you have any friends? Can't people here love each other?" As he said it, he suddenly saw Lyris's tear-streaked face in his memory, a strange echo in his ears. He pushed the image away.

"Of course we do," she said. "But I suppose you mean love between men and women, don't you?" She shrugged. "I love my children, all my children, sons and daughters. I love my kharvah, what's left of the poor man. I have responsibilities to them, they have responsibilities to me. I even love you, Nathan"—she grinned, sharp-toothed—"in my own way. And *everyone* knows their place, it's all written down in laws and contracts and traditions. It's in our Families and our history and in our language. Places are not static, they go up and down like a dance."

She inhaled again, murky water bubbling. "That you should understand. You enjoyed the dancing, didn't you?" He didn't answer, his drunken antics hardly something to boast about. "And what happens when one person screws up? Everyone else falls down. The closer they are, the harder they fall. Energy wasted in standing up, finding a new place, getting the music started again." She *tsk*ed in the odd Vanar manner he found so annoying, sucking air sharply between her front teeth. "Better everyone knows their role in the dance. It's more enjoyable that way."

It wasn't the dance he minded. He just wasn't sure he liked the music.

IX

FOR THE MOST PART, HIS LIFE BORDERED ON DEADLY DULL. FEW Vanar men actually held jobs, and higher-status men of the Nine Families were not allowed to work at all, either outside the House or in it. Like the city, nearly all of the estate's menial labor was carried out by machine, all of the cleaning, washing. Even gardening, to Nathan's dismay, had been largely automated. He almost missed the physical exertion when he had been a mere naekulam hustling odd jobs from merchants.

Now he kept his body in shape by spending hours in the baths and swimming or exercising in the gymnasium. Whenever they weren't intent on the condition of their physical bodies, endlessly sweating off the slightest hint of fat on their stomachs, men were expected to occupy the rest of their vast amount of spare time with learning to play musical instruments, in complicated dances and singing, painting, writing lyric poetry Nathan could barely follow. The music was pleasant but bland, the dance physically demanding but ritualistic, painting skillful and innocuous. It was increasingly apparent that men's main preoccupation was to become as valuable an asset as possible for rarely seen mothers, wives, and daughters. The more valuable a man became, the more secure his position.

Within the House, there was little contact between the sexes, at least not overtly. Nathan found the segregation and obsessive atmosphere of the men's house stupefying, the enforced community grating.

Until his marriage, he would sleep in the boys' communal room, wake early for a quiet breakfast laid out in a self-service manner in the men's refectory. There were no tables or chairs, men ate in groups clustered around the cold food, or carried off their portions to eat in the enclosed garden.

After a time, he noticed how various cliques had staked out their own "territories," jealously guarded and respected by most, while within each clique the pecking order became more evident. Whatever criteria was used to establish oneself within any of the cliques, Nathan fit none, and so remained an isolated observer. On rare occasion, hostilities would break out, oddly subdued arguments and gentle shoving matches too nominal to be called a fight. Staring with a scowling face too close to another, a finger pressed against a shoulder, minor "accidental" injuries until the pattern quietly rearranged itself, losers sullenly accepting the loss of their chosen spot. Nathan was intrigued that while Vanar men went to great lengths to develop strong, muscular bodies, the slightest whiff of any real violence met with instant alarm. Nor did it seem Vanar men were aware of the incongruity.

The rest of his companions quickly discovered Nathan was content enough to back away from their aggressive posturing. He found a corner no one seemed to want and ate alone if not in privacy. The constant mass of people surrounding him day and night began to be oppressive. He remembered with ironic regret hating the lonely isolation of his tiny room. If he ate early enough, or late enough, he could avoid the main pack, but risked either having to wait for the food to arrive or there being nothing left if he came too late.

After breakfast he spent two hours with Yaenida before Nga'esha business booted him out. He wandered what grounds were allowed to him, like the pacing of a caged animal, and it was on one of these neurotic prowls he found the hole in the wall.

It was not so much a hole as a low spot half hidden behind a group of ornamental shrubbery, the fallen stonework forming natural steps. Tucking his sati up to free his legs, he climbed to the top and stared over. Stones sloped toward the other side, and once over, he would have no trouble climbing back in. The indigenous jungle was still far in the distance, although this part of Yaenida's property had not been well kept. No doubt this part of the estate was off-limits. He looked around quickly, then scrabbled over the wall, bare feet landing on a thick layer of dead leaves. He waited for several minutes, his heartbeat rapid, but no one came to stop him. For the first time in two months, he was alone. The solitude was a welcome relief.

This became his private retreat. Each day he went a bit farther until he found the wide river cutting him off from the rest of the Nga'esha's enormous property. An old oak tree, thick trunk split in two, served as his seat, the crotch filled with a litter of detritus for a cushion. He could sit with his back against the rough bark, his feet comfortably propped against the opposite fork, listening to the rush of water. Somehow, it made the memorization easier.

"*Vaktaemi be,* I (low person, male) speak. *Vaktaevah,* we (two low persons) speak. *Vaktaemah* we (low persons plural) speak. *Vaktaeasi, vaktaethah, vaktaeyam,* you speak. *Vaktaevaha,* you two (high persons) speak. . . ." He could sit with his eyes closed, reciting softly to himself, playing the study beads jammed in his ear, or simply stare off across the water longingly toward the distant wild jungles, rich with native flora in all their forbidden secrets.

By midafternoon, he would climb the rubble of the damaged wall, checking through the cover of foliage to be sure no one was looking before lowering himself back into his stifling cloistered life. No one ever seemed to miss him, and he wondered if Yaenida knew about his private sanctuary.

Except for the rainy season, the weather remained monotonously warm and fair, reflecting his repetitiously empty days. Whenever the slightest change occurred, it was greeted with enthusiasm usually outweighing the event itself. When the really unusual happened, the exhilaration rippled through the men's quarters with a festive spirit.

Pratima is coming.

He had no idea who Pratima was, but any novelty was welcome, the undercurrent of excitement infectious. The younger boys had trouble calming down in the evening, making sleeping in peace more of a problem than usual. Mock fights broke out, nervous wrestling while keeping a guilty eye out for adult reproach. Nathan noticed one boy getting more than his fair share of the furtive abuse.

He was past puberty—only Nathan was older—and Nathan wondered why the boy hadn't been moved into the men's house when he'd come of age to be sponsored by his father or an uncle, or even an older cousin. He stood out even without being the oldest boy there, his pale blue eyes setting off skin so blanched it seemed almost blue itself. Nathan would have thought him an albino were it not for his jet black hair. The boy endured the incomprehensible taunts stoically, yet the more the boy ignored the bullies' teasing the worse it got. Finally, more annoyed at being kept awake than from altruism, Nathan had jumped up from his tiny bed and stalked over to where three of the boy's tormentors had cornered him. They turned, staring up with their mouths open in startled O's.

"Get the fuck away from him, you miserable little bastards," he growled in Hengeli, knowing they didn't understand the words. They understood the tone, however, as well as the anger of a fully adult man towering above them. They scattered. The dark-haired boy stared at him without alarm, but with a strange look of detached curiosity.

Nathan's spontaneous gesture elected him the boy's unwilling protector. They ate together, and with some rearrangement of sleeping mats, slept side by side. The boy accepted his daily disappearances without question or reproach, more of a presence than a friend. He rarely spoke, to Nathan or anyone. It took Nathan most of the week just to get the boy's name out of him: Raemik.

Pratima is coming.

Nathan's excursions were interrupted, as well as his morning lessons with Yaenida. Aelgar, Yronae's senior kharvah, began rehearsing small groups for the upcoming banquet with a fervor bordering on hysteria. Aelgar's hair, liberally streaked with gray, had receded from his temples, not helped by his habit of chewing on the end of his braid when nervous. During that week, Nathan kept tabs for his own amusement on how much hair the man gnawed off.

Since Nathan knew next to nothing of the essential etiquette, the senior kharvah appointed him to minor serving duties. While dozens of boys and younger men perfected intricate dances and the older men studied polite conversation and music, Nathan was drilled like a conscripted soldier on basic serving techniques: which hand to use to put a platter on the table, when to fill a cup or glass, how to sweep aside the sati folds when bending over to serve a full plate so as not to trip and inadvertently dump the meal into the diner's lap.

Raemik had silently followed Nathan with the rest, his solemn eyes wide. But when Aelgar had frowned and snapped his fingers, the boy had faded away as silently as a ghost. Excluded from the general activity, Raemik waited each night in the deserted garden for Nathan. When he came to look for the boy, Raemik simply stood and followed him without response, no relief, no resentment.

The emotion Nathan had seen on the boy's face was fear: every time Pratima's name was whispered, his already white skin paled even further.

On the morning of Pratima's arrival, Raemik vanished. Nathan spent an hour searching for him before Aelgar hustled him along with ill-disguised impatience. By the time the banquet began, he'd forgotten about the boy in the frenzied activity.

The music and laughter had gone on for hours before he was booted out the door to retrieve empty plates. For the first few passes, he concentrated on collecting plates without dropping them or screwing up the intricate protocol, without even noticing the people he gathered them from. Then, with delayed shock, he noticed the women were not Vanar. They weren't Hengeli, either, and looked so ill at ease in their unfamiliar surroundings none of them even noticed his gawping.

"Move," Aelgar hissed behind him, startling him back into motion. He quickly retrieved dirty dishes while trying to eavesdrop on what little snatches of Hengeli he could overhear and figure out where the women were from by the native language they spoke among themselves.

He was wondering if he dared risk speaking to them when the second surprise of the night made him stop and stare. A woman in a black sati lounged beside Yaenida, serenely smoking a water pipe. Thin, almost skeletally so, with black hair framing a sharp-chinned face, her pale blue eyes set off skin so white it nearly glowed. It was as if Raemik had suddenly changed sex and grown twenty years older. This, he knew instinctively, was Pratima.

As if he had made some noise calling her attention, she glanced up at him with a colorless expression, then idly looked away.

The fourth time he passed behind Pratima, precariously balancing an armful of plates while observing the woman from out the corner of his eye, she said coldly without looking at him, "You are staring at me, *qanistha bhraetae*, little brother."

Although her voice was soft, he could hear her clearly through the laughter and noise. She raised her face to him, the irises of her eyes so pale they seemed only visible by a thin blue ring separating them from her sclera, black pupils standing out in stark relief. Yaenida leaned back to look up at him as well, her lips quirked up into a wry smile.

"This naeqili offers humblest of apologies, jah'nari l'amae," he stuttered out in bad Vanar.

Pratima's only response was the tiniest rise of an eyebrow. It was astonishingly like Raemik. Then she turned away, ignoring him as completely as if he no longer existed.

Aelgar considered this evidence of dissatisfaction with Nathan's performance, and abruptly switched him to the lowest possible job: banishment to the kitchen where he fed dirty plates into the washer for the rest of the evening. His slim chance of speaking with any of the foreigners was lost. Shortly after, he and the rest of the lower-status men were curtly dismissed, escaping with their own plates piled high with looted treats to gorge themselves in private.

He was not there when Raemik was presented, but Tycar, one of the younger sahakharae who had taken a more than comfortable interest in Nathan, relayed the gossip in slow, simple Vanar. Raemik had been ushered in, dressed in his best sati and drenched head to toe in gold and jewels. He could have been stark naked, the sahakharae commented, for all he seemed aware of his finery. The boy had removed the end of his sati, bared head high and proud, and looked straight at Pratima with his usual inert expression.

"Welcome, Sister," he had said, and other witnesses agreed with Tycar that the boy's voice had been clear and steady. "It is a joy to finally meet you."

Pratima had said nothing for a long moment, then smiled. "It pleases me, young brother, to see how well you have grown."

Raemik bowed, and she returned it before the boy turned and walked away, spine erect.

"It was as if he were like fog," the sahakharae said, illustrating with his hands. "He had such grace, as if he had no feet, floating like morning mist along the ground. Not one sound. Even with all that jewelry, he made not one sound!"

But Raemik had made one sound that night that Nathan knew of. The boy had tapped Nathan's shoulder far late in the night, wakening him, and sat on his haunches silently, eyes glittering in the dark. Nathan snorted awake, and stared at Raemik questioningly before he raised the sheet. The boy slid in beside him, curling his thin body into the curves of Nathan's torso and legs, shivering violently.

Hesitantly, Nathan draped his arm over the boy's side, his hand curled to cup the boy's thin shoulder. For an awkward moment, he wondered if Raemik was expecting him to make a sexual advance before he realized the boy was crying, the sound barely audible.

He was only a scared, lonely child desperate for comfort, and Nathan had a sudden ache in his throat. He rocked him gently, shushing in the boy's hair until they both fell asleep.

X

THE FOREIGN STRANGERS LEFT AND PRATIMA STAYED, ALTHOUGH THE rhythm of the Household soon returned to near normal over the next few weeks. Yaenida seemed distracted, half Nathan's lessons canceled. He saw little of Raemik during the day, but the boy didn't repeat his single nocturnal visit. Nor, it seemed, was Nathan needed as his protector any longer. The younger boys and most of the men avoided Raemik with an almost uncomfortable diligence. Nathan spent more time in his private sanctuary, not realizing how much he missed the boy's company.

On a cool midmorning, Nathan jumped the fence and hiked the distance to the river. When he reached the line of trees bordering the clearing, he stopped in surprise before ducking behind a covering of bushes. A woman dressed only in a black mati stood motionless on one foot, balanced on her toes, an alien shape in the clearing. Her other leg bent up at an acute angle, her foot at waist level, held out on a flexed leg. Her arms were held out from her sides, elbows bent and palms up, her thumb and middle finger together with the rest of her fingers splayed. Her head canted up to face the sun. The light dappled her white skin, reflecting colors, the green of leaves, brown earth, gold sun. A long thick braid of black hair hung down her back, the slight breeze lifting strands from her sharp face, her eyes half closed with a thin sliver of white showing, her mouth slightly open.

Pratima.

For a moment, resentment soured in his mouth. Annoyed with the trespasser intruding into his private domain, he then remembered he was not supposed to be here at all, and wondered if he could steal away before she spotted him. He studied her for a moment, trying to judge if she suspected his presence, and was startled by how absolutely inanimate she was, not simply still. No hint of breath, no slight quiver of muscles maintaining her balance. She looked like a sculpted dancer frozen in midstep, as still as if she were carved from stone. As inert as death.

He hid in the bushes behind the tree line and watched her for several minutes. His legs began to ache slightly from the crouch, and he shifted his own position as quietly as possible, amazed at the same time she had not moved at all. He decided she was unaware of him and it would be best for him to retreat as quietly as possible. He had moved only slightly to turn back before her eyes opened, head swiveling to stare straight at him unerringly.

"Stay, young bhraetae," she said softly. He wondered how long she had known he was there. She swayed slightly, as if released from a spell, and lowered her arms and leg. "Join me." The gentleness of her voice made it seem more a request than an order. She sat down on the ground cross-legged, recovering her sati from the grass and draping it casually around her shoulders.

He'd been caught. If it was forbidden, it was too late now. His heart thumping, he walked into the clearing and sat at a remove from her. Hands together, thumbs against his chest, he bowed slightly, keeping his eyes on her.

"Humblest apologies, l'amae," he said in slow Vanar, struggling for the proper words. "This person (*bottom scrapings of the barrel status male*) means (*keep it in the present tense, stupid, it's easier that way*) no trouble (*damn, is 'trouble' masculine or feminine?*) to you (*dative declension, highest possible status, just in case . . .*)."

She returned the gesture somberly. "Nathan, isn't it?" she asked in fluent Hengeli. Her accent was light, pleasant, pronouncing his name correctly but with an oddly old-fashioned accent, as if she'd learned the language from watching vintage entertainment programs. "Nathan Crewe. And, no, you didn't disturb me."

"You speak Hengeli," he said, astonished.

"Among a few other languages. But I admit, I was expecting someone else."

"Raemik," he guessed. "I don't think he knows about this place. I doubt he'd come even if he does if he knew you were here. Raemik is afraid of you," he added, not sure why he was volunteering the information. She seemed to think about that for a moment, and nodded. "Sorry to disappoint you, it's only me." He tried a smile.

"I'm never disappointed."

He hesitated, then asked, "How do you do that?"

She didn't pretend not to understand him. "I could try to explain it, but I'm not sure you would believe me. It has to do with balancing on the alignment of the earth. It isn't difficult, but it's something that must be learned from birth."

"Like Vanar." He chuckled wryly.

"Not like Vanar," she said seriously. "I was born to it." She gazed at him with her astonishingly pale eyes, making him uneasy. As if she knew the effect, she turned her head slightly and spoke softly while watching the leaves flutter overhead. "I'm a Pilot."

After a moment, he was aware his mouth was hanging open, and he bit his lip. "But I thought you were Vanar," he finally managed, and mentally kicked himself.

"I *am* Vanar," she said, amused. "All Pilots are Vanar."

"I know that, but what I meant was I didn't think Pilots ever left the Worms," he amended lamely.

She smiled fleetingly. "What you meant is you thought Pilots were all hideous freaks who drink the blood of newborn babies to remain immortal. Sorry, that's only a myth."

"Like the one that all Hengeli men are psychotic rapists?" he shot back.

She laughed, the sound oddly musical and alien. "Touché. But it is true that Pilots rarely do go to ground. I don't like being planetbound. It's quite uncomfortable." She glanced at him, and away again. "I spent some of my childhood here, though. This was my private spot when I was young and wanted to escape my teachers, too. When I have to come back, I like to come to this place." She patted the old tree with affection. "Although it's changed a little," she said with a touch of irony.

"How long will you stay?" he asked, suddenly homesick for somewhere he had never lived, wishing he could leave as well.

"Not long. One month. Maybe a year." She shrugged. "I don't have much sense of time on the ground."

"So it's true, then, Pilots live forever?" he blurted.

She laughed again, making him feel as if he'd accomplished something, a strange sense of enjoyment in the sound. Then her face grew serious. "Pilots live outside time, within time, all time, no time," she intoned in an earnest voice. "We exist without existence, eternal through all space and no space. We live forever and die young."

He stared at her, uncomprehending, before the corners of her lips twitched. "Don't you despise mystics? I do." When she looked at him, her eyes seemed less uncanny. "That's a myth, too," she said. "Or an exaggeration at best."

"You're here for Raemik. Is he also going to become a Pilot?"

"No." She inclined her head to one side, gauging him. "My turn. You're Yaenida's son."

That sounded too odd. "Adopted. She's not really my mother."

"She is now," Pratima said firmly. "That makes *you* Vanar as well."

He shrugged. "By way of Hengeli."

She pulled up her knees, wrapping thin arms around them to prop her chin. "So tell me, what's a nice Hengeli boy like you doing in a place like Vanar?"

He laughed, more at ease. "An act of monumental stupidity, I'm afraid," he admitted. "I used to teach botany at a not-very-prestigious college on a remote outpost. I was frustrated, ambitious, and thoroughly ignorant about anything that didn't have roots and chlorophyll. If I had any hope of ever working at a better university, I needed to impress the board. The little I knew about Vanar didn't involve its sociology. I was only interested in a species of native plant. Someone had given it to me, brought it out from Vanar."

Lyris had. She'd seduced him with a shy smile and dark eyes and a small, stubby plant frozen forever in cortaplast, blue leaves and bloodred roots. He'd spent more time cutting the sample and analyzing it, more excited by the shape of its cellular structure than the shape of her nude body pressing against his as she nibbled his ear to distract him.

"It was the only known sample and had some interesting properties. There's next to nothing known on native Vanar botany, and I hoped to be the first non-Vanar to publish original research. I was warned what might happen, but I didn't believe it. Didn't want to believe it." He stopped, took a deep breath before he was able to go on. He shrugged dismissively. "Thought for some reason the rules wouldn't apply to me. My ignorance exceeded my ambition. And now I'm stranded." *Forever.* Suddenly, he found himself staring at the ground, swallowing at the ache in his throat.

"What kind of plant?" she asked quietly.

"What does it matter now?" he retorted with more bitterness than he intended. When she didn't answer, waiting quietly, he relented. "It's called *svapnah* in Vanar. There's no word for it in Hengeli."

"And if you could, would you still study this plant?"

He grinned in spite of himself. "If I could, yes. Unfortunately, it only grows out there." He waved toward the dense jungle across the river. "And I'm confined to here. Svapnah doesn't grow well in managed terraformed gardens, it seems. Too sensitive, or more likely it grows in conjunction with something else. The proteins are too foreign to be of any use to humans, pretty much like the rest of Vanar flora, but it secretes a resin with narcotic properties similar in effect to the stuff everyone smokes here. But why would a plant evolve to develop that sort of chemical when there's no native fauna to react to it? The only insects or birds on Vanar have had to be imported from off-world, they can't even survive in native rain forests. Which is what makes me think there's some symbiotic or parasitical association happening with something else, maybe microscopic, mimicking the kind of defense against attack you might find with insects or . . ." He stopped, embarrassed as he realized he had fallen into his lecturing manner.

"Interesting," she said, amused.

"For someone who doesn't like coming down to ground too often?" She smiled but didn't answer. She winced, then closed her eyes and rolled her head on her neck. He could hear the minuscule pops of her vertebrae. "Are you in pain?"

"It takes a while to adjust to this gravity. I'm not used to only one direction for down. It's nothing serious."

He might have offered to rub her shoulders, but her demeanor didn't invite physical familiarity. Yet the thought of touching her sent a sudden tingle through him. "Where did you learn to speak Hengeli?" he asked instead.

She unwrapped her arms and stretched out her legs, leaning back on her arms to arch her back. Her nipples stood out in relief against the cloth of her mati, and he had to look away.

"Well, whenever we're not sucking out the blood of helpless infants, Pilots lead pretty dull lives," she said, opening her eyes. "So mostly we eavesdrop. Spying may be rude, but it's all the entertainment we get. Follow the Station gossip. Listen to ship chatter. Tune in to the next episode. Place bets on our favorite characters." She pursed her lips with a wry expression. "Sounds heartless, I suppose. To be honest, it is. We Vanar are heartless people in so many ways." She smiled wryly. "As I'm sure you are already aware."

"I wouldn't say that . . . ," he said cautiously.

"I would never expect you to. And I won't bother to lie and claim any altruistic motives, either. I asked you to stay only because Vanar bores me rigid, and you're about the only distraction I'm likely to find on this damned estate while I'm here." She shrugged. "If that insults you, I will apologize and leave you in peace."

She waited while he thought about it, unconcerned with his verdict, not even looking at him. "I'm not insulted," he said. "I'm bored out of my mind here, too. Other than Yaenida, there aren't many people I *can* talk with. I'd sit around and chat with the damned trees if they spoke Hengeli. So, who's entertaining who?"

She smiled, almost a grin, sharp teeth evenly spaced. The aloofness melted. "I like that." She looked at him in a way that made him tense, a dispassionate scan up, down, as if she could see through his clothing, measuring him with a quick inspection. "Yes, I like that very much," she said, and he relaxed with an odd sense of relief without knowing why.

She stood in one flowing motion, taking up her black sati with her. If she had trouble in the gravity, it didn't show in her gracefulness. "If you wish to be left undisturbed in this place, I will come only in the mornings," she said as she folded and knotted her sati around her in a style he had never seen.

Her courtesy, so unlike other Vanar women, startled him. But if his being there was forbidden, she would not inform on him. "Will you want to be alone in the mornings, then?" he asked cautiously.

She smiled. "If I do, there are other places I can go." She gazed around the small clearing, the water rippling in long undulating ribbons in the river, before looking back at him. "It's beautiful, but I don't much like Vanar, Nathan Crewe. Talking with you has been a pleasure in an otherwise bleak place."

She walked toward the trees, back toward the House. As she passed him, he noticed she made almost no sound, but not, it seemed, because she was trying. "If you don't like it here," he called after her, "then you tell me: what's a nice Pilot like you doing on Vanar?"

She laughed, full-throated. She twisted to face him, each hand on the trunk of the trees bordering the clearing, the sunlight reflected in her colorless eyes making them gleam gold, coins pressed against the eyes of a corpse.

"Getting pregnant," she said, grinning, and vanished into the trees like the Cheshire cat.

XI

SHE WASN'T THERE THE NEXT MORNING, NOR THE ONE AFTER, LEAVING him disappointed, with an odd hollow ache. He wasn't falling in love, nothing so clichéd. It was the fascination with the exotic that drew him over the wall, hurrying toward the river, hoping she would be there. But as the days passed, he was afraid she'd forgotten him.

He had never seen, never mind met a Pilot before. He knew of no one who ever had. They were the stuff of myths and drunken tales, shadowy figures made inhuman simply by their mystery. All he knew of Pilots were they were all Vanar women. Typically, the role of Pilots in fictional programs were either portrayed by breathtaking actresses with implausible anatomy, or by a variety of hideous creatures defying any possible hint of femininity. Pilotships were usually depicted as vague objects so brilliantly lit with flashing lights it was hard to make out any shape at all.

He had only once seen an actual Pilotship, when he was on the *Chandelle* as it had gone from the Quintin solar system's station for transfer to the Cooper Station thirteen light-years away. It had not been the radiant blaze of colors favored in adventure shows, but it had been nonetheless spectacular. The *Chandelle* was one of the more midsized class of luxury cruisers, capable of accommodating three thousand passengers for voyages lasting up to several years. A pleasure liner designed for the not-quite-yet fabulously wealthy, she had everything a full-sized and affluent town could boast of, complete with theaters, sports gyms and pools, clubs, and a number of restaurants. He had gone to the civilian nav observatory to watch the docking, clinking champagne glasses with his fellow passengers, nervousness giving an edge to the festive excitement. As it was a small compartment, the invitations were restricted to those who had never seen a Pilotship docking before, a once-in-a-lifetime spectacle.

Nathan didn't know much about traveling between solar systems, despite having been the ersatz cabin boy to his mentor and patron, Ivan Brohm, for a couple years aboard the freighter WT/HG-574, known semiaffectionately to its crew as the *Warthog*. Freighters did not come equipped with a virtual nay obs, that sort of optical illusion reserved for gullible tourists. Living on the *Warthog* wasn't much different than living inside a sealed sewer pipe and about as interesting.

He had escaped Westcastle, and hadn't been planetside until Fat Ivan set him down on Remsill, helped him forge his academic records and identification to get him into a decent university program, and left. He had promised to return for him, but the old fat bastard was killed in a freak blowout during a Station loading just after Nathan's graduation and bequeathed the bulk of his relatively meager estate to Nathan. Nathan had found a job teaching, and space travel had become one of those adventures that eventually fade and become only peripheral experiences in a life.

When Arcavia University had turned him down for tenure, he'd taken a year's sabbatical and spent every last penny he had to pay his way to Cooper. He'd planned to look for employment on a freighter like the *Warthog* as a terraform ecologist like Ivan had been, with the hope of making a study of the botanical ecology on one of the dozens of planetary systems still under Hengeli control.

He'd paid his fare, wandered around searching for his cabin with other lost passengers, worried about his baggage, and trusted the actual mechanics of getting from point A to point B to the people trained for that job. He was a botanist—what would he know about space travel? But he knew a Worm could not be seen in space. It is *there*, it just *is*, and is the only method of cheating the lightspeed limitations.

Pilotships were actually a part of the Worm, the liner's bright and cheerful travel brochure informed him. They were incapable of existing independently, and unable to remain still, even during the docking and debarkation procedures at either end. Other than that, there was no further useful information in the literature, not even a diagram.

He had been keeping one eye on the viewport while trading anecdotes with a neurosurgeon on his way to a research hospital on the Nga'esha-controlled Cooper Station. Sweat prickled Nathan's skin in the close compartment, the surgeon's red face uncomfortably close to his, the man's breath soured from the alcohol.

So when he first noticed the Pilotship, it was only because the stars seemed to be extinguishing themselves, vanishing in an ever-enlarging circle. Then he made out the faint features of the Pilotship, his mind taking a minute to adjust to what his eyes saw.

It was immense, eclipsing the *Chandelle* as a giant's boot might shadow a beetle. Light-absorbing black, quark-eating black, a smooth-hulled machine too alien to call a ship, its enormous maw slowly engulfing them and a thousand other fellow ships like plankton down the gullet of a whale as the passengers stared speechless, overwhelmed.

"Son of a bitch," the surgeon finally breathed, and someone tittered, a strangled sound bordering on hysteria. The surgeon promptly knocked back the rest of his champagne and left in search of something stronger, too shaken to watch any more.

The actual transfer into the belly of the Pilotship took place hours later. There had been a momentary rush as the *Chandelle* was swallowed, then nothing to detect he was traveling inside the Worm at speeds he couldn't imagine. He'd gone to bed eventually. When he woke, he was on the approach to Cooper Station, still several million miles away, the Pilotship long gone.

To have met one of the hermetic human beings who lived in the Worm, who controlled the great ships that made interstellar travel even possible, intrigued him. That she spoke fluent Hengeli made him all the more aware of his deep longing for basic, simple conversation. That she might want to see him again excited him in a way he couldn't quite explain. It wasn't love but desire she stirred in him: a deep physical hunger sparked by her strangeness, erotic and perilous.

Perhaps the curious feelings stirred up whenever he thought of Pratima were from the lack of any sexual contact in far too long. He found himself watching Raemik more often, constantly comparing the eerie similarities between the two, and the boy developed a wariness around him, as if he could sense Nathan's growing sexual tension. Even the sahakharae seemed aware of his need, like vultures scenting blood. Nathan did nothing to encourage intimacy with them, going out of his way to avoid sahakharae, his own past a ghost still haunting his dreams. He wanted a woman. He wanted one particular woman. A woman who looked eerily like Raemik.

Guilt and fear added to his problem. Raemik had crept into the boys' quarters late, long after curfew. He never said where he'd gone, nor had Nathan ever asked. Wherever he had been, none of the other boys took any notice, or if they knew kept it among themselves.

Nathan had been the only one awake, unable to sleep, propped up against the wall listening to the quiet breathing of children. Tired of wrestling with Vanar calligraphy, he had left his reader on, glowing faintly unread beside him. No one stirred as the boy slipped past the sleepers. Nathan watched him in silence as Raemik unclipped his sati and let it unwind at his feet.

The boy stood with his back to Nathan, legs bare under his mati, then turned to stare back at him. Nathan found he was unable to look away, his heart suddenly beating too fast. Slowly, the boy drew his mati over his head and stood naked in the darkened room, his pale skin glowing like moonlight. Slender young muscles still soft with adolescence, Raemik stepped out of the mound of cloth his sati made on the floor, closer to him. Horrified, Nathan felt his breathing becoming hoarse, electricity dancing on his skin. The boy glanced down at Nathan's crotch, then back, unblinking.

To his dismay, the smell of the boy's young flesh transfixed him. He was close enough to touch him, grab him, drag him down roughly on top of him. Slowly, Raemik knelt over him, one hand beside him for balance, and waited, fear in his eyes along with the trust and willingness.

If the boy touched him, he'd be lost. He didn't want him, Raemik was not his sister. But the resemblance sang to the same erotic desire Nathan felt toward Pratima. The intensity of his need appalled him, frightened by what the boy had aroused.

It took every fiber in him to smile and shake his head. "Raemik," he whispered. "Go to sleep."

The child didn't change expression, but simply turned and wriggled under the sheet over his own narrow mat, his face toward Nathan, eyes open. Nathan finally had to turn away to avoid the look, and it was a long time before he could fall asleep.

The next morning, he hiked to the clearing, now as afraid Pratima would be there as not. He was both relieved and disappointed to find it empty. A flutter of color in the notched bole between the old tree's two trunks caught his eye. A reader-sized package wrapped in bright protective envelope had been left wedged in the tree's hollow. Inside was a book, the antiquated kind, thick paper pages pressed between a

cover of leather. It was old, incredibly so, but preserved in better condition than most of the antique books in Yaenida's extensive library. He knew instinctively it was priceless.

He opened it to a colored plate of the svapnah plant he had described to Pratima. The printed words were in Vanar script, but a note inserted between the pages was scrawled in an oddly childish Hengeli handwriting:

"Learning is easier with a carrot rather than the stick."

He spent an hour reverently looking through the book, reveling in the beautiful prints of native Vanar plants. Then, carefully replacing it in the envelope, he settled into the hollow of the tree, his back against one trunk, his feet propped against the other, pulled his sati up around his waist, and masturbated quickly, almost frantically. Branches swayed as the wind flicked leaves, gold and red veins lacing through the deep, wide green. Silk tongues of air flared against his skin as the sensations rushed through him.

His fierce orgasm ripped up into a scream of starved exultation, leaving him trembling, a sheen of sweat on his body, and feeling strangely empty.

If anything, his hunger only intensified. He alternated between wishing he'd never met her to desperately wanting her to appear in the clearing. Not even the years he'd spent on the all-male crew of the *Warthog* had driven him as mad as the thought of Pratima, so close and so far beyond his reach. And the continued unwanted attention from the sahakharae made his frustration even more acute. After he tried yet again to tactfully rebuff the overt advances from a few more aggressive sahakharae, chiefly from Tycar, he lost his patience. He made his point with a bit of yelling and heated shoving.

The sahakharae quickly backed off, leaving him alone with all the aversion to a leper just as the men in the charity shelter had. But he was satisfied with the result. Problem solved. So he thought. When he arrived a few mornings later in Yaenida's library, he found he had been sadly mistaken. He had not even gone in to the room far enough to bow and take his seat before Yaenida stopped him.

"I do not as a rule involve myself with men's disputes," she said harshly. "If there are difficulties, the senior kharvah handles it. It is his domain. But"—she looked up at him, eyes bloodshot behind their thick, tired lids—"there *is* the language problem. So I've been asked to speak to you."

"I can explain—" he started.

"I am not interested," she cut him off curtly. "Half a dozen sahakharae are threatening to leave my House. Twice that number of kharvah complain you are disruptive and violent, and it is being unfairly tolerated because you are an exotic. I'm getting complaints from my daughters that the men's arguments are affecting their private lives, and I am personally extremely cross at being forced to deal with this. My time, limited as it is, is valuable."

He stood stiffly, clutching his reader against his chest. "I apologize, Pratha Yaenida. It wasn't my intention—"

"I don't give a damn what your intentions were," she snapped, the cold anger in her voice far harsher than he'd heard before. "Violent behavior within my House will *not* be tolerated. You know that. You go back and fix it, do you understand? I want my men happy. I expect to see them *very* happy, Nathan."

"I don't want to fuck sahakharae, Yaenida!" he protested.

"Then fuck that boy sleeping with you!" she shouted, slamming one knobby fist against the arm of her chair. "What the hell's the matter with you! You don't like boys, find a damned taemora, there's at least a dozen unmarried women parasites around ready and willing to ease your appetite. You're not required to be celibate. You're a man, you're not *expected* to be. If you have a need, *do* something about it, but I don't want trouble from you again. Do I make myself clear?"

"Yes," he said, whispering.

She seemed to collapse within herself, as if the energy spent had physically drained her. "Good. Now get out," she said brusquely. "I'm too tired today."

He bowed, and turned, but hesitated at the door, knowing he was risking further wrath. "Pratha Yaenida—"

"*What!*" she shouted at him with more exasperation than strength, glaring.

"I didn't know," he said simply. "About the taemora. About anything. How do I play by the rules if I don't know what they are?"

She stared for a moment before her expression softened. "I believe you," she said, bemused. She waved at him weakly, beckoning him back. He sat down on the edge of the hard chair as she canted her head at him. "But I know you've registered at a kaemahjah. If you felt the need, why haven't you gone back there?"

He shrugged. "The only thing they wanted from me I didn't find all that enjoyable."

She seemed amazed. "What happened?"

He told her. When he finished, she was smiling, once again amused, her anger vanished. "A medical examination isn't usually considered an erotic experience." She scribbled on a piece of paper before folding it over. Rooting around in her reader for an address, she wrote it on the note in her delicate Hengeli. "You're not being asked simply to provide sperm. Go here and give them this."

He took it, eying her questioningly.

"Nathan, Vanar men are expected to want sex. That is their primary function in our society. Why would you think anyone required you to be chaste and virginal? Go, please, and enjoy yourself." She sank tiredly into the chair. "But I meant what I said: no more trouble."

XII

THE KAEMAHJAH WASN'T ALL THAT MUCH DIFFERENT THAN ANY LARGE social club on Remsill or the upscale lounge of a liner: drinks, dancing, music, laughter, conversation.

And, of course, sex. Lots of it.

All women were legally allowed to marry three kharvah, although most Middle and Common caste women married fewer. But in the High Families, when senior women took more than one kharvah out of circulation for business reasons, a lot of unmarried women were left over. Most of them were the younger daughters and cousins who stayed at home to support the Family business. Or they were taemorae, hired employees hoping to acquire enough business connections to begin their own households while canvassing the younger men with more prominent family connections in search of a kharvah or two of their own. Or they were women who simply elected to remain unmarried, whether childless or not, either finding mates among their own sex or satisfaction in a kaemahjah, the house of joy.

This particular kaemahjah was a popular outlet for women from respectable houses looking for male company. Some came to relieve the stress of Family business, to have their tender muscles and egos massaged. Some came only to be entertained, to dance or talk, uninterested in sex at all. Some came in for the sole purpose of getting pregnant, earnest women who fucked with an intense determination that was somewhat alarming to Nathan.

The vast majority of men who chose to become sahakharae were not homosexual, which surprised Nathan. Most were younger sons from Common Families without prominent-enough connections to have attracted a marriageable woman. Boys with enough talent or good looks hoped to find a sponsor to train them, with ambitions of attaining a position in one of the Nine Houses. Once sterilized, they gave up any prospect of those family ties that welded Vanar society together. But many of them earned a significant income in the kaemahjah to supplement their official function of keeping tensions at home under control, saving for a comfortable retirement.

There was also a pool of kharvah with ever-changing faces drifting in and out. They came to meet possible marriage partners, or to visit lovers they had been prohibited from marrying for reasons of Family business concerns. Others came because their wives couldn't spread their time far enough between business and several kharvah to keep everyone happy. And there were plenty more like Nathan who simply came because they were frustrated and bored.

After two months, Nathan began to feel the seasoned pro. The staff at the kaemahjah greeted him now by name, even if they all mangled it into "Nay-teen Karoo." An older employee assigned herself as his guide and protector. He had been preoccupied with a tall, exquisitely lovely woman doing her best to chat with him, struggling to understand his clumsy Vanar while stroking his thigh delightfully, before his self-appointed guardian interposed to warn her off. At first, he had been annoyed—the tall woman had been highly attractive—until he discovered she had rather explicit tastes that there were other men more accommodating toward.

Apparently, they had special hospitalization coverage.

He also discovered he had the absolute right to refuse any offer he didn't care for, a strange sensation of control he hadn't had in a long time. Rarely was anything more than a simple "no" needed, and at the slightest hint of insistence, kaemahjah staff firmly intervened. Nor, in spite of his preconceptions, did he feel like a prostitute; no money ever changed hands. Although small inexpensive gifts were sometimes offered, just as often they were reciprocated. His stipend was paid by the government of Vanar, the amount considerably higher now that he was Nga'esha kharvah rather than mere naekulam. The money was deposited directly into an account to pay for his time regardless of whether he had sex or simply sat and drank and listened to the music.

For the most part, all he did do was drink and listen to the music while watching the dancers. His Vanar had improved after Pratima's gift, increasing his vocabulary enough to hold his own in a discussion on native Vanar botany, should any women who shared his passion ever show up.

So far, none had.

At first, it had even been fun, a chance to escape from the constant male company and revel in plenty of guilt-free sex. He had partied with boyish enthusiasm, a few favorites more than once, but after a while, the novelty wore off. He was not among the men sought out for their elegant and witty conversation, although he was welcome to join in the groups, listening attentively, trying hard to understand the jokes. When he did, he was so pleased with his own accomplishment he sometimes forgot to laugh.

He learned to smoke the traditional Vanar water pipe, enjoying the mild narcotic languor and the hallucinatory sharpness of his senses. There was no limitation on either smoking or his drinking, and if he drank himself into a vomiting coma, he knew he would be taken care of without disapproval by the staff. But after a few times of waking up hungover and disoriented in a sterile white room, stinking of sour vomit and sweat, that luxury wore thin as well. Occasionally, he would drink enough to lose his inhibitions and try dancing. The women thought it hilarious to watch his poor imitation of the polished, elaborate movements of men with bodies trained since infancy. But he did try to keep making a fool of himself to a minimum.

He attempted to learn *qaellast*, studying the endless games without much success. The rules seemed deceptively simple, but he had yet to win a single game, even against the worst players. Eventually, only the staff offered to compete with him, patiently explaining in slow Vanar whenever he made his frequent incredibly stupid moves.

No one seemed concerned that he spent most of his time by himself, drinking and smoking. He passed the tedious days in a dreamy, quiet state skirting the edge of depression. At least he could relax here as he couldn't at the House, where he was endlessly smiling and obeisant, lowest of the low, bowing and scraping while suppressing the urge to punch his fist through something. Yaenida had less and less time for him, ensconced with her senior daughters behind closed doors, engaged in one business matter after another. Once his daily kowtow had been performed, he escaped to the clearing. After a time, even that refuge had turned to more emptiness, Pratima's absence disheartening.

On a late afternoon, the clientele thinned out and he was idly considering leaving. He had already politely turned down an offer of company, deducing with a now experienced eye the woman's end objective: not many sought him out for anything more than a quick, indifferent coupling, and these tended to be either women attracted by his strangeness or unmarried women desperately seeking pregnancy. He was beginning to resent the first, and while he could sympathize with the latter, on occasion even enjoyed sex with them, the goal left him less than enthusiastic.

Not ready to return to the Ngai'esha House and face the smug gloating in the men's quarters, he preferred to simply sit and listen to the music. He leaned against cushions piled up against a carved screen, his foot idly tapping the air to the rhythm. This group was better than most, four men who played a fast intricate rhapsody of reedy flute, a three-level dulcimerlike stringed instrument, lute, and a drum that the young player bounced his fingers on to produce a deep, rolling sound that made a pleasant sensation in his gut.

He hadn't noticed her, and when he did, it was obvious she had been watching him from across the room for some time. His heart slammed into his throat, and he stood up slowly on numbed legs. He was light-headed and queasy, wondering if the narcotic smoke had made him ill before he realized it was simple fear and panic knotting around his excitement.

Pratima sat alone, almost secluded by the screens around her. Reclining on the low divan, she propped her head up with one fist, resting her weight on her elbow. Her hair, loosened from the braid, fanned behind her in polished black waves. A qaellast board had been set up, stones gleaming white and red against dark-grained wood. She watched him walk toward her with a faint wry smile.

"Greetings, bhraetae," she said in Vanar when he reached the screens. He stopped and put his hand on one edge to steady himself. "Would you care to play a game of qaellast?"

"I'm the poorest player on all Vanar, l'amae," he said, in the same language.

The skin around her eyes crinkled as her smile broadened.

"The music is excellent. Perhaps you might dance for me?"

"I'm an even worse dancer." He stepped inside the privacy screens and drew them closed, the music still faintly audible behind the dampening barrier.

"Then what *can* you do for me?" she said softly, looking up at him.

He didn't know where the words came from, how he managed to speak at all as terrified as he was. "What you came here for." Taking two steps to her, he slid his hand behind her neck to pull her head toward him, his fingers tangled in her hair. He had a glimpse of white teeth as her lips opened before he crushed his mouth over hers, kissing her with greedy hunger.

Half falling on her, he knocked over the qaellast board, scattered stones hopping over the stone floor. Her hands gripped his arms, hard fingers digging into his skin, pulling him down onto her. His tongue slid into her mouth and she bit it gently, held it captive with her teeth. He moaned, feverishly groping with her sati, pushing it open off her shoulders. His hands covered her small breasts, nipples hard under his palms, the bones on her rib cage palpable through the flesh. She was small and slender, but with the ruthless tenacity of steel cable rather than any fragility.

She released his mouth, and he buried his face in the curve of her neck, filling his senses with her smell, her taste. Strong hands wrenched his sati open. His bare skin burned under her touch as she reached down and grasped his cock, pulling him toward her inexorably.

"Oh, no," he groaned, not wanting it to happen so quickly, powerless to slow himself as he felt her press him against her hot softness. His hips thrust instinctively, sliding, filling her. Pressure shimmered up his spine, her fingers stabbed into the flesh of his buttocks, squeezing, drawing him deep into her, her legs clamped around his waist. He could hear himself making helpless animal sounds as he drove himself into her with bruising force. He shuddered and came, the explosion of relief blinding him.

His muscles had turned to butter, and he slid off beside her, one boneless arm draped over her chest. He lay there breathlessly, shaking in fatigued satiety. Dazed, unable to even move, it took several minutes for his heart to gradually slow. The sweat on his body chilled him, the hairs on his arms standing up.

Suddenly, he was aware she had made no sound at all. *None.* He looked at her, fumbling in embarrassment. His penis slid out, his testicles contracting with the air-chilled slickness. Even spent and ashamed, he was surprised to find he still wanted her, an ache coiling around the base of his groin.

She gently disentangled herself from him and began wrapping her black sati around herself, expertly twisting and pleating it into shape. He watched her silently, miserable, unable to find the words to even apologize to her.

She clipped the folds of cloth together securely with an unembellished pin, then held out her hand toward him. "Now that you have fucked me," she said calmly in Hengeli, "come, and I will make love to you."

XIII

HE FELT A VICARIOUS THRILL OF POWER, ABSORBING PRESTIGE JUST BY being in her presence. The deferential respect she received, the interest turned toward them, strangely intoxicated him.

She appeared not to notice, nothing condescending or haughty in her demeanor. When she spoke, she was faultlessly polite, yet it was as if she had no understanding of any hierarchy. When she walked, she seemed unaware others made way for her, heedless of their respect. She wasn't arrogantly ignoring them, he realized; she dismissed it so thoroughly from her consciousness that their reaction to her simply didn't exist.

He, however, didn't quite have the same dexterity. He was very much aware of the respect around them. The stares turned on him had an almost physical sensation. They left the kaemahjah, and a float taxi settled next to them at the barest motion of her hand. The driver didn't blink as she motioned him inside to sit beside her, rather than relegating him to the back as he expected.

The taxi rapidly skated away from the outlying suburbs at the margins of the Estates. Thin, twisted spires and arched walkways, organic designs crystallized into delicate buildings, dominated the city center. She had the taxi stop in front of a glittering tower of white marble and got out, walking away without looking back as he followed her. The taxi lifted and sped off, seemingly unconcerned she had not paid for the fare.

The streets teemed with pedestrians, mostly women. He tried to ignore their stares as she stopped, facing a blank wall. The building had no entrance that he could see, until she stepped in front of an unadorned expanse of marble and placed her hand against the stone. A thin seam incised a black rectangular line, and the marble fell back smoothly, exposing a bright entry. It closed behind them seamlessly.

She stood in the center of a barren room as large as Yaenida's study and said in Vanar, "Up, please." Only his gut told him they were ascending until they reached the top of the tower. The walls folded back like flower petals opening to the morning sun and merged into the floor. The space was huge, expansive windows curving around a panoramic view of the city so high and so empty it made him vertiginous.

Large paintings, costly museum-quality pieces, hung on the arced girders separating the pseuquartz windows like bars on an immense birdcage. The room was spacious enough to easily accommodate a thousand boisterous party guests, while floor cushions and low settees arranged around antique screens made the area surprisingly intimate.

She watched him as he walked around. His bare feet sank into the plush carpets, and he noticed the faint perfume of flowers before spotting a cascade of orchids thriving on a ten-meter-high tumble of natural rock. The granite glistened as water trickled through the greenery into a mosaic pool large enough to swim in filled with silver-scaled fish.

"Is this yours?" he asked, dazzled.

She seemed surprised by the question. "No," she said simply. "Are you hungry?"

He turned as he heard the faint skittering, staring at a black metal and chrome ten-legged spider striding with delicate grace across the room toward them. Two feet high, it held a silver tray bearing food on its back, balanced with four sets of sharp-spined mandibles. Stopping before a low table, it smoothly lifted the tray off its back, swiveling the mandibles to set it down before sorting and arranging the food into two settings.

"Thank you, Ilitu," Pratima said in Vanar, and the mechanism strolled back toward a small alcove, its multijointed legs moving in smooth rotation, tapered ends barely making tracks in the thick rug.

"Are you always so polite to robots?" he asked as the machine settled into its slot, curling up its legs to mesh like an abstract sculpture against the wall.

She knelt by the table and picked up a tiny canapé. "Only when they're sentient," she said, and popped the hors d'oeuvre into her mouth. He shot a startled look at the mechanical spider, gazing back into its lifeless eyes, four ebony stones. She motioned for him to sit down.

Rather than kneeling formally in Vanar fashion, he tucked his sati under his knees and sat down cross-legged. She smiled, but said nothing. He watched as she leaned over to pour out a tiny serving of coffee. Her hands were steady, long, unadorned fingers with blunt nails holding the fragile cup out to him.

"Thank you," he murmured reflexively, and sipped the thick, black liquid before setting the cup down gently. He was not an expert on ceramics, but he knew he was drinking from antique porcelain worth far more than he was comfortable handling.

"Okay, I'm impressed," he said. "Who does this all belong to, then?"

She tucked a strand of loose hair behind one ear. "It doesn't belong to anybody. It's just somewhere for Pilots to go during our downtime, a place where we can relax." She ate another canapé, chewing slowly as he surveyed the huge room. "Pilots are particularly sensitive to claustrophobia. We need space."

He picked up a strip of thin slices of pickled ginger arranged on a tiny sliver of bread among artfully cut vegetables, then a thick garlicky artichoke paté, cradled in the halves of pinkish hard eggs. They were delicious. "Ilitu made these?"

"Yes."

He made a deliberate effort to turn toward the spidery thing. "Excellent, Ilitu. Thank you," he said in careful Vanar. When he turned back toward Pratima, she was grinning. "No?"

"Not necessary," she said, voice sparkling with suppressed laughter. "But I'm sure she appreciates it."

They ate in silence, trading glances and hesitant smiles like lovestruck adolescents, or at least he felt like an infatuated teenager. "Would you like to listen to music?" she asked.

"Why not?" he barely got out before the opening strains of a quiet concerto. Startled, he shook his head and leaned back. "What, is the room sentient, too?" he asked.

"The entire building is sentient," she said. "We are inside Ilitu. She is a conscious entity much like ourselves."

"This is too strange, Pratima." He set his half-eaten canapé back down on his tiny porcelain plate.

"If it bothers you, I will take you back to the Estate." Her milk-blue eyes regarded him serenely, impenetrable.

"No," he said quickly. "Not yet. I'm just not used to this, is all." He tried a smile, feeling like a fraud. "So is this what it's like on a Pilotship?"

She glanced around, considering her answer. "It has some similarities," she said. Then, rethinking it over, "No, to be honest, it's not like a Pilotship at all. Nothing is like a Pilotship. Now, of course, being eternally ground-bound, you would like to ask me to tell you all about what it's *really* like on a Pilotship."

Her playful malice sparked a flash of resentment, the hair on the back of his neck prickling. "Actually," he said with sudden recklessness, "I'd rather ask if you enjoyed pulling the wings off houseflies when you were a child."

The muscles in her face didn't move, but her expression changed immediately. The suggestion of her smile vanished, and her pale eyes grew cold. "There are no houseflies on Vanar," she said quietly. She picked up her delicate cup and slid away from the table, her back against the floor cushions, legs stretched casually, the hand holding her coffee resting on one knee. "And I believe I owe you an apology, Nathan," she said indifferently. "It was cruel to tease you about your imprisonment here."

His pulse shuddering in his ears, he was furious with himself. "No, I'm sorry, l'amae," he said quickly. "I had no right—"

"You had every right," she cut him off. "And don't call me 'l'amae.' My boredom does not justify using other people as toys for my own amusement. I don't often forget that, but when I do"—the ice cracked, her voice suddenly sad—"it is fitting I should be reminded." She looked away from him, flat gaze leveled on the evening sky, violet striations in the distance. "Please accept my sincere apologies."

He said nothing for a long moment, then with obviously feigned meekness, "Does that mean you aren't going to make love to me now, after all?"

Slowly, her mouth twisted into a grin before she laughed, a deep sound rolling from her throat like the flutter of birds' wings suddenly set free. Her body shook, and a tiny drop of coffee splashed over the edge of the cup, an ebony bead staining her pale leg. He had to suppress the urge to lick it from her skin. Her free hand swept back the long tangle of dark hair spilling over her shoulders. When she had finished laughing, she eyed him thoughtfully, still smiling.

"Of them all, Yaenida has been the most interesting and the most elusive," she said softly, speaking more to herself. "She never does anything without good reason, once you sift through all the devious tricks and turns. Why you, Nathan? What's she up to now?"

He shook his head. "I don't understand."

She laughed again, a mild exhalation through her nose. She leaned closer to him, her languor radiating an uncompromising energy. "What do you know of Pilots?" she asked, this time without the teasing sarcasm, and ran a fingernail across his collarbone at the top of his mati. He felt the blood surge to his penis.

He swallowed. "About what anybody knows. Or thinks they do. Slightly more than nothing. All Pilots are Vanar women."

"And they live forever?"

"You told me that wasn't true," he pointed out.

"I also told you it was." She set down the cup and slid around the table to sit beside him, her legs curled over his. Catching hold of the end of his sati, she pulled it, making him lean into her.

"I live inside the Worm, Nathan," she said softly, her lips an inch from his. He could feel the heat of her breath against his cheek, the earthy scent of sweetened coffee. "My friends are all Pilots, exactly like me. We never meet the people on the ships we take from one place to the next. We don't care about them, it's the *going* we live for. When we must leave our nice, safe Pilotship, we come to Vanar where we were conceived, like salmon returning upstream to spawn."

He realized what the silver-scaled fish in the huge pond were, and glanced in their direction. She smiled, one side of her mouth quirked up wryly. "Vanar is a place where people never ask us questions, because those answers they don't already know, they're too polite to pry. Where Pilots are treated like sacred lepers. Where we never have to answer, even to ourselves, Who are you? *What* are you?"

She slowly unwound the sati from around his shoulders, strong hands stroking his bare skin as she uncovered it.

"Consider the brutal nature of power." She kissed his shoulder, her lips following the curve of his clavicle toward his throat. Her breath was humid against his skin, alternately warm and cool between the words. "When we were monkeys, power was at its most basic level. Big strong male monkey beats up and fucks little helpless female monkey. Being perverse creatures, female monkeys are attracted to the biggest, meanest monkey around. The monkey with the most power got the most sex and had the most progeny. Sex and power. Power and sex. They are the essentials of survival, they can't be separated."

His unclipped sati fell off his shoulders, and she pushed up his mati to comb her fingers through the fine hairs on his chest, following their descent down the hollow of his rib cage, stroking his stomach. His hands shook as he unfastened her plain brooch pinning the black cloth above her shoulder and pulled away the fabric, her puckered nipples charcoal black against translucently white skin.

"Then the monkeys learned to walk and talk and invented money. Now it was the monkey with the most money who had the most power. But still they were monkeys; it was still the big monkeys who controlled the money and the power. And the sex." She pressed him gently down to the soft floor, kissing him as she pushed open his sati, her hands sweeping over his shoulders.

"Then along come the Worms," he murmured, uncurling the length of fabric from her torso.

"Oh, yes," she whispered into his ear, and he shivered as she bit the lobe gently, her tongue tracing a soft line around the shell. "Then came the Worms. Without them, we would all just be grubby clots of life infecting planets in isolation, waving obsolete greetings to each other, exiled across the vast distances. But with the Worms, there is trade. Flight is trade is money is power is sex. . . ."

She cupped him in her hand through the cloth of his sati, her palm squeezing the shaft while the tips of her fingers rolled his balls between them. He moaned softly as his head arched back, needles of pleasure spiraling through his legs.

"And only women can safely Pilot the great ships through the lair of the celestial Worm." Her body pressed against him, her hands sliding up his ribs, over his arms. "All of a sudden, power didn't depend on which monkey was the biggest and strongest or even the smartest any longer, did it?" She smiled, hitched herself up against his chest, and slid down against his cock, taking him inside her in one long, unhurried thrust. She leaned down to kiss him.

Conversation ceased. This time, they made love slowly, kicking away their tangled sati, luxuriating in the freedom of the expanse of thick, deep carpet, hands and lips and sweat intermingled. They rolled like wrestlers, reveling in the space. And this time, she made noise. Glorious sounds growling in her throat. The pressure grew against his spine, seething along the nerve ends in his skin. She rode him expertly, balanced no matter how violently his hips rolled and plunged against her, his spine arching.

Then she threw back her head and moaned, a single long wail of rapture as contractions shuddered up the length of his penis.

He was breaking, falling, and he came and came and came.

His thoughts eventually reorganized back into an orderly state, an awareness he had been staring at the sky above him for a long time, stars shimmering against the blackness between the outline of the silver-filigreed girders. She lay curled against him, ivory on gold, one arm across his chest, one leg draped over his thighs. Her head tucked into his shoulder, tangled hair under his chin. He turned on his side to look down at her face.

Her eyes were open, her dreamy gaze at nothing interrupted as she looked up at him.

"So why can't men be Pilots?" he asked.

She laughed, and rolled onto her back, her neck resting on his arm. He placed his hand splay-fingered over her stomach. Amazed at how huge and ugly it seemed against her body, he studied his own hand as if it were the first time he had ever seen it: heavy corded tendons, the scuffed knuckles, green-blue veins under the network of minuscule creases. The downy hair on her belly was as white as her skin, making him think of a wild animal, caged and unpredictable.

"Always questions." She sighed, a long inhale of satisfaction and soft exhale. "You don't have the right chromosomes."

She curled and rolled to her feet in a single fluid movement, padding naked toward the alcove. The spider machine watched passively as she opened a small cabinet and brought out two fragile glasses and a decanter of dark wine. Nathan sat up against cushions as she poured the drinks, her back toward him.

She was far from beautiful, he realized. Black hair snarled down her back, not quite covering her buttocks, their angular muscles cut into flat planes. Hips jutted out of her too-thin body, legs sinewy under unnaturally pale skin. Her knees were slightly knobby, and when she turned, a glass in each hand, he could make out each rib under tiny breasts, the slight gap between her thin legs.

She smiled as if she could hear his thoughts, and when she walked toward him, the unattractiveness vanished. She moved with consummate grace, total control, and when she knelt to hand him a glass, the ache of desire had already stirred again.

She sipped her wine, then leaned to kiss him, the wine's chill and tartness against her lips. Settling back on her haunches, legs tucked under her, she said, "All Pilots are women, but not all women can be Pilots."

"Why not?" he asked, sipping his own wine.

She grinned. "*They* don't have the right chromosomes. Family connections are all-important to the Vanar, as you may have figured out by now. But Families don't care too much about bloodlines. It's money that runs in their veins, and controlling the money means making sure there are plenty of competent daughters to run the Families. A woman needs an heir, she adopts a daughter. She sleeps with a dozen men, who's the father of the children? Who cares? They all are. Oh, they do keep track for medical reasons, but no one is too concerned with breeding. Eugenics and racial purity has always been a crock. A child is a throw of the dice, each and every time."

She pushed her hair off her forehead with her fingers, her eyes looking beyond him. "Except for Pilots." Her voice was bitter. "Our breeding is sacrosanct. We are so different it's hard to remember I'm actually Vanar, too." She focused on him and smiled. "The genetics are quite complicated, I don't know if I could explain it to you."

"I'm a botanist, Pratima," he said wryly. "Even plants have DNA."

"Ah," she said, as if startled by the idea of an educated man. "Well." She considered for a moment. "Strictly speaking, Pilots have no fathers."

He looked at her, puzzled.

"Sex cells are all haploid. Take a meiotic cell with only half the normal number of chromosomes, force it replicate, double its chromosomes, and grow yourself a baby from it. What have you got?"

"A baby with identical pairs of genes," he said slowly.

"Exactly. Pilots need identical genes. Our equilibrium has to balance even down to the submolecular level. Even further, you have forty-six chromosomes. I have twenty-eight."

He blinked, stunned. "What?"

"I'm still human, as human as you are. If you know anything about basic human genetics, you know that most of what is in our genomes is evolutionary junk. Very little of our genome is allocated to being human. Everything you have, I have too. And then some. A lot of specially designed recessive genes all carefully balanced and tailored for us to make long-term survival possible in a Worm have been inserted. All the rest—all the useless squatters, the vestiges of prehistoric genes, the DNA parasites cluttering up your genome—have been edited out of mine. We only need twenty-eight chromosomes for it all. But that's the reason why all Pilots are female: all of our chromosomes are identical." She stretched her bare legs out in front of her, avoiding his gaze.

"Are all Pilots identical?" he asked carefully, still struggling to absorb this. "Do they all look like you?"

"No," she said. "The Nine Families own and control the Worms connecting the systems, and each one has developed their own paradigm. Pilot lines are distinctly different. But within the Family, Pilots are more closely related than mere clones. The distinction between one generation and the next becomes blurred when everyone is a duplicate of each other. My mother is more than my twin sister. When we ride the Worm, to a certain extent, she becomes *me*. We are all one being."

He was putting the pieces together. "You said you were on Vanar to get pregnant."

"Yes."

"Not mine."

"Of course not."

He stared at her in growing dismay. "Raemik."

"Don't judge me, Nathan," she said softly. "You can't condemn what you don't understand." Her small chin lifted as she twisted her head to glare at him, eyes as blank as a marble statue with her white irises against the corneas. "Raemik is not just my twin brother, he's my son."

"My God." He felt the blood drain away from his face.

"Where did you imagine little baby Pilots came from?" she said sharply. "Did you think we're assembled in some nice sterile laboratory, pour a few chemicals together and stir well? Would that be easier on

your sense of propriety rather than dirty, disgusting incest?" She slith-
ered away from him, a pink sheen washed on her cheekbones. "Clones
age too quickly, their cells are already mature, too much risk of muta-
tion even with genetic maintenance. My mother's son gave me Raemik.
He is my perfect match, his genetics are identical to mine, except for
his one Y chromosome. Our daughter will be my exact twin, my *sister*."

"And it's that important?"

"Critical," she said neutrally. "Pilotships are unforgiving creatures.
I could try to describe the experience to you, Nathan, and I don't
mean to insult you by saying it would be like explaining the rainbow to
the blind. Pilots aren't merely navigators; the Worm isn't a machine.
We're part of the living engine itself, we *become* the Worm. We've
been designed and bred to ride that equilibrium. We live for nothing
else. And if a Pilot loses her balance even for a moment, she doesn't
just fall down and skin her knee. She's ripped apart, slowly, all the
length of the Worm. Not two molecules are left sticking together."

She shuddered and drank the last of her wine.

"I'd like some more," he said, and got unsteadily to his feet.

"Bring the bottle."

He retrieved the decanter and walked back toward her. The
panoramic lights of the city skyline surrounding him on every side, the
openness of the pseuquartz windows, gave him the odd feeling of flying. He stumbled slightly, fighting an irrational fear he might fall and
slide screaming off the edge of the circular room. He settled beside
her, pouring out the wine with a shaking hand.

"Equilibrium is everything," she said softly, and slid her arm
around his waist, holding him gently against her. *"Everything."*

She was trembling.

XIV

THEY FELL ASLEEP, LIMBS TANGLED TOGETHER, BUT WHEN HE WOKE, HE was curled up alone in a nest of floor cushions. He raised himself to peer blearily over the edge, squinting through puffy eyelids in the early-morning sunrise.

She stood naked on one foot in the center of the vast room, facing the sun over his shoulder. Her ashen skin seemed to glow in the light, accented by the black of her hair tumbling down her back. On tiptoes, her head back, she suspended one leg out at an angle, foot waist-high, her arms out, elbows crooked, palms up. He blinked at her as her head rolled forward. She opened her eyes to smile at him, then shut them again. For a few seconds, she wobbled slightly before she did a little hop.

She now stood with her entire weight balanced on the end of her left big toe. He goggled at her, unbelievingly, and crawled out of the heap of pillows, trailing his sati snagged around an ankle. He shook it off and walked around her, an arm length away.

She didn't move, didn't breath, not a muscle twitched as she held her impossible position. He leaned in toward her to study her face, and her lips moved. "Don't touch me, please," she said calmly, and froze again, motionless.

Wrapping his sati carelessly around his waist, he sat down and watched, amazed. After she had stayed in the same position for several minutes with not the slightest quiver of movement, he shook his head and got up in search of coffee. He opened a few cabinets at random, examining their contents.

"Good morning, Ilitu, you're looking splendid today. Sleep well, did you?" He looked down at the spider machine, speaking in Hengeli, not expecting it to answer. "You wouldn't know where the coffee is, by any chance?" To his surprise, the spider unfolded from its insert and strolled smoothly into the center of the alcove. Within a few moments, it had gathered the ingredients and equipment and began preparing coffee.

He took two cups back toward Pratima, and as he stood holding them, he realized she was now balanced on her right big toe. He hadn't seen her move. He almost dropped the cup as she took a sudden deep breath, startling him, and opened her eyes. Dropping with a solid thump to the flat of her feet, she took her cup out of his hand. "Thank you," she said. "This is lovely."

"Thank Ilitu. It . . . she speaks Hengeli as well."

Pratima smiled at him over the lip of her cup. "Nathan," she scolded, "Ilitu doesn't speak Hengeli; she's just intelligent. The word for 'coffee' in Vanar is . . . '*coffee*.'"

"That makes me feel almost fluent." He hesitated, then, "How do you *do* that?" he asked wonderingly.

"Equilibrium is everything," she said seriously. "Everything is equilibrium." Still holding onto the cup, she slowly leaned backward, reaching over her head to place her free hand to the floor. Lazily, her legs lifted in an arc over her head, settled gently onto her feet as she stood. She drank from the cup, not a drop spilled. "It's a form of meditation. You train yourself to balance *everything*, to ride the movement of the earth, as the core moves inside the mantle, as the planet moves around the sun, as the star is slung out around the arms of the galaxy's spiral, as the galaxies spin out into the universe, down into your bones, into your blood, into the dance of molecules that gives us all the illusion we are solid and real. You learn how to float in between the spaces of mass and energy, where time hides."

He stared at her for a moment, then said, "You're right. I hate mystics," and sipped his own coffee.

She laughed, took his cup from his hands, and put it down with hers. She grasped his waist, turning his back to her. "Stand on one leg," she said, and when he started to raise himself onto his toes, "No, keep your foot flat on the floor. Learn to walk before you run. Hold your arms out, like this." Her hands were cool against the skin under his arms as she corrected his stance. "Leg higher, higher, that's it. Now close your eyes."

Her hands slid down to rest lightly on his hips as he wobbled, his muscles jerking him as he sought stability.

"Yes," she said, her voice soft in his ear. He felt her featherlight stroking of his body, leaving ghost sensations behind. "Feel how your body moves. It knows where the center of gravity is, it *wants* to be there. If you do this every day, it will learn to use less and less movement to correct your balance. You must concentrate on aligning your body so that you can tweak the smallest muscle to maintain your equilibrium instead of flailing your arms around like a spastic bird as you're doing now."

She was laughing, and the effort to keep from laughing himself made it difficult. Tilting dangerously to one side, he put his other foot down.

"I can't do this," he said, starting to turn toward her. She grabbed his waist firmly, holding him back.

"*Try*, Nathan," she said fiercely, the laughter still in her voice. "It isn't difficult unless you convince yourself it is. Understand by doing. Close your eyes. Get that leg up higher. . . ."

Obediently, he stood teetering on one foot, his arms wobbling as he swayed blindly. She kept her hands on his waist, steadying him, guiding him. Her hands glided along his chest, his hips.

"Better, good. Now listen to me. Imagine a string running through your center, top of your head to the bottom of your foot." Her mouth was close to his ear, the words caressing his cheek, warm perfume. "It goes all the way through you, down toward the center of the world. *Feel* it if you can. Feel it draw you down into the planet, pulling all the time. Feel it pressing your foot to the ground, making that string tight. It becomes so taut, it's like a steel cord, holding you in perfect alignment."

He tried to envision it, aware of his weight pressing his foot firmly to the floor.

"That's it," she said, and he wondered if she was commenting on his progress or just encouraging him. "Now imagine yourself getting thinner. Your whole body is being drawn into the string, evenly on all sides." Her voice was almost hypnotic. "You flow into it, make yourself the string, all the way to the center of the world. *Concentrate*, Nathan. . . ."

He did, focusing on the image as hard as he could. Suddenly, he realized her hands were no longer on his hips, and he staggered, his foot striking the floor to keep himself from falling. She was seated cross-legged in front of him, sipping coffee, as she had been, he was instantly aware, for some time. His muscles were trembling with fatigue as she inclined her head slightly in an ironic salute.

"That's the idea," she said. "Practice every day and you'll get better."

He knelt beside her, his senses keen, hyperaware. "Will it make me into a Pilot?" he asked jokingly.

"No," she said, smiling, "but it might make you a better dancer."

He took the cup from her hand and kissed her, reveling in the sharp taste, the complex spice of coffee and the salt flavor of her mouth. His heightened awareness made the brush of her skin against his an excruciating joy. He heard her muffled whimper as shades of tone, harmonics resonating through him.

When he finally came, it was with a savage intensity he had never before experienced, shattering his senses into shards of light and color. He dimly heard her wail in exultation, riding him, riding him. . . .

XV

SHE TOOK HIM BACK TO THE NGA'ESHA ESTATE IN THE LATE AFTERNOON and left him there. In the following days, he didn't see her—not by the river, not in passing in the labyrinthine passages of the House. After the first few days of exhilaration, a blanket of depression settled in.

Disappointment at being ignored and forgotten gave way to an uneasy disgust with himself. It had been fun while it lasted, he chided himself. Why had he any expectation it would be more than that? But somehow he knew it had been.

He decided he should have something constructive to occupy his time and energies rather than moping around like an infatuated schoolboy. He was still a botanist, and for the project he had in mind, he would need permission from the senior kharvah. Nathan knew amends would have to be made before he was back in Aelgar's favor. If he ever had been.

Aelgar still treated him with suspicious contempt, and the young sahakharae he had shoved around—what was his name?—Tycar, took a special vindictive pleasure in managing to be present whenever Nathan went through his ritualistic contrition. Thwarted lust hath no fury, Nathan thought acidly. After several weeks, Nathan suspected his tedious humble kowtowing was becoming expected, something he was not keen on having turned into regular habit. He needed a change in strategy.

As the pratha h'máy's oldest daughter and heir, Yronae held the Nga'esha domestic purse strings; Yaenida didn't worry about money on any scale less than interplanetary. Yronae's own eldest daughter and heir, Suryah, supervised the Nga'esha women's personal assets, while her younger daughter, the *qaturthi h'máy* Bidaelah, controlled the men's household accounts. Nathan had to go through the intricate formalities of petitioning Bidaelah to allow him access to his own bank account. After some reluctance—based, he suspected, more on linguistic confusion than any callousness on the woman's part—she authorized the funds to be transferred to his personal account on his datacard from an astonishing amount he had accumulated. As naeqili, he'd barely earned enough to pay for tea and bath fees, but as the youngest son of a pratha h'máy, his allowance was staggering. On any other world, he'd have been considered rich beyond his dreams.

It took a little more pleading to persuade a younger cousin still apprenticing as a taemora to escort him to the shops he had no access to without a female chaperone. While the cousin waited with surly impatience, he first bought the most expensive sati clip he could afford, ornate gold filigree entwined around a profusion of bright precious stones, nearly draining his entire capital. Then he dragged her to a garden nursery where he talked the bemused shopkeeper into selling him a single sprig of white plum blossoms snipped from a tree. The cousin seemed uninterested in his purchase of the gaudy bit of jewelry, although she did raise an eyebrow at how much he was willing to pay for it. While women and men often exchanged small presents, for ritual purposes or out of friendship, gifts were rarely more than inexpensive trinkets. The flowers, however, baffled her. He didn't bother to enlighten her.

He'd rehearsed his speech for days, making sure the complex verb tenses and pronoun shifts were perfect. Then he sought out Aelgar holding court on the third level of the men's garden by a large, ornamental pool.

The day was unusually hot, and a number of boys and younger sahakharae had stripped to escape into the pool. Aelgar lolled the full length of a carved divan set under the protective shade of an ancient maple tree, his sati loosened to expose the man's hairless brown barrel chest. He fanned himself listlessly, wafting the humid air over his face with a bright paper folding fan. Nathan recognized one of the musicians from the kaemahjah, a young sahakharae who played the flute, weaving an intricate melody around his partner's lap harp. They sat close to Aelgar to share the shade of the old tree.

Acer buergeranum lucienum, Nathan noted distantly; could use a good dose of manganese sulfate, to judge by the leaves. . . .

Within the men's realm, the first husband of the pratha h'máy held the final authority. Yaenida's sole surviving kharvah, however, was a near recluse, senile and blind. Her heir's first husband, Aelgar, held the regency. When in the presence of the women, especially that of his wife Yronae, the senior kharvah was servility itself. But in his own dominion he ruled with an arrogant despotism. Tycar sat cross-legged on the ground at Aelgar's feet, a sadistic smirk already on his mouth as Nathan approached. He idly fingered the layers of gold bands encrusting his ankles, a habit Nathan recognized by now as anticipation. The boys swam to the edge of the pool, elbows and eyes over the edge to watch the promised show. The music faltered and died away as Nathan stopped in front of Aelgar respectfully. The balding man glanced up as he approached, his eyes disdainful.

Nathan brushed the folds of his sati to one side and knelt on the grass in front of the kharvah, pebbles in the soil digging into his knees. "Most senior and revered Aelgar," he said, pressing his hands together and touching his fingertips to forehead, bent over so far he nearly touched the ground, "this insignificant person knows I have thoughtlessly caused you distress through my ignorance and violent barbarity.

Although I have tried to atone for my misconduct, I realize now I have not done enough to prove myself worthy of your pardon."

He straightened to reach into a fold in his sati, and removed the clip wrapped in a colorful handwoven birdsilk cloth almost as fine a gift as the jewelry he proffered. He held it in cupped hands, bowing low so that the offering was higher than his head.

"Please accept this small token of my penitence and respect."

Keeping his eyes lowered, he couldn't see the reaction on Aelgar's face, listening instead to the expectant silence of the waiting crowd. For several moments, nothing happened, and his shoulders twinged in the abnormal position he held himself in.

Come on, take it, you greedy son of a bitch, he thought fiercely, and almost laughed when he felt the older man lift the tiny burden out of his hands. He straightened slightly, enough to watch the response of the crowd from the corner of his eye. Tycar was trying unsuccessfully to disguise his disappointment. One of the musicians had lifted himself up on his knees, craning his neck for a peek as Aelgar unwrapped the rainbow silk.

A murmur of ohhs and ahhs fluttered through the gathering as Aelgar held up the gold pin, its oversized rubies, emeralds, and blue diamonds sparkling garishly in the sunlight. Aelgar examined it objectively, appraising its value with an expert's eye while trying not to appear impressed. Finally he nodded, and sat up, his short legs swinging to the ground.

"Small brother," he said, although Nathan stood head and shoulders taller and outweighed him by more than a dozen kilos, "no person could refuse such a heartfelt apology and still call himself civilized." Nathan looked up into the older man's hard eyes, knowing the words were as hollow as his own, the truth gauzed behind the veils of Vanar etiquette. The bribe had been accepted. "Come, sit with me. You are forgiven."

Tycar glared sideways at Nathan, furious at being cheated out of the entertainment of any further humiliation.

"Not quite so, revered Aelgar. My crime was against all my brothers, but mostly against my small brother Tycar." Nathan enjoyed the sight of Tycar's surprise and distrust, and he paused just long enough for theatrical effect before extracting the twig of plum blossom from his sati. He held the flowers out toward the sahakharae. "Please accept this with my apology. Your beauty is like that of young flowers, far too delightful and delicate to ever again be subjected to such clumsiness as mine."

Gotcha, he thought, watching the emotions war across the sahakharae's face. *You don't take it, you look like an asshole. You do take it, you're permanently off my back.*

The sahakharae reluctantly accepted the sprig of flowers, unhappy at being outmaneuvered. His scowl of defeat turned to resignation as the younger boys swarmed around him, debating with spirited glee what one could actually do with such a strange gift. They finally decided to weave the flowers into the sahakharae's dark hair.

Nathan sat by Aelgar for an hour or so, listening to the music and trading what small talk he could handle. He caught the older man studying him with calculating interest, and Nathan returned the look innocently. After enough time had been served to satisfy protocol, he managed to make his escape from the senior kharvah and his entourage with more profuse courtesy and bowing, the solidified smile on his face beginning to ache.

He took several deep breaths to calm his nerves as he walked the serpentine path back up toward the main men's quarter of the House. Although he was pleased with himself, he was surprised by how much deep anger he still felt. He nearly missed Raemik half hidden in the branches of a tree as Nathan took the steps up the second level two at a time. The boy crouched in the branches, pale eyes regarding him soberly as Nathan stopped and smiled up at him. From his vantage point, Raemik could have seen the entire charade, but his impassive face gave Nathan no hint as to what he might have thought of it.

Yaenida, however, more than made up for it. He arrived the next morning for his daily lesson and found the old woman standing by a window. Her medical taemora stood cautiously to one side in case the old woman overdid herself and collapsed. Yaenida turned as Nathan entered the study, smiling broadly in the brilliant sunlight turning her jaundiced skin to gold.

"It seems death will have to wait a little while longer to take me," she said, relaxed.

"May it wait many years, jah'nari l'amae," he said. She gripped the taemora's arm resolutely and took one faltering step after another back toward the table. The taemora eased the old woman's body down into the mound of pillows jammed into the wide, carved chair, tucked Yaenida's sati around her legs, and left without a word or backward glance. Once her attendant had gone, he set his reader on the broad table and took his usual place, such casual Hengeli behavior tolerated only in private.

"You say that with such feeling, Nathan, one might almost think you meant it." She grimaced as she adjusted her fragile body deeper into the cushions.

"I do mean it," he said evenly, opening his reader. "I gain far more with you alive, Yaenida, than with you dead." He looked up at the woman grinning at him sardonically. "I also happen to like you, but I don't expect you to believe that."

She shook her head and said, "It's a shame you'll never be as good with words in Vanar as you are in Hengeli, although I've heard you're not doing all that badly there, as well."

He raised one eyebrow with mock surprise. "Me? Really?"

"You judged Aelgar's avarice and lack of taste exactly right, and the bit with the flowers was a masterful touch. You seem to have taken my advice to heart."

He bowed in exaggerated acknowledgment. "This worthless nae-qili does his humble best," he said in Vanar, which made her laugh, a dry, rasping sound sucking the air from her lungs. He got up without being told to set up her water pipe. She took the stem from him with shaking fingers, sucking in the smoke greedily to calm her lungs. He sat back down and waited.

"You don't much enjoy men's company, do you, Nathan?" she asked when she had her breath back.

He leaned back and thought about it seriously. "Not on Vanar," he admitted finally.

"Why not? You would be better off in the long run to make friends among the men of my House. You should consider taking a lover from among the sahakharae. That would be the expedient thing to do."

The reader was open, but the screen remained blank, ignored. It troubled him how much of his personal life Pratha Yaenida knew, no secrets remaining hidden for long from her far-reaching intelligence network. But the past was the past, he was not the same person he had been so many years ago, a lifetime ago.

"I'm not interested in sex with men, Yaenida, and I don't have much in common with the rest of my Vanar 'brothers,'" he said patiently, "not just because of the language problem."

"No," she said, in a tone that wasn't a question.

"All these elaborate formalities"—he waved a hand in a gesture of frustration—"the ritual posturing, the complicated speech, it's stupefying. Whenever I've tried to have a conversation with someone to practice my Vanar, it's as if the men can't speak in anything *but* formulae and rote response. It's like talking to machines, no one is really there."

She propped her head on her fist, the slack skin of her face pushing one eye half closed as she listened silently, a thread of smoke spiraling toward the high ceiling.

"The men of your Family aren't stupid, and most of them are educated. They're literate, they have complicated debates I can barely follow about all sorts of things. But it's just a game, to see how many verbal points you can score, not out of any passion or enjoyment. They're afraid to make a decision or have an opinion of their own about anything they might actually care about."

"Hmm," was all the comment she made, hooded eyes deceptively jaded.

"No one has much spirit of their own," he said, struggling to find the words. "Or if they do, they spend a lot of effort to hide it. It's like scratching on glass: you can see there's something underneath, but there's no way to reach it. No one *does* anything. They just . . . sit around like lifeless pets waiting to be played with."

She sank farther back into the cushions, hooking the stem of her pipe over the water reservoir. Resting her elbows on the polished table, she steepled her fingertips together. "I think you disparage our men unjustly, Nathan. Nga'esha men in particular, I'm proud to say, are quite astute and creative. Men can do many things far better than most women. They dance, they paint, they play music, they write beautiful poetry that you unfortunately can't appreciate fully."

Nathan sighed. "How nice," he said scornfully. "But art out of boredom isn't a virtue. Can you honestly tell me, Yaenida, that all the dancing and music and poetry is to satisfy any particular creative urge of their own? It's all geared toward making themselves more valuable as marriage commodities for the Family business."

She regarded him silently for a moment, her lips pursed. "Aren't you being a little harsh in your judgment?"

"Not as harsh as life is for the men of Vanar."

She snorted. "I suspect there are those who might not feel so sorry for you. The asteroid miners in the Craswell system, for example. Long hours, hard physical work, the most basic amenities, low-paying labor contracts, high accident mortality. Can you imagine their reaction to your bitching about your soft existence?"

"I'll be happy to trade places with any one of them this minute, l'a-mae, if you'll allow it. They at least have the freedom to quit their jobs."

"The freedom to starve, Nathan? Don't pretend to be naive. They survive any way they can, the same as you do." Her eyes narrowed as she tucked her hands into her sleeves for warmth, although the room was a comfortable temperature. "Freedom comes packaged in a variety of cages. Get used to yours."

"I don't think I can," he said bitterly.

"Why not?" she asked reasonably. "You don't really believe human beings are born kind and good and wise, do you? We are greedy, selfish, and ruthless, which is why our species has survived for so long." She leaned back in her chair, wincing in pain through an amused smile. "Women endured much worse for untold generations. We survived. And so will you."

"The sins of the fathers shall be visited upon their sons?"

She laughed. "Not my religion," she said. "But, yes. The good of the community outweighs the good of the individual. Men's biological nature is violent and must be controlled, to protect society as well as themselves. Women have always had plenty of reason to fear male violence. Women are rarely serial killers. We're not even equipped for rape."

He didn't answer, staring into the lifeless screen of the reader. She sighed, leaned back into the cushion in the chair shaking her head. "Such a stubborn boy," she admonished. "Surely it can't all be that dreadful for you here? You could still be living in Westcastle, you know."

"I don't need a lecture on the horrors of war, jah'nari l'amae," he said thickly, glancing up at her angrily. "As for Vanar being a place of peace and harmony where all women are gentle pacifists, I've got a five-inch scar down my left side that contradicts you."

She snorted dismissively. "That was merely politics."

"And that makes the difference?"

"Absolutely. We've always had the usual squabbles between rival Houses, business conflicts, even an assassination once in a while, but nothing major, nothing to threaten our entire society. Our streets are safe, we live without locks on our doors, those of us who even bother with doors. In all our history, we have never had a war. Can't you see that these are things worth protecting?"

"For godsake, Yaenida," he protested. "Protect from whom? *Me?* I'm not a rapist or a murderer! I am *not* a violent man."

"Aren't you?" She shook her hands out of her sleeves, and leaned forward to rest her elbows on the arms of the chair. "You made a very threatening gesture toward a woman on the street. Don't tell me you weren't angry enough to hit her."

"That woman had no right to hit *me.*"

"Of course she did. To her, it looked like you were assaulting Lyris Arjusana. Men are *never* to touch a woman against her wishes, Nathan. Not on Vanar. You were naekulam, a foreigner without family, rude and unpredictable. They had reason to believe you were ready to respond to an ordinary rebuke with violence. That woman knew you weren't Vanar and likely thought she actually was doing you a favor. If she or Lyris Arjusana had made a formal complaint, you'd have found yourself back in much more unpleasant circumstances. The violence done to you hurts more from insult than any injury. How much physical harm can a woman half your size really inflict? Had it been the other way round, you could have easily caused severe injury to her."

"The real injury caused to me, Yaenida, is being imprisoned here with no hope of escape. I'm a botanist, not a criminal, and certainly not a rapist or a murderer. Tell me, how is that violent? Who is going to be hurt if I go out into the jungle to study plants?"

"Ostensibly, no one," she admitted candidly, her expression nonchalant. "But to allow one man more privileges than another invites discontent and jealousy. Be realistic, Nathan. Vanar or not, we all have limitations; accept yours and you'll be happier."

He stared down at the knuckles of his clenched fists in his lap without speaking.

"You have access to the grounds, and permission to have your private litte garden. Grow flowers. Grow weeds, if that's what you want to do. It's healthy for men to be interested in plants, to appreciate their bond with the earth, respect the source from which all life flows."

"Worship your Mother Goddess?" he said sourly.

She picked up her pipe and rolled a small ball of sticky black resin between her fingers to reload the bowl. "Our beliefs are more philosophy than religion. We don't worship any deity like your hairy old man squatting in the clouds to piss abuse down on those who refuse to crawl before his tyranny. She is merely a symbol—the union of all living beings into one reality, neither male nor female, greater than the sum of its parts. As individuals, we must accept our personal limitations as being only part of the whole. But there is no divine judgment or punishment, only the harm we do to ourselves when we try to divide the mind from the body and the body from the soul."

She gazed off distractedly over his shoulder, puffing the pipe to life. "A clever sermon," he said. "Do you really believe it?"

She smiled. "Certainly." She focused back on his face. "Why not? It's no sillier than any other theology, and centuries of Vanar peace and prosperity haven't harmed its validity." Her eyes hardened. "But while this philosophical discussion has been amusing, Nathan, you would do well to listen to some practical advice."

"Always, Pratha Yaenida," he said, and she glanced at him as she heard the sudden wariness in his voice.

"Don't labor under the illusion that you are more cunning than the men of my House. Aelgar isn't stupid, he simply underestimated you. He's perfectly aware you've used our own conventions to outsmart him . . . *this* time. He's not likely to let that happen again. Sahakharae, on the other hand"—she shrugged—"have their place, but are often envious creatures who enjoy stirring up trouble. You are not liked by the men of my House. They are resentful of your intimacy with me and are afraid of your strangeness. They have little else to do and plenty of time to do it in, should they decide to hurt you."

She studied him silently for a moment. "You will find yourself in a very small minority if you continue voicing your discontent. There are many things about our men you know little of. It would profit you to open your mind as well as your eyes. Vanar men don't think of themselves as oppressed; they consider themselves blessed to be living in a society that allows them to be cherished and protected by the ideals of the Eternal Mother."

He was sure he heard a tinge of irony in her voice.

"You're here to stay, for the rest of your life, whether you like it or not. So you can do one of two things, Nathan. You can sit around sniveling about it, or you can accept what you cannot change and turn what you can to your own advantage. For the moment, you are an asset to me, and I will defend you as best I can. As I *have* been. No one will challenge my authority openly, and it is not wise to annoy me too far. But if you become such a disruptive influence that the stability of my House is threatened, I will not protect you."

A thrill of alarm shot through his gut.

"I cannot afford to," she said softly.

She turned back to her reader, flipping it open and squinting at the oversized Vanar script. "You can start by paying stricter attention to learning Vanar. We begin," she said firmly. "Certain verbs are followed by an infinitive with a linking preposition, others are not. Those verbs with linking prepositions fall into four categories of construction, depending on the subjunctives *aht, tvae, aen,* and *ynah.* . . ."

He made better progress that day. The stick could also be a powerful incentive to learning.

XVI

PRATIMA WAITED FOR HIM BY THE RIVER, SITTING WITH HER LEGS tucked underneath her on the grassy bank as the gray water flowed by. Her face was turned away from him, only the curve of her cheek visible, but he knew she was aware he stood at the edge of the brake behind her, watching her.

She was not beautiful, and he had never wanted a woman more. The thick bracken crackled under his bare feet as he approached her. She turned her head slightly, listening. Her eyes closed as his hands settled onto her shoulders. Kneeling behind her, not bothering to brush his sati out of the way, he kissed the side of her neck, her skin cool under his lips.

His hands slipped inside the edge of her sati, sliding down her ribs to cup each tiny breast, her nipples hardening. She leaned back against him, her eyes still closed, and sighed. His own breath caught at the sound, the urgent pressure growing in his groin.

They made love slowly, without speaking, black and pale blue cloth spread underneath naked bodies. He watched her in amazement as she suddenly gasped, back arching, roll after roll of orgasmic surge carrying her. She hadn't reached the end of the waves before the tingling pressure began in his own legs, rushing through him and exploding in his head.

He dozed after that, his arm across her thin chest, her legs tangled around his. The warm breeze carried the sweet smell of the river across their sweating skin. When he woke, she had vanished as completely as a dream. He wondered at it, but was not surprised she could so easily slip away.

He rolled onto his back, his arms and legs loosely splayed against the sheer linen sati. Staring up into the electric blue of the sky as it began to darken into late afternoon, he sighed, then rose to shake the fragments of twigs and stiff river grass out of his sati.

A small package flew out of the silk folds, and he nearly lost it in the thick vegetation. Only the rainbow flash of paper caught his eye, and when he unwrapped it, he held a tiny wooden box. The fragile clasp was ancient, bronze metal in ornate design. His thumb pushed it up gently, prizing the lid open against the stiff hinge.

Inside, several dozen bloodred svapnah seedpods nested one against the other. He smiled, shaking the box a bit to make them roll across the bottom.

That afternoon, he started his garden.

He raided the groundskeeping system, the gardening tools oddly shaped as they were made for use by machines, but he managed. Choosing a site away from the main garden, screened by a stone wall but exposed to the morning light, he started breaking the ground.

Raemik settled onto the narrow ledge of the wall, sati pulled up from around his knees to allow him to sit cross-legged. Nathan wiped his forearm across his eyes to glance at the boy. His pale skin seemed to absorb the sunlight, glowing a golden color reflected from a silver mirror. The end of his sati over his head cast his eyes into shade, accenting the faint blue in his irises. But he looked distinct from his sister, now that Nathan was more adept at perceiving the subtle differences between them. He was also relieved to find his sexual confusion toward Raemik gone.

The boy regarded him silently, and Nathan went back to his backbreaking work, double digging the ground to prepare his garden site. As he worked, the only sounds were the trills of birds, insects humming in the air, and his own grunts and breathing as he dug the spade into the soil: lift, turn, break the clods with the edge of the shovel, step back, and repeat down the long row.

"You're my sister's lover," Raemik said suddenly.

Startled, Nathan straightened, blinking away the sweat beading into his eyes. He wasn't sure if Raemik meant it as a question. Probably not, since privacy was limited in the men's house, gossip the lifeblood of their daily existence.

"I'm not your sister's lover," he said, recognizing the word Raemik had chosen as one that implied a semipermanence. "I"—he had to think of the various terms he could use, with all their shades of meanings—"had sex with her," he finally settled on. "I don't know if I will see her again."

Surprisingly, the boy smiled, a tight, cold sneer that had nothing to do with humor. "You will," he said. "Like attracts like. You're both exotics."

Nathan eyed the boy, but that seemed to be the end of the conversation for a while. After Nathan had broken the ground for nearly another hour under the watchful gaze of his young overseer, Raemik said, "Tell her she should go away. Go back to her beloved Worm."

Nathan's back ached as he straightened, and he jabbed the spade into the ground to give him a footrest. Leaning on the handle he looked up at the boy, breathing hard. "Why should she go away?" he asked reasonably.

There was more emotion in the single glance the boy threw at him than he'd ever seen: fear, loathing, anger, hate, and a faint sheen of desperation and bravado. "Tell her to come back in a year. I'm not ready. She can't make me, you know. That's one thing they can't make men do."

He understood what the boy meant. "And you'll be ready in a year?" he asked dubiously.

The boy smiled enigmatically. "A year is nothing for her, and everything to me. Tell her I'm not ready yet to throw away the rest of my life." Then he was up on his feet, running along the thin ledge of the wall with an agility Nathan had only seen before in Pratima.

As it was, Nathan didn't see her again for several weeks, although he spent as much of his free time as he could waiting for her at the river or at the kaemahjah. There were few other places where they could meet. He had been reclining against the kaemahjah cushions smoking a water pipe and listening to the music with his eyes closed when he felt someone settling beside him. He knew before opening his eyes it would be Pratima.

What did surprise him was the depth of his hunger as he pulled her down by her neck to kiss her gently. He held her tightly, and when she pulled back, her own eyes regarded him with a touch of alarm and wonder.

"I've missed you," he said quietly.

"Family business," she apologized. She smiled, reserved. "How is your garden coming along?"

He shrugged. "I'll just have to wait to see what comes up."

She smiled, placing a gentle hand on the swelling in his lap. After that, they sat side by side quietly, listening to the end of the music holding hands with almost chaste diffidence. When it finished, they left by silent agreement, taking a taxi hoverfloat into the center of the city to the white tower.

They rose up the marble shaft into the top without speaking, nor even looking at each other much, and Nathan found he was vaguely uneasy. As the floor petaled back, revealing the vast room, he realized they were not alone.

He heard her before he saw the woman in the pool, then glanced at Pratima. She had her lips pursed in an expression of regret for him, but her eyes sparkled with far more animation than he'd seen before.

The woman swam languidly to the edge of the pool, dark red hair fanning out like sea grass behind her in the water.

"Pratima," she said, her voice clear over the sound of the waterfall. As she heaved herself out of the pool, Nathan realized with a shock that she was naked and very pregnant. He looked away as she bent awkwardly to retrieve the silk robe on the floor.

Pratima crossed the huge circular room and the two women raised their hands, palms pressed together for a long moment. "Bralin," Pratima said, more as a confirmation than a greeting. They kissed, more chastely than lovers, but far more intimately than Nathan expected.

Bralin glanced at him curiously, her eyes an unusual shade of green. She draped the black silk over her shoulders, tying it loosely above her swollen belly, and crossed to lower herself carefully onto the mass of pillows kicked into a circular screen.

"Bralin is a Pilot for the Ushahayam motherline," Pratima said to him in Hengeli.

Bralin's eyes widened. "You must be Nay-teen Karoo," she said to him in heavily accented Hengeli, obviously intrigued. He felt his face flush as Pratima looked at him expressionlessly.

"I apologize if I embarrass you," Bralin said hurriedly. "But I never before meet a . . ." She stopped, struggling for the word, then said something in Vanar to Pratima.

"Foreigner," Pratima answered. He was suddenly sure the word Bralin had used had far more meaning than what had been tactfully translated. "Nathan, Bralin and I would like coffee."

His back stiffened, and he stared at her, seeing nothing but an impassive cold in her face. "Nothing would give me greater pleasure than to serve you both, l'amaée," he said in rigid Vanar before he turned his back on Bralin's puzzled glance and marched toward the opposite end of the tower room.

"Coffee please, Ilitu," he said to the mechanical spider and watched as the machine disengaged itself from the slot in the wall. The articulated robot quickly and efficiently made the thick, dark brew, but as it clamped its mandible around the tray to balance it on its flat back, Nathan got an almost perverse pleasure out of bending over to pick it up. "Thank you," he said firmly.

The machine didn't resist, silently refolding its jointed legs back into the slot.

The two women sat together as comfortably and close as lovers, Pratima's palm resting lightly on the pregnant woman's belly. They spoke in an odd, soft, rapid language, not even Vanar, he realized, resentful of even this smallest exclusion. Doing his best to parody the lowest-ranking sahakharae he could envision, he carried the tray across the room. He shifted his weight to sweep his sati to one side with his foot, and set the tray on the soft carpet. His hands shook only slightly as he held out the small porcelain cups ritually to the two women. Bralin looked uncomfortable, he was pleased to see, but Pratima regarded him with remote indifference.

He sat at their feet, head bowed docilely, not touching his own tiny cup, until the other woman finished, made polite excuses, and left. Only when she had gone did he allow the anger out.

"Does the entire planet know I'm your lover?" he demanded, using the same Vanar word Raemik had.

"Probably," Pratima said, serenely.

He glanced in the direction Bralin had left. "And now quite literally the entire inhabited universe knows. Tell me, am I a popular character in the Pilot's latest entertainment? Anyone placing bets on me for the next episode?"

"Not about you and me, although every Pilot is certainly aware of your presence on Vanar," Pratima said quietly. "Nathan, why does it surprise you to find you are known? Of course people are curious about you."

"Is that what I am? A novelty? A rare animal in a zoo to be stared and pointed at?"

She paused, her head to one side, then, "Why are you so angry?"

"How can you ask that?" he said hotly, dropping any pretense of meekness. "You snap your fingers and expect me to jump, then parade me in front of your friend like a prize bull." He stood up, pacing away from her. "I expected better than that from you."

"Did you expect me to be someone other than Vanar?" she said quietly behind him. There was no emotion at all in her voice.

He was shaking. Westcastle had smelled like the sea in the winter when the sporadic acid rains churned up salt into the air from the desolate badlands. Sometimes, when the light was right, he would pretend the shimmering mirages on the horizon really were water, wanting desperately to believe in a magic that, if only he prayed hard enough, would deliver a boat to sail him away and set him free. He had never stopped believing in that magic. He didn't want to now.

"Did you expect *me* to be someone other than Hengeli? I'm not your whore, Pratima, not some plaything to be used and thrown away when you get tired of me."

When he turned toward her, some trick of the light filtering through the pseuquartz threw a slant of rainbow-prismed color across the room, splashed against her white skin like colors spilled from a child's paint box. "I see," she said softly. "Do you want me to take you back to the Estate?"

His pride made him badly want to say yes, but he knew if he did, he would never see her again. She was not a woman who would come around to ask his forgiveness.

"No," he said, miserable. "I love you." She didn't react any more than if he'd told her the correct time or that the weather looked like rain. "I want you to love me." He gestured toward the exit where Bralin had gone. "I don't want to be just a bit of lewd gossip between Pilots."

"You want more respect than that," she said, and he wasn't sure it was a question.

He walked deliberately back and sat down next to her. "Don't I deserve that much? Or are you really so Vanar that every man is nothing to you?"

She was the one who finally looked away. "I've never lied to you, Nathan. But whatever I feel about you, whatever you feel for me . . . is irrelevant."

"Why?" He heard his voice break.

She laughed sadly. "Because I'm a Pilot." When she looked up again, her pale eyes glittered wetly. "I'd have thought you'd have noticed by now."

"I've noticed," he said, and took her hands. "Do you love me, Pratima?"

"I don't know. I do know that I want you, more than anyone I've ever known." Again, it was that cool lifeless voice, totally devoid of feeling.

"Then take me with you."

"I can't."

"For godsake, why not?" he demanded, not bothering to amend the gender of the deity he swore by. "You're a Pilot, you can do whatever you *want!*"

Her mouth twisted in a spasm of anger and pain, but she left her hands trapped in his. "Even Hengeli is discerning enough to make the distinction," she snapped. "I didn't say I *won't*. I said I *can't*. Nathan, I live inside the Worm. If you think it's lonely here, you can't imagine what it's like on a Pilotship. I live with a hundred other women who are so completely like me, it's as if I am alone. When I speak with my sisters, I'm talking to myself. When we make love, it's only masturbation—"

She laughed at his shock. "What did you imagine we were like? We're human beings, too. We have feelings, we are capable of love. There's nothing I want more than to be with you. But you can't survive in a Pilotship. The first time we passed from one End to the other, every atom in your body would be torn apart."

"I could stay on one of the liners in transport—"

"How would I reach you? A Pilotship is part of the Worm itself. There's no access between a Pilotship and the cargo we transport."

"You got from there to Vanar," he pointed out.

"Yes," she said. "On an automated single-passenger shuttle I have no control over. It goes to Vanar and back and that's all. There's only one way on and off this planet for me. And *only* for me."

"Then stay on Vanar. Stay with me, Pratima."

Her eyes widened in surprise. "I can't. That would kill *me*."

"You're here now, and you seem far from dead," he objected.

"I only come to Vanar once a year, and I don't stay planetbound any longer than I have to. It *hurts* me to be here. Every minute I'm here, this planet is literally tearing me apart inside."

His mind shifted desperately for a solution. "I'm supposed to marry in a few months. But if I married you, I'd wait for you, Pratima. I'd be here every year, for however long you could stay . . ."

The horror on her face stopped him, the tear that fell down her cheek catching the rainbow light. "You really don't understand," she said in dismay. "I live in the Worm—"

He shot to his feet, shouting down at her in anger. "I *know* you live in the goddamned Worm, Pratima!"

She went on as if he hadn't spoken. "—time is different for me." Suddenly, he realized, and stared at her. "The last time I was on Vanar was to give birth to Raemik. A year ago. My time."

He felt suddenly light-headed.

"If I don't conceive this trip," she was saying softly, "I'll have to come back next year. *My time.* A year for me is nearly fifteen for you."

"You live forever and die young," he said, and sat down heavily.

"The Worm exacts a heavy toll on Pilots. I have only a few more years left. And yet I will still outlive you."

"That's what Raemik meant." He looked at her numbly, then reluctantly shut his eyes, blocking out the light. "He wants me to tell you he won't cooperate. That you should leave and come back next year." He opened his eyes again to stare at nothing.

She sat quietly beside him for a long moment, then left to retrieve a bottle of *xerx* brandy. Pouring the honey-colored alcohol into a cut crystal glass, she held it out to him. He took it from her but held it passively without drinking.

"You weren't going to tell me, were you?" she asked, no anger in her flattened tone.

"No," he admitted.

"Why not?"

"What difference does it make?" He glanced at her. "As if you didn't know. I didn't want you to leave, Pratima. I didn't want to spend the next year without you."

"And fifteen makes a difference?"

He laughed acidly, a sharp bark of pain. "All the difference in the world. Make it a hundred. Make it forever." Lifting the glass to his mouth, he threw back the burning liquor in one gulp. "The first time I find someone on this fucking awful planet who might actually make my life tolerable, and it has to be you."

He suddenly threw the glass, not caring how old or expensive it was, and smiled in grim satisfaction as it shattered against the pseuquartz wall. When he turned to her, she stood very still, watching him with her too pale eyes. Her fear depressed him.

"Why should you give a damn," he said, his throat constricted. "You're a Pilot, what could a *malinam naeqili* be to you?"

She didn't move, standing with nearly the same inertness he had seen in her meditation. Only her eyes were alive, ghostly shimmer in her colorless irises. "I do care, Nathan. Where did you get the idea Pilots are so powerful?" she asked softly.

"I'm not blind," he snapped, and gestured at the huge room with its luxurious furnishings. "You live like a queen, you go where you want, you *take* what you want, what else could I think?"

"I told you before, this place doesn't belong to me. Nothing belongs to me. I don't pay for anything, because I have no money. Pilots own nothing." She didn't smile. "Legally, Pilots themselves are owned. We are property. Extremely valuable property, but my caste is even lower than a naeqili."

He found his mouth hanging open, and shut it, feeling the muscles in his jaw clench. Turning away, his legs felt wooden as he walked toward the small waterfall and the clear pool. Silver-scaled fish darted away from his shadow on the rippling water.

"But you're a Pilot," he said, incredulous. "Without you, Vanar would be just another planet around just another star."

She hadn't moved when he turned toward her again, watching him with deathly stillness. "Being a source of power doesn't mean I control it. Nor am I even the key. . . ."

"Raemik." He shook his head in contempt. "Men can't survive on the Pilotship, and however long the time dilation lets you live, you're not immortal. They hold your men hostage."

Her mouth quirked thoughtfully. "'Hostage' isn't a word I might have chosen, but it'll do. I can take what I like on Vanar because I can't take it with me. It all stays behind when I leave. I can do whatever I like on Vanar because nothing I do can endanger the Family's control over the Worms or its revenues. And it's important to keep Pilots happy. It upsets a Pilot's equilibrium to be unhappy."

"Are you happy, Pratima?" he asked, less angry, and was glad this time his voice hadn't cracked.

She didn't answer for several long moments. "Not particularly," she said impersonally, gazing off into the distance outside the pseuquartz.

"Am I making you unhappy?" he said, afraid of the answer.

She looked at him directly. "Yes."

He closed his eyes for a moment, letting the mingled sense of relief and shame wash over him.

She said calmly, "I'm sorry if I've offended you. You're not Vanar. I don't know what you expect from me."

"Despite all the enthusiastic rumors, I really am not a homicidal maniac. I would never hurt you."

A fleeting smile curled past her lips. "I know that."

"What about Raemik? Are you and the Nga'esha really going to let him get away with disobedience?"

"The Nga'esha may not like it, but it is not their decision. He is still just a child. We are not barbarians, and I would never force Raemik. Never."

"Then there's no reason for you to stay on Vanar any longer, not if it means risking your health."

"Oh, Nathan." The quaver in her voice was the only indication of emotion. He watched her silently, amazed at her slight trembling, her reserved demeanor still intact. "If you think I've stayed down this long waiting for my brother, you're wrong. I've never met anyone like you. You're the first breath of fresh air I've ever known. I've only been two places in my life," she said, her voice steady. "Vanar and the Worm. I envy you, having seen so many other worlds."

"Not that many. And it seems Vanar will be my last," he said bitterly.

She ignored him. "You've met different kinds of peoples, seen different cultures. Your experience is so rich. You're trapped on Vanar because of the choices you've made, good or bad. I've never had any choices: the narrow limits of my destiny were written the moment I was conceived."

Her eyes flickered, as if she were looking inward, not quite seeing him. "I'm not complaining; it's far from an unpleasant life. The people who designed Pilots weren't cruel; we enjoy what we do. We *live* for what we do. We are part of the Worm, we can't exist without it. It's the only real love Pilots can ever know."

She focused on him as he frowned. "But it's a very solitary existence. I see the rest of humanity go by from behind a barrier, untouched and untouchable. The only other men I've ever known were Vanar. I know them, they know me, there's no complication. Everyone understands their place. Nothing risked, nothing lost. I would have done my duty on Vanar, relieved the boredom the best I could, and been happy to go home to the Worm and the comfort of my sisters' company. I would never have fallen in love. Pilots don't fall in love."

"Certainly not with foreigners."

The silence stretched. "No, certainly not with foreigners." She stood with her back stiffly erect, sharp chin held high. "I wish now that I'd never met you, Nathan," she said serenely. "But that's a child's wish. I wish I had been smart enough to have avoided you, but the temptation was too great. I wish I had the strength to lie to you, tell you I don't want you. I wish I could simply leave and not come back until I know you're only dust and memory."

"You're hoping I'll do it for you," he said. "Tell you I hate you for this, tell you to leave me."

After a long moment, she nodded wordlessly.

"I can't." He was unwilling to cross the small distance between them to touch her. "I'm a selfish man and I've had little enough in my life. Stay with me, please. I'm never going to escape Vanar, Pratima. In four months I have to marry Kallah. Give me that much. Stay with me until then."

"It will cause you problems."

"I'll have the rest of my life to regret it."

"It will cause me problems."

"Stay anyway," he said ruthlessly.

For a moment, she looked as if she would refuse, then she nodded slowly.

He didn't know which of them moved first, but found himself holding on to her tightly, enfolding her with both arms as if she would dissolve if he didn't. They didn't make love for a long time after that, but somehow, simply touching each other was more than enough, nearly unbearable.

XVII

THE RAINY SEASON BEGAN EARLY, AND HE WORRIED THE SVAPNAH seeds might be washed away as his experimental plot turned to mud. He drew up plans with painstaking care for a greenhouse in hopes of being permitted to build it. He had tried to interest Aelgar in the plans, explaining his ideas with much enthusiasm but, so far, no effect.

After another wet afternoon spent waiting futilely for Pratima at the kaemahjah, he gave up and started for home. He nearly walked past Lyris huddled under her brightly colored umbrella, his own obstructing his view.

"Hello, Nate." Her familiar voice stopped him.

He knew who it was before he turned around uneasily. He wondered why Lyris hadn't come inside the kaemahjah, especially since it was obvious from the state of her sati she'd been waiting outside in the rain for some time.

"Hello, Lyris," he said finally, keeping his voice neutrally polite. Warm rain pattered against his silk umbrella, running in droplets at the end of the spokes around his head. He was acutely aware of her inspection. Although wet around the hem, his blue sati was folded and tied precisely, the clasp Kallah had given him pinned at the shoulder, the decorative end of the fabric draped correctly over his head. His hair had grown long enough to lay properly across his left shoulder in a plain braid.

"You're looking well," Lyris said finally, and laughed, "Almost like a native." He didn't answer. Her own red sati was less than immaculate, the mati underneath wrinkled. She wore the subcaptain's pin he had only seen on her ship's coveralls as a sati clip. She seemed more uncomfortable and out of place in Vanar dress than he did. "Pratima was attending a conference between the Nga'esha and my mother-line's Family all afternoon," she remarked, the malice clear. "You've wasted your day."

"My days are spent trying to improve my Vanar," he said dryly, "and are never wasted." He couldn't help adding, "Jealous?"

She squinted angrily, then smiled with false cheer. "Of course not. You ended it with me long ago. In any case, it's not like I would be envious of another *woman*, is it?"

He said stonily, "What do you want, Lyris?"

Her bright smile widened. "To twist the knife, Nathan. What else is there?"

He felt his lips thin tightly against his teeth, and forced himself to smile. "Nice to know you still care. But if you're finished now, I have things to do."

He turned away and grimaced as she fell into step beside him. "Oh, but I haven't even started. I'm leaving tonight, I've got a ship to St. Kiranne." He forced himself to take even steps, keeping his eye on the pockets of rain puddles in the wide street. A taxi hoverfloat whooshed by, inches off the wet street, throwing a small spray like a wake off the prow of a speedboat.

"You'd like St. Kiranne," Lyris was commenting lightly, her lilting accent flowing over the words like a hint of song. He'd once thought he could listen to that voice forever. "They've done such an amazing job of terraforming the place, you'd never know it was just a lifeless rock before. It's like a tropical rain forest without all the nasty bugs. Flowers bloom everywhere all year round. A whole army of botanists and gaiaists to keep it balanced. And the cities, open, free. People make love in the park in broad daylight. It's a totally egalitarian, technocratic Republic, you'd love it there—"

"Lyris," he cut her off, pleased with how bored his voice sounded. "I know where St. Kiranne is. I've lived on Vanar almost two years now, and I've had plenty of time to get used to the fact I'm a prisoner here. You'll have to do better than this."

She danced slightly in front of him, her eyes bright. "I'm so happy you've adjusted," she said, her voice spiteful. "But I also know that sometime next week when you're sitting on your ass getting stoned while waiting around for that freak lover of yours to grace you with a quick fuck, you'll be thinking of me. You'll know I'll be a hundred light-years away from here. I'll find myself a cute young thing to share a bottle of wine with in a seaside bistro. I'll be sitting there knowing you're thinking of me, and we'll raise a toast to you, Nathan, trust me."

He stopped, taking a deep breath, not even trying to hide his anger. "This is petty," he said, "even for you."

The jovial mask slid off her features as she snarled, bitter triumph in her eyes. "Does it hurt yet, Nathan?" she asked softly. "You don't know what hurt is."

He sighed and started walking again, taking long-legged strides that forced her to keep pace at an awkward trot. "Believe what you like, but I never meant to hurt you."

She laughed harshly, a bit out of breath. "It didn't stop you, either. No, you just used me to get you to Vanar. Once we were on our way, you weren't quite the ardent lover anymore, were you? Or at least not with *me* anyway. . . ."

He couldn't remember much about Lyris's shipmate, not even her name. Just a vague memory of a girlish laugh, dark hair, and strong legs around his waist, and a much sharper one of the horror on Lyris's face, both hands clutching the sides of the hatchway to keep herself upright, staring and staring. How strange, that savage jealousy, knowing now what he did of Vanar morality.

"How many times do I have to say I'm sorry?" he asked, unapologetic. "It was a party, I was drunk, she was drunk, you and I were arguing . . ." He shrugged. "It happens." He cursed silently as his bare foot skidded on the wet stones, and slowed his pace. "It would have been a once-only mistake, if you'd have let it, Lyris."

"You know what I think is ironic?" she said, winded. "Do you remember what we argued about?"

"Of course," he said acidly. "You were right, I was wrong. Does it make you feel better to hear me say it? I was an idiot. I should have listened to you."

He glanced up from under the lip of the umbrella, gauging the gray sky as distant thunder rumbled. He regretted now not having taken the public transport across town. No taxi would stop for a lone man, not even in this weather. Ducking under an awning projecting over the street as the rain intensified, he looked down at the Vanar girl he'd once thought he loved, her wet hair plastered against her cheek. Her face had flushed from trying to keep up with him, and he had to resist the temptation to brush the curls back out of her still-lovely eyes.

"I really am sorry, Lyris. And even though I'd let you down badly, you tried to warn me. You still gave me what I wanted," he said quietly. "You held up your end of the deal, in spite of everything. Whatever else, I can't fault your honor."

She stared at him with openmouthed incredulity, then, to his surprise, she laughed, the sound tense and hysterical. She bit back the hard giggles escaping past her clenched teeth. "That's what I loved most about you, Nathan, the way you can sweet-talk your way into anything with that innocent nobler-than-thou attitude. If I were as virtuous as you think I am, you wouldn't be here at all. If you could have just been able to keep from cheating on me, I'd have had your ignorant ass transferred to another Station before we Wormed through. I would never have let you get within a light-year of Vanar."

The fleeting temptation to touch her had gone. "All right, whatever," Nathan said, and glanced up at the sky again, wishing the rain would ease up. It beat down steadily against the awning. A few more minutes of Lyris's spite, and he'd say the hell with it. "Have it your own way. You knew what would happen to me, and you hated me enough to let me do it anyway. Enjoy your revenge."

She sounded sick, choking back the laughter. "Oh, no, Nate, darling. I didn't do it for revenge. I did it for the *money*."

He stared blankly at the gray clouds, feeling his blood turn cold before he let himself look at her. She was grinning, a mask of hate and elation. "What?"

"Are you really naive enough to believe if someone on Vanar hadn't wanted you here, someone very powerful, you could ever have set one toe on this planet? And if that certain someone hadn't been protecting you from the very first minute, how long do you think it would have taken before Eraelin Changriti got rid of you? Nathan, you were bought and paid for."

She danced several quick steps away from him, and he knew he wasn't able to keep the fury off his face. Her own held a mixture of fear and excitement, watching him with all the eager caution of a wild animal handler.

"What are you talking about?" His own voice sounded flat.

"We're a business people—surely you know that by now. Someone on Vanar wanted a native Hengeli-speaking male, so she put in an order and I was paid to fill it. I went a-hunting and you were bagged and tagged, Nathan. Want three guesses who?"

"No," he said, a denial of her story, not the guess. She knew what he meant.

"Oh, but it's true, all right. I couldn't just leave Vanar and let you go on thinking you brought this on yourself. You never had a chance." The rain was letting up, but he didn't notice. She spoke quickly, rushing her words as if afraid she wouldn't have the time to get them all out. "I'm not coming back here, not *ever*. I'm jumping ship off to a nice little Barrier outworld where nobody gives a shit about Vanar, find myself some colonist goat farmer with a stiff dick and a small brain and live happily ever after. Consider this my farewell gift to you."

She skipped backward away from him, still grinning rigidly before she turned and nearly fled. He stood under the awning, stunned, before he started the walk back to the Estate through the rain. By the time he arrived, he was wet, muddy, and furious.

He didn't bother with the circuitous route through the men's section. He remembered the direct way to the women's house, his cold rage building with every step he took. A senior kharvah stood as he approached the doors between the houses, puzzled and alarmed. Nathan shoved him out of the way without a word, not hearing as he called out a warning.

The massive doors made a satisfying thud as he threw them back to reveal the startled face of one of Yaenida's granddaughters at the end of the corridor. His head forward on hunched shoulders like a bull lowering its horns, he marched toward the inner rooms. The woman shouted at him in anger, barring the passage. Her voice cut off in a gasp of shock as he firmly grabbed her shoulders and pushed her unceremoniously to one side.

He paid no attention to the women scattering around him as he strode toward the main chamber where he knew Yaenida would be. He ignored the change in their voices, from alarm and astonishment to purposeful shouts. He was far too angry to concentrate on the Vanar as he flung open the carved doors and glared at the old woman.

Yronae gestured urgently to the other women in the room as he stalked toward the old woman. He noted dimly that several wore sati of different High Families, and knew he had interrupted a business conference of some importance. It gave him a sense of grim satisfaction.

Yaenida watched him approach, curious and unafraid. He stopped a few feet from where the old woman lay half submerged in a drift of pillows, her tiny figure engulfed in billowing silk. He didn't notice the Dhikar pouring into the room from every archway.

"Did you get a good bargain, Yaenida?" he said without preamble, all the hurt and anger boiling out of his voice. His fists quivered by his sides. "What's the going rate these days on Hengeli men? *How much did you pay for me, you cold-blooded goddamned bitch!*"

She stared up at him imperturbably, only her eyes alive in the skull-thin face. He caught the movement out of the corner of one eye, jerking around as the Dhikar grabbed him, their implants humming like angry bees. He dropped like a stone as agony exploded in his head . . .

XVIII

. . . AND WOKE A MOMENT AND SEVERAL HOURS LATER WITH THE abrupt jolt to consciousness from a dreamless coma. He sat slumped over in a small room, long shadows thrown up against the walls, and opened his eyes to stare at a medical taemora watching him impassively. The anger and pain had evaporated, the sudden emotional blankness making him queasy.

The taemora rose, taking him by one arm. As he stood up, it seemed everything was happening at a strange rate of speed. He noticed a weight on his wrist, but it took several long seconds before he could organize his efforts into looking down.

An inch-wide articulated steel band had been locked around his left wrist, adhering firmly to his skin. It was heavy, but not uncomfortably so, moving smoothly as he rotated his wrist to examine it. The taemora waited patiently, and when he let his hand drop, she led him out of the small room.

He recognized where he was, in the men's house. The sudden spatial shift disoriented him, and he swayed unsteadily before he regained his balance. The taemora held him upright, then led him to the boys' lodgings.

He noticed the silence as she ushered him inside, saw the way the children pulled back as she closed the door behind him, leaving them alone. Standing for a moment, mildly puzzled by the emptiness of his thoughts, he took a few experimental steps. His head turned far more slowly than he expected, and a boy recoiled with a wide-eyed stare of alarm.

He took several more faltering steps down the long room before he stopped, unable to arrange his thoughts into any sensible cohesion.

It's this thing, he realized, and gazed down at the metal band on his wrist. When he looked back up, he distantly observed the boys shrinking away from him in fascinated wariness as Raemik stepped in front of him.

It took him forever to focus on the boy's pale blue eyes, then he apathetically let Raemik lead him by one hand to his own tiny alcove.

He sat down on the narrow mat, stretching his legs out in front of him, and leaned against the pillows stacked against the wall. Raemik perched on the edge of the shelf beside him, chin resting on his knees, arms around his legs, watching Nathan with steady, unblinking eyes.

Nathan raised the arm with the metal band clamped to it. "What's this?" he asked, remotely aware of how thick his speech was. The boy glanced at the band.

"It's a *lajjae*," he said calmly. Nathan stared up numbly at Raemik, his eyes dry as he blinked. "Criminals and madmen wear them," the boy added after a long moment.

Nathan let his hand fall back limply onto his lap. "Oh." His own voice sounded dry and lifeless.

He slept, waking several times from dreams so vague he couldn't recall the slightest detail even moments after opening his eyes. He was gazing inattentively at the light moving across the carved screens when the boys began to stir, sleepy whispers and nervous laughter.

He watched Raemik dress. "Get up, Nathan," the boy said softly. It bothered him on some level he couldn't quite touch that the idea of rising hadn't occurred to him himself. He stood, starting to fold the sati between his fingers, and had it halfway around his waist when his thoughts drifted off as he forgot what he was doing. The folds slipped from his hand. Raemik caught the falling linen and quickly pleated and arranged it around the older man with an expert hand. The boy had to stand on his toes to pin it at Nathan's shoulder, then simply handed the end of the sati to him.

He lifted the end over his head out of sheer habit, letting the silk drape carelessly. It wasn't so much that he felt drugged, but as if everything else around him were happening at a slightly faster speed than he could manage to keep up with. He knew he should be grateful that Raemik had taken charge, steering him toward the men's garden, although the only thing he could feel was a lethargic sense of loss. The silence in the refectory was palpable, sahakharae and kharvah alike moving silently out of their way as Raemik led him toward the common table.

He took the plate from the boy without question, eating methodically. Raemik had to prompt him back to the food occasionally as he stared into space, not caring. The boy looked up as a shadow fell across them, while Nathan barely swiveled his head to study a pair of stocky legs silhouetted in the sunlight through the thin sati.

"He's wanted," Aelgar's subdued voice said above him, and it took Nathan a few moments for the Vanar words to filter through.

Nathan stood and followed the senior kharvah, then hesitated, looking back at the boy still sitting cross-legged on the grass. "Thank you, Raemik," he said quietly with an effort, the words lifeless. The boy nodded solemnly.

He paid little attention other than to concentrate on following the short kharvah into the women's house, taking the same route he had barged through only the day before. As the door was slid open into Yaenida's private council room, Aelgar stepped to one side, bowing deftly as he took his place by the wall.

Yaenida sat elevated on a dais in the center of the room, a stick figure engulfed in her volcanic island of pillows. Her rippled reflection in the polished wood floor only increased the illusion of remote isolation. Several senior men sat on their heels to the left of the room, an equal number of women opposite. A private interpreter sat slightly behind to Yaenida's right, her flatreader already humming faintly in the stillness. An impressive number of Dhikar stood guard, he noticed, his unforeseen breach of the pratha h'máy's inner sanctum not likely to be repeated again.

Yronae moved to stand impassively by Yaenida's left shoulder. The sati draped over her head shadowed Yaenida's face, but her eyes were distinct as she watched him approach. Both women wore full formal sati, their House and Family insignia displayed on their pins.

He wished his mind functioned at a better speed as he spotted the thin square mat set in front of Yaenida, exactly three paces distant from her, the Family crest woven into its center. The level of ceremony was as high as he'd ever seen. Taking deliberate steps, he crossed the wide hardwood floor to the mat. He skimmed back the hem of his sati with methodical care as he knelt on the mat and bowed, hands together in a formal greeting, then sat back on his heels, palms against his thighs. Both Yaenida and her daughter inclined their heads in a minimal nod. A small box had been set squarely in front of the mat, but he knew better than to open it without instructions.

"Nathan Crewe Nga'esha," Yaenida said in Vanar, dimly surprising him by the use of his full Vanar name, "we would ask you a few questions concerning your behavior of yesterday."

"Of course, jah'nari l'amae Yaenida Nga'esha," he answered in the same language. He thought he saw a small fleeting smile on her face as he used her motherline, establishing their Family connection. Belatedly, he noted two of the women were wearing Changriti burgundy. *Shit.* Several women he didn't recognize wore other colors, although they might have been part of the group he had interrupted the day before. All of the men, however, wore formal Nga'esha blue.

"I'm in big trouble, aren't I?" he asked her in Hengeli.

"Oh yes," she assured him in the same tongue. The interpreter next to her sat with a tranced look as she whispered almost inaudibly, translating their words simultaneously for the recorder as well as the tiny beads in the Vanar women's ears.

"Getting to be a bad habit." This time she wasn't able to suppress the amused surprise, and he wondered distantly where the words had come from. "Is this a trial?"

"In a way."

He held up the wrist bound with the steel band. "This isn't necessary."

Her eyes flickered down at it, then back to his face. "If you are allowed to leave here, it will be removed."

If you are allowed to leave here alive, he knew she meant. He noted the medical taemora in the background. Strangely, he knew he should be afraid and was not. He nodded casually, and let his hand drop to rest again on his thigh.

She indicated the box, and he reached to open it, finding an earbead nestled like a pearl inside. "You may speak in Hengeli, if you feel you are unable to explain yourself competently in Vanar," she continued. "That is only just."

Just? He wanted to say he would be surprised if there were actually any such synonymous word in Vanar. Instead, he picked up the earbead. "Thank you, jah'nari l'amae." He worked the tiny bead into his right ear. "May this naeqili inquire as to the nature of the charges against me?"

She sat back deeper into the pillows, wincing slightly in pain. "There are no charges, Nathan," she said, dropping her formal tone.

They could have been alone in her library. "This is a private Family matter. Where did you hear your presence on Vanar was by a pre-arranged contract?"

"Then it's true, isn't it?" The lack of anger in him felt as sharp-edged as a hole left behind after its removal.

Yronae looked annoyed as she spoke, the interpreter's light, passionless voice translating the Hengeli intimately in his ear. "You are not to ask questions—" she said before Yaenida's raised hand impatiently cut her off.

"Yes, it's true. Where did you hear it?"

"Lyris Arjusana, subcaptain on the *Comptess Dovian*."

"Why would she tell you this?"

"She hates me," he heard himself say dispassionately. "She's jumping ship, not planning to return to Vanar after this next flight, and she wanted to get in a few last kicks before she left."

He noted the rustle of surprise ripple through the room. As Yaenida eyed him silently, Yronae hastily strode from the room, returning a few minutes later. She faced her mother, lips pressed thin with disgust. "The *Dovian* left last night for St. Kiranne," she said. "Crew of four. It's carrying Cooperative Family cargo. Do we stop her?" The interpreter didn't translate this into Hengeli for him, but Yronae's Vanar was clipped enough in anger for him to follow.

"No," Yaenida said, her voice bored. "She's not stealing anything. Let her go." Nathan felt rather than heard the disapproval in the room. "Why does she hate you, Nathan?"

"It's a personal matter."

Yronae glanced at her mother in irritation, but said nothing. Yaenida smiled, the barest hint on her lips. "Your gallantry is commendable, but misplaced," she said, surprisingly gentle. "When I ask you a question, it isn't a request. You do understand?"

He listened to the words, their meaning following belatedly on the sound. Then he glanced at the medical taemora watching him impassively, no doubt the gear beside her lethal.

"Yes, I understand, jah'nari l'amae."

So he relinquished what few secrets he had left, recounted the whole tawdry story—his infidelity, the botched plans and lies, her anger and hurt—detached from it all as if it had happened to someone else. In a way, it had been someone else, so long ago. He closed his eyes as he spoke, his skin quivering as it remembered Vasant Subah's merciless touch on a deeper visceral level even if his conscious mind had been anesthetized.

Then they grilled him with questions Vasant Subah had neglected to inquire into. Questions about his childhood, questions about the occupation, his mother, university, friends he hadn't seen in decades and never would again. He struggled to remember the minutiae about people and places he hadn't thought about in years, even as he recognized the prying insignificance.

When they had finished with him, his privacy utterly violated, he sat, his legs beginning to ache stiffly, and listened to the flawless but somehow stilted Hengeli in his ear as Aelgar rose to disclose the details of his fight with Tycar, including, he noted, the resolution. The senior kharvah didn't like him, and his annoyance at being outmaneuvered was plain, even in the interpreter's impersonal monotone.

But Aelgar knew how far he could take it, and managed to avoid outright judgment or condemnation. As did the other men of Yaenida's House who rose to answer questions about his behavior, their hostility tacit but carefully neutral.

Nathan looked at none of them until he heard one of them say, "He spends too much time digging in the dirt." It was Yinanq, one of Yaenida's great-grandsons, as yet unmarried. Nathan knew he was envious of his forthcoming marriage to Kallah, and raised his head to study the young man with vague curiosity.

Yaenida blinked at him owlishly, as if perplexed. "He was trained as a botanist. He likes to grow plants. Why should you feel threatened if he chooses to make a garden?"

The young man's face was rigidly bland. "He uses tools he takes away from the grounds machines. Why does he need to garden when the machines can do it? The tools are sharp and heavy and he could use them as weapons."

Aelgar ducked his head to hide a rueful scowl. Even Yronae winced. Any false accusation, even those implied, would reflect badly on the Family's integrity.

"Has he ever made a threat or any gesture like a threat with these tools?"

"He stabs the ground violently—"

"Toward you, or any other person?"

It took Yinanq several empty moments before he grudgingly admitted, "No. But he is strange." The man's demeanor slipped. "He should not be allowed to garden. It makes him dirty and smell bad." Aelgar glanced at him warningly. Yinanq dropped his gaze.

"Being strange is not a crime," Yaenida said quietly. "Nor is being dirty or smelling bad, however offensive it might be. Life sciences may be more common to women, but the nurturing of growing things is one of the devotions to our Mother earth, and all that live from Her. Surely you can't disapprove of that?"

Although she was speaking to the young kharvah, Nathan was sure her remarks were directed toward the women. The man flushed, but said nothing. "We are not concerned if he shocks your sense of propriety. We are here to decide if Nathan Crewe Nga'esha, your *brother*, is a violent and dangerous man. Other than the one time with Tycar, have you ever seen Nathan attack or threaten anyone?"

The man's lips compressed, determined. "No, but I've heard . . ."

"Heard what?"

"I heard he threatened the children in the quarters where he sleeps," the man finished resolutely.

In the long silence, Yaenida looked back at Nathan questioningly. He drew a complete blank, his memory sluggish. He shrugged.

"Threatened how?"

"He shouted at them, waving his fists and threatening to hit them. They complain they are frightened of him."

Nathan shook his head at Yaenida, puzzled; then his face cleared as he remembered. "Ah," he said. "The malicious little brats tormenting Raemik. I got tired of the noise, and yelled at them to shut the hell up and leave him alone. They did."

"In Vanar or Hengeli?" Yaenida asked.

"Hengeli," he admitted.

"Did you ever shout at them again?" she asked wryly.

"I haven't had to."

He caught the amused looks on the women's faces from the corner of his eye, but kept his gaze on Yaenida. She rubbed her fingertips over her dry, thin lips thoughtfully.

"I'd prefer not to bring children into this," Yaenida said.

"Then you'll have to take one of us at our word," Nathan said evenly. It seemed the lajjae was good for something.

"Thank you, Yinanq," Yaenida said finally. He heard the rustle of cloth as the disgruntled man retook his place. "Now, Nathan, we must address the violent behavior you exhibited toward me yesterday."

Despite the dampening effect of the band on his wrist, he knew his life depended on his answers now. "Jah'nari l'amae, you've been on Hengeli worlds. You know Hengeli express ourselves verbally far more directly and passionately than do the Vanar, but we don't resort that often to physical violence."

"Your wars, Nathan, are quite violent."

"Are you judging me, or are you judging the entire Hengeli history and culture?" Even Yronae raised an eyebrow. "I was angry and I shouted at you, l'amae, but I had no intention of striking you or causing you any bodily harm. Despite the fact that I've been abducted, sold like an animal, and held prisoner on Vanar—serious crimes on any other civilized world including Hengeli—all I did was shout at you. And for that small offense, you may murder me." He raised his steel-clad wrist. "I am neither a criminal nor a madman. I'm not sure the same can be said about those who conspired to kidnap me in the first place."

He heard the sharp intake of the interpreter's breath through the bead in his ear as she faltered, then continued translating his words into Vanar. Yaenida regarded him with amused, narrowed eyes.

"You came to Vanar of your own free will, Nathan," she said.

"Did I?" He forced himself to smile, despite the lack of emotion. The expression felt as strange as a mask being held over his face. He held the smile and sat still with his spine erect. After a very long moment, she nodded.

Without a word, the men stood up and filed out of the room. Once they had gone and the door closed behind them, the women stood and followed Yronae, retreating to a small anteroom, folding the screen around them. He could barely make out the murmur of voices as they talked among themselves. Except for the omnipresent Dhikar and the interpreter seated behind her, Nathan and Yaenida were alone.

"So what happens now?" Nathan asked. He noticed the interpreter still recorded their conversation.

"We wait for their decision."

"You don't have a vote?"

She smiled. "I have the only vote."

"Ah." He shifted slightly, his knees beginning to ache, and he stared out at the reddening sky. The murmur of voices went on, like the rush of wind through leaves in a tree. He tried to arouse anger, fear, regret. Nothing. He thought of Pratima, and felt no distress he might never see her again.

When he looked back, Yaenida was still watching him. "Promise me something, Yaenida. Even if you decide to kill me, first tell me why you did this to me. I think I at least deserve an explanation."

She considered it before she nodded.

It took several hours, Yaenida dozing off at one point. The medical taemora discreetly approached the sleeping woman to examine her before gliding silently back out of sight. He placed his hands on the floor, pushing up to relieve the pressure on his throbbing knees, ignoring the interpreter's scowl of disapproval.

The muttering continued, rising and falling soporifically. Forbidden to stand, the ache spread from his cramped legs up his spine. Finally, he shut his eyes, concentrating on making himself into a thin string, flowing down evenly into the center of the world, trying to escape into the spaces between time and matter.

It helped enough to startle him back to awareness as the women filed back into the room. Several looked unhappy, including the two from the Changriti Family, and the rest looked far from pleased. Yaenida was instantly awake, her eyes alert.

"We have discussed this matter completely, Pratha Yaenida Nga'-esha," one of the women said as they seated themselves on the floor cushions. The others nodded their assent. "We must remember that Nathan Crewe Nga'esha is now legally your youngest son. That of course complicates this matter. His personal offense must be considered as the act of a Vanar, not yepoqioh."

The interpreter tactfully translated the term as "foreigner," although Nathan had heard it often enough to recognize the connotation of "ignorant nonperson not fully civilized." Yaenida frowned.

"While the incident is regrettable, we agree he has not demonstrated a sufficiently violent nature to represent any real or lasting threat to your House or to Vanar society."

Nathan felt no sense of relief.

One of the Changriti women spoke. "However, we do feel Vanar culture is incompatible with others of the outside, which his actions have surely proven. For the sake of our own continued harmony as well as doing no injury to other foreigners, we strongly recommend that no more foreign males be allowed admittance to Vanar for any reason whatsoever. While we understand the Nga'esha feel it occasionally necessary to permit foreign guests for business purposes, we strongly urge the Nga'esha to tighten their restrictions on any visiting non-Vanar women and strictly limit contact between the Vanar and foreigners. We further condemn granting citizenship through adoption of non-Vanar into the Families, regardless of gender."

"Is this the consensus reached by you all?" Yaenida asked. The women muttered and nodded. "Sisters," Yaenida said gently to the two Changriti women, "you still appear unhappy. Do you feel this matter of sufficient importance to call an Assembly of Families?"

After an embarrassed moment, one of the Changriti women answered, "No, Pratha Yaenida. We have an obvious interest in this matter, of course, but there are better things to concern the Assembly than something as minor as a private Family quarrel. We trust, however, you will be able to correct this situation before it becomes a Changriti problem as well."

Through the film of his own detachment, he saw Yaenida's flash of anger at the Changriti's intimated barb, and wondered dryly at it. "My thanks to you all," Yaenida said, and watched with hard eyes as the women left. The interpreter packed up her instruments and retreated as Yaenida signaled the taemora, pointing at Nathan's wrist.

He watched as the taemora slid the keypin into the band, springing it open, and removed it from his hand. The skin underneath had reddened, itching in the sudden exposure to air. Tiny pinpricks made neat patterns where microscopic needles had inserted themselves into his flesh. He felt no rush of feelings flooding back as he rubbed the chafed skin, looking up expectantly at Yaenida.

"I'm too tired to go into long explanations at the moment, Nathan," Yaenida said. "We'll talk tomorrow, if you're up to it."

"I'll be up to it," he said quietly.

She chuckled. "Don't bet on it." As he got to his feet, he grimaced, lurching slightly. His legs had gone to sleep, feeling returning with painful needles as the blood flowed to starved muscles. The taemora caught him by the elbow to steady him gently. Bowing with her hand still holding him, he headed for the door.

"Naeqilae ae malinam," he heard Yaenida growl, and for a brief moment thought she was cursing him. Then he remembered the gender shift. Somehow, he understood she meant Lyris.

XIX

THE TAEMORA DIDN'T TAKE HIM BACK TO THE BOYS' DORMITORY, INSTEAD guiding him through a maze of corridors and stairs to a room at the far west end of the women's house. The single window overlooking a small garden was grilled with an iron lacework rather than the usual carved wood. It was pretty, loops and curls of metal shaped into leaves and birds, and quite secure. When she shut the door, Nathan heard the solid clunk of the deadbolt slide into place. He didn't much care.

The room had no decoration at all, but was not quite desolate enough to be called a jail cell. It was not a place he hoped he'd have to spend much time in, although he had lived through worse.

A few ordinary pillows had been thrown onto a narrow ledge built along one wall, serving as both bed and divan. He sat on the low edge, legs crossed, and stared out through the openings in the metal lace barring the window. Rubbing his wrist, he wondered when his emotions would return, then was curious whether or not they *would* return. He hadn't eaten since morning, but he had no appetite.

He sat quietly for over an hour before he heard footsteps and the bolt sliding back. He turned his head as the door was pushed open, but made no other movement. Raemik held a rolled sleeping mat as the taemora carried Nathan's own small chest of belongings into the room. She dropped it unceremoniously onto the floor as Raemik slipped wordlessly into one corner. Checking Nathan's eyes and pulse, she muttered to herself and pressed a medgun against his shoulder, the contents hissing painlessly into his body. He had no interest in what it might be.

She left, bolting the door firmly behind her. Raemik settled into the corner, sitting on his sleeping roll, chin on his knees.

"Are you in trouble, too, Raemik?" Nathan finally asked.

"No. But someone has to watch you."

Nathan smiled briefly, glancing at the barricaded window. "I don't think I could escape. Even if I could, where would I go?"

Raemik didn't answer. Nathan leaned against the wall, withdrawn, gazing at the growing darkness without interest. The lights around the outside walls glowed as night fell, the sounds of insects growing in the quiet. Raemik had curled up on his sleeping roll, asleep. Stretching out across the narrow ledge, Nathan dozed off.

He woke from his recurring nightmare, jerking out of the vivid dream gasping and painfully awake. For a moment, he was sure he was back in prison, sealed in a whitewomb, the suffocating gel clogging his lungs. His heart pounded against his rib cage, racing out of control. His nerves felt as if they were on fire, and he was convinced he was about to die. Raemik's pale eyes glinted in the dark as Nathan stood up, his legs stiff. He fought down an insane panic, unsure of what he meant to do.

Then his stomach rebelled and he smacked his hand against the wall panel, throwing up convulsively as the toilet emerged. He fell to his knees, his forehead pressed against the wall, eyes squeezed shut as he wept helplessly. Raemik's cool hands settled gently on his shoulders.

The boy helped him back onto his bed and sat next to him silently while he shuddered uncontrollably. Suddenly, Nathan laughed, horrified as the harsh sound tore out of him, leaving him breathless and watery-eyed. The laughter subsided.

Exhausted, he fell asleep, limbs jerking as nightmares crawled through his brain. A cloud of shapeless black pursued him as he ran, the smell of smoke. His legs sucked down deeper into thick mud, a roar of death behind him he dared not look back at. His own voice crying out woke him. He lay on his back, drenched in sweat. His skin itched as if insects crawled on him. Raemik sat beside him, watching impassively.

"How long...," he croaked, swallowing against his parched mouth, "...how long does this go on?"

Raemik shrugged. "I don't know. The taemora says a day. Maybe two."

It was closer to three. On the third day, he had recovered enough to keep himself under control, although the irrational fears had given way to a glum depression. They both glanced up as the door unbolted, but instead of the taemora, Pratima stood in the open doorway. A sharp pang jolted Nathan from his gloom, and he smiled.

Raemik bowed stiffly as his sister entered, then slipped around her to leave.

"You have no need to avoid me, Raemik," Pratima said sadly in Vanar before he could vanish, but not turning to look after him. "I am your friend."

The boy stopped, his face unreadable. He likewise didn't turn to look at his mother. "No," he said, his voice old, "you are not." Then he was gone.

Pratima sat cautiously next to him. "Along with all the other reasons my brother has for despising me, I think he is also jealous."

Then she was hugging him tightly, her thin arms around his neck.

XX

THEY KEPT HIM IN THE ROOM, ALTHOUGH THE DOOR WAS NO LONGER bolted against him. He quickly found that he was never allowed out of someone's sight no matter where he went within the House. Although he was free to walk the small enclosed garden outside his window, the main grounds and the river as well as the doors leading to the outside were now completely forbidden to him.

For the most part, Pratima stayed with him at night, Raemik slipping away the instant she appeared. She shared his lonely meals, but disappeared from time to time. He asked no questions, and made no complaint, grateful she was there at all.

When Laendor, one of Yaenida's numerous cousins, arrived to inform him Yaenida had sent for him, she didn't even glance at the Pilot, as if Pratima didn't exist. He squeezed her hand and followed Laendor to the library.

The room assaulted his senses, the smell of old books, stale smoke, and fresh polish as familiar as the buttery light cutting patterns through the wooden screen, but all of it now felt somehow wrong. Yaenida sat packed in pillows in her usual huge chair, her reader already glowing against the wood grain of the long table. His own reader lay unopened on the table.

"I trust you are feeling better, Nathan?" she asked him with a mocking smile.

He wondered if the flutter in his stomach was only a residual effect of the lajjae or if the fear was his own. He stared at her for a long moment, his mouth dry.

Her brown eyes squinted through smoke, drooping eyelids red rimmed. The shriveled skin was tight against the bones of her face, deep wrinkles cutting folds along her cheeks. She wore a plain sati, but rather than the sheer linen he wore, hers was woven of the finest imported birdsilk, gold thread intricately shot through the costly blue material, opaque and faintly iridescent. Several heavy gold bracelets weighted her emaciated arms, and although the pin holding the edge of her sati at her shoulder was elegantly simple, the large black diamond in its center was worth far more than Nathan would ever have hoped to earn in twenty lifetimes.

It hadn't quite sunk in until that moment how close he had come to execution. He put his palms together, fingertips to his chin, and bowed deeply. "Most certainly, jah'nari pratha h'máy," he said submissively in Vanar. When he straightened, her mouth had turned down in a frown.

He slid into the narrow chair and studiously opened his own flatscreen reader, avoiding her eyes. "I'm ready, Pratha Yaenida."

She held the tip of the water pipe to her mouth with one hand, her nails thick and yellowed, while her other hand rested over the edge of the chair, gold bracelets tinkling as she moved her wrist absently. "Yes, I suppose you are."

He inhaled to steady his nerves. "This naeqili is very sorry for the trouble my anger has caused—"

"Don't, Nathan," she cut him off, her voice pained. When he looked at her, she couldn't meet his eyes. "Don't apologize to me. You had reason to be angry."

They sat in silence for several minutes. "If their decision had been different," he was surprised to hear himself say, "would you have had me killed?"

"Possibly," she admitted. "But not without a fight. Especially now. I doubt not even Eraelin would choose to oppose me that badly, and she got much of what she wanted, anyway. That, and for some reason I've become rather fond of you. I value your delightfully male insolence. I never meant to break you of it. Just curb it a little, for your own sake."

It was as close to an apology as she would give. He didn't know what to say, and sat with his hands folded in front of his reader like a docile child.

She sighed, suddenly appearing haggard. "Yes, Nathan, it's true that I paid to bring you here. But I didn't 'buy' you like a piece of meat. I paid for a service, privately and quietly. I thought I could trust Lyris to recruit someone who would have understood completely what he was getting into and be willing to remain on Vanar for the rest of his life, in return for a most generous compensation to his family. He had to have excellent credentials in history, comparative xenosociology, and applied psychology, as well as being sufficiently bilingual." She smiled grimly. "I also had hoped for someone with a similar racial appearance to the Vanar, which might have made his integration less . . . conspicuous."

"That's not me," he said cautiously.

She sucked in a lungful of smoke and blew it out in a fine stream, watching as it curled toward the carved beams in the ceiling. "No, it's not. You certainly were not what I had ordered. I had thought her competent enough to find what I wanted since she's spent most of her life off Vanar and knows the systems very well. I must admit I was vastly disappointed in her when she delivered a botanist. An excellent botanist, I'm sure, but you're lousy with languages and you aren't trained in any field that would have been of value to me."

"And after you discovered I wasn't the goods you'd ordered, you let me rot in prison. You know what they did to me there. For six *months*, Pratha Yaenida." He felt his repressed anger begin to simmer, and fought to keep it down.

Her eyes narrowed. "I also taught you what you needed to know to get out and stay out."

He had to force back the bitter laugh. "Then you packed me off to a charity shelter and abandoned me, which wasn't that much better."

"A shortsighted error on my part," she admitted calmly. "I didn't think you would be of much use, and I know when to cut my losses. I was not interested in social experimentation. As a result, you've learned Vanar haphazardly and have a lot of bad habits that have been difficult to rectify."

In spite of himself, he did laugh, a hoarse, humorless cough. "So why didn't you just toss me back in the pond and fish out another Hengeli if I wasn't up to your standards?"

"I tried," she admitted unashamedly. "Unfortunately, the deal I made with Lyris was barely legal, and only because I am pratha h'máy of the Nga'esha Family. Once the Changriti were aware you were here, I knew I couldn't keep my more peculiar contracts quite so private. It was unlikely I would have another chance to repeat such a transaction. You're the first permanent non-Vanar resident male in our entire history, Nathan, and it looks like you'll be the last."

"It's me or nothing," he said, bewildered by his own wounded pride. "But why can't you let me go now? What good am I to you?"

She smiled, her hands busy as she tapped out the ashes and placed another pinch of resin into the bowl of her pipe. "Flexibility is the key to survival, in business or botany. You may not be what I ordered, but I invested quite heavily in you. I hate to waste money. And you've presented enough new challenges to keep things interesting. It's been entertaining simply to observe how you've adapted. But I'm afraid I won't be able to see the end of the experiment, Nathan. I am running out of time."

That shook him. "Yaenida—"

She cut him off. "I am the matriarch of the Nga'esha, the most powerful and wealthy of all the Families on Vanar. The Nine Families own every Worm in existence; we have controlled the monopoly on trade between inhabited star systems for over seven centuries." Her words came clipped and indifferent. "Only the Nga'esha hold the Worm connecting us with the entire Hengeli dominion, the richest system of settled worlds. No one, *no one* can defy us. Not even the Changriti."

He studied the knuckles of his folded hands. "I know all this, Pratha Yaenida," he said softly. He knew it very well.

"There are more people on Vanar who speak Hengeli than you might realize, Nathan. But there are very few native Hengeli speakers who know Vanar."

"So you're trying to turn me into a translator anyway. *Why?*"

She idly watched tendrils of smoke spiraling on the faint breeze through the wood lace screens. "Vanar is an isolated world ruling behind a screen of mystery. We are the unseen dragon. We move, and all that is heard is the sound of scales rasping. We breathe, and only the fire in our nostrils can be seen. They know we're here, impregnable in our lair." Her voice was flat, devoid of pride. "No one needs to measure the dragon to know it's not wise to annoy her."

She took a long inhalation on her water pipe, her intent gaze on him. He found himself studiously avoiding her eyes. When she exhaled, the smoke curled lazily. Like dragon's breath, he thought.

"The Changriti are blinkered and unreasonable. But I am not the only pratha h'máy too old and frail to be popping up to this Station or that when I need to negotiate with the yepoqioh. And I have never found negotiation by remote control as effective as face-to-face contact. It is useful to have outsiders see how we live, the Nga'esha House far more impressive and intimidating than a Station conference room. Profits are the sole reason the Changriti haven't been able to shut out all foreigners completely. I want more than just profits. Ours is a unique and rich culture we should be proud to share with the outside, not cut ourselves off even further."

He thought about how much of it he would definitely not like to see shared, but kept his mouth shut.

"If I had chosen a woman to import into Vanar, that would have aroused too much suspicion in minds already welded shut. But a man?" She shrugged. "It might raise a few eyebrows, but no one would seriously consider a toy for an eccentric old woman as a threat. Until you. What a troublesome toy you turned out to be."

Feeling his face grow hot, he struggled to remain expressionless. She puffed smoke from around the stem of her pipe without looking at him. She smiled, more at herself

"Ah, Nathan," she said, "and it is also true, I confess, I have a weakness for Hengeli men. I love their spirit and humor, even at the worst of times. Especially at the worst of times."

That disturbed him and he looked away, out at the passing shadows of clouds against the window glass. "I've had a lot of practice," he said distantly.

"I know," she said gently. "I also understand why Lyris has fled Vanar, and it isn't out of fear of me. Vanar is beautiful but stifling, life outside is just too damned much fun. If I wanted Lyris back, it would be easy enough to apprehend her. How long do you think she could really hide on some colony outworld?"

"Why don't you then?"

"Because she's much like myself, as I was at her age." Her old eyes glittered with bitter amusement. "I paid her in full, despite her failure. Her own Family would never have given her enough money to leave, and I suppose I wanted her to escape from Vanar, as I once had, for much the same reasons." She shook her head. "But not all. You see, Lyris is Vanar through her mother, but her father was a flight control officer on Beacon Station. He's Hengeli, like you."

He sat back in surprise, but said nothing.

"I'm not the only Vanar who's found you brash young Hengeli men irresistible. Her father didn't even know he had a daughter. Lyris's mother was recalled to Vanar before the child was born." She grinned at the look on his face. "We don't care about half-breed children, Nathan. Only the mother's line is important. Her mother was a prominent Arjusana, a proud, powerful High Family. Legally, Lyris has all the rights and privileges to her Family motherline. In the extremely unlikely event that she had been the daughter of a Vanar man and a foreign woman, she would have had no birthrights whatsoever. She might have been happier that way.

"Only our most trustworthy and dedicated are allowed off-world. It is discouraged, but not forbidden to fraternize with yepoqioh. But you off-world men are so appealing to Vanar women, so innocent and arrogant and carnal. Passion sometimes interferes with common sense. Vanar women are entirely capable of controlling their own reproduction. That she fell in love with a Hengeli was appalling enough, but permissible. To allow herself to become pregnant by him was quite unacceptable.

"So, instead of being the daughter of an eminent Arjusana, Lyris grew up on Vanar trying to make reparations for her mother's weakness. She grew up dreaming of her Hengeli father, but when she finally found him, he wanted nothing to do with her. Terrified, in fact, that if his Vanar superiors found he had even spoken to her, he'd lose what was left of his career on-Station. Then she met you. Her mother's fatal attraction to yepoqioh men apparently runs true in the daughter as well. In the end, Lyris Arjusana became a very bitter, unhappy young woman who has had a very bitter, unhappy life. I wish her luck wherever she is."

It made sense, the fierce animosity between Lyris and her Vanar shipmates, her fury with him when he, her Hengeli lover, had betrayed her.

"Unlike me, she doesn't have to come back. Her disappearance makes little impact on the overall infrastructure of the Arjusana Family." Yaenida smiled fleetingly at him. "Frankly, I think they're all secretly relieved to see her gone."

She leaned back, staring dreamily toward the ceiling through the haze of smoke, and smiled at the memories hidden there. "But I never had the luxury of such a choice. Although my mother was pratha h'máy, it was my sister who had been groomed since birth as heir. I was a bored troublemaker, a rebellious little shit too smart for my own good. I refused to marry any of the men my Family had chosen. I didn't want to settle down to a life I thought would smother me alive. My mother hoped time off Vanar might satisfy my wandering nature, get the restlessness out of my system, and bring me back with enough worldly experience to make me a valuable advisor to my sister.

"But crewing on a Nga'esha Cartel liner was almost as dreary as Vanar itself. I ran off when we reached Rhodus, got a hitch with a hairy old freighter navigator more interested in filling up his time with drink and talk than with sex. He took me as far as Novapolita, where I completely humiliated my illustrious Family by enlisting as a lowly foot soldier in the Hengeli civil dispute."

"You fought on Hengeli?" He was startled. "For which side?"

"It's all the same, who cares? I picked one at random."

His jaw tightened. "People died in that war. A lot of people." Including his father, he didn't add. She knew it already.

"I suppose so." She shrugged. "But that sort of violence is all so remote, so dull. Push this button, pull that trigger, fire and smoke and destruction, certainly a lot of dead bodies. I probably killed a few people myself, who knows? But after the initial thrill wore off, I found war tiresome and stupid, and such a waste of my valuable time. So I deserted."

She laughed. "Of course, once the Hengeli found out who I was, they diplomatically altered it to a 'voluntary discharge.' I may have been a deserter, but I was still Nga'esha. We do as we damned well please. Everyone else can rewrite history however it suits them.

"But while I was off scandalizing half of Vanar, my sister, Q'sola, had botched several important business ventures. My mother conceded the favorite she wanted wasn't the heir she needed. I was dragged back to Vanar." She chuckled. "Quite literally, in fact, kicking and screaming the entire way. But my experience with the outside worlds my poor sister detested came in handy before too long.

"Q'sola considered the Stations simply utilitarian depots for ships on their way from one system to another. We hold the monopoly, the Stations are a necessity, who cared how uncomfortable or basic they were? She couldn't understand why I pushed so hard to spend precious Nga'esha resources to expand Richter and Cooper, to develop casinos and theaters and restaurants and taverns and brothels—all the sort of recreational amenities that don't appeal much to the Vanar but do to quite a lot to the Hengeli systems. It required negotiating with non-Vanar companies to run and police the Stations. Which meant establishing permanent non-Vanar communities on-Station, with schools and hospitals and shops, more money out of Nga'esha coffers going straight into yepoqioh pockets. You wouldn't believe the protests I had to continually appease. All I did for years was beg, borrow, threaten, blackmail, bribe, scheme, and conspire before we ever saw the first return on such an extensive investment. When we finally did, I plowed it all straight back into building a new Station: Sukrah, the largest ever built. The profits on Sukrah alone made us the biggest fortune in Vanar history. The Nga'esha became the most powerful of the Nine Families, and I'd sealed my reputation. Q'sola was discarded and I was named heir, the next Nga'esha pratha h'máy."

She paused, puffing on her water pipe thoughtfully. Why she was confiding the details of her past life to him, he didn't know, and didn't dare ask.

"But success and pride went to my head. I became arrogant, insolent, convinced I was always right. When my mother died, Q'sola tried to have me assassinated." Her gaze hardened as she glanced at him. "Did you ever believe women were any less bloody-minded or greedy than men, Nathan?" she asked with dangerous softness. "Did you ever suppose *I* did?"

"No, l'amae," he said carefully. She smiled without warmth.

"Fortunately, she was as incompetent at murder as she was at business. I survived, and the experience made me wiser. Q'sola's firstborn was about twelve then: bright girl, sharp. Yronae. I did two things very quickly. First, I adopted Yronae as my daughter and designated heir; then I married two kharvah, the first a youngest son in the Daharanan Motherline, a somewhat minor but respectable High Family, and the second the son of the Ushahayam pratha h'máy, a powerful Family I needed at my back. I chose them both very carefully, and my senior kharvah balanced out his junior partner quite nicely."

"What happened to Q'sola?" Nathan asked, caught up in her narration enough to momentarily forget his own worries.

"Oh, I forgave her, naturally. The matter never became public, as it was a private Family concern. You see, when a man is rejected by his Family, he becomes naekulam. There is no such thing as a female naekulam. The shame is too great. If Q'sola had been exposed, she would either have been exiled or gone into permanent retreat in the Temple.

"Q'sola already had an established network of cronies as well, while I'd been off on my grand adventures. I returned experienced in everything but what I needed to survive on Vanar. So I forgave her and showered her with honors and gifts. She was my right hand at every Council, my most trusted advisor. We were inseparable, true sisters once more. Willingly or not, she taught me everything I needed to know about Vanar Family intrigues and politics."

She blew smoke at the ceiling then lowered her head, bright eyes fixed on his. "Then a few years later, she conveniently died." She raised an eyebrow at the suspicion in his face.

"Q'sola was a surly, unforgiving bitch whose incessant bungling was becoming an embarrassment the Family couldn't afford. She drank too much, so I provided her with vast quantities of the very best with a few untraceable additives to speed her along the way." She exhaled another gust of smoke, squinting at him. "Which is how murder is done *properly* in High Families, Nathan," she said mildly.

"Does Yronae know?"

"Of course. How else would she have learned as well as she has? She has her mother's rigidness, but none of her obstinate stupidity. Q'sola threatened the stability of the entire Family, not just me. Had she succeeded in murdering me and taking my place, sooner or later Yronae would have had to find a suitable way of killing her mother herself. For the good of the Family."

He felt the skin on his cheeks prickle, a sharp ache in the pit of his stomach. "As you would have me killed if I became a threat to the Family?"

"Exactly," she said without hesitation. "Even as fond of you as I am. And it's far easier to get rid of troublesome men than troublesome sisters."

He sat wordlessly as she returned his gaze steadily, smoke wreathing a halo around her head. Finally she smiled, not unkindly. "As a man, however, you're an insignificant liability. There's not much you could do short of a serious act of violence that would warrant disposing of you."

"Gee, thanks," he said dryly, forgetting himself. "That makes me feel a hell of a lot better." Then he bit his lip nervously, not in the least relieved when she laughed.

"Don't worry, Nate," she said affectionately. "Your smart mouth is one of the things I like best about you."

"My smart mouth nearly got me killed," he said sourly.

"Ah, yes. Your smart Hengeli mouth." Her eyes were bloodshot from the smoke, almost glowing. Dragon's eyes. "Your world may be a burnt-out wreck, but Hengeli remains the most common universal language throughout the inhabited systems. Even the Vanar must use Hengeli to negotiate with yepoqioh. Do you know why?"

"I keep telling you, jah'nari l'amae, I'm not a linguist."

"Because Hengeli was the first language of flight. We took our traffic vernacular with us wherever we went. It's a wonderfully plastic, forgiving language anyone can adapt to."

"The lingua franca of the stars," he said dryly.

She laughed. "If you *were* a linguist, you'd understand the irony of what you just said."

"I don't need to be, Pratha Yaenida. I know damned well what I said. But other than as casual entertainment, what do you want from me?"

Her eyebrows rose slightly as she waved a bone-thin hand toward the walls of books, a fortune in gold jiggling on her wrist. "Seven hundred years of Vanar literature, culture, science, philosophy, history—all that makes us what we are—are in this room." She nodded to her flatscreen. "The books are merely artifacts. Far more information is contained in the library archives under our feet, enough to fill a thousand rooms this size. Nearly all of it is completely unknown outside Vanar."

He glanced around, puzzled.

"Like it not, Nathan, you are going to be my linguist," she said, her voice flat. "You will learn not only our language, but the history and the culture, the art, the music, the mentality. Learn it well enough to help translate this work into Hengeli." She waved a vague hand to take in the whole of the library. "You have the working understanding of the outside culture, and you will be able to make us understood where we cannot hope to explain ourselves."

His jaw dropped. "My God," he breathed. "You can't be *serious . . .*"

"It has been my own private project. I've devoted nearly a century and a half to it, already. Bit by bit, I've been exporting it, while I've done what I can to import new ideas. I want to expand Vanar's influence, for us to be accepted and admired, not just feared because we are unknown. Make us understood."

"And how do I do that?" Nathan demanded. "I have even less contact now with the outside than any other Nga'esha man in your House." Aelgar had made it clear that Nathan would never serve at another banquet, the likelihood he would ever see anyone other than the Vanar again near zero.

"The reach of a pratha h'máy is very long, Nathan, sometimes even from beyond the grave, " she said dryly. "You need worry only about the translations."

"And if I refuse, you'll have me drink myself to death?"

"Of course not," she said contemptuously. "Your life will simply become even more interesting than it is now."

"I'm just an overrated gardener, Yaenida! I don't have the training, the background, I can't *do* this—"

"Wrong answer. You *will* do this."

The finality of her voice silenced him.

"I don't expect you to translate everything. But you have plenty of time." She smiled vaguely.

He stared around at the room of books in horror, feeling the weight of the databank below like an anchor sucking him down into black water. "I couldn't finish this if I lived to be a hundred."

"You will live far longer than that," she assured. "As you are Nga'-esha, you've already begun genetic reconditioning treatments." He stared at her, pop-eyed. "You will never get cancer or diabetes or arthritis, or go bald, for that matter. Even so, it will take the rest of your very long and healthy life to get through a fraction of it. But it's not as if you're going anywhere, are you?"

He leaned his elbows against the table, holding his head, palms pressed against his eyes with fingers raked into his hair. "Damn you, Yaenida," he said quietly. "Why didn't you just kill me? I'm already in hell."

"You exaggerate, Nathan."

"No. No, I don't. Everything has been taken from me. My freedom, my education, my privacy, my future." Now even Pratima, he didn't dare add. "For what?" He gestured at the books around the room in despair. "*This?* A load of Vanar poetry and etiquette rule books? This is my life?"

Yaenida placidly smoked her pipe as Nathan hunched on his elbows, head bowed over the table. "This needn't be completely onerous," she said. He looked up resentfully as she spoke. "Were I to make you too unhappy, I would only be ensuring you would do the work with the minimum amount of effort, and the results would be inadequate. That is not good business."

"If I am permitted to speak honestly," he said sarcastically, "I can't imagine how you could possibly make me any more miserable than I am now."

"Perhaps not, but I might be able to make you *less* miserable." She was no longer smiling. "As well as solving a temporary difficulty. You still wish to research Vanar native flora, do you not?"

For a moment, he couldn't breathe. "Yes," he whispered.

"And publish?"

It wouldn't mean any tenure at a university, but at least it might give back some purpose to his life. "Yes, very much."

"Fine, then. I'm sending you to Dravyam. The Nga'esha Estate there is smaller, but secure. The *dalhitri b'ahu* is a cousin and old friend, l'amae Mahdupi dva Sahmudrah ek Nga'esha. I have asked her to take over your instruction preparatory to your marriage. She is an excellent teacher, quite patient and meticulous, but you would be well advised to show her the same respect as you do me." She grinned. "A good deal more, actually, as she may not find your charming brashness as amusing as I do."

"Hae'm, jah'nari l'amae."

"You may take Pratima with you, if you like."

He didn't trust himself to speak, and she shook her head, pleased with the reaction she'd provoked. "Pratima speaks excellent Hengeli, and you will need someone to help you. When you are not studying either Vanar or our marriage rituals, you may go where you wish on the estate, but only with Pratima or another escort at all times. You are strictly prohibited from wandering off by yourself. The estate is extensive and still in a not-fully-developed state. There should be plenty of indigenous vegetation within its confines to interest you."

"For how long, Pratha Yaenida?"

"Until I send for you."

He nodded, doing his best to appear the model of the compliant Vanar man.

"Don't worry, Nathan," she added, not in the least fooled. "You'll be back in time to annoy me further before I'm dead."

XXI

THE NGA'ESHA ESTATE AT DRAVYAM WAS MUCH LARGER THAN HE'D EX-pected, but vastly different. The small city of Dravyam itself was several kilometers away from the sprawling Nga'esha complex. It was as if a small version of the Nga'esha House in Sabtú had been lifted wholesale and dropped into the midst of the indigenous seaside jungle, only the line of the high-speed train to connect it to the rest of the civilized world.

They hadn't taken the train, however. Nathan and Pratima had held hands like excited teenagers, staring out the windows of the private Nga'esha aircraft as the dense jungle flashed by beneath them. Their Dhikar guards seemed indifferent, deceptively relaxed.

"I've never been to Dravyam," Pratima said.

"Why not? Was it forbidden?"

Pratima laughed in surprise. "No, of course not. Nothing is forbidden to Pilots on Vanar. I never had a reason before, is all."

He squeezed her hand gently, pleased, and even under the diligent watch of the Dhikar, kissed her.

The Dravyam estate's dalhitri b'ahu, l'amae Mahdupi dva Sahmudrah ek Nga'esha, waited for them personally at the landing stage, two Dhikar of her own to escort her. She said nothing to Pratima, making only the most cursory nod to the Pilot, and regarded him with unabashed curiosity. "Greetings, Cousin."

If he understood the convoluted Nga'esha family pedigree correctly, Mahdupi Nga'esha would have been his maternal second cousin four times removed, for which there was indeed a precise Vanar term. But she had chosen to use a simpler, more casual salutation that left Nathan momentarily at a loss. After concentrating so long on who was related to whom and to what degree, this unexpected informality threw him. "I hope your stay with us is pleasant," she said.

And short, he thought. "Tah byát, jah'nari l'amae," he said simply with a formal bow. When he straightened, she was smiling in a way that reminded him of Yaenida, although the two women were physically very dissimilar. Stout and radiating a robust health, Dalhitri Mahdupi wore a simple cotton kirtiya over what Nathan was sure were a well-worn pair of work trousers, and none of the jewelry favored by her more fashion-conscious cousins in Sabtú.

"I'm afraid that after the liveliness of our capital city you will find Dravyam rather dull and provincial," Mahdupi said, but her words were directed at the Nga'esha Pilot.

When Pratima said nothing, not even raising her eyes far enough to acknowledge the dalhitri, Nathan said, "I'm sure Dravyam has its compensations," in what he hoped was his best cordial manner.

Mahdupi's eyebrows lifted, and he worried that he'd bungled some form of Vanar grammar and accidentally said something completely different. "I'm looking forward to studying the native flora, very much," he hastened to add nervously. Her smile broadened, but she said nothing. "With your permission, of course. . . ."

Pratima slipped her hand into his and squeezed gently, stopping his gibbering.

Mahdupi chuckled. "Well," she said, not unkindly, "your presence will no doubt liven up the place."

"But hopefully not too much," Pratima whispered to him in Hengeli once the Dalhitri Mahdupi's back had turned.

The men's quarters of the Dravyam estate were not anywhere near as extravagant as those in Sabtú, but the view overlooking the sea cliffs was outstanding. Steps carved into granite cliffs wound down to the rocky beaches below, and the men and women of the Dravyam estate basked in the sun or swam in the clear waters. The Vanar had introduced a modified marine life to Vanar oceans, with limited success. The moons around Vanar were too small to create any truly vigorous tides, and the water more brackish with minerals than salt. But the occasional flash of bright red and yellow shoals of tame fish would have the children scampering into the water to feed their pets.

Blue in the distance, the peaks of the Dravyam mountains cut a jagged line on the horizon. The reddish green native jungle stretched unbroken from the edge of the Dravyam estate to the foothills of the distant mountains.

The morning of his second day, Mahdupi sent for him. He'd been summoned with almost careless indifference by her senior kharvah, a handsome man with disheveled hair and work-roughed nails that made Nathan wonder what he did. Nathan had hurriedly checked his own appearance before rushing to the estate's main hall, but then had found himself alone, the seating ledges around the room empty, and only a single well-flattened cushion in the middle of the floor. Not taking the chance he wasn't being watched and tested, he bowed to no one and knelt at the proper distance to the vacant pillow. And waited.

The hall was smaller than that of the Nga'esha pratha h'máy in Sabtú. Massive rough-hewn timber beams supported the roof, and the plastered walls were painted a pale rose. The polished granite floor was icy under his legs. He began to worry he'd gotten it wrong, wondering if he should leave to search for Dalhitri Mahdupi when she finally showed up, seeming surprised to see him.

"Oh," she said, walking toward him. "You're here already." She didn't sit down, passing the faded cushion to hand him a box. "My cousin has instructed me to give this to you." When he looked at her inquiringly, she nodded at it. "Well? Open it."

Inside, he discovered compact field analysis equipment, far more sophisticated than what he'd lost on the *Comptess Dovian*.

"It's a . . ." She used a word he didn't know.

"We call it called a 'lab kit' in Hengeli," he said.

Mahdupi shook her head, amused. "No, no. I mean you only get to keep it if you satisfy me with how well you learn what you need for your marriage to Kallah Changriti."

"A bribe." He ran his fingers over the lab kit lovingly before he looked up at her. "Then can we start the lessons now, jah'nari l'amae?"

She chuckled, and Nathan found himself liking her. "Go play with your new toys first. Pratima is waiting for you with a hoverfloat. You're free to use it to go wherever you like, within a hundred-kilometer radius. The float won't operate any farther than that, and it will be easier to find the two of you should I need to. Return by sundown, and you'll find a schedule posted on your reader."

He didn't need telling twice. He bowed deeply, grabbed the lab kit, and nearly ran to find Pratima. She seemed as giddy as he, their relative freedom intoxicating.

"Where to?" she asked as she lifted the float from its moors.

He pointed toward the distant mountains. "That way, exactly ninety-nine point nine kilometers."

They set down at eighty-seven point three kilometers instead, as Nathan spotted an intriguing splotch of color in a clearing in the dense forest. As he hoped, it was a meadow of svapnah, just about to flower. He walked through the knee-high plants, brushing his hands across their budding tips reverently, his fingers wet with dew.

"Fantastic," he breathed. He turned back toward Pratima, then frowned in concern at her expression. "What is it?"

"Listen."

He did. "To what?"

She smiled slowly. "Exactly."

No sound other than the whisper of wind through the odd treelike plants towering above them, the dripping of rainwater from their leaves. No birds, no insects, no animal life of any kind had ever evolved on Vanar, the planet still a huge reserve of primeval flora. Terraforming had yet to spread its tendrils this far into the rain forest, none of the native plants capable of supporting alien life.

But it wouldn't be long, Nathan thought, crouching down as he noticed a distinctly familiar grass growing between the red-green stalks of svapnah. Not even this far out into indigenous territory could he find an ecosystem not contaminated by alien species imported for centuries by the Vanar. Vanar's native plant life, although spectacularly diverse, had yet to develop past rudimentary structures, even structures as complex as the small, plain svapnah flowers rare. The mild conditions of their environment created little evolutionary pressure. The balmy climate with little seasonal change suited such slow-growing plants . . . and provided a perfect breeding ground for such foreign competitors as this *Phalaris arundinacea*, an invasive, fast-growing grass that loved wet, warm weather—he could almost feel his botanist's training clicking over in his head—needing very little in the way of soil nutrients to survive and spread, vying ruthlessly for space with the native flora.

Nathan fingered the long, slender blades of grass, strangely indignant. The injustice of his precious svapnah being slowly pushed toward extinction by common invaders boiled up in him. In a sudden burst of anger, he grabbed a handful of the grass and jerked it out of the ground. Then another, and another, clots of damp earth spraying his face, his sati, the fragile svapnah plants around him.

"Stop it, Nathan! What are you doing?" Pratima's strong hands shook him by the shoulders, breaking his frenzy. He gasped for breath, trembling, and realized his face was wet with tears. She squatted beside him, concerned. "What's the matter with you?"

"It doesn't belong here," he growled, his voice thick. "It does not belong here."

"Oh, Nathan." Pratima wrapped her arms around his shoulders, drawing his head down to her shoulder to let him weep like a child.

XXII

THE ATMOSPHERE AT DRAVYAM MIGHT HAVE SEEMED MORE RELAXED than at the main estate at Sabtú, and its dalhitri b'ahu more informal than most, but appearances could be deceiving. His lessons with Mahdupi cut into his expeditions into the forests with Pratima. Not even a dazzling plankton bloom along the coastline could persuade the dalhitri to let up on his instruction, the Vanar strangely indifferent to their own native botany.

One of the men, Rulayi, agreed to row him out on a small boat after the evening meal, the sun barely set. He watched, bemused, as Nathan dipped his collection net into the midst of the luminescent plankton, the water throbbing with silent flashes. He spent several hours out on the water, taking samples, running analyses through the lab kit, making notes. Several Dhikar waited on the beach when they returned well after dark. Rulayi didn't appear anxious, nor did the Dhikar do more than observe as the muscular kharvah hauled the boat up onto the rocky shore before the Dhikar escorted them back to the men's house. The next morning, Dalhitri Mahdupi didn't mention their excursion during their lesson, her eyes shut as she lounged on the sunlit ledge overlooking the bay while he stumbled through a reading of Vanar poetry. She said nothing other than to correct his frequent mispronunciation.

When she allowed him to pause for the afternoon, he had bowed and gone as far as the arch when she said, "We are not as strict here as at my cousin's House, but there are rules. You will follow them."

He turned back, but she hadn't moved from her place in the sun, her eyes still shut. "Pardon, l'amae?"

You are allowed to study your plants while you are here, Nathan Nga'esha, but you've been told: only with Pratima or one of the Dhikar. You are here to learn to be more Vanar, not to involve my men in your bizarre yepoqioh ways. They do not understand, and curiosity is not an attractive trait to encourage in men. You will not be warned again. Understood?"

She hadn't raised her voice, or so much as opened her eyes, but Nathan's mouth had gone dry. "Hae'm, jah'nari l'amae."

He waited for her to dismiss him, but she said nothing more, still basking in the sun as if asleep. After several minutes, he crept out as silently as he could, breathing a sigh of relief if that was to be the worst of his discipline.

While he studied with Mahdupi, Pratima spent much of her time swimming in the clear, tranquil waters of the bay, where the gravity didn't affect her body with quite as much force. Several times, he caught sight of her from the balconies of the men's house, her long hair streaming behind her like seaweed, her naked body shining pearl white. But even here, Nathan noticed, the Vanar avoided her, and she swam in a carefully isolated bubble, alone in a sea of people.

They fell into a quiet routine: she swam, he studied, they escaped whenever they could to the freedom of the rain forest. She helped him to map the unexplored forests, recording every new species of native plant he found, learned how to gather and process his samples. She laughed at him as he sweated and stumbled and whacked his way through dense undergrowth while she slipped through the shadowy rain forest as nimbly as a wraith. They took packed food with them, picnicking on the cold slopes of the mountain. He sat at the top of a cliff with his arms and legs wrapped around Pratima to warm her thin body, both of them shivering as they looked down at the distant fields and buildings of Dravyam huddled next to the sea.

"You love it here," Pratima said quietly.

He held her tighter, kissing her hair. "I love anywhere I'm with you." But he did find it sad the Vanar cared so little for the native land, willing to destroy what they could find no utilitarian purpose for.

Whenever they couldn't get away from the estate, they retreated to a low stone bower overgrown with wisteria in a secluded corner of a garden. They had turned it into their private nest, sleeping nestled together with the scent of flowers around them. Even the children left them in peace, no one to disturb their tiny Eden, as fleeting and illusory as it was.

He had been with Mahdupi and a young sahakharae music teacher as they drilled him in the interminable marriage rituals he would be expected to carry out on his return to the Sabtú Nga'esha Estate when one of her taemora clerks hurried in, unannounced, and murmured in her ear. Mahdupi bent her head to listen without expression, although the taemora was clearly agitated. The sahakharae seemed oblivious to anything other than his *kapotah* lute, tuning the strings in the sudden lull.

When the taemora straightened, waiting expectantly, Mahdupi sat back on her heels, broad hands on her thighs, and sighed. She gazed at Nathan thoughtfully. He carefully kept his own gaze fixed over her shoulder, still holding his own lute awkwardly in his lap. He knew enough by now not to ask any questions, although inwardly he cringed, wondering what violation of Vanar rules he'd inadvertently committed this time.

As if reaching a decision, she stood from the floor and snapped her fingers at him. "Come with me, Nathan." The sahakharae glanced up briefly, expressionless, but neither he nor the taemora followed as Mahdupi led him out of the room.

Mahdupi strode without looking back to see if he followed, her determined stride so quick he had to trot after her down the long hallway into an area he had never been. They reached a balcony already filled with excited spectators, a few women glancing at him in surprise. He realized he was deep in the women's part of the House, where men were generally forbidden. Mahdupi jerked her head, a gesture for him to come out onto the balcony.

The gallery overlooked part of the main garden where what seemed like a small riot had broken out below. After a moment, he picked out two men, their sati torn and disheveled, circling each other as various allies orbited around them in the turmoil with bright, avid eyes. He was guiltily relieved the problem hadn't been his after all. He'd also seen enough fights in his life to know this was not the usual docile posturing of men jockeying for position in the Family hierarchy. This was the real thing: pure raw emotion, real fury and hatred boiling over into the open.

A woman, a middle-aged taemora, pushed her way to lean over the balustrade beside him, her face flushed, watching the activity below intently. Aware of his stare, she glanced at him, the point of her tongue moistening her tips, and he could almost feel the sexual energy radiating from her. The woman smiled and turned her attention back on the men below.

The two men ripped off their sati, crouching in only torn and bloodied mati as they confronted each other. He recognized Rulayi, the man who had rowed him out to take samples of the plankton bloom. The younger man he knew only by sight, Santosh. Both were married to one of Mahdupi's more distant cousins, an extremely pretty woman he had noticed but whose name he couldn't remember. The older man, her second kharvah and therefore his opponent's subordinate, had powerful shoulders, quick for all his weight. He circled the younger man with relaxed ease, his more wiry opponent obviously scared. Their supporters occasionally skirmished with challengers, the two sides shoving and pulling at each other as they kept the center area cleared for the two antagonists.

"What's going on?" he asked Mahdupi, unable to maintain strict Vanar custom.

She shot him an acerbic look. "Be quiet and just watch."

Rulayi kept his focus on his younger rival, smiling grimly as he waited. When Santosh sprang, the older man dodged, reflexes quick. His arm shot out and punched the younger man in the face. Santosh crumpled to his knees, clutching his bleeding face. A woman, the wife of the two kharvah below, rushed from out of the inner rooms onto the balcony, wild eyed as she took in the two struggling men. She clutched the balustrade, half hanging over the edge as she screamed at the two men in rage and fear and desperation, her Vanar too rapid and slurred for Nathan to follow. Rulayi glanced up at her scornfully, his eyes hot, before turning his attention back to Santosh.

Her friends held her arms on either side, murmuring encouragement as they pulled her back from the edge. He suddenly recalled the woman's name: Nicaea. Her blanched face was stricken as she moaned, a strangled sound in her throat. To his surprise, Mahdupi chuckled, a deep, almost inaudible sound. Nathan glanced at her, but there was no amusement in the woman's stolid face.

As Rulayi circled his downed foe, Santosh's hand suddenly clutched his ankle, jerking hard. Nathan caught the look of surprise as the man toppled, then it was a frenzy of arms and legs as the two men fought for a hold. Vanar men were well trained in wrestling, but this wasn't the stylized sport put on for the enjoyment of women. These two men fought in earnest.

Several Dhikar appeared, strolling unhurriedly through the crowd of men who quickly gave way. But when they looked up at the dalhitri, to Nathan's surprise, she shook her head. The Dhikar stood out of the way of the brawl, observing without interference.

"You aren't going to stop this?" Nathan asked in disbelief.

Mahdupi smiled bitterly, ignoring his bad manners. "No."

Whether by accident or design, Santosh punched the older man hard under the chin with his head. Rulayi's eyes rolled up white in his head, and he crumpled as limp as a boned fish. The woman next to him inhaled with more relish than disgust, absently rubbing one hand across her chest, stroking her own breasts.

The sound in the court hushed as the men circled around the pair stopped, watching avidly as Santosh struggled to his feet, sobbing for breath. Blood dripped from a nose Nathan was sure was broken, Santosh's eyes already beginning to swell into bruised slits as he stared down at the unconscious man. Suddenly Nathan knew, *knew*, Santosh was deciding whether or not to kill Rulayi. The younger man placed his bare foot against his fallen opponent's neck. With a little weight, he could crush the man's windpipe, even break his neck.

Nathan glanced at Mahdupi, who wasn't even watching the scene below. He traced her speculative gaze to Nicaea, the distraught woman half flung over the balustrade, disheveled and hysterical.

"Santosh, please don't . . . please . . . ," his wife called out, her voice barely audible.

The younger man glared up at her, anger and triumph and naked despair in his face. The man on the ground moaned and stirred. Santosh pulled his foot away from Rulayi's throat, then hawked and spat on his face, more blood than spittle. He turned his back on the woman on the balcony and strode away with his head high, his back stiff. From the glee on the faces of some of the men picking up their fallen companion and the sullen expression on others', Nathan suspected their emotions were the results of bets won or lost rather than on the fate of their comrades.

The women mingled slowly, talking among themselves, flushed with high spirits. Only Nicaea stood like carved stone, pale and mute.

"Stupid woman," Mahdupi said. "She should never have played one against the other, encouraged their jealousy to amuse herself. What did she expect they would do? You see, Nathan, why we discourage violence among our men?" She looked around sourly at the women still giddy with excitement. "It does not bring out the best in any of us."

"What happens now?"

"They will be punished. All three of them," Mahdupi said softly. "But you may go now. I shall be quite busy for some time, I think." She glanced around grimly at the women following them, lowered her voice, and much to his surprise, spoke to him for the first time in impeccable Hengeli. "Do us both a favor. Find Pratima. Spend the day doing whatever it is you do in the forest. Spend two. Don't come back until I send for you."

"How will you know where we are, l'amae Mahdupi?"

"If you assumed I know everything, you would be wrong," she said. "But you'd also be safe in your assumptions."

Pratima and Nathan escaped to the forest, where it would be four days before Mahdupi recalled them. They heard that for several nights, the men's quarters had been half deserted, and those kharvah not called to their wives' beds had grumbled among themselves. But the morning after the fight, Santosh had been found in the almond orchard.

He had hung himself.

XXIII

TWO WEEKS BEFORE HE WAS EXPECTED TO MARRY KALLAH, HE AND Pratima had been returned to Sabtú. He wasn't too unhappy to leave; his excursions into the rain forest had been curtailed, the mood in Dravyam turning oppressive. Nicaea and Rulayi had both disappeared, no one willing to talk about what might have happened to either of them.

Mahdupi had taken the responsibility of teaching Nathan what he needed to know for his marriage to Kallah very seriously, drilling him in the endless greetings and ceremonies as relentlessly as Yaenida had taught him Vanar, and inspecting his rehearsals with a critical eye. Now that Nathan knelt in the airy sunlit room off the Changriti men's garden, he was glad his zealous cousin was far away in Dravyam and not there to wince at his bumbling.

He had set out at sunrise to walk barefoot all the way across Sabtú from the Nga'esha Estate to the Changriti, as tradition dictated, while carrying the inlaid box filled with small gifts and jewels and a full coffee set as well as the kapotah lute he was somehow expected to play to accompany his own singing as he entertained Kallali's two kharvah. His suggestion that he be allowed to sing something from his limited Hengeli repertoire had been met with shocked horror from his tutors. As he tramped along the road, his face already hurting from smiling as he bowed at the ceaseless wishes for good luck and success from every stranger he passed, he'd thought sourly that his musical ability might amuse the two unlucky men only if they had a healthy sense of humor.

He'd arrived shortly before noon, his feet blistered and the calves of his legs sore. Although Ukul Daharanan was the younger of the two kharvah, he had been Kallah's first husband as well as the nephew of a Daharanan dalhitri h'máy. Once Nathan married into the Changriti, both he and Raetha Avachi, Kallah's second kharvah and the minor son of a Middle Family, would defer to Ukul. But Ukul apparently was not blessed with the sense of humor Nathan had hoped for as the younger man sat listening to the foreigner's inept attempt to approximate the children's melody Mahdupi's music teacher had painstakingly taught him to pick out on the lute's multitude of strings. His sharp face was as expressionless and as warm as arctic granite.

Raetha's friendly grin, on the other hand, seemed a permanent fixture in the big man's round face as he peered at Nathan through a shock of dark hair constantly falling over his forehead into his eyes. The two men sat on plump cushions, while Nathan, as a supplicant for admission to the Changriti men's house, knelt on the hardwood floor. He balanced the lute across his lap, metal picks slipping around the end of his sweaty fingers. Although they were the only ones in the huge hall, Nathan heard the whispers and saw the shadows of the curious Changriti menfolk behind the carved window screens.

Nathan finally completed his idiotic little verse about a thin cat dancing with a fat donkey and put the lute down to one side and bowed. When he straightened, Ukul's expression had not changed in the least, but he said, his voice colorless, "How interesting the way you have given a beloved melody of our childhood new interpretation, unlike anything I've heard before."

Raetha's eyes widened, and Ukul shot him an acid look as the larger man choked back a snort of laughter.

Nathan blinked and reddened, then stumbled through the ritual response, "I am happy it was pleasing to your ear," although he knew that Ukul had said no such thing.

It took another two hours to hand out the gifts he'd hauled all the way across the city: bits of jewelry, the latest popular drama in entertainment cubes (or so he'd been assured; traditional Vanar theater bored him even when he understood the plot), expensive handmade birdsilk sati in the Changriti burgundy with matching mati in each man's Family colors. He'd also added a bit of pink apple blossom to weave into each man's braid, the fashion having caught on since his strange gift to Tycar. Ukul barely glanced at the loot spread out neatly in front of him, although Raetha was obviously far more pleased with the flowers than with the rest of the expensive gifts.

"I would dance for you, esteemed brothers, had I not so stupidly injured my left ankle, which would, of course, only spoil your enjoyment. My most humble apologies." Aelgar himself had suggested this pretext, promising him that, if put properly, it might be enough to get him out of having to lumber about the room like a lobotomized ox. But he held his breath, waiting for Ukul's response. The weasel-faced man would get more satisfaction out of forcing him into an absurd performance than from watching a good one, Nathan instinctively knew. But he tried to keep his relief off his face when Ukul expressed his regret.

Then Nathan had begun the tedious coffee ceremony, reciting the poetry in proper order as he went through the praising of the earth, the praising of the coffee bush, the blessing of the beans, the grinding, the sifting, the spicing, the boiling of the water, the blessing of the sugar, the blessing of the sand, the hammered copper pot, the tiny porcelain cups, heating the coffee to a boil exactly three times before he poured it out with absolute precision. He'd almost finished, his back hurting from the continuous bowing, his cheeks numbed from his frozen smile, his knees throbbing from kneeling long hours on the floor, grateful to be nearing the end of an extremely unpleasant day, when disaster struck.

As he held out the steaming cup of black coffee for Ukul, his mind went suddenly blank. His mouth hung slack and he couldn't remember the damned script. Ukul stared back at him, narrowed eyes as black as the coffee as he waited unrelentingly. Frozen, Nathan groped for the words, the cup rattling ominously in his hand.

"May the perfume of this offering . . . ," he suddenly heard Raetha whisper. The large man was gazing up obliviously over Nathan's shoulder, as if unaware of anything wrong.

Ukul flicked an angry slit-eyed glance toward his junior.

His memory jolted, Nathan babbled quickly, "May the perfume of this offering be as fresh to your nose as the morning sun on the grass, may it be pleasant to your tongue, sweet as honey . . ." The words were unintelligible sounds, learned by rote, Nathan too rattled to remember their meaning.

Raetha hazarded a friendly smile as they each drank the coffee in turn, although Nathan could barely taste his. Then, thankfully, the ordeal was over. They bobbed and waved and sent him home, the sun already beginning to set. The two men would discuss his various merits and defects, and give their verdict to their wife before each of them sent gifts to him, to be examined closely by Aelgar as an indication of how well or how poorly he'd done. Who would then report to Yronae, who would then consult Yaenida, who would then invite Eraelin for a similar private women's ceremony. It all seemed very mind-numbingly tedious.

He took the underground train back to the edge of the Nga'esha Estate, having to wait on the platform as three trains went by before one with a men's car stopped. His feet hurt, his back hurt, his ego hurt, and, he thought ruefully, the fun was just beginning. . . .

XXIV

HE HAD THOUGHT PRATIMA WOULD WANT TO BE GONE BEFORE THE ACtual marriage and was baffled and uneasy when she announced her decision to attend the ceremony. Three days before the wedding, they escaped to their favorite rendezvous, down by the river in the copse with the old split tree. Pratima lay in the tree's hollow, playfully dropping leaves on him while he leaned against the trunk below.

"It's not that I want you to leave," he tried to explain, hoping to convince her without hurting her feelings, "but there's no reason you have to attend."

"Of course there is," she replied serenely. "It's a Nga'esha wedding, and Pilot or no, I'm still Nga'esha. It would be rude for me not to attend. Besides, it's not every day that a son of the Nga'esha pratha h'máy is married, you know. The celebration should be quite something to see."

He twisted around to gaze up at her, perplexed by her calmness. "Pratima, doesn't it bother you, my marrying someone else?"

"No. Why should it?"

He stood up and hauled himself into the tree, crowding her in the hollow. "Because it's to someone else. Aren't you the least bit jealous?"

She ran light fingers across his cheek. "Do you love her?"

"Who, Kallah?" He laughed. "I don't even *know* her."

"Then why should I be jealous?"

"Because one of my principal duties once I'm married," he explained with the patience he'd use with a dull child, "is to do my best to get her pregnant."

"Naturally."

"That means I'll have to have sex with her."

She smiled impishly. "That's the usual way it's done."

"Pratima," he said, exasperated, "you're not this dense. You know what I'm saying."

"Yes, of course I do. You're the one making the mistake of confusing love with sex."

That stung. "I know the difference, Pratima. Maybe you can convince yourself this was all nothing more than a passing fling, but I'm not ashamed to admit I love you more than anyone I've ever loved in my life."

Frowning, she sat upright and placed her hands on his face, her palms cool against his skin. "I wish you spoke better Vanar, Nate. It would be easier to explain. I never said I thought what has happened between us isn't important; it is. Which is going to give you problems with your new wife. She's the one who will be jealous, not me. Vanar women would like to believe men are emotionally stunted animals whose only desire is for sex. It would make life so much simpler if that were true. Kallah doesn't love you any more than you love her. But her pride would be wounded if she thought you incapable of ever caring for her. It's emotional infidelity that threatens us, Nathan, not physical. Vanar men are allowed all the sex they want . . . as long as they don't ever fall in love. That's the one betrayal women can't endure, in any culture."

"But Kallah doesn't love me, and she's got two other kharvah as well. Why should she be jealous of you?"

Pratima shrugged. "True, I'm no real danger to her, since you and I could never marry or have children, and I'll be leaving Vanar soon enough. She knows about us, of course. Everyone does. But it must be disconcerting for her. In her mind she'll be worrying that you're comparing her with me, that she'll be competing with a beloved memory she can never hope to surpass. Which isn't the best way to start off a new marriage."

With consummate suppleness, she did a leisurely backward flip out of the bole to land as softly as a cat on her feet. He wasn't quite as graceful clambering down out of the tree himself. "Be cautious about revealing your feelings quite so openly, Nathan. It can be dangerous, as you saw in Dravyam. Be careful of her other two kharvah, especially Ukul Daharanan. Ukul has not yet been able to father a child, and worries his position is threatened. He is truly devoted to Kallah, and isn't happy about her choice in you."

"How do you know all this?"

She shrugged. "Pilots love gossip. It amuses us." She didn't look amused. "Kallah may not love you, but she is certainly fascinated by the exotic. Let's just hope the novelty wears off before his tolerance wears out."

She laced her hands behind his neck, leaning back on her arms as he held her waist. "And I want to be there, Nathan, not just because I'm Nga'esha and it's my duty, but because I do love you. You will need someone there who does. But I will say good-bye to you now, because once you are married, we won't have the time later. I'm leaving as soon as it's over."

His heart thudded dully, and he felt suddenly ill. "How the hell am I going to survive here without you?"

She smiled wistfully. "You will. Your heart beats, your lungs breathe, and somehow you'll manage to live from one day to the next. We all do."

He took a ragged breath. "Give me something to look forward to, Pratima. I'll wait fifteen years for you, if that's what it takes. Promise you'll come back to me, for a month, for two, I don't care. Just come back to me."

She stared at him for a long moment, her pale eyes wary. He watched her internal debate, emotions flickering across her face before she kissed him gently. "Have many children. Be happy. And I promise, I'll come back," she whispered against his cheek, her breath warm on his skin.

They made love gently, almost without passion. By an unspoken agreement, she waited until he'd fallen asleep before she left as if evaporating into thin air. When he woke, he wrapped his arms around his knees and wept.

XXV

As weddings go, Nathan later thought wryly, he'd been to better. He wasn't even sure at which part of the ceremony he actually became a married man. Not that he'd seen much of it, either.

The basics had been described to him, and he knew somewhat of what to expect. But the reality was far worse than the anticipation. He'd spent the previous day being soaked, washed, scraped, massaged, oiled, polished, painted, and purged until he'd gone to bed with every inch of his skin tender, the bedclothes nearly painful. Shortly before daybreak, he was rudely woken from a sound sleep by a cacophonous chorus of the Nga'esha men singing loudly while bashing hand drums and cymbals. With Aelgar directing the action, he was seized and lifted bodily out of bed, carried off to the main atrium of the men's courtyard. There, a canopied sedan chair had been elaborately decorated with hundreds of bright silk streamers and brass bells. The men carried him around it three times before setting him on his feet in front of it.

Where he stood for the next three hours while Nga'esha men decorated him even more elaborately than the sedan chair. The weight of gold bracelets from wrist to elbow, and more on his legs from ankle to knee, dragged on him uncomfortably, making him wonder how he was going to walk with all this metal. The conventional sati had been dispensed with, and he was outfitted in a glittering costume not designed for the normal human male body. The exaggerated shoulders were settled onto him like a yoke for an ox, and someone cinched in his waist with such an abrupt jerk he gasped as the breath was knocked out of him. Once he was fastened into the rest of the costume, his thighs were squeezed together so tightly he could barely shuffle along by moving his knees.

Huge headgear completely covered his face with a garish curtain of beads, and he wondered how he was expected to even be able to *see* to walk. The answer, he discovered when he was picked up like an oversized doll and installed standing in the sedan chair, was that he wasn't expected to do anything at all.

He clung to the canopy supports to keep from being pitched out, swaying dangerously as the chair was lifted onto as many shoulders as could be wedged under it and carried out of the men's house to be paraded through the women's half of the estate. Judging by the cheering as he was conveyed lurching through the halls, every Nga'esha female relative had come for the wedding, his already diminished sight further hampered by a shower of paper streamers and confetti flung over him.

Although it was still early morning, half of Sabtú seemed to be crowded into the expansive women's gardens. Pratha Yaenida sat enthroned on a portable dais even larger and grander than his sedan chair. She, he would notice, spent most of the festivities dozing, comfortably snuggled into her nest of cushions. They set him down in the middle of the garden as the main exhibit. Long tables groaned under the weight of the food. The aroma made his mouth water, but he knew he wouldn't be given any.

His role in the ceremony was a test of endurance. He would remain on display while the party went on around him. The Changriti guests arrived a few hours after the celebration had begun, when the drinking began in earnest as the level of boisterous revelry escalated. If Kallah was among them, he never saw her.

When his part in the ceremonies had been explained, his only worry was that he'd be bored stiff and hungry. He hadn't grasped how excruciating the torture of simply standing upright for hours on end would be with the burden of the heavy jewel-encrusted costume and gold metal weighing him down. By midafternoon, the vague headache he'd had since early morning blossomed into a thumping migraine. By sunset, the small of his back ached and his ankles had begun swelling, the heavy gold squeezing them painfully.

At one point, he reeled precariously and begged as politely as he could to be allowed out of the chair. Many pairs of hands pushed him back upright. Someone used the long sleeves of his costume to tie his wrists to the sedan chair's posts to keep him from falling. He felt as if he were being crucified.

"Drink this," a male voice murmured, and poked something up under the headgear toward his face. He nearly gagged on the stem of a squeezebulb shoved between his lips, the burning liquid forced into his mouth. He managed to swallow most of it, the rest dribbling down his chin. Pinioned as he was, and burdened by the awkward headgear, he couldn't even wipe his mouth.

But it helped to clear his head. The quivering muscles in his legs steadied, and the headache lessened. It lasted about an hour, when another dose was thrust into his face. The intervals between doses became shorter and his agony more intense as night dragged on, the party still in full swing and showing no signs of subsiding any time soon.

Eventually whatever was in the burning liquid had no effect on him at all. His head spun, his vision black-specked as he fought to stay conscious. He blacked out several times, the relief fleeting as the weight pulled his arms out of their swollen joints. Searing pain forced him back to consciousness. The sky had lightened to a deep indigo, sunrise still an hour or so off, when he sagged against his silk restraints, weeping helplessly from the pain. He seriously wondered if they intended to kill him.

"I can't take this," he shouted, but his voice came out in a hoarse croak, lost in the music and laughter around him. He wasn't even aware he spoke in Hengeli, unable to think in Vanar at all. "For god-sake, please, I can't take any more!"

"Then don't." He heard Pratima's voice and wondered where it came from. Through his tears, he saw the gleam of a knife slash at his bonds, and heard the silk rip as his weight tore the sleeves from his costume. He collapsed, plunging out of the sedan chair headfirst. He never felt himself hit the ground, only remotely aware of the cheer that went up as many gentle hands lifted his body to carry him off.

His vision clouded, he saw only a blur of white rather than her face, and felt her lips brush his cheek. "Now aren't you glad I came?" he heard her whisper in his ear, and she was gone.

He passed out. When he roused from the black stupor, he lay naked in a massive bed while Raetha Avachi dabbed his forehead with a warm wet cloth. He groaned, pain shooting through his joints as he struggled to sit up.

"Where am I?"

"Kallah's private apartments," another voice said.

Ukul Daharanan appeared behind Raetha, scowling down at him.

How had he gotten from the Nga'esha women's gardens to the Changriti Estate clear on the other side of Sabtú? He hissed as Raetha patted the wet cloth against his cheek, then touched the swollen bruise under his eye with inquisitive fingers.

"Where's Kallah?"

"Still at the marriage celebration," Ukul said with unmistakable contempt. "Where you should be, had you any real stamina. *I* didn't break until well after the second evening at my wedding."

Nathan thought to say something on the lines of Ukul being the better man, but couldn't muster the energy to find the words in Vanar. The effort would have been wasted, he suspected. Raetha smiled wryly, glancing over his shoulder briefly as his surly partner stalked away. He leaned closer to Nathan and said softly, "But you did better than I did. I didn't last even until sundown, quite a scandal that was."

The stamina of Vanar women was apparently vigorous as well. Nathan spent the next three days in bed, recovering from his ordeal. Until Kallah staggered home to welcome him to his new life as a mar-ried man.

PART TWO

XXVI

AT SOME POINT, THE WALL IN HIS MIND CRACKED. HE HAD FOUGHT THE
Vanar language like a crippled man trying to scale a mountain, struggling between ambition and despair. One night, he had gone to sleep,
his head aching with complex syntax, abstract nouns and gerund verbs
tattooing a frustrated beat in his nerves. His dreams were vague, restless, resisting his attempt to impose enough order and logic on them
to let him sleep in peace. Toward morning, they'd exhausted him and
he let himself sink into the morass of the bizarre.

He dreamed in Vanar. He'd dreamt in Vanar before, of course, but
in remembering the dream the next morning, the words had only been
gibberish, a product of wishful thinking, as if hoping by magic the language would simply embed itself into his brain and stop torturing him.
But this morning, when he awoke, he knew, *knew* the Vanar in his
dreams had been correct, had been *real*.

He stopped having to translate every word he heard into its Hengeli counterpart, the sounds taking on their own meanings for him.
The rat's-nest curling of Vanar calligraphy began to make sense, all one
hundred and fifty-three letters and the innumerable underlying
ideograms unraveling into their separate parts so that he could see the
whole.

His command of Vanar tripled in a week, and at one point, when

Yaenida had asked him for the Hengeli translation for a word, he found himself groping for it, astonished and even alarmed that he could so easily forget bits and pieces of his own language.

He only wished Pratima could have been there to congratulate him. Maybe she knew, anyway; there had to be some kind of communication possible between Pilots and their Nga'esha controllers, but none that would ever be permitted to him.

He also knew he would never be completely fluent, never master the nuances various pronunciations could spin on a single word, would always miss half the jokes, the puns, the innuendoes, the double-edged double entendres. But the block was gone, and his awareness of the conversations around him had given him new insights, the first being that the Vanar had become accustomed to his incomprehension, talking amongst themselves as if he weren't there. Many things were said in his presence that might have been wiser to say elsewhere, and he quickly decided not to educate his Vanar companions to his sudden perception. Where once he had pretended to understand when he didn't, now he pretended not to understand when he did. He kept his face neutral, silent and seemingly disinterested in the conversation around him. Only Yaenida knew, and she had promised to keep his secret. At least for a while.

Only once had he slipped, laughing unexpectedly at a joke he'd overheard between two women. Startled, they had stared at him, and when they spoke again, it was as if he had suddenly lost all his newfound understanding, their conversation unintelligible babble. Then he realized it was a *second* language, a language he thought he'd never heard before until he remembered the unfamiliar dialect Pratima had used with the Ushahayam Pilot Bralin. When he asked Yaenida, she merely nodded and said, yes, it was a woman's language, spoken for privacy, and not to concern himself with it, as it was nothing he would be expected to learn or would ever be taught.

The year after Pratima's departure went by quickly enough. After his marriage, he saw little enough of his new wife, and then only when he was summoned to her personal rooms for an intimate little soiree with only himself and a dozen sahakharae, three or four taemora, a pair of the omnipresent Dhikar, and one or the other, or sometimes both, of his fellow kharvah.

The sahakharae provided most of the entertainment, dancing or playing music, while Ukul scowled sullenly and Raetha smoked himself into a stupor, smiling absentmindedly into space. What the taemora were there for, Nathan never could figure out. Once the evening's festivities had finished, everyone but the Dhikar left. He'd found it difficult to keep his mind on his more private obligations with two Dhikar behind the sheer linen bed curtains listening to their every grunt and moan, but somehow he managed it. To his astonishment, and Ukul's open bitterness, Kallah became pregnant with her first child four months after the wedding, and his nocturnal visits to his wife's bed came to an abrupt end. Instead, the three kharvah were forced to endure each other's company for the next eight months as they catered to Kallah's every demand.

Pregnancy didn't agree with her, her moods swinging from irrational hostility to maudlin weeping as her belly slowly inflated. Even the medical taemora lost patience with her whining, and had to be replaced after she tactlessly suggested that Kallah's problems were more mental than physiological. Pratha Eraelin stormed into her daughter's quarters one afternoon, ignoring the three kharvah scattering out of her way as she and her daughter engaged in a ferocious argument. The two women screamed furiously at each other in the impenetrable language of women until the pratha Eraelin kicked over a table and stalked out, leaving Kallah still shrieking and smashing anything breakable in her mother's wake. The three men spent the next several hours placating their wife, Ukul murmuring to her consolingly while Raetha poured an endless river of herbal tea and Nathan kneaded her tense shoulders until his fingers cramped in agony.

Raetha Avachi had come from a large Middle Family where daughters and sons mixed with far more familiarity and affection. There he'd learned more practical ways of attending to women than the traditional songs and dance at which he was nearly as inadequate as Nathan. He taught Nathan how to cradle her against his chest to use his own body heat to warm her back, and caress her swollen belly with soothing fingers. In her fifth month, the four had been out in Kallah's private courtyard, the heat of the sun making them all lethargic. Kallah sprawled against him, her abdomen bare under his hands, while Raetha sat behind them both, kneading Nathan's neck gently. Ukul paid meticulous care to the pressure points in the soles of his wife's feet. Kallah dozed, half asleep and her head nodding, waking her every time her chin dipped. Nathan had his eyes closed, leaning back into Raetha's hands contentedly.

Then he stiffened, his eyes opened wide as he sat upright, startling his companions.

"What is it?" Ukul demanded.

"Hey," Nathan breathed, and spread his fingers firmly against her sides. "Feel this. . . ."

Uncertain, Ukul placed his palm against Kallah's exposed flesh to feel the outline of the child moving underneath. Kallah smiled as serenely as a cat, pleased, as Raetha reached down to explore the unseen baby kicking within her. For a brief moment, Ukul and Nathan grinned at each other before Ukul remembered who had fathered this child and his scowl returned.

As soon as Kallah knew she had conceived she had taken each of her three kharvah to bed, including poor Raetha, whose sexual orientation had not been taken into consideration when the Changriti had hammered out a favorable marriage contract with the wealthy Avachi. He had dutifully struggled to manage his end of it, as Vanar custom dictated, so that each man could share equally in the honor of her child. However, from the first moment Aenanda arrived in the world with her mass of bright red hair and green eyes, it was impossible to pretend she could ever have been anyone's child other than Nathan's.

To his own astonishment, he'd fallen in love with the squalling, red-faced infant the moment he first held her in his arms, and he spent every moment allowed to him playing and laughing with her, another Hengeli peculiarity barely tolerated by the Vanar women and baffling to their men. Sons were deposited into the men's care as soon as they could be weaned, to be taught what skills they'd need in later life, while daughters, regarded as a valuable Family resource, were raised by their mothers and various female relatives. Kallah seemed perplexed by his adoration of their child, although she didn't attempt to discourage it.

Although Aenanda's birth secured both Ukul's and Raetha's political position in the Changriti household as fathers, the tension between Ukul and himself grew ever more acrimomous. By the time Aenanda was nearly a year old, the senior kharvah spent most of his waking hours conspiring with his coterie of sahakharae to devise malicious ways of making Nathan suffer. Most of the sly snubs or taunts that might have infuriated the ordinary Vanar made little impact on him, and his tormentors were reduced to more adolescent forms of persecution: wrigglies in his food, minor vandalism to his property, schoolboy pranks Nathan had outgrown before puberty.

More annoyed than angry, Nathan first tried to appease the disgruntled Changriti kharvah with the same sort of ritualistic deference and tedious groveling he'd perfected within the Nga'esha House. Unfortunately, the harder he tried, the worse the torment became. He knew enough not to complain to his wife, or worse, to Eraelin's senior husband, as the chief kharvah was one of the leading bullies in Ukul's clique. Finally, he gave it up.

Kallah granted his request to reside at the Nga'esha House without even a token objection. Nor did anyone from the Changriti House seem unhappy to see the back of him, with the possible exception of Raetha, who spent more and more of his time in a drug-induced trance. The traditional despotism of the Changriti House was hard on a boy torn away from the more free-spirited life of his Middle Family. Nor did Ukul ever pass up an opportunity to berate Raetha for his ungratefulness, marriage to a dalhitri of one of the Nine Families an incredible honor for someone of his modest caste. Raetha would simply agree with him, apologize, and smile vaguely into space. Nathan made the trip across the city once a week to visit both his daughter and Raetha, his concern growing for the gentle man.

Returning to the Nga'esha House felt like a welcome breath of fresh air after the oppressive atmosphere of despair and hostility with the Changriti. To his immense delight, Yaenida finally gave him a room of his own, an almost unheard-of luxury. He needed the space for his work, and had complained that the children in the boys' dormitory couldn't resist poking about into his possessions, baffled and hurt at his selfishness when he repeatedly scolded them.

The sahakharae were almost as bad, and *they* had complained about *him* when Yaenida attempted to move him into their quarters.

As Nathan had no uncles or nephews willing to sponsor him, Aelgar attempted to fob off the worst corner of the men's quarters on him; when it rained, a leak soaked his sleeping mat and the smell of mold was faint but tenacious. Nathan chose to protest this indignity by stringing up a makeshift hammock between two trees in the garden to sleep in at night, which had the desired effect of the senior kharvah pleading with Yronae to please speak with her mother to do something about that impossible *aevaesah jaelmah*, wretched troublemaker.

He simply didn't fit in anywhere, and the rest of Yaenida's male relatives were happy with the solution rather than envious. They were used to communal living, and viewed his private room as punitive isolation, quite fitting for the foreigner dropped in their midst.

Tensions between him and the Nga'esha men eased considerably after that. Often, he would look up from his reader and find one of the lower-status members, usually a younger second cousin or brother-in-law's son, waiting politely in his open doorway for him to notice their presence, bringing him a late-night snack, or offers for a friendly drink of tea or alcohol, or simply a social visit required to keep the fabric of Family relations close-knit.

He'd been struggling with translating a difficult Vanar passage from an historical treatise Yaenida had assigned him, baffled how the hell he would ever be able to explain in Hengeli terms concepts completely unknown outside Vanar, when a silhouette fell over his reader. To his surprise, Yinanq hovered at the edge of the open doorway, nervous and unsmiling.

"*Yahaem ayo,*" Nathan called out quietly.

Yinanq came in, his entire posture rigidly correct as he greeted Nathan, bowed, and knelt on the proffered floor pillow. Nathan had seen little of the young man since his near-fatal trial, both of them careful to avoid the other. Nathan offered him coffee, which was politely declined, then a fruit brandy, which was reluctantly accepted.

After a great deal of gracious compliments on the brandy, the room's furnishings, speculations on the antiquity of the carvings on the window screen, predictions on the ceaseless rainy weather and other such inconsequential murmurings, Nathan knew the young man was nearing the purpose of his visit. "I am getting married," Yinanq announced finally.

"Congratulations, elder brother," Nathan responded, although he was older than Yinanq by more than a decade. It wasn't the number of years, Nathan understood by now, it was the position in the Family, the constant shuffle up and down the familial ladder monitored with obsessive attention by everyone anxious to improve his own standing. "What Family has found you so excellent in their favor?" He wouldn't ask what woman; asking after a specific woman would be too impolite. Even the most important of wives were of secondary importance to their Family.

Yinanq smiled, the first look of genuine satisfaction Nathan had seen. "The Sahmudrah," he said, trying and failing to keep the pride out of his voice. "I have been asked to be first husband to the daughter of the dalhitri." The First Mother's granddaughter, Nathan knew, and knew the Sahmudrah had only one unmarried granddaughter, so far the only daughter of its heir. Nathan hadn't bothered struggling through much of the gossip in the news articles he'd subscribed to on his reader, but judging by the recordings of Elon dva Arjusana ek Sahmudrah, she was young and exceedingly attractive. It had been a topic of hopeful gossip among a good many Nga'esha where she might come looking for an eligible kharvah. No doubt there were quite a number of disappointed Nga'esha commiserating one another while Yinanq circulated his good news.

Nathan offered even more congratulations with a sense of relief. Yinanq had made a far more favorable bargain than had he been selected as Kallah Changriti's third husband. The younger man hadn't come to gloat, Nathan presumed, but to let him know their rivalry had been settled.

But that was not the purpose of Yinanq's visit, Nathan realized as the man lingered. He grew impatient as they continued the painfully stilted formalities, Yinanq reluctant to leave. Just as Nathan was trying to think of a polite way of asking him to either get to the point or piss off so he could get on with his work, the younger man fidgeted with the hem of his sati, cleared his throat, found something interesting under the edge of his thumbnail, and spoke while keeping his eyes on his hands.

"The flowers you gave Tycar look good in dark hair," he said. And stopped, all his attention on his thumb. His hands were trembling.

"Yes," Nathan agreed, baffled.

"It's very popular. Many of the sahakharae now demand flowers for their hair instead of jewelry."

Nathan stared at the younger man now picking furiously at his cuticle.

"They count the number of blossoms to decipher hidden meanings," Yinanq continued, "and compare the color between themselves. Giving hair flowers is becoming a ceremonial art in itself. You have given Vanar a new fashion. Everyone is talking about it."

Inwardly, Nathan groaned, both at having invented yet another interminable Vanar ritual and at the inane conversation. Then Yinanq dropped his hands into his lap and looked up, gazing with reflexive precision just over Nathan's shoulder, but unable to hide the misery on his face. "I apologize for saying you were dirty and smelled bad. And . . . and telling our jah'nari pratha h'máy you threatened the children."

The young man's voice was shaking as badly as his hands.

"But both of those things were true, elder brother. I'm sure you only did it for the sake of the Family."

Yinanq lowered his head, close to tears. Suddenly Nathan realized just how young the man was, barely more than a boy. "No, I did it because I was jealous, because I was afraid of you and thought it was unfair that a rhowgha yepoqioh should have the luck to marry the Changriti heir instead of me."

After having lived so long in the stifling formality, the convolutions of half-speech, this naked and honest confession left Nathan stunned. He stared at the man only a few years older than Raemik. "Oh, for godsake . . . ," he started, then stopped, realizing as Yinanq looked up in confusion that he'd spoken in Hengeli. "Yinanq, I accept your apology. Now you know you were not chosen for the Changriti only because the Goddess had something better in mind for you. May you father many daughters and die an old and happy man."

If he had thought this ritual blessing would make the boy feel better, he was even more confused as Yinanq's eyes reddened, his face frozen with embarrassment as tears threatened to spill over.

"Now I know you are not yepoqioh, you are my revered uncle, my great-aunt's excellent little brother, and this stupid naeqili was wrong to doubt the wisdom of our pratha h'máy when she brought you into our Family. All the Nga'esha know you are *koshah*, a treasure more valuable than a mountain of pearls, wise and good and truly civilized, most venerable Nay-teen Karoo . . ." Yinanq's damp eyes were wide, almost wild as he babbled.

Nathan sighed. "Yinanq . . ."

"I have to persuade my *práhsaedam* to come with me when I go to the Sahmudrah," the boy blurted out. He stopped, gulping.

Nathan waited. When Yinanq didn't continue, he said quietly, "I'm not so wise as you think. I don't understand what any of this has to do with me."

"I've known Jayati all my life. We grew up together, he's my only real friend," Yinanq said, his voice hoarse with the attempt to keep it steady. "I don't know anyone in the Sahmudrah Family, all of the Nga'esha kharvah there are old men. If he won't come with me, I'll be totally alone, I'll have no one."

Nathan understood. The bond between many of the marriageable men and the sahakharae, even when it wasn't sexual, was often closer than marriage. Considering the nearly hostile nature of relationships between men and women, it would have been surprising if it weren't. The strain between Yinanq and his favorite was one of simple hurt and jealousy, the irrational anger from the fear of losing a loved one. Nathan understood it well enough.

"What would it take to convince your friend?"

"A perfect gift. Hair flowers like you gave Tycar."

"But that's easy. You know where I bought them, they must have plenty more where those came from."

Yinanq shook his head. "It's true, that shop is doing an excellent business now, everyone goes there, the *saudaegar* can't keep up with the demand, and she curses your name as much as blesses it. Many others are selling hair flowers, too. But Jayati says the custom started with you. You are the expert, and only you know which are the perfect flowers, they must be as exquisite as those you gave to Tycar. He says you must choose for me, only you. . . ."

Nathan sat back on his heels. Yinanq's head drooped so low it practically touched the floor, his skin flushed a deep, mortified red.

"You know what I think?" Nathan said slowly, and smiled as Yinanq lifted his head just far enough to peek at him. "I think Jayati doesn't give a shit about the flowers." He used the Hengeli profanity, hoping that might catch on as well. "What he's doing is testing you. He knows there have been bad feelings between us, and he wants you to prove to him that you love him more than you are afraid of me. To see if you can swallow your pride enough to ask for my help."

As Yinanq blinked at him, Nathan could see he knew that already, wondering at the former rhowgha yepoqioh's incredibly dim wits. "But I still need a gift," he insisted plaintively.

"And I need to be left alone to work. What do you think will happen if I help you choose the 'right' flowers? Everyone will come to me to choose for them. I'll be plagued by a thousand others who would want the same privilege."

"Then you refuse to help me?" It was nearly a sob.

Nathan grinned. "No, I think I have a solution, and a suitable vengeance on you for calling me dirty and smelly."

Yinanq flinched, but said nothing as he listened.

Two days later, Nathan sauntered out into the men's enclosed garden and, as if by total coincidence, bumped into Yinanq and his favorite sahakharae sitting by the fountain. Several other men loitered in the sunshine, one of them idly plucking on a kapotah lute with far more skill than Nathan would ever have. Yinanq glanced up nervously as Nathan greeted them, Jayati bowing in return.

Jayati looked even younger than Yinanq, but his expression was cooler, the self-possession of someone who knew he was in control, whatever the realities of his social relation to Yinanq. He was handsome, as most sahakharae were, his face still pudgy with the roundness of baby fat not yet hardened by age, but at the moment hardened by an expression of profound dissatisfaction.

With a somewhat less than unrehearsed voice, Yinanq invited Nathan to share the sunlight on the edge of the fountain with them.

Nathan was careful to sit beside the sahakharae where he could easily see the violet flowers woven into the boy's dark braid, along with a spray of tiny gold beads. The beads were actually quite a nice touch, Nathan thought. For the several minutes of bland pleasantries he exchanged with the two boys, he kept glancing at Jayati's braid while trying not to be too obvious about it.

Finally, he paused, looked directly at the flowers and said, "Lilac."

"*Khee?*" Jayati said. *What?*

Nathan nodded at the flowers. "That's what they're called in Hengeli. I don't know the name in Vanar."

Which of course was a barefaced lie. Horticulture was the one subject in Vanar he knew better than any other. He inhaled the fragrance, then looked at Yinanq. "What a wonderful choice. Are they from you?"

Wordless, Yinanq nodded as Jayati glanced between them and fingered the braid speculatively, uncertain.

Nathan shook his head in a pose of wonder and admiration. "How much better, far more sophisticated than the simple gift I made so long ago to *my* small brother, so ingenious of you to bring perfume and beauty together. The pale violet neatly complements the Nga'esha blue. How lucky *your* small brother is to have such a talented friend in you, Yinanq. And the gold beads are truly a Vanar finesse I could never hope to match, the way they bring out the depth of the color . . ."

He carried on in this way for a few more moments before he was afraid he'd break out laughing and spoil the whole game. Yinanq looked slightly ill, but smiled wanly.

"If ever again I need to make such a gift myself, Yinanq, may I come to you for your advice?"

Yinanq nodded again, then opened his mouth. "Yes." It came out as a croak. Nathan thanked him, careful not to notice the open-mouthed eavesdroppers, and stood up to leave. He turned away, but not so quickly that he missed Jayati's hand slip onto Yinanq's knee, or Yinanq's face light up in relief.

The market value on plum blossoms plummeted sharply, while lilac became the sudden rage, along with innumerable strands of gold beads. When Yinanq made his barefoot trek to the Sahmudrah estate for inspection by his future wife's various menfolk, he had to lug enough lilac along to be smelled coming from two blocks away.

The competition for the most inventive or showiest flowers became cutthroat fierce. Nathan strolled several times past the garden, staying just far enough away to be inconspicuous and trying not to grin as Yinanq was pestered at every turn for advice on just the right color, how many cuttings were too much, which was better: lily of the valley or alyssum? Did marigolds smell good or bad, and were salpiglossis too big? Could pearls be used rather than gold? Were hair flowers only for sahakharae or could just anyone wear them?

Could even *women* wear them?

The one and only time two bitter adversaries arrived on his doorstep to settle a heated dispute, Nathan simply pleaded he had to bow to Yinanq's far superior aesthetic taste and sent them on their way. Yinanq's eyes began to have an edge of panic around them whenever Nathan spotted the boy striding rapidly through the gardens as if trying to outrun his pursuers.

A week before Yinanq's marriage, Jayati came to visit. Yinanq's práhsaedam was far more comfortable in his presence than his friend had been. After half an hour of sipping brandy-laced coffee and swapping salacious gossip about the various foibles in the Sahmudrah and Changriti Families, Jayati finally said, "I have something for you."

He carefully extracted a small silk-covered object from the folds of his sati and unwrapped it. The petals unfolded into a single huge bloodred hibiscus flower, the stem secured to the thin wire used to anchor it into a braid. A burst of jade beads hung in a cascade under the flower.

"Is this from you or Yinanq?"

"Both of us, but it was his idea." Jayati smiled, the knowing amusement belonging on a much older face. "He *is* capable of a few of his own, you know."

Nathan laughed, and had the boy help him position it into his still unimpressively short braid and wore it proudly the entire day until it wilted. Then he scandalized the men's house by showing how one could make tea from it, making the flower's color appear from the brownish infusion with a drop of lemon juice into the white porcelain cup.

That was one idea that didn't catch on.

XXVII

Nathan woke to the sound of ritual wailing, the eerie warbling carrying from the women's house like a pack of strange animals on the hunt. The hair on his arms stood up in alarm. He stepped out dressed only in his mati, the hallways in confusion, and saw the Nga'esha men standing with varying expressions of shock, silently unbraiding their hair. His heart sank as Raemik walked toward him, black hair cascading freely across his shoulders.

"What is it?" But he knew, even as he asked.

"Pratha Yaenida is dead."

Even so, it stopped his breath as much as if he'd been punched in the gut. He knew it had to happen sooner or later. But he had hoped, every day, it wouldn't be today. He stood rooted, paralyzed, as his mind spun, his first reaction fear and loss. Now that Yaenida was gone, who could he talk to, who would protect him? Guilt followed—the old woman had died and he was thinking of only himself. It didn't last long. Grief was a selfish emotion.

"You should unbind your hair," Raemik said quietly.

He nodded, his hands numb as he loosened his braid. "What happens now?" he asked, his voice shaky.

Raemik glanced over his shoulder as Nga'esha men wandered the halls, clutching each other and weeping. The boy's eyes were solemn, but dry and indifferent. "We wait. This is not a matter that concerns men." He smiled, the momentary expression caustic. "When *they* want you, you'll be sent for."

Dazed, Nathan watched the boy walk past him, suddenly aware how much Raemik had grown in the past months. The pubescent softness was almost gone, and although he walked with his sister's supreme grace, the long sinewy legs and angular shoulders were as masculine as Nathan's.

Neither he nor any other of the men was allowed at the funeral. Although none of the others had expected to be, Nathan felt the taboo like a personal slight. The sense of incompleteness left him bewildered. For two weeks, conversations in the men's house were kept at a low murmur, an air of expectation as social positions shifted into new patterns of influence and power.

Two days after the funeral, Nathan went to the men's baths late in the evening, to try to soak away some of his tension in the hot water. Lounging on the steps at one end of the pool he let his thoughts wander, as intangible as the steam floating across the surface of the water. Aelgar waded slowly toward him, emerging from the vapor, his retinue trailing like specters behind him. Nathan wiped the condensation out of his eyes before he recognized the senior kharvah and bowed over pressed palms. Aelgar did not return the ritualistic greeting.

The stocky potbellied man glared at him. "Move," he said sharply.

"Excuse me?" Nathan was confused more by the abrupt tone than the order.

"You are occupying a space I want," Aelgar said. His face twisted with hostile arrogance. "Give it to me."

Nathan blinked in surprise. "Of course, jah'nar Aelgar." He stood up, and waded through waist-deep water from the steps. As he passed Aelgar, however, his feet became tangled with someone else's. He tripped, falling face first into the water, and narrowly missed hitting his chin against the edge of the pool. He came up sputtering, unhurt, and flailed as he was suddenly shoved and again stumbled into the water.

This time, instead of trying to stand, he kicked out and swam to clear the small group. Sculling on his back, he glared, his legs churning the water in Aelgar's direction.

"Yronae dva Ushahayam ek Nga'esha is the pratha h'máy of this House now, *qanistha pautrah*," Aelgar said as he settled himself in the spot Nathan had just relinquished. The others watched Nathan expectantly.

Nathan stared back, his eyes narrowed. The senior kharvah had addressed him as the youngest son of the youngest son rather than as the brother of the pratha h'máy, the difference in rank making his intent clear.

"I am quite aware of that, *paramah shaelah*, most foremost brother-in-law," Nathan said, choosing his words carefully.

He caught the quick smirk from one of the men around Aelgar, but watched the senior kharvah's face closely.

"My daughter, Suryah, has been named as dalhitri h'máy."

Yronae had had only one kharvah when Suryah was born, Aelgar. Although her two subsequent husbands shared in the Nga'esha birthrights of her subsequent daughters, Aelgar held his high position in the men's house through his claim on his first child, not through his wife.

Nathan was suddenly sick of all the petty backbiting, the interminable jockeying, the shifts and skirmishes of Family relationships, the sad and desperate bids for precarious security held only through other people's lives.

"Lucky you, then, Aelgar dva Navamam Hadatha," he snapped. "May your wife, my *sister*, live as long and as well as my mother." For as long as he had to wait for Suryah to become the Nga'esha pratha h'máy, Aelgar would be simply a senior kharvah, not the more powerful kinship status of First Father. Nathan would remain a direct relative of the pratha h'máy, even if only through adoption.

Aelgar did not react for a long moment, then smiled thinly. "Your benefactress is gone, and Pratha Yronae does not much like you," he said with uncustomary bluntness. "I am blessed with a wife who listens to my counsel. You will need friends and supporters among us, if she even allows you to remain within the Nga'esha House."

"And what part of your anatomy do you propose I should kiss, Aelgar?" Nathan retorted, equally blunt. He was rewarded by the surprised murmurs and the flush of red on the senior kharvah's face that had nothing to do with the heat. Nathan didn't attempt to hide his anger. "The Pratha Yronae has other brothers. I am not interested in contesting them or you for position. Perhaps it is a failing of my Hengeli background, but I honestly want nothing more than to be left in peace."

Aelgar worked his teeth against his bottom lip as he listened.

"Leave me alone and do what you like. The Pratha Yronae does not listen to my opinions, and I have neither the experience nor the talent needed for running the men's house, which you have done an excellent job of in the name of my sister's father for many years." Aelgar looked both relieved and satisfied. "Listen to me carefully, Aelgar. I am not your enemy. But I swear to you, you really don't want to make me one."

Nathan stopped, breathing hard, sculling in the deep water. No one spoke in the silence, astonishment on the faces around the pool. The Vanar were not used to direct threats, preferring to hide their intentions behind innuendo and allusions. But slowly, Aelgar nodded.

"Bhraetae," he said simply. Brother. Then he relaxed, leaning back against the steps, and closed his eyes.

The conflict was over.

Nathan swam to the other end of the long pool, and hauled himself out, still quivering with anger. One of the veteran sahakharae, Margasir, waited for him impassively, already pouring oil into one palm. Nathan lay facedown, his cheek resting on crossed arms, staring across the pool at the small group around Aelgar as the muscular masseur positioned himself on Nathan's naked buttocks. The sahakharae began to knead his shoulders and back, digging strong fingers into the taut muscles. The older man grunted with disapproval.

"Relax, qanisth' aeyaesah, before I hurt you," Margasir grumbled.

Nathan grinned despite himself. "How am I the 'troublemaker,' Margasir? I was minding my own business." He winced and squeezed his eyes shut as the sahakharae's blunt fingers crushed his trapezius muscles under a viselike grip.

"We all mind our own business," the sahakharae said. "As Aelgar is minding his." They didn't speak for several minutes as the masseur worked. "I am thinking of leaving the Nga'esha House," Margasir said finally. It was not a casual statement.

"Why?" Nathan asked carefully. He felt the man shrug through the hands on his back.

"The l'amae Yaenida was a good pratha h'máy," he said. "Tolerant and often generous to sahakharae. The jah'nari Yronae is an excellent businesswoman."

Nathan analyzed the oblique statement. "Where would you go?"

"I was considering perhaps the Changriti."

Surprised, Nathan pushed up on his elbows to glance over his shoulder at the sahakharae. Grinning, the man effortlessly shoved him back down to the mat, knocking the breath out of him. "Oof!" He hesitated. "Why the Changriti?"

"I am old," Margasir said calmly. He skidded a few more inches down along Nathan's thighs to knead one hand against the small of his back, the other hand on the smaller man's neck easily pinning him to the mat. "And I have no práhsaedam here to hold me."

Nathan struggled futilely for a moment, then let himself go limp. "Get off of me, Margasir," he mumbled wearily with his face pressed into the mat.

The naked sahakharae slid off to sit beside him cross-legged, white teeth sharp in his dark, wrinkled face. Nathan rolled onto one side, leaning on his elbow. "Aelgar is right," Margasir said. "You will need friends now."

"And you know I am not interested in sahakharae."

Margasir shrugged. "I am not interested in you either, Nathan Crewe Nga'esha. You are far too ugly," he said mockingly. Then his smile dimmed. "The new *jyesth bhraetaeé* will have their own favorites, or they will look for younger men." He glanced around at the men in the baths, shrewdly calculating. "The changes here, not all will be good for me." He glanced back at Nathan, dark eyes hard. "I have lived with the Nga'esha long enough to gather those secrets best left buried. I am only Middle Family, and don't wish to return there. I've grown to like the life in the High Families. I have need for friends, too. Especially a young man of High Family who is married to the heir of another."

"As her most subordinate and least influential kharvah, Margasir," Nathan reminded him. "And I'm not exactly in high standing with my newly elevated sister, either."

Margasir chuckled. "It's high enough for me. Make me your práhsaedam, Nathan. If the Nga'esha insist you leave, take me with you when you go back to the Changriti. I am sure I will be of use to you before too long, troublesome bah'chae." He leaned over to place one incredibly powerful hand on Nathan's knee with mock seduction.

"Even if it is only to keep away less refined sahakharae who lust after your golden hair."

"You got yourself a deal," Nathan said in Hengeli. The other man did not have to understand the words to know their meaning.

XXVIII

THE NEW PRATHA YRONAE SENT FOR NATHAN TWO WEEKS AFTER PRATHA Yaenida died, the Dhikar escorting him to the Nga'esha principal court. He'd been in this huge room enough times that he shouldn't have wondered at the odd sense of déjà vu. But as he walked across the familiar polished wooden floor toward the woman he had never been able to consider a sister, he realized what was lacking. He had half expected to see Pratha Yaenida tucked into her heap of pillows on the dais, nonchalantly smoking her water pipe and chuckling wryly.

Instead, Yronae sat on the dais on a single embroidered cushion, one leg tucked under her, her arm resting across her other knee, her spine ramrod straight. Her daughter Suryah stood behind her mother, one hand resting lightly on the carved rail of the dais, her expression as rigidly austere as her mother's as he approached.

Various household taemora and Nga'esha relatives arranged themselves around the margins of the room in clusters according to their degree of privilege or seniority. He recognized most of them by name now and, more importantly, knew his own position relative to theirs down to the last *ek* and *dva*.

No one spoke as he walked toward the Pratha Yronae. It was so quiet he could hear his bare feet whispering on the burnished inlaid floor. No breeze stirred the long streamers of silk, even the tiny brass bells silent. Exactly three paces from her, he bowed over his palms before hooking the end of his sati with his ankle and kneeling with a fluid elegance he'd gained from exhaustive practice, his sati opening just enough to expose his thighs without being offensive, his hands placed precisely on bare skin, his head canted respectfully with his gaze indirect but not inattentive.

"Qanistha bhraetae, Nathan Crewe Nga'esha," she said.

"Jah'nari bhagini, pratha h'máy Yronae dva Ushahayam ek Daharanan traeyah Nga'esha." The acknowledgment of his kinship with her and ritual listing of her Family alliances came effortlessly. He felt oddly calm, knowing he'd said it flawlessly—no Vanar could have done better.

Yronae smiled and nodded her approval with the most remote of gestures, and for an elusive moment he could see Yaenida in her.

"Your daughter is soon to reach her third birthday, is she not?"

"Hae'm, pratha h'máy."

"The Nga'esha hear she is an exceptionally bright child, and as precocious as her father." He wondered if she was making a subtle criticism, but said nothing. "The House of your mothers wishes you continued good fortune with her."

"Thank you, l'amae"

The cordial exchange out of the way, Yronae put out her hand toward one of the taemora. The woman placed a reader in her palm and backed away respectfully. Yronae didn't so much as look at her.

"My mother was a most remarkable person," she said. Nathan risked glancing at her directly, unsure of her meaning. "Perhaps her personality was influenced by her extensive travels and exposure to Hengeli worlds in ways most other Vanar have difficulty understanding. She was fond of many things Hengeli, and I know she reserved great affection for you."

He had no idea how to respond to that, so remained silent. Yronae looked down at the reader in her hand. "Usually when the pratha h'máy of a great House such as the Nga'esha dies, the conventions of endowments are reasonably straightforward. However, Pratha Yaenida made certain unique provisions that the honor of this House is bound to fulfill. We have had her testament adjudicated by counsel to the Assembly of Families, and it is their determination that, while certain of these bequests may be peculiar, they are all within the ordinances of Vanar law and must therefore be complied with."

She was reading Yaenida's will, he realized. He glanced up at Suryah's glacial face, then away, wondering what on earth Yaenida had embroiled him in now, her long reach from even beyond the grave.

"As the youngest son of the late pratha h'máy, you are entitled to an increase in the lifetime percentage of the Nga'esha household revenues, as custom dictates. The net value has been adjusted from a rate of one-eighty-fifth to that of one-half of one percent per annum." She looked up from the reader and added impassively, "Not a huge improvement, I'm afraid, but you should have enough to keep your new práhsaedam in fresh hair flowers."

One half of a percent of the entire Nga'esha annual income from the Worm would do a great deal more than keep him supplied with flowers, had he been anywhere else other than Vanar, he realized. He nodded without speaking, stunned.

"Further, the Pratha Yaenida has made a special endowment for you. You are to inherit her private library."

"The library?"

"With certain provisos, of course. The contents of the library cannot be destroyed or sold off, nor any of the furnishings. As per her instructions, all monitoring devices have been removed, and the library is to remain your sole property to use however you see fit during the duration of your lifetime. Upon your death it will revert back to the Nga'esha Family." For the first time, Yronae smiled, contemptuously. "Short of burning it down, it is yours to do with what you like. However, may I suggest that any of your more unorthodox ideas such as perhaps raising goats in it might not be appropriate?"

He wasn't sure if she was actually making a joke or not. "Hae'm, pratha h'máy." he murmured absently, still absorbing the shock. "The library was monitored?" he asked.

"Of course. It isn't now. You will have complete privacy."

"Are all the rooms in the House monitored?"

Suryah didn't bother to hide her flash of irritation, but Yronae kept her face an impersonal mask. "The depth of your ignorance is a constant source of amazement to me, Nathan Crewe Nga'esha. I will never understand how my mother could find such unsophisticated and ill-mannered people so entertaining."

He knew when to shut up, willing himself back into proper Vanar etiquette, head bowed submissively.

"One thing further: no one may enter the library except in your presence or by your permission."

He blinked, astonished. "No one?"

"No one," she repeated. "Not even myself, although might I assume that as your pratha h'máy this permission is granted as a matter of course?"

He sat back on his heels, his mind whirling. "Hae'm, pratha h'máy," he said before he had thought about it. Then he added cautiously, "I would be honored to accompany you at any time you desire, jah'nari l'amae."

Her smile thinned, but without hostility. He had managed to defer to her without allowing her into the library on her own. She tilted her head in the suggestion of a bow, acknowledging his victory, then snapped the reader shut.

"That is all. You may go."

He stood and bowed, pausing briefly when one of his nieces handed him a small, ornate paper box without explanation. A brief glance back at Yronae didn't encourage him to ask questions.

Wandering out to the men's courtyard, he scanned the various men watching him expectantly, sahakharae and kharvah alike. Raemik stepped out from the portico into the bright sunlight, shading his eyes with one hand while his skin shone like ivory.

"She left me the library," Nathan told him as if no one else had been listening. Raemik didn't appear impressed.

"To do what with?"

"I don't know. Anything I like, supposedly." The men whispered to one another in puzzled surprise, as unsure as he about what this strange legacy meant. Suddenly, Nathan grinned and grabbed Raemik by the hand. "Come with me," he said, and pulled the boy along at a trot.

They ran along the corridors down to the carved door of the main wing, turning past the halls leading to the women's inner sanctum. The routine Dhikar loitering along the atrium turned, startled, but made no effort to stop him as he dodged past her and opened the doors to the library.

"Nobody can enter without my consent," he said, and waved his hand with a flourish toward the open door. "Do come in, Raemik."

The boy had never been inside the library, and ventured into the spacious room warily, as if expecting some exotic monster to jump out at him. Nathan waved cheerfully at the bemused Dhikar before he closed the door with a solid thump, making the boy jump.

"What do you do in here?" Raemik asked, puzzled.

"Work."

"Doing what?"

"Translating." He waved a hand at the thousands of antique books around them, the mere tip of the iceberg. "All this, into Hengeli."

The boy stared at him, then at the books, with genuine bewilderment. "Why?"

"Because the Pratha Yaenida said I had to."

Raemik looked around thoughtfully. "Won't that take you a long time?"

Nathan laughed. "Oh, yes, a very long time. It's an impossibly absurd Sisyphean task that will take me all the rest of my miserable life, and if I lived to be two hundred and never slept another day again, I would never see the end of it."

The boy was now regarding him with a cautious expression, as if the strange monster he suspected lurked in the shadows had transmuted itself into Nathan. "And this makes you happy?"

"No, but you really have to admire the bitch, don't you?" he said, startling Raemik.

He had used the obscene Vanar term *bich'chú*, which transposed itself quite neatly in Hengeli, he thought. "Don't you understand, Raemik? I can do anything, say anything I want here, and no one is going to stop me." He fumbled in a drawer for the meager collection of his Hengeli music cubes that had made it through Vanar's formidable censors. Raemik crouched in alarm as the opening violins of Saint-Saëns's ancient "Danse Macabre" echoed through the book stacks.

Nathan hiked his sati up around his knees to jump up onto one of the chairs, then onto the top of the massive table, and began to dance with wild extravagant abandon. As Raemik watched the crazy yepo-qioh pirouette and prance to music the boy had obviously never heard before in his life, his astonishment gave way to a slow grin.

"Come on," Nathan said, and reached down to yank the boy up to the tabletop. Together, they capered across the table with chaotic exuberance, shouting with glee and kicking ancient books and readers off with bare feet as the orchestra built to the thunderous crescendo, drums rolling, cymbals crashing, trumpets blaring, violins shrieking, the two of them laughing until tears rolled down both their faces. Nathan had never seen the boy so animated, and by the time the music finished, they were both out of breath and sweating.

He flopped down on the edge of the table, Raemik beside him, both gasping and giggling like fools. "Aren't you afraid of what Yronae will do if she catches you doing this?" Raemik asked.

Nathan began laughing again. "That's the whole point, Raemik. She won't. They took all the monitors out of the library. Yaenida has made sure I'll keep on doing the job she wanted me to by making this place my own private sanctuary. Nobody can see us or hear us, this is the one place on the entire planet that is totally mine. I can do and say anything I want here."

He watched the comprehension dawn in the boy's face. "Anything?"

"Except raise goats." He noticed the small box he'd been given in the women's hall on the floor where it had tumbled out of the folds of his sati during his mad dance. Hopping down, he retrieved it and leaned against the table to open it. Inside was a small, brown biscuit wrapped in tissue paper. He held it out toward Raemik. "What is this?"

"It's a memorial cake."

"What am I supposed to do with it?"

"You're supposed to eat it."

"Now?"

"Whenever you feel like, really."

He sniffed it doubtfully. "Why did they give it to me?"

"You're Nga'esha. Everybody gets one."

"You got one, too?"

Raemik smiled, his enigmatic expression back. "Even me."

"You've already eaten yours, I take it?"

"Last night."

The boy wasn't going to enlighten him, Nathan decided. He nibbled the edge of cake, finding it tasteless and gritty. A coarse fragment wedged itself between his back molars, resisting his efforts to dislodge it with his little fingernail. He finished off the cake with distaste, then he poured himself a glass of xerx brandy from Yaenida's private decanter to help wash down the dry biscuit. "God, that tastes like shit. You want one?" he asked, holding the decanter up toward Raemik.

The boy shook his head solemnly. "You were supposed to be remembering Pratha Yaenida when you ate it."

"Believe me," Nathan said after he'd swished the liquor around in his mouth to rinse his teeth, "I'm not likely to forget Pratha Yaenida anytime soon. I really am going to miss the old girl." Raemik ducked his head to hide the smile. "So now would you be so kind as to explain to me yet another of these inscrutable Vanar rituals?"

"From her we came. To us she returns," Raemik said simply.

The significance of the words made Nathan's stomach lurch. "Oh," he said, and looked into the now empty box in disbelief. "You mean she's actually *in* the cake?"

"Her ashes are."

"Oh, no . . ." Clapping one hand over his mouth, he swallowed hard to keep from vomiting while he quickly poured himself another glass of brandy. He managed to keep it down, barely.

He discovered an interesting fact he had never been aware of before: there were no cemeteries on Vanar.

XXIX

AFTER FIRST CONSULTING HIS WIFE, AELGAR FINALLY GRANTED Nathan permission to build a greenhouse at the far end of the estate where he had already established his garden plot. He was allowed the use of a single garden drone, the barely sentient machine doing the arduous labor of lifting heavy stones into place for the last of the foundation walls while Nathan struggled with mixing enough mortar to keep up with it. Three walls had already been completed, the framing in place and waiting for the large partitions of paned pseuquartz lying on the grass to be erected.

The sahakharae had been briefly interested in all the activity, once he'd explained he could grow different species of flowers inside. Most lost interest and wandered off after he'd enthused about trying to raise the svapnah he still longed to decipher. But his rambling lectures on modified pseudo-sporophyllous leaves and xenoamphicribral tissue development didn't much interest many of the sahakharae. Other than Raemik, who he suspected would have been just as devoted had Nathan been a fanatic sewage engineer, he rarely had much of an audience.

Today, however, Raemik had disappeared again while one of the younger sahakharae had decided to sit on the grass, arms around his knees, and watch Nathan work. A small lute lay beside him, strings gleaming in the sunlight.

The door frame had already been constructed, a large stone plinth in place. While the drone went back for another load of stone for the back wall, Nathan examined the glassless door on the ground, then glanced at the sahakharae.

"You want to give me a hand here . . . ? He struggled to recall the boy's name. The one always busy making up songs, was all he could think of.

"Qim."

"Qim."

Between the two of them, Nathan got the bare door hung and balanced on the hinges.

"How did you learn to do this?" Qim asked.

Nathan chuckled. "I wasn't always a Nga'esha." He gauged the boy shrewdly. "Are you really interested, or are you only here pretending as a means to an end?"

Qim smiled, most of the sahakharae long habituated to Nathan's directness. "I will pretend to be interested, if you will pretend to believe me."

Nathan dusted his hands off on the pair of makeshift work shorts he'd sewn himself, plenty of pockets bulging with spare tools and hardware. "Never mind. Is there something I could do for you, Qim?"

The sahakharae's eyes shifted, his manner subtly altered in a manner Nathan recognized. The Vanar found it damned difficult to come out with a simple request. Nathan groaned inwardly, hoping whatever convoluted circuit Qim used to arrive at his purpose would be shorter than usual.

"Everyone has remarked on what a strange legacy the old pratha h'máy left you."

After a beat, Nathan said without enthusiasm, "Uh-huh. Look, do you mind if I work while we talk?"

"No, please. It would be an honor to watch and learn from you. Perhaps I might play something to make it more pleasurable for you?"

"Sure, whatever." Nathan had already stepped over the plinth to examine the door, engrossed in lifting the first quarter of glass into the frame and tapping small nails into the wood to anchor it in place. The costly pseuquartz glass was as unbreakable as steel, and although Nathan didn't worry about stray blows from his hammer, habit made him wince in reflex.

The boy fine-tuned the strings on the lute for a moment before he began picking out an intricate melody. After Nathan had the fourth quarter of glass tacked into place, he paused to listen, baffled. The sahakharae drummed his thumb and little finger on different areas of the wooden lute to keep a rhythm as the rest of his fingers danced over the strings, creating the sense of more than one instrument.

Qim glanced up to gauge the effect, then back at his hands with a satisfied look. When he finished, he set the lute on the grass beside him, leaned back, and waited confidently for Nathan's reaction.

"You're very good," Nathan said.

"Thank you."

"It sounds familiar."

Qim looked down at the lute, toying with the strings idly. "I don't know why it should. You never listen to me when I play music in the men's garden." The boy's tone wasn't reproachful, nor, did it seem, was he making any sly sexual approach. Farce as it might be, Nathan and Margasir had declared themselves in an exclusive arrangement, and the young sahakharae wasn't likely to trespass. Whatever Qim wanted from Nathan, he wasn't after that sort of rapport.

"Yes, I do," Nathan said, drawn into the verbal game despite himself. He took a roll of malleable caulk out of his workbox and began pressing it into place. "And that's not the sort of music you usually play."

The sort of music Qim usually played was geared to pleasing Pratha Yronae and her coterie, who preferred the elaborately pretty if bland music popular with many Vanar women. Then he recognized where he'd seen Qim before.

"I wrote that piece myself. Did you like it?" Qim asked.

"You've played in the kaemahjah, haven't you? You and your friends." He remembered the quartet of flute and dulcimer, lute and drum, and where he'd last heard Qim play. And who he'd been with. And what they'd been doing. His hands fumbled with the caulk, and he paused, closing his eyes for a moment until the ache went away.

Qim watched him curiously. "Sometimes. Although you have not come to listen to us in a long time."

Not since his marriage. Not since Pratima had left. "No, I haven't." Nathan resumed caulking the glass with determined concentration. "What do you want, Qim?" he asked impassively, and wished now the boy would go away and leave him in peace.

"Raemik says you play Hengeli music in your library."

Nathan pressed the caulk into the gap, his thumb leaving an undulating pattern. "He does, does he?" he said with overt skepticism. Raemik spoke to very few people, and Nathan knew he especially avoided sahakharae. "And he's told you this himself?"

To his credit, the boy had the grace to look chagrined. "Not . . . personally. But I have never heard Hengeli music before. I would very much like to hear some."

"I'll be happy to lend you a few cubes." He took a putty knife from a pocket in his overalls and trimmed the caulk, the excess curling away in neat corkscrews. He glazed the rest of the door in silence, aware that the sahakharae remained where he was. When he'd finished, he swung the door open and closed experimentally to inspect the balance, and was satisfied.

The drone returned with the final load of stone, hooked itself into the small mixer for the mortar, and resumed constructing the back wall. Nathan cut open another bag of dry cement and poured it into the mixer, the drone measuring the proper amount of water itself. He shook his head, fine powder dusting his skin and hair, then glanced in irritation at the sahakharae still watching him silently.

"Is there anything else you wanted?" Nathan said crossly.

"Have I offended you in some way, jah'nar bhraetae? Is my music unpleasant to your ear?"

The boy seemed genuinely anxious, which only fueled Nathan's exasperation. "No, Qim. Your music is . . . I like your music. It just reminds me of . . . someone."

"Ah," Qim said quietly. Nathan continued working while the sahakharae sat cross-legged on the ground, watching. After several minutes of silence, he said, "You should come back to the kaemahjah. It isn't good to love anyone so much, Nathan Nga'esha, especially not a woman."

"I hardly need advice on love from a damned sahakharae," Nathan snapped. "And you have neither the age nor the experience to justify it."

Nathan would have welcomed a quarrel, but instead the sahakharae swallowed, visibly shaken. Hands together and pressed to his forehead in the most deferential fashion, he bowed in contrition. "You are of course entirely correct. Please forgive my presumption, jah'nar Nga'esha, I meant no offense."

Nathan's shoulders slumped in defeat. "Forget it, Qim, it's . . . not a problem. I'm touchy about foolish things." The boy straightened uncertainly. "If you want to come by my room later on tonight, I'll lend you whatever takes your interest."

Qim bowed again, this time with ordinary courtesy, and got to his feet. "Thank you. I will be honored." Nathan didn't watch him go.

He continued the work on his greenhouse, expending his anger on hard exertion, stopping only when it became too dark.

It wasn't Qim who showed up that evening, however, but Margasir who appeared in the doorway waiting to be noticed and invited in.

"*Yahaem ayo,*" Nathan said, surprised as he took the soundpearl out of his ear. He had been listening to some of his Hengeli music to decide which the boy might like.

Margasir came in, bowed his thanks as Nathan waved him to sit down. Even with his new práhsaedam, he had to follow the usual Vanar ritual of sipping liberally spiked coffee and commenting on innocuous subjects until the sahakharae got around to the point. Margasir, thankfully, knew how little patience Nathan had with formality and kept it to a minimum.

"I had a chat with one of my protégés this afternoon."

"'Protégés'?" Nathan grinned. "Is this where I throw a temper tantrum to protest my jealousy?"

Margasir at least smiled at Nathan's attempt at a joke. "No. This is where I prove myself as useful to you as I promised I would be. You may not realize it, being only an ignorant yepoqioh naeqili, but you've managed to attract a práhsaedam with a distinguished reputation. Families with promising boys engage me to train them to become sahakharae. Every one of my protégés has gone on to find placement in the High Families. You know this one. Qim, the musician?"

Nathan grimaced. "And no doubt he complained to you about what an uncivilized ill-mannered yepoqioh naeqili I am."

"Actually, no. He's come to me at a much older age than I usually teach, and still has much to learn. He told me he had offended you, and wished to be instructed in how to make amends." Margasir laughed ruefully. "I didn't tell him I have absolutely no idea. If you were Vanar-born, I would know. But if you were Vanar-born, the question would never have come up in the first place."

Nathan leaned back against one of the floor pillows scrunched behind him against the wall and rested his arm over one raised knee. Here, in the privacy of his own room, he preferred comfort to tradition. Likewise, Margasir copied Nathan's more casual pose, although he looked far less at ease with it.

"I wish people would learn that it's much easier for me to offend them than for them to offend me. He didn't offend me. All he wanted was to borrow some music cubes. And being Vanar-born, of course, he couldn't just come straight out and ask for it, he had to play childish games first."

Margasir frowned disapprovingly. "Childish? It might interest you to know that Qim is seven years older than you."

"Qim? But he's just a boy!"

"He's had the best regenerative therapy from a very young age. Of course, his Family could afford it. Qim's full name is Qim dva Daharanan Changriti."

Nathan's jaw dropped. "He's Changriti?"

Margasir raised an eyebrow and smiled. "Son of the late Changriti pratha h'máy's grandniece."

Nathan absorbed this. "What the hell's a Changriti son doing becoming a sahakharae?"

"Ah, now that's an interesting story." Something in the sahakharae's tone told Nathan he wasn't likely to enjoy it. "Some years ago, Qim met a woman from a very badly positioned Common Family. They were both promising music students and fell madly in love. Now had Qim simply obeyed his Family and married the High Family woman selected for him, he and the girl could have remained lovers and no one would have objected. But he was foolish. He refused, insisting he would marry only her. To prevent such an unprofitable marriage, the Changriti made her family a lucrative offer arranging for the girl to be transferred to one of their more remote stations off-world, out of the way. Her family was delighted with such an excellent deal. The girl was not."

Nathan shook his head in sympathy.

"As it was, she never left Sabtú. Before the contract could be finalized, she killed herself. After that, there was no reason for the Changriti to pay off the contract. And rather than yielding to his Family's will, Qim took his revenge by becoming sahakharae, which makes him worthless to the Changriti. Naturally, they disowned him. If the old Pratha Yaenida had not offered him a place here as sahakharae, Qim would now be naekulam. So you see, Nathan Crewe Nga'esha, Qim dva Daharanan Changriti does indeed have both the age and the experience to justify offering you well-meant advice."

Nathan stared at him for a long moment before his shoulders slumped in defeat. "Shit," he said wearily in Hengeli.

"In any case," Margasir went on, "it was never Qim's intent to offer you advice. He wished simply to impress you with his music in the hope you might allow him to listen to your Hengeli music."

"Once again, it seems I'm the one who needs to be making amends, not Qim. So. Any suggestions how I fix this?" Somehow, he doubted another offering of hair flowers would suffice.

Margasir shrugged. "You are the son of a pratha h'máy. Qim is only a very minor sahakharae. And since it was he who offended you—"

"Damn it, I've told you he *didn't* offend me—"

"Since *he* offended *you*," Margasir insisted, interrupting Nathan's protest, "a gracious man would allow him the opportunity to offer an apology. Might I suggest a suitable place for this might be in the privacy of your library?"

The library. Qim had also mentioned the library. "Of course."

"Good," Margasir said with satisfaction. "Now, having demonstrated how valuable a práhsaedam you are incredibly lucky to have acquired, I humbly ask a small favor of you."

"Anything . . ."

"Please be so kind as to groan ecstatically and tell me how fantastic I am in a very loud voice." Margasir grinned wickedly at Nathan's astonishment, adding, "Other ears are listening, and I *do* have my reputation to consider. Who will send their sons to me if I can't please even one very ugly, barbaric yepoqioh?"

Nathan laughed. "Get out of here, you old fraud."

XXX

HE HAD LEARNED TO RECOGNIZE THE INDIVIDUAL DHIKAR ASSIGNED TO stand watch outside his library by the way each of them knocked on the door. The Dhikar, unaccustomed to either locked doors or knocking to gain admission, had developed their own style of announcing visitors. He'd nicknamed the one who tentatively patted the door with her palm so lightly he nearly couldn't hear it Flutterfly. Heavy Hand Hannah bludgeoned the door so hard he always started, and didn't stop until he'd opened it. This time it was Two-Knock, the one who rapped on the wood with two distinctly spaced blows as solemn as announcing death itself. If any of them had real names, Nathan had never been able to discover them.

He opened the door and bowed courteously to Two-Knock, who nodded gravely back at him and allowed Qim past her.

The musician looked around curiously as Nathan shut the door, then asked, in nearly the same puzzled tone as had Raemik, "What do you do here?"

"Depends." Nathan settled into the massive chair once belonging to Pratha Yaenida, sprawling casually. This was his inner sanctum, and he refused to obey Vanar protocol here. Qim's eyes widened, but he said nothing, still standing politely with his hands clasped in front of him, head slightly bowed in proper sahakharae fashion. "I'm supposed to be translating it all into Hengeli, but mostly I just rummage through the archives for anything related to botany. Most of the rest is boring crap anyway, and I haven't the patience for it. Would you please sit down and relax?"

Startled, Qim sat down in one of the chairs around the table so hurriedly Nathan nearly laughed. The sahakharae took a breath and began, "I asked your práhsaedam, my revered teacher, for guidance on how best to offer my apologies—"

"Yes, I know," Nathan said, cutting him off. "Apology accepted, forget it ever happened." The boy blinked, taken aback. "Look, Qim, I'm just an uncivilized yepoqioh. I can't stand all these elaborate formalities, they drive me crazy. If you really want to offer me an apology, the best one would be to come straight out with whatever it is you wanted in the first place."

Qim lowered his gaze to his hands clutched in his lap. "I only wanted to hear what Hengeli music sounds like."

"Okay." He opened the antique coffer where he kept his collection, scanning through the titles. "Although there's no such thing as one Hengeli style. It's not like Vanar, where there's only one people, one language, one culture. There's many different kinds of people with their own language and their own music on Hengeli."

"Why?" Qim seemed genuinely baffled.

Taken aback, Nathan floundered. "Well . . . because it's Hengeli. It's where we all originated from, so they've had many thousands of years of history behind them. . . ." He studied the boy carefully. "They don't teach you much non-Vanar history here, do they?"

"No. What do we need it for?"

"Right," Nathan said, unable to think of an appropriate answer. "Anyway, it's all different, and what I have doesn't even come close to a full spectrum. I'm not allowed to import anything modern, meaning anything less than about a hundred years old. So mostly all I have is very ancient classical because that's what Vanar Customs authorities consider 'safe.'"

"Is it? Safe?"

Nathan looked up sharply. Qim's face was as bland as his voice, but his eyes didn't blink. "Some of it. We Hengeli also wrote a lot of pretty music designed to do nothing but please pretty girls. Is that what you'd like to hear?"

Qim shrugged one shoulder noncommittally. "If that's all you have."

Nathan smiled. "No," he said carefully. "But without knowing what you'd like or not, I'll just try a few things at random, okay?"

Mahler bored him. Wagner shocked him. Paganini confused him. Vivaldi entranced him. African Industrial Retro Wave excited him. Japanese Nouveau Zen music lulled him. Old Colonial music made him wince. But his favorite was Celtic jazz. Qim drew out a small felt bag from where he kept it tied under his sati and slid two small wooden flutes from it. Picking up one, he experimentally blew several running notes, following the long-dead musicians who had recorded the cube centuries ago. Then he caught the melody, his foot tapping a rhythm to the bodhran drums, closed his eyes, and played.

The boy was good. More than just good, Nathan realized, watching him sway with the music, oblivious as his fingers skimmed across the flute effortlessly. But while he played, Nathan picked up the other flute, examining it with intense interest. The surface was as burnished as copper, smooth and warm to the touch.

The music finished, and Qim opened his eyes, caught Nathan holding his other flute, and smiled.

"Do you make these?"

Qim nodded.

"It's not bamboo."

"No." When he didn't continue, Nathan held it up questioningly. "The proper sort of bamboo is too hard for me to get," Qim continued. "It all has to come from off-world, and I can't afford it. Anymore." Not as a novice sahakharae rather than a high-ranked Changriti, Nathan understood.

"This is native wood."

Qim nodded again.

"Where did you get it?"

Now the boy's narrow eyes shifted around at the books, cautious. "It's said the monitors were taken out of the library."

"Yes."

"How do you know?"

Nathan laughed. "For sure? I don't. I have only Pratha Yronae's word for it." When Qim's expression didn't change, he added, "She's a hard-hearted bitch, but I trust her."

Shocked, Qim gasped. "Aren't you afraid of saying things like that?" he asked once he'd recovered.

"If she is listening, then she'd reveal herself a liar and deserves what she hears. This is the one place I have ever been able to speak my mind. The old pratha knew how important that was to me."

Qim considered this, then said slowly, "I'm not sure that is a good habit to become accustomed to."

"Neither am I. Where did you get the wood?"

Taking the flute from Nathan, Qim concentrated on replacing them in the felt bag before he answered, keeping his eyes averted. "I can show you." So much left unspoken in those few words, Nathan knew.

"When?"

"Tomorrow night." He looked up, dark eyes enigmatic. "Pratha Yronae knows, of course. The old pratha never objected, but our new one . . ." He shrugged again.

After a moment, Nathan said, "Knows . . . what?"

But Qim's ingrained caution was too strong, regardless of the library's privacy. He stood, tucking the bag back under his sati. "Tomorrow night."

Nathan spent much of the next day working on his greenhouse, but with his mind distracted, oddly cheered by the mystery. He had barely started his dinner sitting under the ancient maple in the men's garden when Qim passed him, nodded without expression, and walked on. Still chewing his last mouthful, Nathan abandoned the rest of his meal and hurried after the boy.

He was not the only one aware of the gap in the men's garden wall, he discovered, absurdly resentful his secret was shared. But rather than follow the path down to the old tree by the river, Qim turned along the ridge of the hill, walking straight for a thicket of compact shrubs Nathan had thought impassable. That weren't. But without his guide, he quickly realized, he'd never be able to navigate this maze a second time. At one point, they had to crawl on hands and knees through a cave in sheer rock, water dripping from tiny stalactites overhead. Not normally claustrophobic, Nathan was grateful all the same to reemerge out the other side. He stood, his sati soaking wet, and glanced up at the crude figure of a blank-faced woman chiseled out of the rock face, the cave entrance between her distorted legs.

Qim quickly peeled off his dripping sati and hung it over a branch where several dozen other sati fluttered in the twilight breeze. All he wore underneath was an unbleached linen mati, as did many sahakharae, his connection with the Changriti long severed. Most of the sati hanging from the branches were Nga'esha blue. A few colors from other High Families dotted the trees, as well as a sprinkling from Middle Families.

"You won't need it," he said to Nathan as he quickly loosened his hair from the intricate braid, discarding beads and flowers and bracelets. While Nathan stripped off his own sati, Qim's fingers raked his hair back and tied it off at the nape of his neck. As fine as a Persian cat's tail, it seemed to float down the young man's back, the simplicity almost erogenous.

They made their way in the growing dusk to a clearing in the forest where, Nathan's botanical eye noticed with excitement, imported trees stood side by side with their odder indigenous counterparts. A small gathering of about fifty men chatted quietly but fell silent as he followed Qim into the middle of the clearing where several large drums had been erected, other musical instruments assembled around them.

Strangely, Nathan realized, no one bowed in the Vanar custom he now had to fight not to reflexively perform himself. Qim avoided their mute reproach as he inspected the drums with minute care. Although Nathan had long been used to being stared at, the silence was unnerving.

An older, muscular man elbowed his way through the crowd, totally naked but for glistening wet body paint, his adornment having been interrupted, by the incomplete look of it. He glared at Nathan, dark eyes hard, before he turned to Qim. Neither spoke, nor did Qim look up, still engrossed in examining the drums. Finally, the man frowned, snorted in disgust, and turned away without a word. But Nathan didn't miss how the young sahakharae briefly closed his eyes and exhaled with relief.

The tension in the crowd diminished. Murmured conversation resumed while newcomers continued to arrive, each one startled to see him in their midst, then pointedly ignoring him. Nathan gave up trying to smile reassuringly and found a fallen log at the edge of the clearing where he could sit at a remove as merely a visiting observer.

A small bonfire had been assembled, more branches being pulled out of the shelter of the forest, native and imported wood stacked equally onto the growing pile. By the time the sky had darkened to true night, stars winking into existence, enough firewood had been accumulated. The fire several people tended finally caught, yellow fingers of flame delicately exploring the branches. The crowd continued to grow, many of them other musicians bringing their own instruments.

One of them, to Nathan's surprise, was a woman dressed in a simple white mati similar to Qim's. Without her sati, he had no way of telling which, if any, of the High Families she was from. Which, he realized, looking around, was true of just about everyone there. She spoke briefly to Qim, and shot a startled look in Nathan's direction, seeing him for the first time. As he had the painted man, Qim avoided her eyes as they talked. The woman shrugged one shoulder, then shook out a long wooden flute of her own. She and the boy ran through a series of riffs, comparing tunes, and Nathan smiled when he recognized a fragment he knew Qim had adapted from the Celtic jazz cube he'd heard only the day before. The woman listened intently, and within seconds, she had caught the melody, her fingers skimming across the flute effortlessly. Another young man joined them, a small mandolinlike instrument in hand, and inside a minute, he too had grasped the unusual music, grinning in delight. Their easy companionship made Nathan feel even more the outsider. Then Qim shot a quick glance at him with a flash of a smile, and his isolation seemed less lonely.

At some signal Nathan couldn't discern, Qim settled behind the drums as his friends stepped back into the crowd, vanishing. The boy's fingers began rolling a quiet rhythm against the taut skins, an expectant hush settling over the people gathered in the clearing. As Nathan admired the complexity of the tempo, an eerie, low rumble echoed back from the hidden depths of the trees, making the hairs on his arms prickle. A bass lute answered from another corner of the darkness, then other instruments Nathan couldn't identify joined in. Qim's eyes closed, and he rocked his body in time to the music that seemed to surround the clearing from every angle.

"You can't talk about this to anyone," a quiet voice said next to his ear, startling him. He turned to the woman who had played the flute with Qim. She crouched beside him, her flute balanced across her knees. Up close, he realized she was younger than he'd first thought. "Qim didn't tell you that, did he?"

"No. He didn't actually tell me much of anything, except that Pratha Yronae knows about it already."

The girl frowned. "Of course. Or we could never be here at all." She shrugged. "The old pratha h'máy first allowed it, but for how long the new one will permit us to continue, who can say? Many of the other Nine Families don't approve. But if it isn't spoken about, it doesn't officially exist."

"Who are you?" he asked, curious.

"Here?" She smiled. "No one." She lifted the flute to her mouth and, the firelight glittering in her eyes, joined her voice to those already playing, stepping back into the anonymity of the night shadows.

The music grew, the energy building until it rolled a tension in Nathan's chest. This was nothing like the innocuous, thin music popular with most Vanar—or at least with Vanar women. This music was rougher, with a power and electricity he'd never heard any Vanar play before. Just as the intensity seemed to build toward a climax, a sudden loud howling behind him made him duck in reflex.

A dozen painted dancers leapt over him, naked but for bizarre masks over their faces. He fell off his seat, arms flung protectively over his head, then caught sight of Qim's laughing face beyond the fire. He grinned ruefully as he realized he was the target of the joke, and joined in the clapping as the dancers began.

The last fading blush of sunset had vanished, the night sky filled with stars. With only the bonfire to illuminate them, the painted dancers took on a surreal appearance. Firelight shone on their bodies, cast their muscles in gold, their shadows wavering like wild animals through the trees.

The drumbeat magnified, and it took Nathan several minutes before he realized they were playing with their own echoes bouncing off cliff walls. It rumbled through the trees in a passable resemblance to thunder, distant and menacing.

If he had been anywhere else, he would have thought the dancers aboriginals, remnants of prehistoric tribes dancing to appease their hostile gods. As it was, the decades spent in training gave them an acrobatic skill and sophisticated choreography all of their own, the distinctive Vanar style shining through even this most unorthodox expression of their art.

He started again when the musicians and spectators alike began to chant, everyone obviously familiar with this particular song. As they chanted the words, the dancers stamped their feet while the audience beat the ground with sticks or fists, pounding the rhythm of the verse with a fierce energy.

"We are *men!*" The refrain resonated around him, driving the dancers. "We are *men!* We are *strong! We* plow the earth, *we* sow the seed! We are *men!*" The ferocity of feeling around him both excited Nathan and alarmed him. He could well see why this ritual, if not a secret, would be a private matter. Even the woman who had been playing with Qim chanted the words with equal vigor, her flute forgotten, her eyes half shut, her body rocking to the drum beat filling the air, building to an unbearable crescendo. "Feel us, feel our spirit, feel our courage, we are the rain storm, we are the thunder, we are *life*, we are *men!*"

The music reached its peak, and abruptly ended, the dancers frozen with their hands thrust into the air, the last drumbeat echoing off the cliff like spent thunder. The sudden silence was as powerful as the boisterous music had been, his ears still ringing, the only sound the breathing of winded dancers and the crackle of the fire. Then the spectators and dancers alike leapt to their feet in a wild cheer of appreciation, orgasmic in intensity.

Qim pushed his way through the tumultuous crowd, his face shining with sweat and joy. "Did you like it?" he demanded, shouting to be heard over the clamor.

"Is it yours?" Nathan asked.

"Yes! 'Thunder in the Mountains'! Did you like it?"

Nathan grinned and nodded. He liked it. He liked it a lot. And he knew why women like Eraelin Changriti would not, this music dangerously subversive.

The girl appeared behind Qim, slipping her hand around his waist. He threw his arm around her shoulder with an affection that went beyond simple friendship. Whoever she was, Qim loved her. They disappeared back into the crowd as new musicians took their place. The revelry went on well into the night. Only when the sky began to lighten with the coming dawn did the music give way to a softer, sadder style, people drifting away until the final musician tucked his flute into his belt and made his way back to where the last few sati hung in the tree branches.

Nathan followed Qim back to the men's house. They slipped into their beds before the rest of the house had woken up for the day, catching an hour or so of sleep.

There are many things about our men you know little of, he heard Yaenida saying, almost able to conjure her image behind drowsy eyelids. *Open your mind as well as your eyes. Vanar men don't think of themselves as oppressed; they consider themselves cherished and protected by the Eternal Mother.*

She had known about these performances, and he wondered if she had ever actually seen one. Somehow, he couldn't quite picture Yaenida crawling through a damp cave tunnel and out between the Eternal Mother's legs. Vanar men might well have considered themselves cherished and protected, but until they could sing "Thunder in the Mountains" proudly, in public, without fear, Nathan knew they would always be oppressed.

Even asleep, Nathan could feel the beat of the drums, his entire body still vibrating, and smiled in his dreams, deeply satisfied.

XXXI

"Nathan Crewe Nga'esha?"

He'd been standing in the men's section of the platform waiting for the next train and quietly minding his own business, skimming through the news headlines on his reader. A dozen or so others queued randomly around him, each of them either browsing their own readers or chatting idly with companions. They all looked up, startled by a woman's voice.

"Hae'm l'amae?" he said warily with a cursory bow. The rest of his fellow passengers drifted prudently away from them.

Judging by the unexceptional style of her sati, she was Middle Family, respectable but far from wealthy. Slim and well-built, she was nearly tall enough to look him directly in the eyes, had he not kept his attention focused over her shoulder. Oddly enough, he noticed, she had trouble keeping her own gaze on him and fidgeted nervously.

"May I speak with you for a moment, please?" Her voice shook, and her face was bloodless. She was more than anxious, he realized. She was terrified, which made him all the more guarded.

"About what, if you will pardon my discourtesy for asking?"

"Roses."

"Excuse me, l'amae?"

"Roses." It came out as barely a squeak. She ran the tip of her tongue over her lips, then blurted, "I have heard you appreciate gardens, and are quite knowledgeable about cultivation. I have a garden, a small one, but which is said to be one of the better private gardens on Vanar. I would like to invite you to my garden as my *mehmaen koshah*, treasured guest." She gulped, then bowed to him in embarrassment, astonishing him. When she straightened, she looked as if she was about to weep.

Instead of attempting to reassure her, he stepped back, wariness now turning to alarm. If she were interested in striking up a more intimate liaison, she would have come to the kaemahjah he had begun to frequent again after the dance in the forest whenever he wanted to escape the pressures of either of his two Houses. Whatever this was about, it smelled like trouble.

"Deepest apologies, l'amae, but I was trained as a research botanist, not a horticulturist," he said. Then added with carefully restrained anger, "And while under other circumstances I would be flattered by such an invitation to see one of the better gardens of Vanar, I doubt the Nga'esha pratha h'máy would approve of my consorting privately with an utter stranger." There. If this was either a test or a trap, Nathan was determined to sidestep it.

Quaking, her eyes damp, she turned as if to bolt, faltered, and turned to him again. "My name is Daegal dva Pakaran," she said, her voice so hoarse he nearly couldn't hear her. "My husband's brother-in-law is second cousin to Margasir dva Saenusi. He said I should make the invitation."

"Margasir, my práhsaedam? He suggested you speak to me?"

"Hae'm jah'nar bhraetae." She bowed again, this time so abjectly even the men standing at a remove whispered. "Our family is far from as illustrious as the Nga'esha, but Margasir Saenusi has said you are not at all arrogant." Taken aback, Nathan blinked in surprise. "My family owns an agricultural business, we raise *dhumah* wheat for the local wholesale market. Margasir said I should tell you this as you are very educated in the science of plants. Although I apologize if I have presumed such a humble enterprise might be of interest to an eminent Nga'esha."

He remembered his long-ago thwarted expedition into the rolling agricultural fields beyond the city limits, and even after he had become Nga'esha, he had never dared to visit them again.

"Actually," he said slowly, "that interests me very much."

She stopped shaking as her jaw dropped. "It *does*?" Then she resumed trembling so hard her teeth chattered.

He backpedaled quickly, still cautious. "Of course, I will first speak with Margasir, as well as confer with my household h'máy for her consent. But if it is possible, I would be honored to accept your invitation. When would you like me to come?"

"Whenever you choose, jah'nar Nga'esha."

"Tomorrow afternoon?"

She nodded mutely, staring pop-eyed at him.

After a moment he prompted, "I'd need an address."

"Margasir knows where we live."

Of course.

The train arrived, soundless but for the whisper of displaced air. He bowed to her quickly, and left her standing on the platform looking after him with a dumbfounded expression.

Margasir stopped churning lengths in the Nga'esha men's pool when Nathan threw one of the children's polo balls at his head to gain his attention. The big sahakharae shook water and hair from his eyes, grinned, and swam toward the edge, powerful muscles making short work of the distance.

"Is this all you ever do, Margasir? Exercise?"

The sahakharae hauled his massive torso out of the water far enough to rest his chin against his folded arms on the pool's edge. "I must work hard if I ever hope to attract a patron better looking than you, Nathan Nga'esha."

"Mm-hm. Do you know a woman named Daegal dva Pakaran?"

Margasir's eyes widened and he laughed, then launched himself backward, splashing Nathan as he sculled out into the water. "You may make me rich after all," the sahakharae said. "That scrawny excuse of a kharvah of hers bet me she'd never manage to work up the nerve. So. When are we invited to see this magnificent garden of hers?"

Amitu wasn't nearly as scrawny as Margasir had made him out to be, but the couple was definitely, by Vanar standards, a very odd mix indeed. Daegal was unbelievably shy while the single kharvah she had married was as gregarious as his brother-in-law's second cousin. The two men clearly had been friends for a long time, greeting each other at the entrance to the Pakaran home with hearty affection.

It was the first time in all the years Nathan had been on Vanar that he'd seen anything other than the poverty of the charity shelter or the luxurious wealth of the High Families. The Pakaran lived in a modest bungalow adjacent to their agricultural fields, large sun-washed rooms tastefully decorated and comfortable and filled with several generations of the Pakaran extended family, both sexes mingling freely together. All of them were awesruck by the blond Nga'esha bowing and smiling in their midst.

Amitu conducted him into the family's main room, keeping up a constant flow of chatter as he directed Nathan to sit on the best divan, by the room's panoramic windows. Nathan had to admit the view of their agricultural fields stretching away toward the native forest on the far horizon was quite impressive. When Daegal sat on a matching divan across from Nathan, her kharvah knelt in effortless Vanar fashion at her feet, looking far more poised than his wife. Daegal's grandfather arrived with a tray of coffees for everyone, tiny cups of the aromatic brew. Margasir, as Nathan's práhsaedam, stood behind him and took a cup from the elderly man to serve Nathan himself.

Inured to Vanar etiquette, Nathan waited politely for Daegal to speak first. After a long, uncomfortable silence, he realized she wasn't likely to do so any time soon. He cleared his throat, gazed down into the coffee wondering how to bypass this obstacle, then looked up at Margasir questioningly. The sahakharae merely raised an eyebrow, as good as a shrug.

"So. How much land does your family farm here?" Nathan asked innocently as if unaware of this breach of protocol.

Daegal gulped, paled, and remained mute. Amitu glanced up at her, smiled benignly, and placed his hand in her lap. She clung to it like a lifeline, her knuckles white.

"One thousand, three hundred and fifty-two hectares," Amitu said, completely at ease. "Although not all of that is dedicated to raising dhumah wheat. That's our main income crop, but we cultivate several hectares of vegetables. Some is for the family use, but we also produce enough to supply five local shopkeepers with fresh vegetables all year round." He looked up affectionately at his wife, giving her just enough time to nod in frantic agreement before he continued. "We put in a fruit orchard seven years ago. Except for the year when rust disease nearly wiped out our crop, that's provided us with enough fruit to sell at a decent profit to a xerx brandy distillery. My wife converted fifty hectares to growing several varieties of wine grapes three years ago, and we've just started bottling our own wine. We haven't sold any commercially yet, but it isn't too bad, if you'd like to try some?"

"I'd like that very much," Nathan said.

Amitu beckoned to a pair of twin boys of about twelve standing timidly by the doorway. "Kael? Would you please go ask your aunt Sabir to give you the special bottle from the cellar for our esteemed guest?"

"The one with the red label?" The boy's voice was nearly inaudible.

"That's the one, love. Xaenus, you fetch the glasses, please."

"Yes, Papa." The twin was nearly as reserved as his brother.

Their parents watched attentively as the twins returned with exquisitely handblown glasses and a bottle of dark red wine. They had obviously been dressed in their best sati, and with choreographed precision, the boys knelt in front of Nathan. While one twin held the glass, his brother poured with meticulous care. The glass wobbled slightly, and Nathan noticed Amitu's wince; not from chagrin but because his wife's grip had suddenly clamped painfully onto his hand. The boys glanced at her anxiously. Her husband gently disengaged her grip, stroking her fingers to encourage her to relax.

A small girl of around four wandered in from the wide porch outside, thumb in her mouth as she cuddled against her mother and stared at him with wide-eyed suspicion. After they had served Nathan and Margasir, the twins brought a glass each for their parents, rewarded with radiant smiles for their efforts.

The Nga'esha stocked only the most outstanding wines Vanar had to offer as well as importing the finest from off-world. While it wasn't the best wine Nathan had ever tasted, the Pakaran had produced a decently substantial, earthy vintage. He complimented it and wished Daegal success whenever they brought it to market. The woman merely stared at him, having not uttered a single word since he arrived. Her husband didn't seem to notice, making up for his wife's verbal shortcomings.

After much polite small talk, Amitu said, "Which would you prefer to see first, our field operations, or my wife's garden?"

While dodging the pitfalls of Vanar customs had never been Nathan's strong suit, it had at least taught him a certain amount of tactful diplomacy. "Naturally, your fields. I much prefer to save the best for last."

Not even this managed to elicit a sound from her, but Daegal blushed, pleased, while her husband grinned. Amitu stood when his wife did. "If you don't mind, I would be honored to show you our modest establishment. Normally, of course, it would be my wife who would accompany you," he said, "but she wishes to make a few last-minute preparations in her garden."

Yeah, sure, Nathan thought as he bowed to Daegal courteously, and smiled at the little girl clutching her mother's sati to hide behind. She popped her thumb out of her mouth long enough to say, "Do you really eat little girls?"

Her mother blanched. Nonplused, Nathan looked at the child, then squatted down to her eye level. "Who says I eat little girls?"

"My auntie Sabir."

"Ah," he said knowingly. "I only eat little girls if they've been very, very naughty. Have you been very, very naughty?"

Gravely, she shook her head.

"Then I'm not allowed to eat you." He winked up at Daegal, who swayed as if she might faint, and smiled at the child before he stood up.

The Pakaran had three stone barns, each kept in immaculate condition by an army of drones. Two were empty but for dormant agricultural machinery and a large coop containing chickens the Pakaran bred only for eggs, as they, like all Vanar, were vegetarian. The third barn was staffed by two stolid women in grimy work coveralls whom Amitu introduced as his wife's younger cousin and a niece, whose names Nathan acknowledged and immediately forgot. The pair was even more timorous than Daegal, if such a thing were possible. Amitu treated the women with the utmost deference, which they ignored, standing as if turned to stone to stare at Nathan, tools and machinery clutched in paralyzed hands.

The young kharvah expertly backed an open maintenance float out of the barn and helped Nathan up into the seat beside him. Battered and paint-flecked, the hoverfloat rode through the furrows of wheat smoothly, Amitu handling the machine with seasoned dexterity. The breeze rippled through green wheat, Amitu pointing out where one season's crop finished and another would begin at the end of the next rainy season.

Far out into the fields, the distant vineyards a blaze of red-gold and the house a smudge on the horizon behind them, Amitu stopped the float, the two of them suspended several inches above the wheat grain. Neither of them spoke for several minutes, the younger man leaning on the damper panel of the float to gaze off across his fields fondly. The heat of late-afternoon sun waned as insects buzzed and distant birds wheeled up on thermals to chase their supper.

"I apologize for my daughter's remark," he said finally.

Nathan chuckled. "My own daughter is nearly her age. Her mother probably uses me as an ogre to frighten her into good behavior, too." He sighed. "I frighten a lot of people, for some reason."

The younger man cleared his throat uneasily. "It isn't just that you are Hengeli, jah'nar bhraetae. Of course, we know the ways of outsiders are not always compatible with our own. Everyone has heard how you have often been in trouble for violent and disrespectful conduct, but Margasir speaks well of you. It is rather that my wife is afraid of offending you."

"Offending *me*? I've had a pleasant afternoon with a family who have made me welcome in their home. How should I be offended?"

Amitu kept his attention on worrying a scrap of dry skin flaking from knuckles that had obviously seen many years of hard manual labor. "The Pakaran are a very minor Middle Family," he said, addressing his calloused, tanned hands. "And I'm from Common Family, the youngest son of three, virtually worthless. My wife's relatives are good people—they've all done the best they could to help us build up this business. But the Pakaran have little money. When Daegal bought the land, it was still native forest. We had to clear it ourselves, recondition the soil, inoculate the ground with proper bacteria, introduce the best worms, buy the first year's seed. It took all the capital she had. When we lost our crop five years ago, that pretty well wiped out our entire investment."

He raised his eyes to scan his fields. "I've tried to talk her into marrying another kharvah, someone from a better family that could provide us with some financial relief. She won't do it. Despite appear-ances, my wife can be very stubborn when she makes up her mind. If it hadn't been for Margasir, we would have lost everything."

"Margasir?"

Amitu glanced at him sidewise. "All that he'd saved for his old age after so many years in the Nga'esha service, he lent to us. Secretly. My wife would be humiliated if it got out she's taken money from a sahakharae. Margasir's patron replaced him last year, preferring a younger man. We were pleased when you took him on as your práh-saedam, truly. He is not young anymore, and has to work hard now, training many new apprentices. But he cannot afford to retire until we have repaid him, which will take many more years yet."

Amitu went back to studying the fields as solar-driven drones trundled through the rows around them like comic metallic beetles, perpetually collecting insect pests to be destroyed. "My oldest daugh-ter is in university. She would prefer to be a community doctor, but she will continue her mother's business because it is her duty. Unless the little one decides to take over when she is of age."

"And your boys?"

The younger man smiled wistfully. "Love this place the way I do." He said nothing for a long moment. "I don't want my sons to become sahakharae," he said softly, "but unless we become successful enough to arrange good marriages for them, I don't see much other alterna-tive."

Nathan thought he understood. "What is it that I can do for you?"

At that, the kharvah smiled widely, looking up into the sky as he exhaled his laugh. "That's just it. We don't want anything from you. My wife loves her garden the way I love these fields. She likes enclosed safe shelters. I like the openness. We are happy here." He looked at Nathan directly, solemnly. "We've never had many guests before, and certainly never any from the High Families. It took a lot of courage for her to invite you."

"I realize that."

"All Daegal wants is to show you her roses. That's it." He snorted with exasperation. "They've got some sort of . . . blight or fungus or who-knows-what, and to listen to Margasir, you can simply breathe over them and they'll be magically cured."

Nathan held up his hands defensively. "Hey, hold on, I know close to *nothing* about roses!"

Amitu laughed. "Which is slightly more than I do, jah'nar botanist." He sobered. "But we asked you to come because you are Margasir's friend, not because you are rich and famous Nga'esha."

"I understand."

"Thank you."

They sat in silence for another moment, taking in the color of the sky as it deepened, the wind in the wheat. "It's lovely here," Nathan said.

"Yes," Amitu agreed. "It is. And I know I am the luckiest man alive." He grinned, restarted the float, and turned back toward the house. "Shall we go examine my wife's precious roses?"

If Amitu's fields had been beautiful, Daegal's secluded walled garden was flawless, half an acre of immaculately groomed borders overflowing with flowers. A small army of tiny drones disguised as garden ornaments, including a family of roly-poly hedgehogs meandering through the shrubs, kept the even emerald lawn meticulously trimmed. Tiny goldfish pirouetted under the shelter of sweet-scented lilies in a small pond, a cascade of water spilling down black rock rippling the surface. A majestic old lemon tree still laden with late fruit dominated the tiny meadow where dozens of bright-colored exotic birds flitted inside the invisible confines of an electronically controlled aviary. Nathan walked through her garden in wonder while Daegal trailed behind him anxiously.

Nathan quickly figured the best way to speak with Daegal was to couch every question so that she could answer with a simple nod or shake of her head. Amitu followed at a distance, the little girl in his arms giggling merrily as they played tug-of-war with her father's braid. Margasir was off somewhere with the boys, the faint sound of laughter drifting even over Daegal's high stone walls.

"This is beautiful," he finally said. Daegal ducked her head, blushing furiously, as if it had been herself he'd complimented. At the end of the winding path through her gardens, a large wooden door with ornate ironwork hinges led into yet another annex of her garden. The perfume of roses when she opened the door flooded his senses. A pebbled walk meandered through an acre of rose garden of every conceivable genus. Yellow and white climbers enveloped the stone wall. Big flamboyant variegated flowers drooped under their own weight, dainty pink tea roses nestled in between. A wild dog rose laced its way through a stone pergola, the ancient rootbase as thick as his arm, simple mauve flowers with a dusting of yellow pollen. Bees and butterflies drifted through a row of damask roses, every plant, every insect imported from off-world.

Daegal cultivated the rarer forms of rose as well, and he stopped to admire a large moss rose bush with its sepals and flower stalks covered with dense, mosslike hairs. Her pride and joy, though, was her delphinidin blues, their colors ranging from palest blue to nearly jet black, deep amethyst and turquoises.

But while all the others in her collection were at the peak of health, the blue roses unquestionably suffered from some ailment. The leaves had wilted; yellowed new shoots had shriveled, as if the plants were drought-stricken although the ground was clearly well-watered. He could see no obvious signs of a fungal disease or viral blight. Which meant, he thought, looking at the diligently nurtured topsoil, that it was probably something in the ground.

"Have you tested for nematodes?"

She nodded.

"And?"

She nodded again, which Nathan took to mean she'd found them.

"Have you tried a soil fumigant?"

Nod.

"I take it that didn't work."

She shook her head, looking even more unhappy.

He looked around at the garden. "Only the blues are diseased?"

Nod.

"Any idea how they were infected?"

She glanced at Amitu, forlorn. "I ordered the stock through a nursery that specializes in imports from off-world," he admitted reluctantly. "It was a present from our eldest daughter, on her birthday, to her mother. Imports are normally very carefully screened for contamination before Vanar would ever allow them to be marketed. But, every once in a while . . ." He shrugged.

"And you haven't taken a complaint to the nursery?"

Amitu and Daegal exchanged a wry look, as if sharing a private joke. "We tried," he said obliquely. "They weren't sympathetic."

Nathan could imagine. Daegal would go out of her way to avoid a quarrel with anyone, while Amitu, as a low-ranking man of Common Family, would be lucky to be simply ignored.

"Would you mind if I took some samples to take away with me?" Nathan asked. "I can't promise anything, but it's an interesting challenge."

Daegal brightened considerably. "Yes, please," she whispered, which would be the first and last words she spoke that afternoon.

Her greenhouse was larger and better equipped than his own, and Daegal was an obsessively tidy gardener, every tool clean and hung, every bin of compost neatly labeled, not a speck of soil on the slate floor. He used her supplies to take snippets of affected leaves and rootstock, and filled several vials with soil taken at various distances from the ailing rosebushes while Daegal hovered anxiously.

Margasir had organized a small snack under the lemon tree. Daegal, her daughter clinging to one hip drowsily, politely bowed and returned to the house. Amitu and Nathan settled onto the cotton cloth spread out on the grass. They praised the small pastries and tea fare served by the twins doing their best imitation of miniature sahakharae. Amitu wasn't able to mask his regret, but Nathan knew that without patronage and training from an accomplished, well-placed sahakharae such as Margasir, even that recourse would be closed to boys from such humble lineage. The twins, for their part, simply enjoyed the attention without worrying about a remote future.

The sun had already set by the time the Pakaran saw them to the door, waving and smiling as they walked down to a waiting taxi float at the end of the long road. As Nathan climbed onto the back of the taxi beside Margasir, he glanced toward the house in time to see Daegal lean her head on Amitu's shoulder, his arm around her waist protectively before the taxi lifted and sped off.

"So, what do think of my friends, the Pakaran?" Margasir asked lightly.

Nathan didn't answer for a long moment, and when he did, his voice was somber. "I think I've just met the only happily married people on all of Vanar."

Margasir shot him a look, but said nothing.

The problem with Daegal's blues was indeed an unusual nematode. It took him the better part of two weeks to track down exactly what type of particular microscopic roundworm it was, and more than that to figure out where it came from and how it got to Vanar. Seeking out the younger cousin who had escorted him to buy a sprig of plum blossom for Tycar, he sweet-talked her into an expedition to the garden shop that had sold the Pakaran the contaminated roses.

He might have been merely a man, but he was still Nga'esha, and the brother of a pratha h'máy. Any indignation by the proprietor gave way quickly to worried politeness. He had no wish to cause her trouble with Vanar Customs, he assured her in a veiled threat well out of earshot of the cousin more preoccupied by a display of exotic orchids. He didn't like Vanar Customs officials any better than she did, he commiserated, as they were constantly disallowing any number of things he tried to import himself. He only wanted to know exactly where the roses had originated. She scribbled down the information without a word, and handed it to him.

Following the paper trail back, he narrowed the source of infestation to a small outbreak that had wiped out an ornamental crop of hybrid petunia. Daegal's elegant blues had used the delphinidin gene transferred from *Petunia solanaceae*, unwittingly attracting the nematode to jump species.

Without the benefit of his library, Nathan might have found the task of locating the appropriate supplier off-world and ordering a quantity of the antidote impossible. The best genetic engineers anywhere could be found on Vanar, but as it was forbidden for a Vanar man to even initiate conversation with a woman, Nathan could not approach them. But by a quirk of the law, although he was not allowed direct contact with anyone outside Vanar, as long as he remained anonymous, he could go through the same blind channels he used when requisitioning his Hengeli music and book cubes.

It would have been simpler and cheaper to have dug up and burnt Daegal's blue roses, excavated the contaminated ground, sterilized the area, and started again from scratch with healthy new stock—as Nathan was informed by several agribiotech companies perplexed why anyone, even someone as rich as the Nga'esha, would want such a tiny supply of custom-designed material. He finally contracted an independent engineer who asked no questions, happy enough to charge his nameless Nga'esha customer a breathtakingly extortionary rate.

As it was, he once again had to petition for an audience with the men's household h'máy, Bidaelah, to beg permission to use his own funds. He was lucky; she was in a foul mood when he was admitted to see her. Although he was very careful to observe the strict Vanar formalities, she didn't even take any notice of his efforts.

"You want to buy *what*?" She scowled at him with incredulity. When he started to explain again, she impatiently waved him off. "Never mind. Whatever weird yepoqioh thing it is you want now, fine, go, buy it. Don't bother me with it."

"It isn't just a question of how much the product costs, jah'nari l'amae. There are other expenses—shipping fees and import tariffs—as well." Not to mention the compulsory bribes to Vanar Customs officials, which he knew he didn't need to mention. "All of which will be quite expensive. It may cost this month's entire deposit in my account."

"As long as you don't want to dip into your capital, I don't care what it costs." She was barely paying him any attention at all, her focus on the work in her reader.

Nathan paused, bewildered. "My capital?" he said. "This isn't my capital?"

Bidaelah glared up at him, irritably. "Of course not. You would hardly be allowed access to that much money without a damned good reason, for which this certainly does not qualify." She nodded at the card he held in one hand. "You're only authorized to use the interest you've accrued on your investments—minus expenses, of course, now that you have a prásaedam to support. Now, please, I'm very busy and I don't have time for such unimportant rubbish. Buy whatever you like, I don't care. Just leave me in peace."

He was courteously but firmly ejected from her offices. Looking down at his datacard in disbelief, he mentally computed what the capital would approximately be based on the interest in his accounts. "My God," he breathed. He was the richest poor man he knew.

The package arrived a few weeks later, and too impatient to go look for Margasir himself, Nathan sent for his práhsaedam to join him in the men's garden. When Margasir arrived, Nathan had his eyes closed with his face to the sun, leaning back to enjoy the warmth.

"You requested to see me?" Margasir said, his tone baffled.

When Nathan opened his eyes, Margasir stood stiffly in front of him, hands clasped together, head bowed in a posture Nathan had never seen the big sahakharae adopt before. For a moment, the deference surprised him, before he remembered he was, still, Nga'esha, and Margasir was, still, his subordinate práhsaedam. Despite all the good-natured banter, the sahakharae's livelihood depended on such kharvah as Nathan. A request was as good as a command, but as he'd never gone through Aelgar before to summon the sahakharae, it was only reasonable for Margasir to assume something was amiss.

He sat up, guiltily. "Please, sit down."

Margasir settled himself gingerly beside Nathan and waited for him to speak.

"I'm not overly experienced with Vanar customs, as you might possibly be aware," Nathan said, rewarded by a fleeting grin. "But it's my understanding that I have actually been paying you something for your services as my práhsaedam, haven't I?"

The sahakharae's expression became guarded. "Of course."

"Good, good." This wasn't going quite the way Nathan had planned. Margasir's discomfort took a lot of the fun out of it. "But I think it's also customary that if you've done me a favor above and beyond your normal obligations, I am expected to reward you in some manner, isn't that also true?"

Margasir's eyes narrowed as he studied Nathan. "Occasionally, this is so," he said carefully, obviously wondering what was up.

"Well, then." Nathan extracted a small wooden box from under the folds of his sati and held it out to Margasir. "I wish to thank you for arranging my visit to your friends, the Pakaran."

Margasir smiled, more from relief Nathan suspected, and took the box from Nathan's hands with a slight bow. He opened it and gazed down inside it for a long moment.

"It's a box of dirt," he said finally.

"Yes."

Margasir looked at him with a sidelong suspicion. "You're giving me a box full of dirt?"

"Yes," Nathan said cheerfully.

The big sahakharae looked back down at it. "I see." He closed the box and considered for a moment. "Nathan Crewe Nga'esha, it has been my experience that you are indeed a truly bizarre individual, but you don't usually do something without a logical reason, if known only to yourself. May this *jaelmah ajnyaenam*, this ignorant wretch, inquire as to what exactly this is supposed to signify?"

Nathan looked at him with mock innocence. "Only a trivial gift to indicate my gratitude for your devoted attentiveness and companionship." He waited a beat. "But of course, if it doesn't please you, I suggest you toss it away."

The sahakharae mulled that over. "Just . . . toss it away?"

"Absolutely."

"Mm-hm." Margasir had borrowed quite a few of Nathan's more Hengeli habits, this small grunt being one of them.

"Might I suggest, however, that a suitable place for you to toss such a loathsome gift might be under the afflicted rosebushes of your friend Daegal dva Pakaran?"

At that, a slow smile creased the sahakharae's face. "Naturally. So what else is in the box, Nathan Nga'esha?"

Nathan shrugged theatrically. "A few specially imported designer viruses, maybe. Nothing worth mentioning."

Margasir stroked his braid thoughtfully, smoothing the end of it against his chest. "That must have been expensive," he suggested with uncustomary bluntness.

"More than you really want to know. And much more than you will ever tell the Pakaran, yes?"

He nodded. "Yes." He stood, the apprehension gone. "Well, at least it's a nice box." The big sahakharae turned to walk away.

"Margasir . . ." When he looked back, Nathan said, "Why did you want to be my práhsaedam?"

"You needed one," Margasir said, again wary.

It was true—life had been much easier for Nathan. His quarters were always tidy now, fresh flowers by his bed, clean clothing laid out for him every morning. More importantly, he had been able to spend a good deal more time with his daughter at the Changriti House, Margasir always with him to cater to Ukul and his coterie, serving as a buffer between Nathan and the Changriti men and smoothing away any ruffled feathers.

"And you needed a patron who leaves you alone," Nathan said with a smile.

If Nathan had wanted his práhsaedam to attend to his every whim, play endless qaellast games with him, sing and dance like a pet monkey, or supply nightly company as a sahakharae should, Margasir would have fulfilled his obligations. As it was, Nathan hardly ever knew where the man was half the time, nor cared.

"We suit each other well," Nathan said.

Margasir returned his smile. "Yes," he agreed dryly. "We do."

"There is no one I would prefer more as my práhsaedam than you, Margasir. No one. My mother, Pratha Yaenida, left me far more than any one man could ever use in a single lifetime. I would be profoundly insulted if, should you ever need anything, anything at all, you did not come to me and ask."

Margasir stared at him, then his gaze dropped, his attitude once again disconcertingly humble. "There were many who said I was foolish to offer to become your práhsaedam, Nathan Nga'esha," he said. "They were wrong. My life has been greatly enriched by your strangeness. And your generosity."

Nathan felt uncomfortable. "Even if I am so very ugly," he said, trying to lighten the tone.

Margasir looked up, his face split into a broad grin. "Fair enough, since I'm so lousy in bed."

As he watched the older man walk away, Nathan felt an odd warmth that had nothing to do with sexuality, wondering at it. He hadn't felt this way since Fat Ivan had awkwardly hugged him on the loading platform on Remsill, thumping him hard on the back before reboarding the *Warthog*. He had never seen the old fat bastard again, Ivan killed less than a year later. Nathan had a sudden memory of being a child again, back in Westcastle, feeling nothing at all as his mother either caressed him weepily or slapped him in her rage at the injustice of the world. He couldn't even remember her face, while he had never been able to get Fat Ivan's out of his memory.

He missed the old man more than he'd ever imagined he would.

XXXII

WHERE HIS DAUGHTER GOT ALL HER ENERGY FROM BAFFLED NATHAN. At this time of the evening, the playroom was empty but for Aenanda and her father, and one of the ever-present Dhikar guards standing watch.

"Then Qandra said red hair looked silly, and Sharu said Qandra was just jealous because she heard her tell Hasasi she wanted red hair too and that's why she stole all the red colors out of the paint box, except it didn't work and just made her hair all sticky so her mother got really mad, then Qandra said it wasn't so and she hit Sharu on the arm, like this."

Aenanda demonstrated, thumping her small fist lightly against her father's arm and giggling at his comic charade of injury. "And she made Sharu cry, so I told Qandra she couldn't be my friend anymore and I wasn't going to talk to her ever again . . ."

It was late, the Dhikar eying him reproachfully as he continued to sprawl on the floor with his five-year-old daughter. He helped her paste scraps of colored paper together as she related the day's playground politics.

He sighed, picking dried glue from his fingertips. "Aenanda, Daddy's tired. Speak Hengeli."

"Okay," Aenanda said, switching to fluent Hengeli without batting an eye. She wriggled on the floor as she sorted through the paper bits. "So then Sharu and me wouldn't let Qandra play with us in the garden, are you going to use the yellow, Daddy? 'Cuz I want it for my . . ." She hesitated. *"Garmisan?"*

"Butterfly," he translated, and handed her the yellow paper. "No, you have it."

"Bubberfly," she repeated. She pushed back the mass of curling red hair from her eyes and attacked the paper with a blunt pair of scissors, cutting out a lopsided pair of wings. "We saw this really big bubberfly in the garden and Sharu tried to catched it, but it flew really really fast and she couldn't jump high enough . . . oh!"

"What?" Nathan asked sharply, alarmed by her sudden uneasiness.

"I'm not supposed to talk Hengeli anymore," she said sheepishly, still using her father's native language.

"Why not?" he asked, puzzled.

"Grandmama doesn't want me to."

"Ah." He sat up and said carefully in Vanar, "In that case, we won't speak in Hengeli." He had no doubt he was constantly being monitored inside the Changriti House, with Pratha Eraelin scrutinizing every word for the slightest infraction. "We must do as Grandmama wishes."

"Why?" Aenanda asked, then ducked her head at her father's warning look. *"Khee'un?"*

"Because she's the boss. What she says, goes."

"How come Grandmama can't speak Hengeli?"

"Aenanda," he chided, "we are not going to have this conversation. In either language, okay?"

The little girl pouted, chopping her bubberfly wings to shreds. "Father Ukul is learning Hengeli," she muttered rebelliously, and glanced up at him slyly through gigantic eyelashes.

He should have scolded her, but his curiosity won out, just as he knew Aenanda knew. "Is he, now?"

"Uh-huh," she said, her sulkiness a sham. "But his teacher isn't as good as you. He makes lots of mistakes and he sounds funny. How come you don't teach Father Ukul to speak Hengeli?"

"I didn't know he wanted to."

"Oh, yes," Aenanda said cheerfully, her moodiness evaporating. "Mama likes it."

That was news to him. As far as Nathan knew, other than the few memorized phrases Kallah had spoken at his adoption party,

Aenanda's mother didn't understand a single word of Hengeli. And this discussion was once again skirting into dangerous territory.

"Right, you," he said, and stood up to scoop his daughter into his arms. "You know what else Mama likes? She likes you to go to bed when you're supposed to. So you'll just have to finish your garmisam tomorrow."

"Bubberfly," Aenanda squealed.

"Garmisam." He kissed her nose, then tried to hand her over to the waiting Dhikar. She clung to him tightly, the strength in her arms around his neck surprising. "Come on, Aenanda. It's a long way back for me, and it's getting late enough as it is. Time for bed."

"Don't go, Daddy," she begged. "Why do you have to leave? Father Ukul and Father Raetha live with me. You could stay here all the time if you wanted to."

His heart sank, but he tried to smile. "You know why, sweetheart. We've been through all this. I have work to do, and the only place I can do it is my library." Someday, Aenanda would pick the logic of his arguments into as many shreds as she had her bubberfly wings. His reader was the best Nga'esha money could buy, more than capable of accessing anything he needed from any distance. But what a five-year-old couldn't solve with logic, she tried with tears and tantrums, very much her mother's daughter.

"No! I don't want you to go, I want you to stay here!" She was struggling in earnest as he tried again to give her over to the waiting Dhikar.

"Aenanda, stop this right now," he said sternly.

The child leaned away from him, quivering with rage, and slapped him in the face with all her small strength. It was painful enough to make him gasp, and he nearly dropped her in his surprise. They both froze, glaring at each other nose to nose. He heard the subharmonic hum, but the Dhikar drew back, cautiously measuring his reaction.

He simply stared at the child, waiting in silence. Aenanda's temper collapsed with guilt, although she was still determined to get her own way.

"You have to do what I say," she insisted.

"I do? And why is that?" he said calmly.

"Because Mama says so," she said with less confidence.

"Mama says so."

The last of her defiance crumbled under his skepticism. "Well . . . but you have to do what Mama tells you to, don't you?"

"Yes, I do. And if Mama says I can't come and see you anymore because it makes you behave like a violent uncivilized yepoqioh, what do I do then?"

Shamefaced, Aenanda hung her head, chubby legs kicking feebly.

He glanced over her shoulder at the Dhikar. The usually stolid guard raised an approving eyebrow before she twitched her wrist, silencing the implants.

"Aenanda, you don't like it when other people hit you. You don't like it when they hit your friends, like Qandra and Sharu, do you?"

"No," she said petulantly. "But when I'm pratha h'máy, then I'll be the boss and what I say goes."

"Uh-huh. When you're pratha h'máy, I'll worry about it. But until then, I'm still your father, and you'll treat me with respect. Do you understand?"

She nodded, chastised but unhappy. Then she hugged him fiercely, her tears wet against his cheek. "I'm sorry, Daddy, I didn't mean it . . ."

He closed his eyes, breathing in her scent, loving this child more than anything in the world. Sighing, he kissed her hair.

"Speak Vanar, Aenanda."

XXXIII

WITH SO FEW OTHER PEOPLE ON THE TRAINS AND STREETS THIS EARLY in the morning, Nathan enjoyed the relative silence as he made his way across town from the Changriti Estate to the safety of his library deep inside the grounds of the Nga'esha. He had reluctantly spent the night in his daughter's House, having been summoned by Kallah after their daughter's outburst. Their discussion was far more civil than he'd expected, Kallah more weary than displeased by her daughter's violent behavior. The amount of time Nathan spent with his daughter was unorthodox, but his visits with Aenanda would not be curtailed, to his relief. Unlike her mother, Kallah was willing to admit their daughter's temper more likely a product of Changriti traits than Hengeli. Ukul had hovered unobtrusively in the background, silent and attentive as usual, but the senior kharvah avoided any eye contact with Nathan, probably mortified his private linguistic studies had been exposed.

Nathan left before sunrise, the last lingering stars fading in the still dark sky. A few shops were opening, preparing for the day's coming business. Sodden leaves beaten from the trees by the rain in the night littered the walkway in tatters. He kept his eyes on the stone paved streets, wet and treacherously slick.

Half a dozen naeqili te rhowghá loitered along the wide boulevard, hoping to be hired to clear the walk by shopkeepers not willing to wait for the automated cleaners to make their pass before the shops opened. It seemed a lifetime ago since Nathan had done such menial labor before he had exchanged his humble sati for Nga'esha blue.

A man in a tattered white sati methodically swept the remains of leaves from the walk into the gutter. This one didn't seem to be getting many jobs, judging by the man's gaunt frame. Preoccupied, Nathan barely noticed him, quickly striding around him in his hurry to make the men's train on time. Then something made him stop and turn, regarding the stooped man with puzzled curiosity.

When he did recognize Rulayi, it hit him as an almost physical shock. The once powerful shoulders had lost their vitality, Rulayi nearly skeletally thin. As Nathan stared, the former Nga'esha slowly ceased the methodical sweep of his broom and looked up. The genial man who had rowed Nathan out to collect plankton off the shores of Dravyam so many years ago gazed back at him apathetically, his eyes vacant. After a moment, Rulayi pulled the white sati over his head, and Nathan spotted the lajjae on his wrist.

"Rulayi?" he said, although there was no question. The man shifted his attention to his broom and turned his back toward Nathan, beginning the dilatory sweep along the stones at his feet, as ponderously stoic as a castrated bull. So this was the punishment the Nga'esha had meted out as just, the man's mind permanently crippled while stripping him of any rights to the protection or support of his Family.

Appalled, Nathan took three quick steps and was around him, grasping him by the forearm to force the man to stop. He wondered how many times he'd walked straight past Rulayi without even seeing the man, so inured now to the anonymous naeqili te rhowghá on the streets that he barely noted their existence anymore.

A movement in the doorway caused them both to turn, Rulayi half a beat behind Nathan. The shopkeeper stood with her arms crossed over her chest, studying him narrowly. Her eyes flickered from his hair to the costly pin holding his Nga'esha blue silk sati over the Changriti burgundy. She glanced at the stack of heavy gold bracelets on his wrists, the gleam of jewels on his ankle winking between the folds of birdsilk, the expensive sandals protecting his elaborately hennaed feet. She knew exactly who he was.

"You are interfering with his labor, young kharvah," the woman said carefully, her tone both chiding and respectful. "I am not paying him to stand and talk." She wore a cheap floral sati, a daughter of a Middle Family, he knew, and not that well placed in her own hierarchy. She resented the disturbance by an obviously rich Nga'esha kharvah. Most likely, she was a younger cousin who would have had to do the job herself had the rhowghá not shuffled through the streets in search of early work.

Nathan stared at her before her lips thinned with irritation. He then bowed, hands together. "Apologies, l'amae," he said quickly. She smirked at his heavy accent. "Please, allow me. . . ."

Before she could object, or Rulayi could react, he had the broom in his hands and swept the remainder of the damp leaves quickly and competently into the gutter. He handed her the broom, slightly out of breath and sweating, keeping his eyes properly averted. "As you can see, nidhih l'amae"—he made sure to use a flatteringly high salutation, one he was sure they both knew she didn't merit—"your path is clean. If you will now pay my naeqili brother, we will leave in peace."

She stood without speaking for so long, Nathan finally glanced up. "I didn't hire you," she said calculatingly.

"I didn't ask you for payment," he said, still using as high-low a terminology as he could. Rulayi stood impassively, hands dangling beside him. "I merely wished to help my friend."

The shopkeeper held out her hand imperiously, frowning with barely suppressed impatience as Rulayi fumbled with his card. As she noted the money into his account, she said, "You only did half. *He* did the rest, and I didn't hire him. I'll only pay you for the work you did." She looked up with a malicious smile, as if inviting argument, obviously enjoying being able to insult a famous Nga'esha, if only a male.

When she held the card out arrogantly, Rulayi took it back without protest. Nathan quickly bowed to hide his reaction. When he straightened, he had managed to mask his anger.

"May the Goddess who is the Mother of us all reward you as you deserve for your compassion, l'amae," he said innocently, gratified by the flush of color on her face. Keeping a straight face, he grabbed Rulayi by the arm and tugged him away.

"Don't worry," he said under his breath, "I'll give you the difference myself." The only response Rulayi made was an apathetic nod. Nathan spotted an open cafe at the corner of the square. Usually, men could eat in the farthest back room, behind the shop, out of sight. "Are you hungry?"

It took Rulayi a few minutes to sort through the slowed responses of his brain to answer. "Yes. Always."

The expression on Rulayi's face didn't change as the woman stopped them at the men's door at the rear of the cafe and refused to serve them. "Not with *him*," she said firmly. She nodded her head toward the lajjae bracelet fastened to Rulayi's wrist. She wasn't hostile, and shook her head reproachfully. "Surely you knew that," she said at his surprise. He hadn't known, never having had enough money when he had lived as a rhowghá outcast to have afforded even the dingy, windowless rooms in the back.

He held his hands together, his fingertips touching loosely in the respectful gesture reserved for strangers. "Would it be possible then, l'amae, to buy a few things and take it away with us?"

For a moment, he was afraid she would refuse, looking over his shoulder stonily into the distance as she considered. Then her eyes slid to Rulayi, standing silently with his head bowed. She sucked air in between her front teeth, frowning, and said, "How much?"

Quickly, Nathan pulled his card from the pouch and scribbled his finger across the surface before he handed it to her. "As much as this amount will buy, l'amae."

She glanced at it and chuckled. "You must be very hungry."

"Very," he said steadily, keeping his eyes lowered.

She smiled and pocketed his card. "Go to the kitchen door. Let no one see you there." Nathan had to pull Rulayi with him, and they waited in the alley for several long minutes. About the time he was sure she was not going to return and give back his card, the beaded netting defending the interior from prying eyes was pulled back. The woman handed his card and a heavy grass-weave sack bulging with far more foodstuffs than the amount he had given her could have bought. The smell of hot, spicy food made his mouth water.

"Thank you," Nathan said, and stumbled over the ritual expression wishing her the Goddess's blessing. Rulayi waited as silently as a shadow behind him.

"My neighbors tend to think of this alley as a place to dump their own rubbish," the woman said. "Every morning, I find someone has crept into the alley and left their litter. Every afternoon, the cleaners charge my business more than my share to take it away. I am the head of my Family, but it is small, and I cannot spare extra daughters to come that early in the morning to remove it before the cleaners come." Again, her eyes flicked toward Rulayi. "If someone were to take care of this problem, I'm sure there would be enough left over from the night before to repay him for the work. Perhaps you have a distant cousin . . . ?"

Both men knew what she was saying. As long as she didn't see Rulayi, she didn't have to acknowledge his presence. Scavenging was legal for the rhowghá. He nodded, both grateful and angry. "I will ask around, l'amae."

He started to turn and stopped when she touched his forearm. Startled, he looked directly at her, his arms full.

"You have eyes like a summer sky just before the sunset," she said quietly. "I have never seen eyes that color before." He didn't know whether it was a proposition or not, so he stood mutely. For a married man of High Family to be out on his own and speaking to a strange woman was considered highly unsuitable conduct, while even more scandalous to be in the company of a naeqili te rhowghá.

Then she smiled kindly and closed the door.

As it was, when he returned the next week to check how Rulayi was doing, she was less pleased to see him. Rulayi had never shown up. Nathan futilely searched for him at every charity shelter in the city, looked in every alley, asked every slow-witted or surly rhowghá he saw.

But no one was either able or willing to tell him where Rulayi had gone.

XXXIV

"When you were my age, Nathan," Raemik asked, "what were you doing?"

They faced one another across the huge table in the library, which at the moment was being used as a lab to prick out fragile svapnah seedlings from the gel trays to transplant into individual growing plugs. These would be carefully labeled and transferred back into Nathan's little greenhouse at the bottom end of the men's garden. Most of them, Nathan suspected, would be dead inside two days, but he was determined to discover the secret to cultivating the native plant.

"Getting the hell out of Westcastle," Nathan said.

"Why?"

"Because we were in the middle of a civil war and I was tired of people trying to shoot my ass."

"Why? What were people fighting about?"

"Water."

"Water?"

"Water." On a planet with as much constant rainfall as Vanar, he could well understand how insignificant that must have seemed to Raemik. He didn't attempt to explain.

"How did you do it, then, leave Hengeli?"

Nathan concentrated on his work, trying to work the dials on the tweezers under the magnifying glass without jostling the brittle cotyledons on the root apex. He listened with only half an ear, but the boy's transparency was glaring. "Not in any way that you could ever leave Vanar, Raemik, or I'd have been long gone myself by now. Would you hand me another set of plugs, please?"

The boy flushed, and silently passed him the plugs he'd filled with the special rooting medium Nathan had devised. After an interim, he asked, "What was it like where you lived?"

"Dry. Very, very dry."

"Were there many plants there?"

"No."

"Then how did you know you wanted to study them?"

"I met someone." Fat Ivan. "He was a terraform technician."

"Is that like a botanist?"

"A bit."

Silence.

"Did he train you to be a botanist?"

"No."

"Then where did you learn so much about plants?"

"I went to university."

"Did that take a long time?"

"Raemik . . ."

"Sorry."

Nathan grimaced as yet another frail quasi-proembrionic meristem snapped in two, the microscopic seedling destroyed. "Damn," he muttered. He sighed and sat back, his eyes aching, and rubbed his stiff neck. Once he'd had to struggle to get two coherent sentences out of the boy. Now he couldn't get him to shut up.

"It took me seven years to earn my degree, in answer to your question. Why, do you want to be a botanist?"

"I don't know, maybe." He shrugged. "It doesn't matter anyway. I cannot go to university."

"That's not true. There are Vanar universities even for men, very good ones. If you can pass the entrance exams, there's no reason you can't go."

"I could pass the exams, Nathan," Raemik said quietly.

"Then figure out something you want to do with your life and go."

"*They* will never let me go to university."

Although they were in the library, where Raemik felt safe to speak his mind, the habitual shutters had closed over his face.

"The Nga'esha?" He took Raemik's silence as an affirmation. "Why not?"

"*They* are already angry enough with me as it is. Making Pratima wait another year."

"And fifteen for you. You'll be a fully adult man when she comes back. You have plenty of time to go to university and study while you wait. Then, when Pratima comes"—he cleared his throat, finding the words difficult—"once you've fulfilled your obligations, I'm sure Pratha Yronae will permit you to do whatever it is you decide you would like to do."

"No," Raemik insisted grimly. "She won't."

The boy's pessimism irritated him. "Pratha Yronae is strict, but she isn't unjust. If you presented your request in a respectful way, I'm sure she would listen to you." The boy remained stubbornly silent. He frowned. "If you prefer, I'll make the request for you."

"No. It won't do any good and will just get you into trouble."

"I've been in trouble before," Nathan said, trying to lighten the atmosphere. "I'm probably due about now anyway. If I don't get into trouble regularly, they think something is wrong with me."

His joke did nothing to appease the boy. Raemik blinked, his pale face as rigid as stone, and to Nathan's concern, a tear slid down his cheek. Nathan came around the table and put his hand on the boy's shoulder.

"Raemik, what is it?"

For a long moment, he didn't think the boy would answer. "I hate them," he finally said so quietly Nathan almost couldn't hear him.

"Who? The Nga'esha?"

Raemik swallowed, his throat flexing as another tear spilled down his cheek. "All of them. All the women. I hate them."

"Raemik . . ."

The boy looked at him, his face distorted in a snarl of repressed fury, teeth clenched with the effort to speak. "You don't know. You don't know *anything*, Nathan Nga'esha. Women are evil, they don't care about anyone but themselves."

"Not all of them. Pratima isn't like that—"

"I hate her most of all." Raemik shook off his hand, pulling away from him. "She claims to be my sister, my *friend*, but she doesn't care what happens to me. She doesn't care at all." He ran the back of his arm across his eyes angrily to wipe away the tears. Fresh ones poured down his face.

"You feel sorry for her because she's a Pilot, don't you? She's just Nga'esha property, poor Pratima. But do you know what I am, Nathan? I'm just seed, like those things." His hand gestured fiercely at the pale red svapnah seedlings. "Pratima goes anywhere she wants on Vanar, and I'm not even allowed to set foot off the Nga'esha Estate. When Pratima comes back, *they* won't allow me to refuse her another year. I'll be too old by then. They'll take what they want from me, and my purpose is over. I won't even be Nga'esha anymore. Do you know what happens to Pilot males? We get castrated and sent away to serve in the temple, forever and ever. So no university for me. No being a botanist or anything else for me. And why? So Nga'esha women can get rich from the Worm."

Raemik suddenly whirled and snatched the gel tray of seedlings from the table, hurling it away toward the shelves. It hit the floor and splattered, Nathan's entire reserve of seedlings in ruins. It didn't matter anyway, he was distantly aware, as the boy turned back to him seething with rage and despair.

"I hate *all* women. I wish they would all die!" he sobbed, his voice no more than a strangled whisper, and fled the library.

Nathan didn't stop him, his own breath difficult in his chest. He thought of the bhaqdah temple disciple—a man with green eyes and red hair, like that of Bralin Ushahayam—who had mistaken him for another. He thought of Rulayi, the once robust man turned to a lifeless automaton, locked into a permanent stupor by the lajjae impris-

oning his mind. He thought of the young Pakaran twins, compelled
into a trade they had no say in. He thought of the long rows of white-
wombs with the opaque shadows of inmates moving lethargically inside. Men without futures, boys without hope.

"This is wrong," he said finally. "This is so wrong."

He left the gel tray where it had been thrown, abandoning his
work and the library. Walking through the men's garden, he surveyed the men relaxing in the sun, small groups chatting idly, Qim
bent over his lute picking out a new melody. Under a tree, Baelam
stroked a slender cat, the animal's natural instinct to hunt bred out
of it to leave nothing more than a docile, pretty plaything. Aware
Nathan was staring, Baelam looked up, puzzled. "Are you feeling
well, *shaelah*?"

"No."

He couldn't stand to be in the Nga'esha House a minute longer.
He pulled the end of his sati over his head as he left by the men's
gate to take the first train he could into the city. He walked along the
wide boulevards and down narrow streets, as if he'd never seen them
before.

Cafe tables littered the sidewalks, filled with confident, lively
people. Customers came and went from teeming shops, laden with
shopping. A pair of sahakharae stepped off the men's section of a
transit bus, cheerfully gossiping as they passed a group of women,
keeping their eyes respectfully averted with habitual decorum,
bobbing a quick bow that wasn't even acknowledged. An elderly
Middle Family kharvah carefully scrutinized vegetables on offer at
the men's end of the market, testing the ripeness of melons with
discerning fingers while the merchant waited patiently for him to
make his selection, her arms crossed over her formidable bosom.
A thin woman endeavored to keep a small horde of spirited little
girls in grass-stained kirtiya from straying outside their play area
in the city park. A young man from a Common Family squatted
next to a small boy howling for sympathy and gravely studied the
scuffed elbow held up for his inspection before dispensing medicinal kisses and hugs. Clean, safe, bustling, the perfect picture of an
ideal society.

Can't you see that these are things worth protecting? Yaenida had asked him. He shook his head to clear the memory of her voice from his mind.

"From what, Yaenida?" he murmured. "Where is the danger here?"

A woman walking past him glanced at him curiously. Without thinking, he nodded his head deferentially, then paused, troubled. She had gone, unaware of his uneasiness. Just how Vanar had he become? Enough that he had not only given up his dreams of escape long ago, but had become so hardened to the system he no longer questioned it?

Wandering into the city center, he stopped outside the huge Assembly building, its towering white walls gleaming in the sunlight. Outside their family Houses, there were more men to be found on the steps of the Assembly than anywhere else on Vanar, Nathan noted. All of them petitioners, most of the women seated along the steps in order of their station acting as counselors and mediators.

He spent the rest of the day inside, sitting in one men's public balcony after another to study what had once been as impenetrable a mystery to him as the language. Now he watched and listened as harried *vaktay* scuttled up and down stairs, held impromptu consultations in the halls, badgered abritators for decisions and hearing dates on civil petitions, divorce decrees, business torts, public service contracts, criminal prosecutions from petty theft to serious assault. He had been paying attention to an appeal from representatives of a small prefecture halfway around the planet—provincial farmers trying hard not to look intimidated by the imposing architecture or the arrogance of the court officials as they lobbied for an increase in budget for a new high-speed train—when a woman spoke, standing next to him.

"Qanistha bhraetae."

He looked up at the Dhikar, the hem of her white kirtiya rimmed with burgundy. "Jah'nari Dhikar," he responded respectfully, but his momentary rush of alarm was replaced with cold anger. He had to repress the impulse to look around for Vasant Subah.

"What are you doing here?" the Dhikar asked. Her tone was polite, not a hint of menace in her voice. But the Dhikar didn't need to resort to bullying to be feared.

"Watching."

"Do you have some involvement in this case?"

"No."

The Dhikar glanced at the meeting, then back at him. It was not one of the more contentious issues of the day, and the public gallery was nearly empty of spectators.

"I see. You find this interesting?"

"Fascinating." At the moment, the provincial vaktay was listing the price of various components for train engines, not even her junior associates able to stifle their yawning. The Dhikar smiled faintly, then nodded in the slightest of bows, and left.

He had been right; it was long overdue since he'd been in trouble.

Outside, he sat on the steps, wondering how to approach a vaktay, when he recognized one of the women of a trio near the foot of a column on the bottom step. She had recognized him as well, trying hard and failing to appear haughty as he walked toward her. He bowed deferentially to all three, and straightened with his fingertips pressed loosely together.

"Good health, Nathan Crewe Nga'esha," she said.

"Good health, Namasi dva Ushahayam ek Sahmudrah."

She raised an eyebrow, the adolescent girl who'd befriended the desperate, hungry naekulam so many years ago having matured into a poised young woman.

"I'm pleased you still remember me," she said.

"How could I forget your generosity to me when so few were willing to aid a bungling naeqili te rhowghá?" She smiled prettily, and he couldn't help adding, "And for so little return, jah'nari l'amae." He dropped his gaze modestly but not so far he didn't catch her heated blush. She glanced at her companions, who seemed too fascinated with him to notice her reaction.

"I see your Vanar has improved greatly since then as well as your fortunes. Are you here on Family business?"

"No, not exactly. I'm looking for advice." He stopped, smiling complaisantly.

She had not only grown up to be a poised young woman, but a perceptive one as well. Murmuring apologies to her friends, she took his elbow and steered him to a private area inside the colonnaded halls. "What sort of advice, qanistha bhraetae?"

"I am still quite ignorant in many Vanar ways, l'amae. How does one such as myself go about finding an advocate to represent him in the Assembly?"

"It must be our fate to meet again after all these years. I am a fully licensed vaktay, authorized as an advocate to speak for a client on any legal issue."

"You may not want to speak for me at all, once you've heard what is on my mind."

Namasi Sahmudrah raised her chin proudly, doing her best to appear authoritative. "It is your right to speak, even if it's only to me. I may not be able to help you, but it's my sworn duty to listen objectively and, if I see an injury has been done, do my best to find a way within the law to correct it."

"Also you need the work," he guessed.

Her professional manner wavered, but she kept her head high.

"And representing a prominent member of the Nga'esha wouldn't be such a bad boost to your career, either."

Her self-assurance crumbled, again just another aspiring counselor, and he regretted teasing her. "It is true I've only recently graduated from university," she admitted, "and haven't had much practice yet at speaking for many clients. Naturally, a prominent member of the Nga'esha would wish to engage someone with more experience. I'm sure I can direct you to someone more qualified, qanistha bhraetae." She wasn't able to mask her disappointment.

"You were kind to me, Namasi Sahmudrah. And I never had the chance to thank you."

She faltered, unused to such frankness. "It was nothing. . . ."

"An unmarried woman of a High Family, unchaperoned, consorting openly with a dangerous, uncivilized yepoqioh? You showed compassion and pity for a naeqili te rhowghá beyond just the desire to indulge your teenaged curiosity." She had the grace to look chagrined. "You took a risk many others would not have dared, l'amae."

"Unfortunately for me or my Family, I was not as discerning as Kallah Changriti in recognizing your potential. The Changriti tactics worked very well with the Nga'esha."

"If you believe the official propaganda." Her eyebrows rose, intrigued. "In any case, the dalhitri Kallah dva Ushahayam Changriti has never had to worry about her career prospects, unlike, say, a struggling young advocate fresh out of university."

She smiled, looking even younger than he knew she was. "One who may not have the skills or experience you might need, which, knowing what I do of you, is likely to be more than a simple contract dispute or domestic mediation."

"I'm not sure yet exactly what it is I want to do, or even what I can do. I will need your guidance and knowledge in Vanar law and custom. But you were brash and fearless, and caring when you didn't have to be, and these are qualities I value far more in an advocate than experience. I would be honored if you would consent to speak for me."

Nonplused, she stared at him. "Thank you," she finally stammered. "I think speaking for you will prove an extraordinary experience, Nathan Nga'esha."

He nodded. "Then we should discuss your fee."

She laughed. "You *are* still ignorant in Vanar customs. We Vanar may be a business people, but a main principle to good business practice is fairness and availability to everyone. No one pays for legal counsel. Advocates are compensated by the state, so that all have equal access to the law. How would anyone expect justice if it were something that could be sold to the highest bidder?"

"An enlightened attitude."

"We are an enlightened people."

"I hope so, jah'nari l'amae" he said earnestly. "I really do hope so."

XXXV

NAMASI SAHMUDRAH, NOT UNEXPECTEDLY, WASN'T OPTIMISTIC ABOUT his chances, and warned him that the Assembly was even less likely to be sympathetic.

"You already enjoy more freedom to pursue your research than any other man on Vanar," she pointed out.

"It's not enough. How can I gain access to valuable research facilities if I can't approach a woman, or so much as initiate even a simple conversation?"

"We might be able to find a way around it, that is more a question of custom than law. But as for owning property . . ." She shook her head, doubtfully.

"If I can buy jewelry or flowers or music cubes, why not land? Especially worthless land? Is there any law preventing that?"

She sat in his library, in Yaenida's old place, while he once again occupied the narrow chair, his posture correct if informal. "In a manner of speaking, there is. You are the legal property of either your wife or your Family, and by extension anything you buy is, again, property of your wife and your Family. You still need permission, implied or otherwise—whether it's hair flowers for your práhsaedam or a house or land makes no difference."

"But I do have the right to—"

"No," Namasi said sharply. "No, you do *not* have the right, Nathan! I keep trying to explain this to you, but you don't listen. *You* don't have rights. Your *Family* has rights. If you are injured or wronged, it is a crime against your Family, not against you as an individual."

"But even naekulam—"

She leaned onto the table, her forehead in her hands in frustration. "That is different. Naekulam are without family, but they are not *maenavah qili*, nonpersons. They are protected by the state, and a crime committed against naekulam is a crime against the state, not the person. This entire concept you have of individual civil rights is likely to be regarded as nothing more than your usual yepoqioh eccentricity, which has not endeared you to too many people as it is."

She sat back, tapping fingernails against her reader. "And you and I both know this isn't about you buying land or gaining access to university libraries, nor will the Assembly be fooled by it, either. I sympathize with you, I do. But we are not a people who accept reform easily, Nathan Nga'esha. Worse, you could not only fail, and probably will, but challenging the validity of unwritten Vanar customs that are more flexible than law by forcing a legal definition may end up taking away what few privileges you and many other men already enjoy. And that certainly won't do much to increase your popularity."

Nathan frowned. "I'm used to being unpopular. Will you still speak for me?" he insisted quietly.

After a long pause, she sighed. "If this is what you want, then yes. I'm a professional; this is my job. But I want you to understand it won't be easy. Are you certain you want to stir up this sort of trouble for yourself?"

Nathan smiled wryly. "If not me, who?" He looked up at her. "And if not *you*, who else?"

She would need every ounce of her boldness and sympathy, they both soon enough discovered. Within days after Namasi's filing a petition for a hearing at the Assembly of Families, he became a target of ominous hostility. He had accompanied Namasi on her way to the Assembly to consult with a more experienced vaktay when a woman collided with him in the crowded street, then brushed past him without a word.

"Pardon . . ." he reflexively started to apologize, turning around.

The speed and military efficiency astonished him. Within seconds, he had been neatly separated from Namasi, herded into a ring of strangers. He felt rather than heard the subsonic hum, and recoiled with automatic terror. Agony exploded through him, bursting into his brain. He dropped to the ground, every muscle and nerve in his body crippled with pain. Distantly, he heard glass breaking. For a moment, as they beat him, he was convinced he was being murdered.

Then the torment stopped as abruptly as it had started. A woman bent down to where he writhed on the ground. "Give it up," she whispered in his ear. Her face was nothing more than a vague blur. "Or next time neither of you will be so lucky." He couldn't even cry out as she stomped her sandaled foot on his hand, grinding her heel to break his fingers.

Then they were gone. He couldn't stand, couldn't see, couldn't speak, the slowly abating waves of pain still paralyzing him.

"Nathan?" Namasi called out in the distance, puzzled and annoyed.

His mouth opened, but his only sound was an animal whimper, absurdly embarrassing him. Hands touched him, and he cringed away.

"Nathan Nga'esha, where did you go?" She must have spotted him then, because her voice changed from irritation to alarm. "Nathan!"

She flung herself on her knees beside him, unmindful of the dirt or blood, and rolled him into her lap. He gasped, but the hurt now was normal, bearable pain. She brushed the hair from his face, her hands shaking. His sati had come undone, bloody and torn, and he noted with detached amusement how she tugged at it in a ludicrous effort to defend his propriety. His attackers had melted away into the crowd now milling about the two of them, onlookers murmuring more with curiosity than concern.

"Nathan—"

"Namasi," he managed to croak out, "are you all right?"

"*Me?*" He heard her strangled laugh. "I'm fine, Nathan. What happened? Who did this to you?"

"An accident," a woman said. "He fell."

Her body went rigid. "Accident! This was no accident!"

"I witnessed it. He fell," the woman repeated firmly.

"I am also a witness," another said.

His blurred vision cleared enough to make out a pair of elderly women, Middle Family, prim and respectable.

"You're lying," Namasi retorted heatedly.

"Excuse me, jah'nari vaktay, but he's bleeding rather a lot. Perhaps you should get him medical attention?" one of the elderly women suggested, unfazed.

As if by magic, an ambulance clinic arrived. The medical taemorae inspected his injuries curiously. Large bruises blossomed on his chest and stomach where he'd been kicked, several gashes from broken glass lacerating his arms and legs. One eye had swollen nearly completely shut, the other blinking away blood dripping from the wound in his scalp. He did yelp as the senior taemora examined his broken hand, grateful as the analgesic she hissed into the skin took effect.

"How many were there?" Namasi asked him.

"Don't know," he mumbled. "One of them was Dhikar. . . ."

"We have two witnesses who say it was an accident," the taemora's aide said, phlegmatic, nodding at the pair of elderly women still standing outside.

Even the senior taemora looked incredulous. "Accident?"

"He was attacked!" Namasi protested.

"They say he fell."

The senior taemora had recovered her composure. "So which is it, qanistha bhraetae?" she asked him.

He opened his mouth, then shut it again, unable to speak.

"Tell them, Nathan!"

When he still didn't answer, the senior taemora said tiredly, "Record it as an accident."

"How can you look at him and say that?" Namasi insisted, outraged.

"Namasi . . . ," he said quietly, "let it go."

She turned her indignation on him. "But it's not true! They're lying!" She whirled in frustration. "This isn't right!"

He smiled in spite of the pain, caught her hand in his remaining good one, and touched his swollen lips to her palm, leaving a smear of blood. "Welcome to the real world, vaktay."

He chose to go home, as the medical facilities at the Nga'esha estate were as good as if not superior to any men's hospital to be found in Sabtú. He sat on the edge of a clinic bed as the Nga'esha taemorae treated his internal injuries without comment, Namasi hovering anxiously.

"I'll ask for a postponement for the hearing to whenever you think you'll be well enough," she said briskly.

He didn't reply, avoiding her by keeping his eyes on the taemora as she swept the therapeutic device across his abdomen. He could feel the odd bubbling deep in the tissues as they repaired themselves.

"Nathan?"

"They've threatened to hurt you as well next time, jah'nari l'amae," he said tightly.

Even the usually stoic taemora glanced at them both. Namasi said nothing for moments.

"I won't be intimidated into quitting," she said. The anger in her voice made him look up. Her chin quivered, her cheeks glowing with a pink flush that made her seem even younger. "If that's what you're afraid of."

"I'm not afraid of you quitting, Namasi. I'm afraid of you getting hurt."

"Well, I'm not—"

"Have you ever been touched by a Dhikar?" he asked quietly.

"No."

He broke protocol, looking into her eyes earnestly. "Be afraid, Namasi."

Her eyes reddened as she struggled to suppress her tears. "Are you finished yet?" she asked the taemorae. They bowed, tidied their equipment, and left his room. Once they had gone, she took his hand in hers, stooping to look into his face.

"This is not the way justice is supposed to be conducted on Vanar," Namasi said, her voice thick with outrage.

He smiled weakly at her idealism wounded by her first taste of intolerance. "You've said yourself, vaktay, we don't have much chance of winning anyway."

"Then we lose! But we lose in court, honorably, in public, not intimidated by thugs on a streetcorner! If this is your real world, Nathan, then don't give up on me. Don't make everything I've studied so hard for and believed in just a lie. Please."

He stroked her cheek with his uninjured hand tenderly, defeated. Then he reluctantly nodded.

Pratha Yronae had been unusually restrained when he returned bruised and bloodied. Whatever her personal views on his first venture into Vanar law, Nathan had expected some form of reprisal for dragging the Nga'esha name into public dispute. But Yronae had allowed him to retreat into the Nga'esha men's quarters, where he'd done his best to be quiet and inconspicuous. But although the days passed without his being summoned, sooner or later, he expected the ax to fall.

His broken hand throbbed even taped, his knuckles blue and swollen, which made taking notes awkward. An ancient Hengeli music cube resonated around the cavernous library, Borodin's booming bass line echoing nicely off the bookshelves. Humming along contentedly with the melody, he leaned with very non-Vanar carelessness on the table, head propped on one elbow and a leg dangling across the arm of the chair, foot bobbing idly to the music as he worked.

Deep in concentration, he didn't hear Yronae behind him. When he realized she was there he stood so quickly he banged his knees on the table. He bowed hastily, grimacing in pain, then slapped the music off. His ears rang in the sudden quiet.

Yronae had never once entered her mother's library since the old woman had left it to him, never. He'd actually seen very little of the Nga'esha pratha h'máy and was just as happy to keep it that way. His sporadic encounters with Yronae were rarely enjoyable for him.

She stood in the open doorway with her legs braced apart, hands clasped behind her back, inspecting the room as if she'd never seen it before.

"May I enter?"

"Of course, jah'nari pratha."

She strode into the room with arrogant confidence. Like she owned the place, Nathan thought. "Your research is going well, I hope?"

"Hae'm jah'nari pratha."

"Good, good." She glanced around the room with a detached air. "Is it necessary for your work to play music at such a volume?"

Yet another small pleasure taken away, he groaned inwardly. "No, jah'nari pratha. My apologies if it has disturbed anyone. . . ."

She shrugged one shoulder, her habitual Vanar gesture halfway between no and indifference. "It's not audible outside this room. Play it as loud as you like, if it helps you think. I only find it incomprehensible how you can appreciate such disagreeable noise."

That he found her own preference in Vanar music insipid, toneless, and about as interesting as a mosquito whine he wasn't about to comment. Whatever she was here for, it wasn't to discuss their conflicting tastes in music.

She strolled around the table, her back to him as she ran fingers along the surface with a detached air. "I see you are once again in the news," she said dryly. "Your vaktay has demanded the Qsayati Vasant Subah carry out an inquiry into your attack."

"I'm sure the Dhikar will pursue the investigation with their usual diligent impartiality."

Her mouth twitched, the only sign of fleeting amusement. "I take it you intend to continue with this unusual litigation of yours?"

He swallowed hard. "As long as Vaktay Namasi Sahmudrah is still willing to speak for me, yes."

She turned to regard him with distant skepticism. "Mmm." Her gaze flicked curiously over his wounded body. "How is your hand?"

"It is healing, Pratha Yronae."

"And your other injuries?"

He wished she would just get to whatever penalty she intended to inflict on him. "Do not interfere with my work, l'amae."

"Show me."

"Khee, jah'nari pratha?"

She nodded at him. "Show me these injuries."

The Vanar didn't have the same sense of bodily modesty, he well understood by now, but he still reddened as he unclipped his sati pin and let the linen unravel before he pulled the mati over his head. He stood naked with his mati clutched in one hand as she examined him solemnly. The deep sutured gashes had already fused, and the bruising and abrasions were still painful, but not disabling.

Yronae frowned. "This will not do." She looked at him directly, unyielding. "You will be confined at once to a whitewomb for a period of no less than three weeks."

He stared at her, paralyzed with horror as she turned to go. "No," he breathed, "Oh God, no . . ." Before she had reached the door, he leapt in front of her, barring her way. He just managed to keep from touching her as he reached out toward her. She backed away from him, eyes wide in disbelief and anger. His hands closed into impotent

fists to keep from grabbing at her, which only caused her to retreat farther away in alarm, her jaw tightening.

Ignoring his injuries, he dropped to his knees. "This ajnyaeman
naeqili regrets displeasing you, jah'nari pratha h'máy, and whatever
other punishment you think I deserve, I'll accept, but not that!"

"*Jameen se ut'tho!*" she snapped. "Get up off the floor and do as
you are told!"

"Don't do this to me!" he shouted before he realized he'd spoken
in Hengeli, then had to struggle to control himself to use Vanar. "You
don't understand. Please don't send me back there. . . ."

"What is wrong with you? Get out of my way. . . ."

"*I won't go!*"

"Shut up, Nathan Crewe Nga'esha! If it is truly that terrible, then
you will not be forced to go. But stop this childish behavior and get up
immediately!"

He nearly wept in relief, thanking her in the most abject Vanar he
knew as he rose, mati clenched in front of him. She stared at him in
incredulity and, to his surprise, appeared as shaken as he was.

"Are all Hengeli men *insane*?" she demanded.

They would be if subjected to this kind of torture day in and day
out, he was far too prudent and far too frightened to retort. She shook
her head in contempt. "You are an embarrassment, disgusting even to
look at. If you refuse to accept proper medical treatment, then you will
leave the Nga'esha House immediately. Return to your Changriti wife,
and do not return until you have healed. Do you understand?"

"Hae'm, jah'nari pratha."

"Now will you get out of my way or do I need to call the Dhikar to
remove you?"

He didn't have to be told twice. Throwing several cubes he'd been
translating as well as a couple ancient books into a small pack, he bundled his sati around him clumsily and fled. If anyone looked at him
askance on the train back to the Changriti Estate, he didn't take any
notice, still shaking so hard his teeth rattled.

If the Pratha Yronae considered his injuries too repulsive to look
at, hers was not a universal opinion, he realized that evening. Raetha
had entered their shared apartments, standing politely outside the

cramped cubbyhole Ukul had allotted to Nathan. "Father of Ae-nanda," he said softly, which was always a bad sign.

"Hae'm?"

"Our wife hopes you would consent to share her bed this evening."

"You must be joking."

Raetha's eyebrows contracted in perplexity. "No," he said seriously. "Why should that be humorous?"

"It isn't, Raetha. Not in the least."

He could have said no. One of the few technical privileges a Vanar man had was to refuse sexual relations with anyone, including his wife. The reality, of course, was that if he pleaded fatigue or headache or, even justifiably, inability to consummate her desire due to his injuries, Kallah Changriti would take it personally. Very personally. Having just been unceremoniously tossed out on his ear from his maternal House, Nathan couldn't dare risk being ejected from his matrimonial home as well. He ran the fingers of his hand through his hair, hissing with sudden pain as a nail scraped across the raw suture on his scalp.

"Tell her . . ." He groped for some other solution, then sighed. "Tell her I would be honored, if she could spare me a single hour to make myself more presentable." What he really needed, he knew, was to find Margasir.

His práhsaedam was exactly where Nathan suspected he would be, busily working out in the Changriti men's gymnasium. Somehow he always knew where Nathan was by whatever mysterious communication the sahakharae used to keep tabs on their partners. Several other younger, equally muscular men who had adopted him as their physical fitness trainer surrounded him, grunting and sweating and admiring themselves and each other in the mirrored gymnasium. The older sahakharae dropped the heavy weights he'd been lifting and wiped his forehead with his arm, eying Nathan curiously. His acolytes paused as well.

"You are even more hideous than usual, Nathan Nga'esha."

"And I love you, too, Margasir," Nathan shot back, which made the sahakharae grin and the boys chortle. He grabbed the other man by one sweat-slicked arm and tugged him away from the group. "How quickly can you make me not so hideous?"

The sahakharae eyed his injured body skeptically. "I'm not trained in that sort of medical art, Nathan."

"You've got one hour."

Margasir's doubt turned to disbelief. "Nor am I trained in magical ones, either."

"Kallah wants me in bed, on form, *now.* I have had a rough day and I'm not in a good mood. The Pratha Yronae has thrown me out because my appearance offends her. I can't go into Kallah like this! I have to do something, anything . . ."

Margasir shook his head, barely able to keep from laughing, which irritated Nathan even more. "Claim you've strained your eyes from too much of your reading and turn off all the lights." His levity lessened as Nathan gestured in wordless frustration. "Nathan, she must know of your condition. Surely she won't be that shocked. All I can do is help to deaden the pain and give you something to increase your chances of satisfying her request."

"That's just great," Nathan muttered, resigned. "Do it."

The sahakharae steered him toward the baths and said kindly, "Come with us, Nathan Nga'esha, and we'll do our best to make you not quite so ugly."

Half an hour later, his hair arranged to hide the worst of the cuts on his head, a judicious application of cosmetics on his face, the most ornate of sati and several pounds of bracelets, anklets, and armbands artfully concealing his various bruises and incisions, he presented himself to Ukul Daharanan for inspection at the great door between the men's and women's houses. As usual, the stolid man examined him briefly, only the small twitch of a muscle in his jaw giving away his hostility.

"Paramah kharvah," Nathan murmured, bowing low in proper deference. "May I humbly ask that if I'm not able to comply with our cherished wife's wishes, you might be kind enough to relieve me of this most pleasant of duties?"

The senior kharvah's eyes narrowed, his smoldering resentment flaring. "She doesn't want me," he said with uncustomary bluntness, then jerked his head toward the door before stalking off.

Oh, well, he thought. It had been worth a try.

Nathan hadn't been invited to share Kallah's bed in years, not

since the birth of their daughter. He'd done his duty, given the Family a daughter and an heir, and firmly established his affiliation within the Changriti hierarchy. Once his function had been accomplished, Kallah had quickly lost interest in him.

Or in conceiving any further children. Kallah had been determined her first child would be female, as she was reluctant to repeat the experience any time in the near future. Nathan suspected that if the Changriti heir elected to produce any more children, she'd employ various aspiring taemora to carry the fetus to term for her, regardless of the cultural stigma. Whenever she did feel in the mood, Ukul had usually been the one summoned. Other than the one time Vanar custom required, Nathan couldn't remember Raetha ever being asked to join his wife for an evening of connubial delight.

Why in the world she had suddenly discovered renewed passion for him, especially at this moment, he couldn't fathom. But as he slid back the door to her private rooms, it was all too obvious that was exactly what was on her mind.

Pregnancy hadn't been all that kind to Kallah. Stretch marks had been removed and her body skillfully resculpted, but she had never quite been able to lose the weight she'd gained after the birth. The grain of her skin had coarsened, her muscles still slack. Someone had spent as much effort on hiding her flaws while embellishing her best features as Margasir had done for him. Kallah lay artfully arranged on the spacious bed, half hidden by the long curtains of sheer silk drifting around the sides. Archaic candles bathed the room in a soft glow while the aroma of the narcotic incense impregnated into the wax filled the room. She wore the sheerest of tasmai, softening but not concealing the ornate corselette fashioned out of more gold wire and winking gemstones than fabric. It did its job admirably, Nathan had to admit, pushing up her breasts while accentuating the roundness of her belly in true Vanar style.

"Be welcome, koshah," she said, her voice husky. Her sentimental flattery didn't soothe his uneasiness. "Would you care for a little wine?"

Without waiting for whatever answer he might give, she gestured to one of the ubiquitous Dhikar, who poured them both a glass each,

serving Nathan first before his wife. He mumbled his thanks and drank half of it in one gulp.

She smiled flirtatiously, and he did his best to return it.

"You may leave now," she said, which baffled him until the Dhikar bowed and glided out of the room, which baffled him even more. Kallah motioned to him to join her on the bed. "We are completely alone."

"I did notice," he said guardedly.

She patted the bed. "Come sit with me, beloved."

He smiled back wanly and pulled the sheer bed curtain aside to sit beside her. She unfastened his pin and drew the end of his sati off from his shoulder, running her hands along the fabric covering his chest. Wincing as her fingers grazed a tender spot, he gritted his teeth in a determined smile. Her hands stopped as she looked up into his face with relish. "Did that hurt?" she whispered throatily, and rubbed her thumb against the wound more vigorously. This time he couldn't keep the twinge from showing, hissing through his teeth as he reflexively grabbed her wrist.

"Yes, l'amae, that hurts."

He expected her to rebuke him for daring to wrest her hand away, but strangely, she seemed more aroused than annoyed. "Show me. I want to see. . . ."

"It isn't a pleasant sight."

"Show me." This time there was no mistaking the command in her tone.

Laboriously, he drew the mati over his head. She examined the wounds on his chest and abdomen with intimate care, her fingers caressing the healing incisions gently. Her elaborately lacquered nails traced the old scar on his left side, long healed.

"My mother hates the sight of this," she said.

"Believe me, it was no pleasure acquiring it, jah'nari l'amae."

"Whenever she goes to watch the men bathe, if you are there, she will not stay. She thinks you purposely flaunt this scar just to insult her."

He didn't respond, uncomfortable with the sudden knowledge that the Changriti men's baths were observable to their pratha h'máy and making a mental note to avoid them in the future. And while

Kallah knew his marriage had not been some clever scheme the Changriti pratha h'máy duped the Nga'esha into, a lie the scar on his side proved, she didn't seem to care.

Kallah bent her head to his chest, her hair screening her face as her lips brushed his injured skin with soft kisses. Maybe it was the maternal instinct coming out in her, he wondered.

Then she bit him.

"Ow! Goddamn it, Kallah!" He reacted before he had a chance to think, shoving her away from him. When she laughed and went for him again, he caught her by both wrists and had to wrestle her down to the bed. His broken hand throbbed, and he panted more in pain than exertion, straddling on top of her. Whatever painkiller Margasir had given him wasn't nearly as effective as he'd hoped.

"Kallah, *nidhih paramah*, darling, beloved, I wish you'd stop, please, this is most painful. . . ."

She managed to shake off one hand, reached up to grab him by the hair, and yanked him down on top of her, her mouth clamping to his.

"Mmph! Ouch! Stop it! *Shit!*" This time, they ended up sprawled half off the bed, his forearm jammed under her chin to keep her from biting him any further while he parried her flailing arms with his other hand.

Then she stopped struggling, her face flushed. "Take me, Nathan," she breathed.

"*Khee?*"

"Take me the way you would an Hengeli woman. There's no one watching, you can do whatever you wish to me. . . ."

She threw herself back limply as she wriggled her hips beneath him in what he assumed she assumed to be a provocative manner. "Oh. Right," he murmured, completely bewildered now.

"I want to feel like an Hengeli woman," she said. "Be forceful, Nathan. Overpower me, ravish me, *hurt* me . . ." Then she eyed him warningly. "But don't hurt me too much. . . ."

This was going to be a rather long night, he suspected.

Mercifully, while Margasir's analgesics hadn't done much for him, whatever he'd given Nathan as an aphrodisiac was working excellently. Not that Kallah was helping much; every time he managed to position himself where it might do some good, she either whacked him on his broken hand or punched him in his extremely sore ribs. Finally he staggered off the bed altogether, landing on his backside on the floor in a snarl of sati silk and bedlinen.

"Fine, if that's how you want it, we'll do it your way," he said in Hengeli, furious as he stood up and shook the tangle of cloth from around his legs.

"Yes, yes!" Kallah cried, rapturous. "Talk dirty to me in your savage language, treat me like an Hengeli woman!"

Then she gasped in surprise as he grabbed her by both ankles to flip her over on her stomach, and launched himself onto her back. As he landed, he gasped himself, agony shuddering through him. Once he'd gotten his breath back, he seized her by the hips, hoisted her rear end into the air, and without any additional finesse plunged into her.

"You goddamned people are all crazy," he grunted, his words chopped into a fierce tempo. "If I tried this sort of crap with an Hengeli woman, she'd have my balls off in a pickle jar so quick I wouldn't know what the hell hit me."

Kallah, whose command of Hengeli might possibly have included the profanity, squealed in ecstasy, her now safely ineffective fists pummeling pillows instead of him. Sweat poured off him, making his grip on her slippery. He nearly lost his hold as she tried to slither from under him. "Oh, no you don't," he scolded, grabbed her by the nape of the neck and pushed her head down, scooting his knees under her thighs to make it impossible for her maneuver.

It must have been gratifying for her, as a few moments later her entire body shuddered violently and she shrieked so loudly it panicked Nathan, thinking he must have genuinely hurt her. He froze, fearful the Dhikar would rush in at any moment to rescue her, before she collapsed as boneless as a dishrag. Realizing, he strained to conclude the deed, managing it a few laborious minutes later. He felt hollowed out, and prayed he had done enough for one night to satisfy her as he rolled off to sprawl on the bed, winded, aching, and exhausted.

He didn't remember falling asleep, only being suddenly aware he was still in bed lying on his back, Kallah nestling against his chest with her hands tucked like a child's under her cheek. His head throbbed, and every joint in his body had stiffened.

She must have known he was awake, as she began kissing his chest gently, her lips soft and dry. He groaned, slipping his one good arm under her neck to hold her against him, hand on her shoulder.

"Nathan?"

"Mm-hm?"

She remained silent so long he wondered if she'd forgotten what she wanted to ask and had fallen asleep.

"Do you still think of Pratima?"

Every minute of every day. "Sometimes."

He had almost drifted back to sleep himself when she asked, "Were you thinking of her tonight, with me?"

He drew away from her just far enough to look down into her anxious face, her eyes vulnerable. He laughed, a single snort, before he tenderly kissed her on the forehead and caressed her cheek with his broken hand. "No," he reassured her. "Hand on my heart, Kallah, not for a single moment, I swear."

Relieved, she smiled back and closed her eyes as she snuggled closer. "You have pleased me well, nidhih kharvah. You are permitted to stay the night with me."

"Gosh, thanks," he said in Hengeli. She was asleep moments later, snoring lightly, her breath wafting warm and cold air through the damp hairs on his chest. His fingers idly toying with strands of her hair, he stared up in the dark, now unable to think of anything but Pratima.

XXXVI

UKUL DAHARANAN WAITED TO BE ACKNOWLEDGED, STANDING IN THE archway of the Changriti's men's garden. Nathan looked up, startled, from where he sat in the shade of the courtyard arcade, then bowed politely over the reader in his lap and hurriedly swept the scattering of cubes on the ledge out of the way. "Please, be welcome, paramah shaelah."

Strangely, the senior kharvah's usual expression of hostility was absent as he bowed in return but didn't sit down. "Pratha Eraelin wishes to see you," he said in barely a whisper. "Now."

Oh, shit.

In all the time he had ever spent in the Changriti House, he had never once been summoned to Eraelin's presence, never even seen the inside of the Changriti private council room. It was, surprisingly, larger even than that of the Nga'esha, with an excellent view of the mountains beyond the elaborately vaulted windows.

Several Changriti women lined the wall bench or the wide ledges of the windows around the room, and an impressive number of Changriti Dhikar stood vigilantly. Ukul escorted him into the hall, and took his place with Eraelin's senior kharvah and a few other privileged members of the male household. Nathan spotted Margasir among them, relieved to have at least one ally present.

Eraelin sat on a dais similar to the Nga'esh's in the center of the hall, the Changriti Family emblem carved on the latticed wood behind her. Kallah stood beside her, her hand resting on the back of her mother's dais, as custom dictated. Eraelin watched him approach with glacial disdain, while his wife looked miserable.

He stopped three paces in front of her and swept back the edge of his sati to kneel on the hard floor with not even the traditional woven mat to cushion his knees. He bowed deeply before sitting back on his heels, and waited for the pratha h'máy to speak.

The tense silence continued for several minutes, but Nathan kept his gaze exactly where it should be, without fidgeting, in defiance. Eraelin nodded to one of the Dhikar sentries. At her signal, Vasant Subah appeared in the archway holding Aenanda by the hand. His daughter looked around anxiously, then brightened when she spotted Nathan.

"Daddy!" she called to him in Hengeli.

The Qsayati shushed her, and he shook his head at her warningly. Aenanda sobered, unhappy and confused, as she was led to a spot where they both could see each other. He fought down the flash of anger as Vasant Subah pulled the little girl into her lap.

"The Changriti are greatly displeased," Eraelin said finally.

When she said nothing further, he waited pointedly several moments to highlight her own discourtesy. "I am sorry to hear that, jah'-nari l'amae." He kept his tone neutral, but unapologetic.

"Your ludicrous claim you were assaulted has been unsubstantiated, and any continued insistence of an investigation into what was clearly your own clumsiness is causing embarrassment to respected members of this Family. You will retract these allegations immediately."

He risked a glance at the Dhikar Qsayati. "I will of course accept any official result the Dhikar have reached from their investigation. But I do not withdraw my statement." Vasant Subah snorted her contempt and looked away.

"The Changriti are not in the habit of being humiliated by unseemly public disputes," Eraelin snarled, her voice thick. "I insist you retract your allegations and further instruct your vaktay to terminate her disgraceful legal proceedings at once."

He recognized the syntax she used to address him as insultingly low, one that he, as the son and brother of two pratha h'máy could expect never to be addressed in. He forced himself not to react, aware that Kallah dropped her own gaze in embarrassment.

"My deepest regrets, jah'nari l'amae, but I must refuse."

"I will not tolerate your *anmaenavah* insolence," Eraelin snapped. "I have never believed you capable of becoming truly civilized, and I have finally been proved right. Even your own Family has evicted you. Do you presume the Changriti are any less vigilant? If you do not renounce this shameful behavior immediately, you will be expelled from the Changriti House as well."

He still held himself rigidly correct, determined not to give her the satisfaction of pushing him into breaking the inflexible rules of Vanar conventions.

When he didn't answer, she said, "Furthermore, you would give us no choice but to have you repudiated as Kallah's husband, causing enormous distress to your wife and your own daughter, as well as the Nga'esha Family when they are compelled to pay compensation for your abrogated marriage contract. You risk becoming naekulam, and you will never be allowed to see Aenanda again. Stop this foolishness now, and you may remain in the Changriti House with all honor intact."

He looked up at Kallah's dismayed expression, then glanced at his daughter wriggling restlessly in Vasant Subah's less than maternal grasp, the child obviously not understanding what was happening.

"I renounce nothing, jah'nari l'amae," he said tightly.

The hush in the hall was so complete he imagined no one dared even breathe. Then Aenanda whimpered, trying to squirm out of the Dhikar chief's grip. His teeth clenched, making his jaw ache.

"How dare you defy me?" Eraelin hissed. "How *dare* you?"

"Because I don't want my daughter to see her father as a coward and a hypocrite—"

Eraelin shot to her feet, all semblance of formal decorum gone. *"Shut up! Shut up, you filthy goat turd! Don't you presume to speak to me in that manner!"*

He stared at her, unsurprised by her ferocity but startled at her loss of control. She quivered with so much rage he thought for a moment she would leap down from her dais to attack him herself.

Aenanda began to cry. "Daddy, I want my daddy . . ."

At that, his composed facade cracked, and he risked looking at Kallah imploringly. Her chin quivering, she snapped her fingers. For a moment, Vasant Subah didn't react until Kallah turned to glare at her dangerously, then she handed the child to a Dhikar. Aenanda struggled as she was carried bodily from the hall, her limbs flailing in ineffectual outrage. "Let me go! I want my daddy!" Her small voice faded, leaving a poisonous silence in its wake.

With visible effort, Pratha Eraelin settled back onto the cushions and arranged her sati carefully. "Leave this House immediately," she said finally, her voice trembling. "You are never to return here again."

He stood up, bowed to her deferentially, and walked from the room in a dignified calm he didn't feel. As he passed the men, both Ukul and Margasir also stood and followed him out. Once outside, Ukul asked softly, "What shall I do with your things?" There was no triumph in the man's voice, no satisfaction his rival had been ousted. He seemed genuinely shaken.

"Send them to the Nga'esha House. Ukul . . ." The senior kharvah glanced up, and Nathan's throat constricted painfully. "Please take care of our daughter for me."

Ukul's eyes reddened as he nodded, and left Nathan and Margasir at the entrance to the men's house. The two hadn't made it out of the Changriti Estate before a young woman ran up from behind them, catching Margasir by one arm to stop him.

"Margasir," she said, pleadingly and out of breath, "you don't have to go with him, don't leave. . . ."

The woman spoke as if Nathan weren't there, ignoring him as completely as a ghost. The sahakharae glanced at Nathan then back to her, his face phlegmatic. "He's my práhsaedam, l'amae," he said coldly. "As well as a brave man. Would you ask me to be any less than he is?"

"But you've told me yourself, you don't even agree with him!" she protested.

"No, I don't. But I do believe in honor and loyalty. Something the Changriti House should learn to appreciate." He turned away, his face stony as she screamed tearful abuse after him.

As they walked toward the men's trains, Nathan said, "You don't think what I'm doing is right." He made it a statement.

Margasir shrugged one shoulder. "I will defend your right to be wrong. If I do not, who will defend me when I am wrong?" Nathan stopped, looking down at the road in confusion. "What is the matter with you now?" Margasir demanded, annoyed.

"I can't go back to the Nga'esha." He looked around vaguely. "I have nowhere to go."

After a moment's silence, Margasir said more gently, "Perhaps my friends the Pakaran will—"

"No. They are good people who don't need my bringing them trouble. I certainly can't sleep on a park bench and risk Vasant Subah arresting me for vagrancy. The only place I can think of is a charity shelter."

"You can't go there," Margasir objected. "You're High Family, not naekulam. You would create a scandal!"

Nathan laughed harshly. "A scandal? Pratha Yronae threatens to imprison me, Pratha Eraelin disowns me, my wife is divorcing me, they've taken my daughter away, and you're worried that *I* will create a scandal?"

Margasir sighed disapprovingly. "I think you have brought much of this down on yourself. You have more than most men can hope for in this life, and you were not even Vanar-born. It isn't your place to tell those of us who are what we should or should not do. Your thinking is too foreign. Your ways may be acceptable for you yepoqioh, but not for us. We are content the way we are."

Nathan nodded, more to himself than in agreement with the big sahakharae. "Some of you are." He set down the road again at a brisk walk, taking long Hengeli strides with his head held high. Margasir had trouble keeping up, not out of any lack of physical strength, but because he found it difficult to override a lifetime of learned mannerisms. "Go home, Margasir," Nathan said heatedly. "You shouldn't suffer for my stubbornness. Even if you don't stay with the Changriti, you don't have to remain with me."

"Shut up, Nathan Nga'esha," Margasir said testily, clutching at his sati to keep the cloth from tangling around his legs. "I am just as capable of choosing my own method of suicide as you are. Besides, how bad can these charity shelters be?"

An hour later, sitting in a stuffy, cramped, shabby room far worse even than the one he'd been allocated after his release from prison, Nathan smiled at a thoroughly disgruntled sahakharae. "Pretty bad, isn't it?" His hands laced behind his head, he leaned back against the barren sleeping ledge, not even a musty, threadbare cushion to soften the crumbling plaster walls.

Margasir scowled, sitting on the floor with his massive arms wrapped around his knees. "One would think you almost enjoy this hardship."

"No, I don't enjoy it," Nathan said, dropping his attempt at levity. "But I know I can survive it. I'm still Nga'esha, Eraelin Changriti can't take that away from me. Pratha Yronae hasn't thrown me out forever, just until my injuries heal well enough that I don't scare the children."

"Bah. I still can't understand why you don't just spend that time in a whitewomb. It isn't a punishment, you know. The days would pass as if they never existed, and you would come out without a scar left, clean as a newborn baby."

Nathan exhaled slowly. "What's your worst nightmare, Margasir?" he asked softly. "Is there anything that truly frightens you?"

The sahakharae glanced at him sharply. "Why do you ask?"

"Whatever it is, that's what a whitewomb feels like to me: the most terrifying torture imaginable. Three weeks in there, and I'd be either dead or insane. Compared to that, this charity shelter is a holiday resort. I lived in a place like this for over a year. We'll only be here three weeks, max. You'll live."

As it was, they didn't even last the night. Daybreak was still several hours away when the Nga'esha taemora nudged him awake with her toe. Margasir grumbled, still half asleep beside him. Nathan rolled onto his back, blinking up at her groggily.

"Come home."

XXXVII

A WEEK LATER, AELGAR SOUGHT HIM OUT, SEARCHING UNTIL HE FOUND Nathan at the farthest end of the men's garden, planting raspberry canes and wiring the shoots against a wall. As the senior kharvah approached, his entourage at a respectful distance behind him, Nathan stood up, brushed the soil from his hands and knees, and bowed. "*Jyesth pihtae*," he greeted him, questioningly, *eminent father*.

Aelgar barely dipped his head in response. The burden of regency for eldest father had taken its toll, and Aelgar seemed to have aged decades. He looked constantly exhausted, his skin sallow, the wrinkles around his eyes deeper. It could not have been easy being Yronae's first husband. "My wife requests that you attend the women's meal this evening," he said stiffly.

Nathan was surprised. "What for?" he asked before he thought.

"It is an honor to be asked," Aelgar said sharply, "and not your place to question your pratha h'máy's reasons."

Nathan murmured his apologies, ritualistic, meaningless, while the worry in his gut tumbled. Aelgar nodded, not listening. That Aelgar was nervous made Nathan even more afraid.

Although the Nga'esha would never allow the Changriti to publicly humiliate any member of their own Family, he was a repudiated husband, back in the Nga'esha House as a younger, unimportant brother in disgrace, and Yronae was not likely to be forgiving. So his being summoned to attend the women's meal was astonishing, to say the least: an honor usually given to those men of her Household held in high enough regard. The last time he had served at a Nga'esha meal had been the reception where he had first met Pratima, how many years ago now?

"I don't remember how to do that, shaelah Aelgar." He deliberately used his personal connection to the older man, not through the symbolic Family hierarchy. It was a plea, he knew, as did Aelgar, and a feeble one at that.

"Then you will come with me now, little brother," his brother-in-law said, his sternness not completely masking his own anxiety. "And we will refresh your memory."

Nathan followed the older man without further argument into the long pavilion where a half dozen other male members of Yronae's house practiced for the evening's meal. To most of them, it was routine, and they ran through the bits and pieces of their own ceremonies with a bored ease. The dancers, half naked and sweating, conferred with the choreographer on a variation of one of the more intricate dances, while two musicians restrung and tuned their multinecked lutes, silver picks on their fingers giving them bird's claws. Qim looked up from his drums as Nathan walked into the cool interior of the pavilion, his expression neutral. As if it were a signal, conversation and music dwindled to silence, the men watching him furtively. Nathan felt his skin prickle with a cold that had nothing to do with the weather. Aelgar scowled, snapped his fingers, and the men resumed their activity.

Baelam, Yronae's third kharvah, was in charge of the service, the unattractive, earnest young man drilling his chosen team on what foods were to be prepared and how they were to be served. If he was aware of Nathan's dread, he gave no sign of it, concentrating all his energies on perfecting the performance.

"You will serve the gold-dusted figs," he said to Nathan. He then explained how to choose the best figs to reserve for Yronae, and how to cache them under the main plate Nathan held in one arm, serving from lowest to highest rank without running out before he got to the pratha h'máy.

"What should I do," Nathan asked, "once I'm finished with the figs?"

Baelam gazed at him absentmindedly. "Then you sit by her right shoulder and wait. She will tell you if there is anything else she wants you to do." Nathan knew if Baelam understood why he was being summoned he would never say.

The younger man chose to wear the Nga'esha sati to honor his wife, and wore it in a fashion that nearly hid the yellow Navamam mati, the least important of the Nine Families. The boy had married extremely well and knew it. He was devoted and dutiful to Yronae, unlike Nathan, who had just thrown away every advantage he had ever gained. There was no animosity in the man's expression, nor even contempt. Baelam accepted his fate, good or bad, with a deference bordering on religious zeal, and could not comprehend why Nathan had so resisted his own.

Baelam drilled him on serving the figs until it was time for the men to wash, the dancers changing into their ornate costumes and headdresses. The men ate a quick supper in the room adjoining the women's kitchen, bolting their meal with little ceremony or enthusiasm. While those in charge of the food continued their preparations, the rest sat silently until Aelgar appeared in the door and nodded. Qim picked up his drums and followed the rest of the musicians out, but shot a quick wink toward Nathan before he disappeared. It had been the only sign of kindness he had seen the entire day, and he felt oddly grateful for it. A few minutes later, Nathan heard faint music begin, muffled by the walls. Baelam had his head tilted back to listen, more intent on timing than on any enjoyment of the music. At some point, he pointed to two other men, who got up silently and left to begin their own roles in the formalities.

It seemed hours before Baelam glanced at him and nodded. Nathan picked up his plate of sugared figs and walked out into the huge room where Yronae waited.

The women's meal was smaller than her mother's huge reception Nathan had seen so long ago. Nor were there any dignitaries, foreign or from other Families, only the Nga'esha present. Yronae sprawled across the low divan at the center of the large room, a half dozen of only the most senior members of the women's house scattered around behind her in a proximate semicircle. He recognized them all, knew his relationship to each through Yronae: Suryah, his niece and Yronae's heir; Bidaelah, Suryah's younger sister; Dhenuh, the daughter of Yronae's first cousin, now pregnant with her third child; and every other minor cousin no matter how tenuously related. Although a private meal, this had to be a meeting of some importance, as he was surprised to see even the influential dalhitri Mahdupi dva Sahmudrah Nga'esha of Dravyam. His former tutor acknowledged his presence with the faintest of nods, unsmilingly. These were all rich and powerful women, their delicate, angular faces bearing the Nga'esha family stamp: smooth skin and dark eyes, deceptive fragility.

The men set down full dishes and removed the empty ones with smooth motions, quiet, graceful. As Nathan entered, Yronae looked up at him, her eyes impassive. He faltered, his heart beating too rapidly, before he averted his gaze and began passing out figs, his arm under the platter sweating.

Qim and the others knelt at one end of the long hall, where the acoustics made even the slightest note audible throughout the room. Two other sahakharae played a counterpart pair of lutes, bass and tenor, while Qim sat behind his drums, his fingers caressing the taut hides stretched over hollowed wood to coax sounds like birds rustling in trees. He looked half asleep, his face bland. They played an old intricate melody while the singer chanted a poem of the Ancient Mothers and the morning sky and evening stars in a smooth, rich voice. Three dancers, glittering in their theatrical costumes, undulated their athletic bodies gracefully, every movement precise and fluid from years of tedious practice. Their hands wove the silent text of the story their bodies acted out, their ritualized movements telling a tale of early Vanar that Nathan could barely follow.

He served the last of the figs to the last of the women, turning smoothly as he had rehearsed while switching the small plate he'd hidden under the larger onto the platter. One of the figs had dislodged from the elaborate arrangement, and before he reached Yronae's divan, he surreptitiously poked it back into place with a finger. It left a mark in the gold dust as he set it on the low table in front of her, a smudge of dark sugar on the rim.

Nathan swept back his sati and knelt beside her divan, his palms resting on his thighs while keeping the sticky finger slightly up and away from the silk. He had to resist the urge to put it in his mouth and lick the gooey sweet from it. Yronae studied the plate for a long moment, and Nathan's heartbeat felt hollow in his chest, waiting for this infraction to be exposed, for himself to be ordered hauled out of the room in disgrace. But she reached toward the plate to choose a fig, held it delicately with her fingers, and ate it without comment, much to Nathan's absurd relief. Only on Vanar, he thought grimly, could a blemished fig be a major catastrophe.

There was another course, then a sequence of wines poured into tiny glasses, and Baelam himself took charge of dispensing the coffee, thick and potent with cardamom. Bored, his knees starting to stiffen, Nathan resisted the urge to stretch his aching back. Yronae signaled for her water pipe. Baelam had retrieved it effortlessly and put it together for her within seconds.

"Qanistha bhraetae," Yronae said, and as Baelam looked up from setting up the pipe curiously, Nathan realized with a start Yronae had been addressing himself.

"Hae'm, bahd'hyin pratha?" he said hastily. His voice sounded too loud in his own ears.

"Younger brother, would you dance for me?"

Nathan stared at Yronae in incredulity. "Khee, pratha h'máy?" He must have misheard her.

Her expression was empty. "Dance for me, little brother."

Mechanically, he got to his feet and walked the few steps out onto the bare floor. He turned and stood helplessly as Baelam's fingers flicked, a signal to the musicians. Qim tapped out a slow beat on his drums, the lutes picking up the melody.

Nathan continued standing as the music began, knowing Baelam had chosen something very simple for him. He appreciated the boy's small kindness, even through his panic. Conversation had ceased, all attention on him as the music played on. A fine haze of smoke drifted from Yronae's nostrils, her face enigmatic.

The music continued relentlessly. Isolated in the middle of the floor, his reflection in the polished wood wavering like water, Nathan stood numbly. He spread his hands out from his sides awkwardly, and took a few fumbling steps in bad imitation of the skilled dancers now watching him from their place beside the musicians. There was no derision in their faces, nor pity, either. They watched gravely, as did the women in the room, while Nathan groped with the dance.

He stopped, red faced, and let his arms drop to his sides. The music faltered and died. No one spoke in the heavy silence.

"I'm sorry." He glanced up at Yronae, embarrassed. "I don't know how to dance, pratha h'máy."

She brought the tip of the water pipe to her mouth, murky bubbles rippling through the squat cut-glass reservoir as she inhaled. Her chosen mix differed from Yaenida's blend of narcotics and therapeutic drugs, the aroma less pungent but far more bitter. "Then play something on the lute for me, qanistha bhraetae." The words came out as smoke, cut into swirls by the motion of her lips.

Nathan had no idea why she was humiliating him. He hadn't so much as touched a kapotah lute since the day he sketchily picked out a children's song for his two potential co-kharvah. "I cannot play, pratha h'máy," he said, as he knew she knew.

The silence in the room stretched for several long moments. He stood with his muscles tensed, keeping his head down, unwilling to look up at her, as if that would somehow make her stop whatever she was doing to him.

"Qanistha bhraetae," she said, her voice utterly calm. "Perhaps you might recite a poem, just one, that you have written. A simple one, very short. Surely, that should be easy enough?"

Why? Why was she doing this? "I have never written any poems, pratha h'máy," he said, his voice thick.

This time the silence went on even longer. He heard the distant rumble of thunder and the first hesitant tap-tap of raindrops on the rooftops, striking the calibrated copper tiles in a natural music of their own. Even nature knew how to better write songs than he did.

"Come sit by me, little brother," Yronae said finally. He didn't trust himself to look up, uneasy as he crossed back to take his place, sweep back the sati hem, kneel, and press his hands against his thighs to keep them from trembling. He had expected the conversation in the room to resume, and knew by their total silence she had not finished with him. "Do your injuries still trouble you, little brother?" She didn't sound that concerned.

"No, jah'nari pratha."

"Do you still intend to speak at the Assembly of Families?"

He forced himself to look up at her profile. She gazed off across the vast emptiness of the room, absorbed in watching the raindrops batter themselves against the glass catches and drip down the intricate network of tumbling cups into a tiny pool of fish. Her black hair, streaked with silver, had been drawn back from her face in intricate plaits. Heavy earrings drew the holes in her lobes into straight lines, fine strands of gem-studded metal looping from ear to ear under her chin. He could see the glint of the support behind her ear to hold most of the jewelry's weight off her fragile earlobes. He stared at her until she finally turned her head to look at him, the tiny bells suspended from the chains under her chin tinking softly.

"I am Nga'esha," he said, keeping as much of the anger as he could out of his voice. "It is my right."

For a moment, he thought she wasn't going to answer. She brought the pipe up to her mouth, thoughtfully. No one spoke, the tension so palpable he wanted to scream. She blew out a fine stream of smoke and regarded it with distant attention.

"It is your right," she said finally, her voice far too soft. "However, I would prefer you did not. I will do what is necessary to keep further dishonor being brought on this Family by involving the Nga'esha name in this matter. It is also my right to forbid you to leave the Estate, to confine you to the men's house or to your library. Should that prove not enough to deter you . . . other means exist."

He felt the omnipresent dread in his chest hollowing him out. How could anyone have lived with this fear for so long without exploding? He felt both nauseous and relieved, finally meeting the problem head on.

"If you feel it shameful for me to speak my heart to the Assembly, then I will renounce my Nga'esha name, become naekulam again. Even naekulam have the right to be heard." His voice was unsteady; he hated that.

"That would be very foolish, little brother," she warned him. "Your right to speak does not mean you will be heard. You have no chance of success; this obsession of yours is futile. Beyond the usual consequences of loss of Family, your Nga'esha name also protects you. It would be risky to throw it away."

His eye still throbbed, the dark bruising turning a mottled green. He touched his swollen cheek casually, as if brushing away a small itch. The gesture was not lost on her. "I understand that, pratha h'máy," he said cynically.

She examined the pipe in her hands for a long time, then set it down beside the divan and rolled onto her stomach to look directly at him, leaning on her weight on both elbows with her face close to his. "Then I will offer you another alternative, Nathan Crewe." She mangled the pronunciation the way most of the Vanar did, but he was surprised she used his name at all, then just as abruptly realized she had not added "Nga'esha" to it. "You may leave Vanar."

It took several moments before the shock of her words registered. "Excuse me?" his voice croaked in disbelief.

A hint of a smile twisted the edges of her mouth. "You are free to leave Vanar. My mother left you a percentage of the income of the Nga'esha Estate, and that is yours, no matter where you go. You will be a rich man, Nathan. Very, very rich. You may go wherever, do whatever you like. But you may never come back to Vanar."

Now he was terrified. This was a death sentence. She must have read the alarm on his face, knew what he was thinking. "No one will harm you," she said. Her words were soft, calm. "You will have the complete protection of the Nga'esha all your life, on my honor as the pratha h'máy of this House."

"You're letting me go?"

"Yes."

He couldn't absorb it, couldn't understand it. "Why?"

Now she smiled in earnest, amused. "Because I choose to."

That had always been the answer to everything. He was here because one Vanar woman had chosen for him to be, he could leave because another chose to release him. He would live or die, because the women of Vanar determined he could.

"My daughter, Aenanda?"

"Will stay here and be raised in her mother's House, as all Vanar girls are."

He would never see her again. Although he might likely never see her again anyway, even here.

"I'm free to leave Vanar?"

"Whenever you wish," she said. "There is transport waiting for you. It will take you anywhere you want, any world you choose."

He stood up shakily, feeling as if he were locked in a dream, and stared down at her. She returned his look evenly, and suddenly he knew it was true, saw the honesty there, realized he truly was being liberated, not executed. *Free.*

"Now?" It came out in a whisper.

"If you like," she said mildly.

He turned away, gazing around at the people still watching him quietly. He looked at the women. Suryah regarded him with tilted almond eyes glittering in the subdued light. Resting on one elbow, her head propped in her hand, Dhenuh's expression was one of mild interest, not hostility. Mahdupi lounged beside her on the wide divan, the older woman's intelligent face unreadable, her gnarled hands clasped loosely one over the other. He turned to study the men: Qim, Baelam, Aelgar. They looked back at him neutrally.

Slowly, he took one step toward the archway leading to the long hall, toward freedom, his body quivering with adrenaline. Another, a third, and another. The reality crested, broke over him like a cold ocean wave, threatening his footing in the undertow. He turned, walking uncertainly toward the men, hesitated, suddenly wandering blindly, not knowing where he was going any longer. His steps teetered like a child's toy pulled haphazardly on a string. He faltered and stopped, unable to see the exit, and stared down at his feet, his arms hanging loosely. No one spoke.

"I would no longer be Vanar, would I?" he asked.

"No."

He looked up to see Yronae watching him speculatively. "I would become naekulam without Family."

She smiled thinly. "All non-Vanar are without Family, Nathan Crewe. It would be no different than if you'd never been here at all."

He stared at her, then turned toward Qim. "Play," he said, his voice harsher than he had intended.

Qim jumped, startled. "What?"

"I would dance for my bahd'hyin. Play the song you wrote, Qim. Play 'Thunder in the Mountains' for me."

The musician's eyes flashed in alarm. "But that is a man's song. I can't—"

"Play it!"

Qim flinched, exchanged a worried look with the other musicians, then glanced at Yronae for approval. She raised an eyebrow but nodded slightly. He gulped, then bent his head over the drums as if he could somehow hide there. His fingertips began their soft beat against the skins, the echoes rolling off the high ceiling and the far walls, blending with the sound of rain falling heavier now against the roof.

Nathan bowed once to Yronae, his hands together, thumbs against his chest, then drew the edge of the sati from his head and wrapped it twice around one arm to anchor it. He closed his eyes, listening to Qim's drums, waiting for the bass lute to begin. He wasn't sure exactly what he was doing, simply knowing that whatever it was, it was right. He tried to recall the hollow, imagining the weave of bodies around him, the smell of smoke, the gleam of sweat on bare arms and backs as the dancers began their step.

He kept his eyes closed while he started to sway, trying to get the rhythm of the drum into his head, get the beat of it into his heart. Holding his hands out with awkward formality, determined, he forced himself to start the dance, let his feet slide on the floor. Tried to forget everything except the sound of the music.

It was too difficult; it felt stilted, artificial, as he moved. He opened his eyes to keep his balance, catching Qim's astonished, frightened eyes, Yronae's impassive face. His jaw clenched so tightly it hurt. He turned, stamped, turned again, stamped, listening to the swell of the drums, the melody of the lutes coming in behind it.

It hadn't been like this in the hollow, not for him, not then. He had not understood, not wanted to understand. He had made himself stand apart, watching. Like the scientist he prided himself to be, an uninvolved observer. He didn't belong here, had always been a stranger. He could leave, stop at any time and walk out, walk away, never come back. Everything he had lost and longed for all these years would be returned a hundredfold. He would be a fool not to.

He gritted his teeth and tried to imitate the movement of the dancers in his memory, wanting to become like them, wanting to *become* them. Waiting for the singing to begin, he realized the musicians would not, could not sing the words, not here. Qim would play to Nathan's execution, but he would not bring the blade down on his own neck.

Oh God, what am I doing?

Nathan stumbled, uncertain, then heard fingers pluck stringed instruments, their rapid tempo beginning to fill in the gaps between the relentless drumbeat rolling in the pit of his stomach.

Equilibrium is everything, Pratima had told him. *Everything is equilibrium.* Suddenly, he knew he didn't need the words. And he was in it, felt the music move like a live thing through him.

Flow into it, all the way to the center of the world. Concentrate Nathan . . .

He didn't know if this was what the others in the clearing had felt, and at this moment, he didn't care. He only knew that he had found something in the music, *this* music, and he grabbed hold of it tightly to let it drive his feet, his body. He didn't need to see any longer to keep his balance, he had found it outside of vision. He danced not with the expert, fluid gestures of the slender trained acrobats with their ritualized movements, but with all the energy and freedom of his private rapture.

He could see in his memory's eye the dancers in the clearing, turned when they turned, raised his arms when they did, felt the drums lifting him up until it filled his ears, pressed away all other thought. He danced past time, past knowing how long he had been dancing in the catch of the melody, heard the song building for its own end. He felt it in the movement of the earth, felt the mantle slide around the core, found it in the dance of molecules in his blood that gave him the illusion he was solid, found it in the spaces between mass and energy where time was hidden.

The thunder of the drums rolled as his pulse kept rhythm, his body knowing where to go, where to be, felt the finish approach like a sexual climax building, let it hook him in its jaws. He heard his own breath whistling in his throat, let it go, until it was almost unbearable, the drums crushing him, the music hurled up wailing.

He let his anger out, let out the frustration and the pain, let out all the despair, let the *fear* out. He wasn't dancing for Yronae any longer, he was dancing for himself, for his life. He heard the end, it was the end, he was the end, and he shouted with the drums, hands in the air, body rigid, as the last of the music rolled away like spent thunder echoing through the mountains. He stood with his arms up in the sudden silence, his head thrown back, his sati unbound and disheveled. His braid had loosened. Sweat dripped from the ends of his hair into his eyes, running down his face and chest like the rain above him tapping against the roof.

Will it make me into a Pilot? he had asked her in jest.

No, but it might make you a better dancer.

Thank you, Pratima. Thank you, my lost love.

Slowly, panting, he lowered his arms and caught Qim staring at him, a mirror of his own emotions. The two men smiled at one another, fleeting, feral, before Nathan turned toward the women.

"Leaving Vanar would make me more than naekulam, older sister," he said, still out of breath, his words hoarse. "It would make me maenavah qili, a nonperson. It would *not* be as if I'd never been here at all. I am different. I am *Nga'esha*. And I have worked too hard for too long to throw everything away now."

Yronae listened, stoic, but her eyes flickered. Around her, he caught the expressions of other women—some of alarm, some of curiosity, some even of hatred—but he kept his attention focused on the Nga'esha pratha h'máy. He wiped his arm across his wet forehead, his eyes stinging with more than sweat.

"I will not leave Vanar. The price of the freedom you offer me is too high. It is true, I cannot play pretty songs for you, I cannot write pretty poems. I will never be able to perform pretty dances to make women smile for me." He was still out of breath, his legs feeling rubbery as the high dissipated. "But if you wish I should dance for you, I will do so because it is my duty even when I know it will not please you. This dance, it may be a man's dance. But it is also a *Vanar* dance. As I am Vanar. And unless you wish to repudiate me, I will speak in the Assembly of Families because it is my right as a Vanar and Nga'e-sha. It does not matter to me if I win or lose. It should not matter to the honor of this House. I will not be silenced, not by the Changriti, not by you. Not at any price."

Slowly, Yronae shook her head in disbelief. "That is your right," she said, her tone flat, unemotional. "You are Nga'esha."

He listened, hearing something he didn't quite understand in her voice, his ears still burning with the music. But for some reason, all he felt was overwhelming relief.

XXXVIII

NATHAN LOOKED UP AS MARGASIR TAPPED GENTLY AGAINST THE GLASS. His fingers in the soil, he nodded for him to enter. The big sahakharae had to duck his head to get through the greenhouse door and grimaced in the humid heat. "It's boiling in here."

"It's supposed to be."

The older man grunted, unconvinced as Nathan potted up the last of the few surviving svapnah seedlings, their forked roots snaking like corkscrews into the carefully prepared compost.

"I take it you're not here because you've missed my company," Nathan said.

"Aelgar sent me. Pratha Yronae requests your presence," he said, eying Nathan's gardening overalls skeptically. "But I think she might be willing to wait long enough for you to bathe and change into something more suitable." He *tsk*ed as he looked at the dirt under Nathan's ragged nails. "And do something about your hands."

Nathan slumped over his potting shelf, exasperated. "Oh, God," he muttered. "*Now* what have I done?"

"You are becoming paranoid, Nathan Nga'esha," the older man chided.

"It isn't paranoia when they really are out to get you, Margasir." He brushed his palms off on the cloth of the overalls before leaving the greenhouse and locking the door. It wasn't to prevent theft, since stealing was a crime nearly unheard-of on Vanar, but to keep the more inquisitive boys from constantly opening the door to see what strange and wonderful things the yepoqioh could be doing inside and disrupting the greenhouse's meticulously maintained climate.

He hadn't seen Pratha Yronae since the night he danced for her, several months before. Nor had he been to the Assembly. Namasi Sahmudrah had come by only once to apprise him of the delay; the Assembly of Families were conferring in a special session to discuss his petition to speak again, which might be good, or it might be bad. They were using delaying tactics hoping to wear him down, but there was little other choice. He would have to wait and see, but soon, soon, she assured him.

He showered quickly, sitting impatiently as Margasir combed out and braided his hair with quick, practiced fingers, working in a sprig of crimson penstemon. The sahakharae tugged the elaborate folds of Nathan's sati into place and secured the end with the red beetle pin. The older man looked him over critically, then rooted in a coffer for several gold anklets. "Wear these," he insisted. Nathan stooped to fasten the heavy anklets. "Daughter's father, right foot," Margasir corrected him wearily.

"You enjoy this, don't you?" Nathan grumbled.

"Of course, Nathan Nga'esha. It was always my childhood dream to oversee a scrawny ugly ajnyaenam bah'chae who can't be trusted to find his ass with both hands."

His práhsaedam walked with him to the connecting doors between houses, stopping at a distance from the waiting Dhikar to fret with Nathan's sati pin like a mother hen. Nathan brushed his hands away irritably. "If you're this nervous, I must be in serious trouble," Nathan said in an undertone, his back to the Dhikar.

"Not this time, Nathan, miraculously enough," Margasir ducked his head to mutter discreetly with a wary glance at the waiting Dhikar. "But please try your very best not to fuck this one up," he said, using the Hengeli expletive perfectly. He winked slyly and walked away before Nathan had a chance to say another word.

The Dhikar escorted Nathan to Yronae's private rooms and stood on either side of the door, his cue to enter. He paused, taking a deep breath to compose himself, preparing for the role of a compliant Vanar man, pasted on his best smile, and walked in.

The effort was wasted. Several taemorae attended to Pratha Yronae, dressing her in an exquisite Nga'esha kirtiya belted over baggy saekah, blue birdsilk shot through with gold filigree. Another taemora organized the pratha h'máy's jewelry, clipping several strands of gold chain from one ear, under the chin, to the other. Yet a third knelt to add the finishing touches to the intricate painting on the skin of her bare feet. Yronae barely glanced over her shoulder at him, said curtly, "Good, you're here," and motioned with her chin for him to stand out of the way.

"You are aware that the Nga'esha are receiving a delegation from your home world?" Yronae asked, shifting her head to allow the taemora to anchor the weight-bearing support in her hair.

"Hae'm, jah'nari l'amae."

"The ambassador is a woman named Suzenne Rashir, as I'm sure you already know."

"Of course, Pratha Yronae." Everyone in the Nga'esha House knew. There had been many other Hengeli delegations on Vanar since his arrival, none of which he had ever been allowed to meet. But while he didn't expect to see another Hengeli again in his life, he kept up with the gossip as well as the next.

The Hengeli had obviously looked into what little Vanar history they could find and rooted around for someone they felt the Nga'esha would respect, someone descended from the same ancient rootstock. Rashir was proud of being from a traditional matrilineal Khasi clan, almost pureblooded and actually born in Shillong.

Nathan knew the pratha h'máy Yronae dva Ushahayam ek Daharanan traeyah Nga'esha could not possibly have cared less; the descendant of the ancestor who had settled Vanar and founded the Nga'esha branch of the Nine Families did not consider tenuous blood connections to modern Khasi relevant. In her eyes, Rashir was as Hengeli as any other of the women in her entourage.

The taemora finished fiddling with her jewelry and stepped away. Yronae turned to him.

"You will attend the conference."

He nodded, wondering how many figs he'd have to poke back onto the tray this time.

"Just you."

Baffled, he momentarily forgot his manners and looked at her directly. "Excuse me, pratha h'máy?"

"This isn't a social reception, it's a business meeting. You are to listen and say nothing. You are to react to nothing that is said. You will conduct yourself with the utmost propriety at all times, is that understood?"

He was nearly breathless with astonishment. "Hae'm, jah'nari l'amae." He was about to meet the first Hengeli he'd seen in over five years. "Thank you."

Yronae snorted. "You don't sing, you don't dance, you're not even pleasurable to look at. If you insist on remaining here, I must find some use for you. My mother understood these Hengeli in a way I would be foolish not to admit I never can. I want you there to listen and observe. You know the language, the culture, the way they think, how their hands move, all the unspoken significances. When it's over, you and I will go over every word together, and you will clarify for me whatever we as Vanar might have missed."

"Hae'm, jah'nari l'amae."

She finally smiled grimly. "So, Nathan Crewe Nga'esha, shall we go see just how Vanar you really are?" She snapped her fingers, and he fell behind the entourage following her into the great hall.

The ambassador and her interpreter had already taken their seats when they arrived. Yronae settled as leisurely as a cat onto a thick floor cushion, facing the ambassador. With one leg under her, the other knee up in a formal pose, Yronae looked impressive and arrogant and uncompromising as hell.

Removing the edge of the sati from over his head, Nathan took his place beside Yronae's left shoulder, kneeling smoothly onto the hard floor, no cushion to ease his legs. The pratha h'máy ignored him as thoroughly as furniture, although he bowed politely before he sat back on his heels, palms on his thighs. Yronae's interpreter sat at her right hand, while Suryah, as her senior daughter and heir apparent, observed from the sidelines. Several taemorae hovered unobtrusively to keep water glasses filled and small sweetmeats on hand, while an impressive number of household Dhikar stood sentry, as immobile as statues.

Although he kept his eyes properly averted, the habit of watching but not looking now ingrained in him, he was aware of the Hengelis' surprise at his presence. As soon as the Hengeli ambassador began to speak, he looked up and kept his attention steadily on the delegation. The interpreter murmured quietly beside Yronae, an odd echo in his own mind. When Yronae spoke, he noted the ambassador's interpreter had to struggle to keep up with the flow, stumbling over words, often missing the nuances completely. He had some sympathy for her; Vanar was a damned difficult language to learn, particularly for someone without the benefit of living for years within the culture.

The Hengeli ambassador was a stout, dark woman obviously ill at ease. Her autocratic bearing and square-shouldered dress were a shade too formal to be anything less than military. She fidgeted slightly, try-ing to ease her legs under her on her floor cushion, unused to anything other than sitting in chairs. After half an hour of polite overtures and allusions to their common genealogy, Rashir began to realize, to her obvious irritation, that being Khasi gave her absolutely no advantage whatsoever.

Two other Hengeli officials flanked her, one of them the ambas-sador's own interpreter, completing the delegation. The other, her as-sistant, Heloise Ruuspoelk, a freckled woman with frizzy mud-colored hair and sharp green eyes, sat respectfully behind her. Even kneeling, Nathan was a head taller than Yronae, his light hair and pale eyes in his round Caucasian face in stark contrast to the normal dark Vanar features. As silent an observer as he was, she studied him with a puz-zled expression; then her face cleared. He kept himself from reacting to her shrewd smile.

"The fact remains," the ambassador was saying with frustration, "there seems little point in 'negotiating' if the results are preordained."

Yronae's interpreter translated flawlessly, but Nathan listened to the emotions behind the words: anger, tension, repressed desperation. Emotions he was all too familiar with himself.

Yronae nodded gravely. "We Vanar have no reason to pretend to a position of weakness," she said levelly. "But we do not believe this makes us tyrants. The Systems do concern us, even if that concern merely is one of self-interest. Vanar has always remained neutral in the affairs of outsiders."

"Not always, jah'nari pratha," the ambassador said. "Even your late mother is known to have had direct involvement in conflicts outside Vanar's interests."

Yronae's cool demeanor didn't alter. "My mother's exposure to alien cultures affected her judgment in many peculiar ways," she said evenly. "Some, undeniably, have aided our Family's prosperity. Others have not yielded quite as beneficial results." The frizzy-haired aide glanced at him. "But I am not my mother. If the Nga'esha are being asked to become more involved in your external affairs, it isn't unreasonable for us to take the time to understand them."

The ambassador's smile was bitter. "And for each minute we wait for you to educate yourselves, a hundred more Hengeli civilians are dying." The aide's glance flicked briefly toward her superior. Yronae was still listening to the murmur of the interpreter, and the ambassador continued before she could respond. "Women and children as well as men, pratha h'máy."

Yronae's expression hardened. "War is repugnant to the Vanar, we are a culture that values peace and civilized mediation over violence. We will not lower ourselves to become involved in outside conflict by choosing sides. I understand your difficulty, Madam Ambassador, but your political conflicts are not our concern."

"Even if our political conflicts are making you rich?"

"We are a trading people," Yronae said bluntly, "not philanthropists. We have a service you need. We expect to be paid for that service, in full, in advance. If you can't meet the price, either make an offer of a different nature, or go home. We value those who are capable of hard negotiations, while we have little patience with disrespect, in men *or* women."

The ambassador recovered her composure. "Nor do I, I assure you. Past experience has led me to suspect negotiating with those who have already made up their minds before negotiations even begin is a futile and demeaning process that I have no interest in. I've learned to speak bluntly, because I've found when faced with bloody-minded re-calcitrance, honesty works when nothing else will."

Nathan risked glancing at Yronae, wondering how she would take the insulting innuendo. Surprisingly, Yronae looked puzzled rather than angry. "Your past experience, however relevant to other peoples, surely cannot have had much to do with the Nga'esha."

The ambassador smiled dryly. "I was not implying the Nga'esha," she said, although Nathan knew damned well she was. "I'm speaking of Novapolita, our mutinous colony. The one pounding ancient and ir-replaceable Hengeli cities into dust every time a Nga'esha Pilotship spits one of their warships through the Worm."

"They pay the price," Yronae said calmly. "You pay the price and you may spit your warships through the Worm to pound *their* cities into rubble."

Yronae knew his past. What minor details the Vanar couldn't have found in records, Vasant Subah had efficiently extracted from him. He wondered if she had brought him into the conference just to see what his reaction would be to hear Hengeli was under attack.

The friction between Novapolita and Hengeli had been dragging on for more than two hundred years. But other than a long series of blockades, general strikes, and sporadic terrorist assaults, the tension had never escalated into outright war.

The Hengeli had declared a cease-fire to their internal civil war more than a decade ago. The refugee camps of Nathan's childhood, apparently, were long gone. Enough of the remaining population had immigrated off-world to reduce the pressure on what little water re-sources remained, while enough goods funneled from the Hengeli ter-ritories into the depleted motherworld relieved the need to guard the Haves from the desperate, homeless Have-Nots.

If what the Hengeli ambassador was saying was true, the Hengeli regime, having paid so dearly to crush civil war, was now losing the battle with the mainstay of their survival, their off-world colonies. Without the influx of vital resources, the Hengeli economy and the technology to run it would grind to a halt. Only what remained of the infrastructure, the military, was holding on.

To his own surprise, Nathan found he still cared.

Hengeli had been the birthplace of civilization, the ground from which the seed spread to the stars. Once Hengeli had been the center of all civilization, her ancient cities, her art, her languages, her cultures the foundation of all humanity populating the three hundred settled systems. Including Vanar. Rashir was doing her best to lean hard on that family connection stretching back nearly a millennium.

It wasn't working.

"We treat Novapolita with as much courtesy as any other client," Yronae said, pausing to give the ambassador's interpreter time to translate. "If they stop paying our price, they will find themselves in the same position as the Hengeli."

"They have access to revenues we don't, pratha h'máy. They have a debt to us, and we are simply demanding the fair and just repayment we are due. Theirs is a relatively young world. Surely you know Hengeli's problems are not of our own making; our resources were decimated by natural disaster. It is true, we might have managed things better, but our colonies have benefited from the lessons we learned without having to pay the same penalty. May I remind you it was Hengeli technology that provided every single system in existence, including Novapolita, with the means by which they were able to settle their colonies in the first place? It is only right and just that they should come to our aid now in return, not take advantage of our weakness."

Nathan could hear the mother's lament behind the clear, modulated elocution and her military bearing. *After all I've done for you, and this is how my children return my love?*

Yronae smiled, humorless. "That might be true of your colonies, but not Vanar, Madam Ambassador. *Not* Vanar."

"I beg your forgiveness for contradicting you, pratha h'máy," Rashir persisted, "but even Vanar. Your people did not settle this world by wishful thinking alone. They had to use Hengeli technology, Hengeli material, Hengeli bioscience ever to have reached Vanar and survive in the first place, regardless of any other circumstances."

Yronae listened to her interpreter, the taemora mumbling with her eyes half shut, almost trancelike. The silence that followed was longer than the time lag in translation.

"I was not aware the Hengeli created the Worms, Madam Ambassador," she said finally.

The ambassador was quick to retort. "Neither did the Vanar. Whatever they are, or whoever built them, they are artifacts vastly older than either of our civilizations, pratha h'máy. And with respect, while you may have been the first to exploit them and have refashioned the Pilotships into a mold more accessible for human beings, the Vanar cannot take credit for the Worms any more than you can take credit for the creation of the universe."

"An honor, as every Vanar knows, belonging solely to the Holy Creatress," Yronae answered blandly. "But we are not here to discuss theology. You want to use the Worm for your own purposes. We have no objection. Pay our price."

The ambassador fidgeted on the floor cushion, unaccustomed to Vanar furnishings. "Novapolita is rich in natural energy resources. She is, legally and legitimately, under Hengeli administration. For political reasons that are making her own government unstable, she has defied all legal pressures to compel her to resume repayment of a significant debt owed to Hengeli fiscal authorities. The situation has become critical. We would only need the use of the Worm for a single operation. Once Novapolita is back under rightful Hengeli control, and her internal crisis rectified, we would be able to repay Vanar threefold the price."

Yronae heard the bribe and ignored it.

"And if you failed, Vanar would lose its investment."

"We would not fail," the ambassador insisted. "We may be lacking in natural resources, but Hengeli has had a much longer time to perfect our military capabilities. Our military force is five times that of Novapolita, both in the total number of warships and in support vessels, and the magnitude of our technological capability and expertise is unmatched by theirs."

Nathan realized how desperate the situation must be. They were going to throw all they had at Novapolita in one last-ditch campaign, gambling everything on victory.

"Once Novapolita is back under our control, we would reimburse Vanar for the expenses she has incurred in our behalf for a pre-arranged, mutually agreed upon amount."

Yronae did not take the bait. "That sort of business practice is illegal on Vanar, Madam Ambassador. It is not only unlawful, but morally contemptible for a buyer to use the assets of a company it wishes to purchase as its own collateral against it."

"Novapolita is not a company, pratha h'máy. But to use the same analogy, it is an illegal and immoral rebellion of one of Hengeli's subsidiary concerns attempting to break away from the parent corporation without the stockholders' permission or even offering a fair buy-out deal. It would be like one of your own Stations deciding they wanted to become a separate government without your permission, and cutting you off from your own assets. We only offer what is ours to begin with, a share of Novapolita's resources, which we are illegally being denied access to."

"This is a matter of opinion, Madam Ambassador, as well as a matter of politics. Vanar is a neutral government. We are not in the business of deciding the legality of one non-Vanar complainant over another. Nor are we willing to break our own laws to gamble on the outcome of your dispute."

Rashir looked down at her blunt fingers wrapped around each other with white-knuckled strength. Ruuspoelk had not changed expression, still scrutinizing Nathan.

"We do not have sufficient ready funds to buy passage for the number of ships we require," Rashir said. "Unless we are in possession of another asset you may be interested in?"

Yronae shrugged, halfway between the Vanar gesture for no and indifference. "If you are in possession of something that might be of value to us, however uncustomary, the Nga'esha are willing to consider all offers, Madam Ambassador."

Rashir nodded grimly. "I would need to confer with my superiors, pratha h'máy. We shall return to our ship in the morning, with your permission. Message transmissions with Hengeli may take a few hours. May I request a delay until tomorrow evening?"

Yronae consented, and remained seated until the Hengeli party had bowed and filed out of the room. She sat for some time, eyes narrowed as she deliberated. No one dared so much as to fidget.

"Little brother," she said finally, without looking at him.

"Hae'm, pratha h'máy?"

"You will have tea with me. I would like the benefit of your observations and feel it may take longer than I had initially anticipated."

His stomach lurched, the thought of an intimate tête-à-tête with Pratha Yronae not his idea of an enjoyable afternoon. But however courteously it might be worded, her request was not optional.

"A pleasure, eminent sister."

XXXIX

FIVE HOURS LATER, HE WAS ESCORTED THROUGH THE RESTRICTED annex of the House where foreign visitors were lodged, opulent guest rooms at the far west end of the women's quarters well guarded by Dhikar. All the rooms overlooked a large, cloistered garden, with a stunning vista of mountains over the rooftops, but any view of the city or its inhabitants was meticulously concealed. The Hengeli entourage were entertained and pampered, taemorae at their beck and call, but kept confined as securely as in any prison and more isolated from contact with the Vanar than an asteroid mine.

Knowing the entire wing was monitored and hyperaware of invisible eyes watching, Nathan followed one of Yronae's many nieces, stopping as the woman knocked on the doors. As the doors slid open, the niece half bowed silently and left him facing Ruuspoelk. He had barely touched his dinner, too nervous for any appetite.

"Come in, please," she said, and turned to let him past her. The power of habit had him bow toward her, fingers together loosely, before he walked into the room.

"Would you like to sit down?" She seemed uncertain of what etiquette was expected.

"Thank you," he said, and crossed to a pair of floor pillows heavy and flattened from use beside the low table. He brushed the hem of his sati back with one foot and knelt, Vanar fashion, Vanar manners, then waited pointedly until she lowered herself awkwardly to the floor cushions. Sitting back on his heels, he slipped the edge of the sati from his head and arranged it on his shoulders. He quietly adjusted the numerous heavy gold bracelets on his wrists before placing his palms against his thighs. And hoped he didn't look anywhere near as nervous as he felt.

He kept his eyes focused steadily just past her shoulder as she examined him with frank interest. While some Vanar might consider his alien features unattractive, he had never had that complaint with Hengeli women, and he knew it. Regenerative therapy preserved his youth, and the Vanar male obsession with exercise kept him fit and trim. He wore a formal Nga'esha sati of rich watered birdsilk, hand-embroidered at the edges with gold thread, only the neckline of his wine red mati showing. His feet were bare but freshly hennaed, the bangle around his right ankle glinting with blood rubies the same color as his mati. An elaborate five-strand braid fell across his shoulder, following the curve of his chest. A tiny scattering of blue flowers and small silver beads glinted where they had been mixed with his blond hair.

Heloise Ruuspoelk had the harried look of an overworked bureaucrat, several pounds overweight from too many hours spent over files on a reader. She wore the same unexceptionally tailored trousers and jacket she had worn to each of the three meetings, and he wondered if she actually owned any other clothing.

"Drink?" she offered as an afterthought.

"No, thank you."

"Well." She cleared her throat. Smiled. The expression was flat, without warmth.

"You requested to see me," he said quietly. "What can I do for you?"

"Actually, I asked to see 'that man who said nothing at the meeting.' I'd like to know who you are, first."

He said promptly, in Vanar, "Son of Yaenida, brother of Yronae, husband of Kallah, father of Aenanda."

She stared at him blankly. "I meant, what is your name?"

"Nathan Crewe Nga'esha," he said.

Her smile widened, but grew no warmer. "That's an Hengeli name," she said with satisfaction.

"Nga'esha isn't."

"You're Vanar?"

"Yes."

She studied his sati. "And Nga'esha?"

"I am the youngest son of the former pratha h'máy, Yaenida Nga'esha. Yronae is my sister."

"Amazing. Your late mother must have been exceptionally fertile at such an advanced age." Nathan didn't respond to her sarcasm. "You speak excellent Hengeli."

"Thank you."

"You *are* Hengeli, aren't you?"

He thought about how to answer that, aware others were listening. "Yes," he said after a moment. "I'm also Hengeli." He kept it in the present tense.

She laughed, the sound small and tight. "Ironic, isn't it? The first Nga'esha man I ever get to meet turns out to be Hengeli." He didn't respond. "If you don't mind my asking, Mr. Crewe, what is an Hengeli man doing at these meetings?"

It had been a long time since someone had addressed him as "mister," the sound of it jarring.

"I'm an interpreter."

"Bullshit," she said. He translated the word literally into Vanar in his head and thought of Yronae trying to puzzle out the meaning of the word, wondering what bovine droppings had to do with anything.

"I don't translate conversation. I'm there to give the Nga'esha pratha h'máy the benefit of my knowledge of Hengeli culture. Cultural analyst, if you prefer."

"It was my understanding that foreign men were strictly prohibited on Vanar."

"They are," he agreed. He didn't elaborate.

"Aren't you homesick, Mr. Crewe?" Ruuspoelk asked. Her tone was casual, if the question was not.

He considered the nuances of the question carefully before he answered. Even with Yronae's assurance he was free to discuss anything with this woman, he knew this skated a dangerous area. "I'm married to the Changriti dalhitri h'máy. We have a daughter. Her name is Aenanda. It means 'joy' in Vanar. This is my home now."

It didn't answer her question, but it did. She stared at him for a moment before she leaned back.

"Hm." She nodded, her eyes wandering to take in his dress. "You seem to have adjusted well enough. Gone native."

He heard the implied insult. He didn't allow any anger to show, feeling, in fact, little of anything.

"How in the hell did you end up here, of all places?"

He thought of Pratima in the clearing by the river. *So tell me, what's a nice Hengeli boy like you doing on Vanar?* It was certainly a question he'd never been able to answer to his own satisfaction. He gave his long-established excuse. "I came looking for a plant. About so high." He held his hands up to measure. "Dark reddish leaves, primitive pseudoflowers. Indigenous to Vanar."

"A plant?" she echoed cynically.

He replaced his palms against his thighs. "I was a botanist before I came to Vanar. I still am."

She didn't answer for several seconds, studying him thoughtfully. "That's not what we've heard," she said finally. "We've heard you were abducted and sold into slavery."

He felt his face go cold. There was only one way she could have known that, only one source she could have heard it from. Lyris. Even angry, he chose his words cautiously, knowing as well as she did that their conversation was being recorded.

"An exaggeration at best," he said. "And if you already know who I am, you also know I've had several studies on indigenous Vanar botany published in Hengeli academic journals over the past four years, which I'll be happy to supply you with should you care to read them. Now, if your curiosity is satisfied, may I go, or is there anything else you wanted to see me for?"

"Your help, Mr. Crewe," another voice behind him said.

He twisted to stare at the ambassador standing behind him, her back against the closed door. He got to his feet more quickly than was graceful. "Excuse me, but I was not given permission to speak with anyone other than Heloise Ruuspoelk."

"I don't give a damn."

"I do. This conversation is over," he said, now openly angry.

"No, I don't think so. This conversation is just starting," Suzenne Rashir said, her face hardened. "And unless my sources about Vanar manners are in error, you won't lay a hand on me to force me away from this door, which means you aren't going anywhere until I say we're done here." She smiled, a twin to the frosty expression of her aide. "So, which are you? Vanar or Hengeli?"

"It doesn't matter which I am. If I touch a woman against her will, Yronae Nga'esha will have me skinned alive. *Not* a reliable test of my loyalties. But if you don't get away from that door voluntarily, I will be forced to call for assistance. This room is being monitored, Madam Ambassador, as I'm sure you're aware, and I can't believe you really want to cause an incident. Not on Vanar."

The smile had vanished, replaced by a flat, unreadable veneer. "Shout as loud as you like," she said calmly. "No one will hear you."

"Among my various other duties," Heloise Ruuspoelk said, "I'm also a debugging expert. Vanar monitoring systems are admittedly extremely good, as most of them are based on Hengeli technology to begin with. But our neutralizing is even better." She pulled a small slender device from under her tunic and held it lightly in her hand. The dull burnished copper cylinder looked like an ordinary reader pen, more ornamental than functional, which, he suspected, it was supposed to.

"Then the pratha h'máy must be aware by now something is wrong," he said, now afraid as well as angry.

"We'll take the risk."

He was shaking, outraged. "You're not the one taking it," he snapped. "Instead of spending a few minutes explaining the nuances of a recorded conversation to the pratha h'máy, all you've done now is ensure I'm going to be spending the rest of the night resurrecting it word for word from memory."

"Then she's going to want you to listen carefully, isn't she?" Heloise Ruuspoelk said. "All we're asking you to do is stay a few minutes, have a friendly chat. That's all. Then you can tell her anything you want." She chuckled. "Even the truth."

"Please sit down, Mr. Crewe," the ambassador said.

He reluctantly walked back to the floor cushion and knelt, brushing his sati back with one foot, in pointedly Vanar formality. The ambassador pushed away from the door and sat down next to her aide, legs crossed clumsily.

"Nga'esha is one of the Nine High Families," Rashir said. "How did *you* become a Nga'esha?"

"I was adopted. It's common practice here."

"You must miss your real family."

He almost laughed, but not in humor. "As far as either I or the Vanar are concerned, the Nga'esha *is* my real family. I haven't seen my birthmother in twenty years." How easy it was to say "birthmother" rather than "real mother," he realized. "I doubt she knows I'm on Vanar, or cares. I don't know where she is now."

"How sad that you can disown your own mother like that." The expression in Rashir's eyes was chilly. "But I suppose being Vanar and a Nga'esha does afford you a more lavish lifestyle than that of the average Hengeli," Rashir said, glancing significantly at his massive gold bracelets. He kept his hands still, not acknowledging the look. "The Nga'esha are the most powerful of the Nine Families. Being a Nga'esha as well as married into the Changriti must give you a great deal of money and power, doesn't it?"

He allowed himself a snort of amused scorn. "You really don't understand how things work here, do you?"

"Evidently not," Rashir agreed promptly. "We don't have the benefit of your extensive experience. Which puts us at a somewhat unfair disadvantage."

He hesitated, weighing his loyalties. "I have an income from my Nga'esha investments, modest by Vanar standards, which I agree outside Vanar would be an enormous fortune. I make more money in a single month in interest alone than either of you will ever earn in your entire lives."

Rashir remained impassive, but Ruuspoelk's eyes blinked rapidly for a moment before she regained her self-control. It was a small pleasure, but satisfying.

"But since I can't spend it anywhere but Vanar, I hardly qualify as being wealthy. While being the brother of the pratha h'máy might give me some minor privileges, I'm only a man as well as the youngest brother, and still obviously Hengeli. I'm third and least important husband to a Changriti. Marriage does *not* make me Changriti, only my daughter. I'm my wife's property, not family. Any 'influence' I have over either the Nga'esha or the Changriti is limited in the extreme."

"Property," Ruuspoelk said with distaste.

He looked directly at her. "Property," he repeated firmly.

"There are men who enjoy being dominated by women. Is that why you're here, are you one of those sort of men?"

If she was trying to goad him into a reaction, he had had too much practice at keeping his temper hidden. He smiled dryly. "Not according to my pratha h'máy," he said, knowing that would have amused Yronae.

"I see. Are you happy here?"

He wished Yronae had not insisted he meet with these women on his own. "Sometimes." He also wished he were a better liar.

"Would you like to go back? With us?"

He wondered if Yronae had known they would make him that offer. "I left Hengeli when I was nineteen. Regardless of how I got here or why, I'm not a prisoner. I've had to learn how to balance my allegiances, but I've chosen to stay, of my own free will."

"We know all about balancing allegiances, Mr. Crewe. Things have changed since you were last in Hengeli. The civil war has been over for years. Former enemies work together now quite compatibly." She exchanged a wry look with Ruuspoelk. "Hengeli has enjoyed twelve years of unbroken peace, the damage so completely repaired you wouldn't know the war had ever happened. We've all worked hard for peace. No one, *no one* wants another war. But every day, innocent Hengeli are dying in a conflict they didn't start and certainly don't deserve, unable to protect themselves or their families." It was a set speech delivered with a politician's plastic earnestness.

"I'm well aware of the consequences of war, Madam Ambassador."

He knew he could keep his face and voice matter-of-fact. "My father was killed by a sniper when I was seven. He was holding my hand when he was shot. My mother was a mathematics teacher. There wasn't much call for her qualifications in a refugee camp. She and I weren't close. I didn't see much of her; she worked most days in forced labor crews defusing mines in the occupied zones and most nights in someone else's bed to keep us from starving. So excuse me if I feel no moral obligation to help you to decide whose father deserves to die and whose does not."

Rashir listened with cordial disinterest, but Ruuspoelk flushed.

"But you knew all this, didn't you?"

If he had hoped to shame either woman, he had failed. "Of course we did, Mr. Crewe," Ruuspoelk said. "Your presence at such a high level Nga'esha meeting came as a surprise. That prompted us to do some digging. Not easy, since few people outside Vanar even know you exist. Your disappearance didn't create much of a stir, frankly. But our intelligence division is good, very good. And very quick. We know all there is to know about you, right up to the time you dropped out of sight. Our data on you after Vanar is admittedly a bit hazier. You're wrong about your mother, by the way. She does care." She smirked at his reaction. "She's alive and well in Villemare-del-Sol. Happily re-married. You have a half brother. His name is Francesco. He's twelve. Looks a lot like you."

He was silent for a moment. "Please give them my best," he said finally, his voice toneless.

Rashir had sat quietly while her aide spoke, without intervening. After a moment, Ruuspoelk exhaled through her nose in contempt. "We also know about your felony convictions."

He had been the same age as his unknown half brother, running in a small gang of children for the protection of numbers rather than trying to survive alone. The first offense had been for stealing potatoes from a black market trader, the magistrate correspondingly lenient. The second had been for heisting an expensive sport scoot in a desperate bid to escape Westcastle. Unfortunately, it had belonged to one of the military police sergeants assigned to the border patrol of West-castle. After a ludicrous low-speed chase, he'd crashed, the scoot demolished while he escaped unhurt. His pursuers remedied that disparity. After he was released from the infirmary, he spent six months in squalid internment before his mother could raise enough to pay the fine for his release.

"And your mother wasn't the only one who traded on her favors in Westcastle, was she? We know how you coerced Ivan Brohm to get him to smuggle you off Hengeli. We also know how you forged your credentials and lied your way into Remsill University. By the way, your degree has been revoked."

If they hoped to shake him a second time, it was their turn to fail.

"If your past behavior is anything to go by, it's not beneath you to use less-than-ethical methods for your own personal gain." Her scorn was almost palpable. "From thief and bumboy con man to a prominent member of the Nga'esha Family is an extraordinary achievement, wouldn't you say? Just out of curiosity, is your pratha h'máy aware of your criminal record?"

He almost laughed. "Every detail, Madam Ambassador."

He was certain this woman had never been in a refugee camp, was one of the privileged whose homes hadn't been blown out of existence. He wondered how well she would have resisted Vasant Subah's interrogation techniques.

Nor was their information as good as she thought: she was dead wrong about Ivan Brohm; Nathan hadn't had to coerce anyone. Regardless of Fat Ivan's other personal vices, he had never laid a finger on Nathan. Once he had discovered Nathan had a fascination for living plants, he had been delighted to take the boy under his wing. The terraform systems technician became the closest thing to a father Nathan had ever known. He latched onto both the older man's affection and the science like a lifeboat, the two mixed together. He had learned to put the war behind him, carve out his own bit of normal existence. Her derision didn't shame him.

"And I don't need to justify anything to you," he added softly.

Ruuspoelk leaned back, her mouth pressed thin. He didn't wait for her to answer, and rose on his knees.

"I'm sorry if you had the wrong impression that I have any influence over the Pratha Yronae just because I'm Nga'esha, or that I would even try to influence her just because I'm Hengeli. Now if there is nothing further I can do for you, would you mind allowing me to leave? I have a long night ahead, and I'd like to get it over with as quickly as possible."

"Not just yet," Rashir said, her tone mild.

He sat back onto his heels, annoyed.

"How much do you know about the trade dispute between the Nga'esha and the Changriti over the Dunton Station issue? I think the Vanar call it Sukrah Station?"

"Absolutely nothing," he said coldly. "Men here are barred from any involvement whatsoever in High Family business affairs." Even the news available to men was heavily censored.

"You are at least aware that the Changriti and the Nga'esha have long been hostile business rivals?"

He briefly contemplated several caustic responses, but settled for the one that would give him the least trouble with Yronae.

"Yes."

"We are in possession of information that could possibly resolve the current dispute in the Nga'esha's favor," Rashir suggested, studying her blunt nails. "Then again, the Changriti might want to pay to ensure this information doesn't reach the Nga'esha, should your pratha h'máy not agree to a reasonable commission."

If Rashir didn't enjoy negotiations with Yronae, he thought, he'd love to be present when she tried to threaten Eraelin. He leaned back, pensive.

"Unfortunately you're talking to the wrong person. Pratha Yronae is simply not going to allow me to be involved with High Family business. If you have something to offer the pratha h'máy, you should be speaking to her about it."

"We can't. Not openly." She exchanged an enigmatic glance with Ruuspoelk. "Official negotiations are too exposed to public scrutiny. It would jeopardize a delicate intelligence operation. You're in a unique position. We can use someone inside the Nga'esha who can relay private documents and information for us without attracting undue attention. Not only can you act as our courier with the Nga'esha, you have access to the Changriti, which may be of value to Pratha Yronae as well."

"Whatever Pratha Yronae chooses to use me for, I still can't help you with the Changriti. My wife has begun divorce proceedings against me—"

"Then *un*-begin them," Ruuspoelk said sharply. Her green eyes were intense. "Kiss and make up. Because there is more at stake here than your personal life."

This time Rashir shot her a warning look, then went back to inspecting her nails. "Believe me, Mr. Crewe, it is no pleasure to see any Hengeli citizen being subjected to what is not much better than slavery," Rashir said. "But my personal sympathy is not the issue here. The thousands of Hengeli men, women, and children dying every day is. Their survival is my sole priority. For humanitarian reasons alone you should help us to help them."

She was making the same error he once had, presuming that Hengeli philosophy and values gave her a cultural superiority to the Vanar. To her Hengeli mind, the Vanar were antiquated savages who had done nothing to deserve their vast wealth. Their tyrannical customs offended her, and she resented being compelled to appeal to an outlaw colony whose primitive ethics had to be tolerated, if despised.

Nathan said nothing, not trusting himself to speak. For a moment, he wanted to warn her that patronizing the Vanar would be a grave mistake, but knew the attempt would be futile. Suzenne Rashir was not a woman easily convinced any society other than her own could ever possibly be as sophisticated or civilized.

"And if we can't appeal to your compassion," Ruuspoelk added caustically, "would it help to clarify things if I told you that while you sit there mulling it over, little Aenanda Changriti could be in danger? Surely your pratha h'máy is not so inflexible she would risk the safety of a five-year-old child, her own *niece*, would she?"

Even Ambassador Rashir glanced at her aide in annoyance. He stared at Ruuspoelk, aware of the pulse beating in his ears, and had to clear his throat before he could speak. "My daughter is not part of the Nga'esha family, and my pratha h'máy will not be concerned with her welfare. But I'd advise you to be extremely careful about making threats against my daughter," he said slowly, finally allowing his anger to show.

Ruuspoelk looked up with a good deal more surprise than was natural. "You misunderstand. I'm not threatening anyone. How could anyone threaten the Vanar?"

"Enough," the ambassador said tersely. "I think we've made our point. Hopefully you can make it to your pratha h'máy."

"You should have just left the monitors functioning," Nathan said grimly. "My opinion one way or the other doesn't matter to Pratha Yronae. She isn't likely to regard me as anything more than a recording device."

"That's fine, Mr. Crewe," Ruuspoelk said. "We didn't neutralize this room to prevent the Nga'esha pratha h'máy from knowing what we've discussed."

He absorbed their meaning. "Then if you're finished with me, it's late and I'd like to be allowed to leave."

"By all means."

He stood, his legs shaky, and bowed. He paused by the door, however, and looked back. "I suppose it is an Hengeli failing. It seems it's not beneath you to use less-than-ethical methods for your own gain as well."

Rashir barely acknowledged him with a hint of a nod, while Ruuspoelk glared at him acidly.

Two of the Nga'esha household guards waited for him on the other side of the soundproof doors, dark eyes impassive. He bowed slightly and said, "I believe the pratha h'máy is anxious to see me."

It was one of the rare times he had seen one of the dour, muscular Dhikar smile.

XL

THEY ESCORTED HIM DIRECTLY TO YRONAE'S PRIVATE APARTMENTS. THE low bed had been recently occupied, to judge by the bedclothes in disarray, and Yronae wore an oversized tasmai tied at the waist, her hair unbraided but tied back loosely from her face. But he saw no sign of drowsiness in her eyes or in the compressed set of her mouth.

The dalhitri b'ahu of Dravyam, Mahdupi, sat sipping brandy from a heavy blown glass while a nameless medical taemora waited at a polite distance. With the Dhikar on either side of him, he bowed, doing his best to hide his dread.

He was both surprised and grateful when Yronae dismissed the Dhikar. "We won't need them, Nathan." She indicated he should kneel on the thick floor cushion rather than the floor. "We may be here for some time, and I want your mind on your task, not your shins." Her tone was curt, but not cruel.

He knelt, settling himself comfortably as the taemora pushed up the sleeve of his mati and pressed a medgun against his upper arm. It hissed, and seconds later he felt the rush clearing his head, his thoughts suddenly coalescing into concise patterns. The taemora gave him two steel oblong spheres to hold one in each hand. Yronae would hold the third, his emotions amplified through the skin of her palm, reading his heartbeat, breathing, muscular electrical activity, hormonal activity in his blood, brainwave patterns. It was similar to the process Vasant Subah had employed to extract information from him. Minus the soul-crushing pain.

"Ready?"

"Hae'm, pratha h'máy," he murmured, closing his eyes.

He replayed the discussion, word for word, as accurately as he could remember, which, he knew, was accurate enough. For her part, Yronae allowed him to go at his own pace, uninterrupted. Nathan could feel his own fatigue under the drugs, like shadows hidden by the light reflecting from the surface of a pool.

"The ambassador then said that they hadn't neutralized the room to prevent you from knowing what we'd discussed."

"Meaning?"

He stopped, inhaled a deep, slow breath, and opened his eyes. The taemora was still beside him, her attention on the medical monitor in her lap. She began fitting up another dose in the medgun.

"Meaning they don't trust our security," Mahdupi interjected before he could think of a more judicious way to phrase it.

Yronae sucked air through the space between her front teeth, making a common sound Nathan had always disliked in the Vanar. Then her brow wrinkled momentarily, glancing at him, and he realized that although he had not reacted visibly, she could feel that dislike through the sphere in her palm, if not the reason. He wondered if she could also feel the involuntary thrill of alarm, his body ingrained to expect Dhikar retaliation.

"Typical Hengeli paranoia." She shifted the sphere from one hand to the other and rubbed the empty palm on her tasmai as if it itched, then frowned, irritated. "Run an inspection anyway, just to be thorough," she said to Mahdupi.

The older woman nodded. Yronae turned back to Nathan: "Go on."

"I requested her permission to leave. I did so at that point. The Dhikar were waiting outside to escort me immediately to you."

"And that was all?"

He hesitated, then said firmly, "That was all."

Her eyes narrowed suspiciously. The sphere in her hand told her he was lying, but he kept his eyes on the locus over her shoulder and his breathing even. His parting retort to the Hengeli was a private matter. After a moment, she grunted and relented.

"Who's in charge of security on Sukrah Station?" Yronae asked Mahdupi. Dunton was the Hengeli name for the Station, one Yronae would never stoop to using.

Mahdupi gestured to him. "You may go."

He had bowed and started to rise when Yronae whirled on him. "No, sit." Surprised, he sank back, the spheres still clutched in his hands. She glared at Mahdupi's questioning look. "He stays."

Mahdupi frowned, and began to speak in the incomprehensible language of women before Yronae cut her off impatiently.

"He stays," she insisted. "Up until now, he's been nothing but an annoying nuisance. At least I've finally found some use for my mother's worthless toy."

Mahdupi scowled her disapproval, shaking her head. "Rohnae dva Navamam Nga'esha," she said. "Head of Sukrah security for the past eleven years."

"What do you know about her?"

"She's from the Nga'esha Estate in Praetah, where she was born and raised. Her *traeyah* second cousin once removed is the household h'máy. She has no direct familial connection with the Changriti that I'm aware of."

"Check. Now."

With a sigh, the older woman fished in the belt of her kirtiya for a monocular lens, settled it over one eye, hooking it into the soundpearl in her ear, and slipped into a near-trance state as she began tapping into the Nga'esha security system. Green and red lights reflected from the surface of her eye, the data impressing itself directly into her retina and processed by long training by her brain. He glanced at the carved window screen, trying to judge by the light between the latticed wood how late the hour it might be. Or early, he thought glumly.

"She has no Changriti ancestry for five generations. Two kharvah at present, both from respectable Middle Families. She has one daughter and one son. Both kharvah are registered as the fathers sharing parentage for both children." Mahdupi's voice was atonal, focused on the data. She paused, switching into a different network. "The son would have been conceived during the first year she was on Sukrah." Pause. "Ah." Mahdupi's eyes focused past the flickering lights. "There is a notation in the medical files that neither kharvah is the genetic donor to her son, a fact apparently unknown by either of them."

Yronae sucked air through her teeth again. If she noted his involuntary reflex, she ignored it. "Changriti?"

Mahdupi was silent, her attention again back to the data oscillating through her retina. Despite the cushions underneath him, his legs ached, exhaustion shivering over him. Yronae paused from her restless pacing, the sphere still in her hand, and nodded curtly at the taemora. The drugs hissed into his arm before he realized, the pain abating.

"Not Changriti," Mahdupi said finally, then added, "not Vanar."

Yronae snorted her disgust, with an acrid glower at him.

"So who is the genetic father?"

Mahdupi shrugged. "If you like, I'll run a match, but it will take time, Yronae. Especially if the child's father isn't Vanar. We might get lucky, and find it's a Sukrah employee. Or it could be one of any number of transient passengers. There are fifty-two individual Hengeli systems connecting through Sukrah."

"Search them all," Yronae insisted. "Find him. I want every detail of Rohnae Nga'esha's movements, any contact, any connection she has ever had with the Changriti no matter how trivial. If she has been passing on Nga'esha secrets to the yepoqioh, I want to know what and who. And how." She looked grim. "I don't care why."

"Yronae, he should not remain here any longer," Mahdupi pressed. "This is not anything to concern him. He's tired; let him go."

Yronae waved the suggestion away irritably.

"Neither Ambassador Rashir or Heloise Ruuspoelk gave you any idea of what this information might entail, other than vague threats?" She pronounced the foreign names as badly as she did 'Nathan Crewe.'"

"No, jah'nari pratha."

"And they said nothing else about the Sukrah Station dispute between the Nga'esha and the Changriti, nothing at all?"

Normally, his personal evaluation would not be welcomed. He faltered, uncertain of how to couch his reply. Yronae snapped her fingers at him brusquely. "Come on, come on, now is not the time to prove how outstandingly Vanar you've become."

Nettled, he retorted sharply, "As I don't know a damned thing about what the Nga'esha and Changriti are involved in concerning Sukrah Station, all I can do is repeat as precisely as I can what was said," he said sharply. Yronae rocked back on her heels as Mahdupi hid a smile. "Jah'nari pratha," he added more prudently.

"Have you considered the possibility this could be nothing more than a trick, the Hengeli infecting you with their paranoia to persuade us into a concession?" Mahdupi suggested. "Rohnae dva Navamam Nga'esha may be guilty of nothing more than bad taste in men."

"For which she should lose her authority and be immediately recalled in disgrace," Yronae snapped.

"She's hardly the first woman to have an affair with an Hengeli man on Station. Or off," Mahdupi said lightly. "Even your esteemed mother Pratha Yaenida seemed fond of them in her immature youth, particularly large furry ones who liked to drink and talk too much."

Yronae glanced away, but not quick enough to hide her anger. "My esteemed mother, Mahdupi, never betrayed Nga'esha secrets in exchange for sex."

Mahdupi must have known how treacherous was the ground she walked on, but shrugged, unruffled, and retrieved her brandy glass. "No, but it wouldn't have been beneath *her* to attain secrets in return for sex. It served her well the first five decades of her rule. We think we know them, because we come and go as we please, while Vanar remains closed to them. But bear in mind, my child, we have only one of theirs." She nodded in Nathan's direction. "*They* have many, many more of *us* out there. And it's so very tempting, out among those enchanting peoples."

Yronae scowled. "What could our women possibly find so tempting about such a dangerous primitive culture?"

"Freedom," Nathan whispered.

"*Khee?*"

He felt the sweat on his palms against the spheres, the drugs still scintillating through his bloodstream making him reckless. He looked up, straight into Yronae's eyes. "Freedom, pratha h'máy. The freedom to go anywhere you want, any world and any Station, to say what you feel, to be with who you want, to love who you want, to do whatever you please. To escape all the traditional restrictions and have all the pressure of Family obligations a billion billion miles away."

Mahdupi watched him gravely, her head tilted as she listened. Whatever the sphere still in Yronae's hand was indicating, it was unpleasant enough for her to wince. Yronae passed her other hand across her forehead, shielding her eyes for a moment. When she looked back at him, he had lowered his gaze, once again the epitome of a properly deferential Vanar man.

"Paranoia or not, bluff or not," Yronae said, "even the allegation Nga'esha security on Station has been compromised can hurt us. The Changriti will use any charges of corruption for their own gain, whether they can prove it or not."

"It may not be a flaw in Nga'esha security," Mahdupi said calmly.

"No?"

Again, Mahdupi glanced at him, averse to discussing Nga'esha Family business in front of him. "They made every pretense his presence was an act of luck they hoped to turn to their advantage. And it is true the ambassador and her aide spent several hours in contact with their ship, accessing their own data records, before they asked to meet him."

"But?"

"If they have equipment sophisticated enough to evade the surveillance in our guest quarters, surely they can conceal their real communiqués behind a technological smokescreen."

Yronae snorted in contempt. "Now who is infected with Hengeli paranoia?"

Madhupi shrugged a shoulder, unconcerned. "Your mother and I have been playing these games since before you were born, Pratha. I may see patterns you do not." When Yronae looked thoughtful, she continued, "So how did the Hengeli know Aenanda Changriti is only five years old?"

Startled, they both looked at Mahdupi. She smiled and sipped her brandy.

"The Changriti would *never*—"

"Perhaps not knowingly."

Yronae was silent for several tense moments. "There is still too much we don't know."

"Agreed."

"But whatever the Hengeli have sealed in their barrel, we cannot afford *not* to buy it. If it is a subterfuge to buy them passage through to Novapolita, we'll deal with the consequences later." To Mahdupi: "Keep a close eye on Sukrah. Declare a complete lockdown if you must." To Nathan: "And you will meet with the Hengeli again when they return. It shouldn't arouse suspicion to say we are simply reassuring them one of their own is being well-treated."

Nathan nodded silently.

"If they give you something to pass on to us, go through Mahdupi. Mahdupi has always had the right of private access to the pratha h'máy—that will go unnoticed."

"Hae'm, jah'nari l'amae."

She paused, observing him. The drugs and tension elevated his blood pressure, his heart thudding dully, making him slightly nauseous.

"You have an unnaturally close rapport with your daughter. Children often know more than we give them credit for. She will trust you and will tell you anything you ask. We should arrange for you to see Aenanda as soon as possible. You will naturally be overcome by paternal love, beg Kallah's forgiveness and to be allowed to return to your rightful duties as her kharvah—"

"No."

Yronae stopped with her mouth open, stunned at being abruptly interrupted. For several seconds, she stared at him. "What did you say?" Her tone was very low, dangerous.

"No, Pratha Yronae. I will not do that."

Mahdupi found something fascinating at the bottom of her brandy glass.

"You will do as your pratha h'máy requires of you," Yronae said softly, her face pale.

He exhaled a deep breath before he spoke. "Forgive me, Sister, but you can't have it both ways. Either I am Vanar or I am not. I will not exploit Aenanda as a pawn in your strategy. Use me in whatever manner you like, but not my daughter."

"I do what is in the interest of the Nga'esha Family. Your daughter is Changriti—"

"She's an innocent child!" He struggled to get his anger back under control.

"You enjoy all the rank and privileges of a Nga'esha," Yronae snapped. He bit back a laugh, and her scowl deepened. "With that privilege comes duty. If you are not prepared to fulfill your duty on behalf of your Family, perhaps you should not profit from the benefits of that Family."

Mahdupi glanced up at her, startled, before her gaze slid back to the now empty glass in her hand.

Nathan stared at Yronae in disbelief.

"Well?" Yronae finally snapped.

Slowly, he shook his head, a completely Hengeli gesture. "I have always considered you difficult and demanding, sometimes even ruthless, but never dishonorable," he said quietly. Yronae was silent now, sitting a shade too fixed. "You've treated me harshly at times, as is your right as my pratha h'máy. But if you would make me naekulam as punishment for protecting my daughter, then I welcome it. Yours would no longer be a Family I would be proud to be a member of."

Mahdupi's mouth pursed thoughtfully as Yronae flushed, struggling with her own emotions. He hoped the sphere still clutched in her hand convinced her that he, at least, was not bluffing.

"I will not tolerate this sort of debate from a bah'chae," she said finally, her voice hoarse. "It is not your place to judge me." She flung the metal sphere back into the box with enough force to make him jump.

The muscles in her jaw worked. "We will meet with the Hengeli tomorrow, and talk about the rest later."

Mahdupi's subtle smile told him he had won.

"Hae'm, pratha h'máy." He swallowed hard and bowed deferentially.

XLI

He never got the chance to meet with either Rashir or Ruuspoelk again, however. In the early hours of the morning, he started awake at the sound of a woman's voice. "Little brother."

He blinked awake to see a woman standing in the open doorway of his private room. Women very rarely ever came to this part of the men's house, particularly this late at night. It was Bidaelah, Yronae's youngest daughter, he was astonished to see, and was just as suddenly afraid.

She stood flanked by two Dhikar, the blue borders around the ends of their white kirtiyas marking them as Nga'esha household security. They each carried heavy articulated rifles strapped onto their arms and shoulders, the first time Nathan had ever seen any of them carry weapons. He could hear the faint whispers of the soundpearls nestled inside their ears, connecting them to their Nga'esha overseers.

"Come with us," Bidaelah said grimly.

"What have I done?" It was out before he had thought about it, and flinched as one of the guards deliberately flexed her hand, the subdermal implants squirming to life with a harsh hum. The Dhikar's expression was totally blank, without malice.

"Be quiet and do as you're told," Bidaelah said sharply.

Wordlessly, he stood, still clutching his reader and the ancient book he had been transcribing when he'd dozed off. No one objected as he held them against his chest, bowing jerkily before he followed Bidaelah into the long hallway. He watched her thick braid swing with her stride, the beaded end brushing the curve of her rear. Behind him, he heard one of the guards murmur something indecipherable, speaking through the transmitter to someone at a distance. He saw no one in the men's section, the halls and rooms surreally silent. The huge carved doors separating the women's house from the men's opened to admit them, then closed with an audible thunk of a lock dropping into place.

He was marched quickly past the halls leading to the library, past those branching off to the gardens and the women's private rooms, past the huge receiving hall, down long, twisting corridors into a part of the House he had never been in before. Two other heavily armed Nga'esha household Dhikar stood before a large door, the wood functionally solid rather than carved into lace, ignoring them stoically as they approached. He stopped behind Bidaelah as she placed her palm against a security scanner by the door.

It slid open to reveal an empty elevator larger than his own room in the men's section. He flinched when one of the Dhikar laid her hand on his shoulder. Her fingers pressed into his skin, firm but not unkind, there simply to prompt him into the elevator and hold him in place.

His mouth was dry, his chest constricted, and he had to force himself to take deeper breaths. The doors slid shut behind him. After a moment, he felt the elevator begin its descent with only the faint sensation in his stomach as evidence of motion. He had no idea how far into the earth it sank, but knew it was deep under the House. It opened to a large, busy room filled with white-clad security and the noise of many voices speaking at once. Several people stopped to stare at him, their expressions inscrutable. He noticed he was the only man.

The Dhikar's hand on his shoulder prodded him forward to follow Bidaelah at a quick pace to the far end of the vaulted space. It was cool, a tang of damp ozone in his nostrils, and he tried not to imagine how much rock lay above his head.

The corridors here were plain, smaller and far more utilitarian than the luxury of the House above. He was admitted past another set of doors, these made of heavy reinforced steel. They closed behind him on silent oiled tracks before another identical set rolled open. Behind these, he found himself inside a circular room, many arched doorways around its circumference, and in the center, pacing agitatedly, was Yronae. She held one finger to keep the bead in her ear in place, muttering softly to the black transmitter looped around her neck. One eye was concealed behind an odd contact lens, green and red light flicking across her iris, bright enough to reflect against the bridge of her brow and nose.

She glanced up at him as he entered. The lens continued to blink its data, unheeded. Her other eye was bloodshot, tired, and she stopped speaking to whomever was on the other end of the transmission. The guard's hand released him as they neared her. His arms still clenched the book and reader against his chest, but he bowed to her respectfully.

She didn't return his gesture, staring at him for several moments. Then, in two quick strides, she stood in front of him, glaring up at him, her lips thinned into a tight, angry line, fists curled in anger. She was close enough for him to hear the tinny sound of a voice whispering in the soundpearl. He braced himself, thinking she was about to strike him, waiting with as much dignity as he could under the circumstances.

When she spoke, it was in the private Nga'esha women's dialect he didn't understand, her words addressed to her daughter. Bidaelah nodded, grasped his forearm, and tugged him to one side of the room. He glanced over his shoulder, surprised to see his guards were no longer behind him, and allowed himself to be led to a small semicircular alcove behind an arched, open doorway. The only furnishings were a pile of floor cushions.

"You will stay here, out of the way," Bidaelah said.

He nodded, trying to be cooperative. "What is happening?"

"Shut up," she snapped. Startled by her rudeness, he gaped at her. "You are to do as you are told and say nothing, do you understand?"

Stunned, he bowed slightly before he sank down to the floor cushions, still holding the book and reader tightly. Biting her upper lip, she turned away, taking only two steps before she stopped. "It is necessary," she said to him over her shoulder without looking at him. The color was high on her cheeks, and he knew Bidaelah was not used to being discourteous.

He took that for an apology. Left alone, he drew his knees up toward his chest and watched Yronae pace the circular room. No one spoke to him, no one even acknowledged his presence, as they listened to the beads speaking in their ears and murmured in the women's language he couldn't understand. He kept his attention on the pratha h'máy.

Her concentration had focused back on whatever messages were being transmitted to her lens, her expression distant, listening and responding to a world beyond the enclosed room. Other women wore similar lenses. He spotted Mahdupi standing hunch-shouldered, her weight shifting from foot to foot as she read the information being projected against her retina, her eyepiece a larger monocular lens held in place over one eye, anchored to the earbead she touched occasionally. She looked up sharply, snapped her fingers, and pointed toward an archway. Four of the Dhikar security left briskly, already settling their rifles into place around their shoulders. As she turned, he caught her attention for a moment. She stared at him for several seconds, not hostile, but impersonal.

Nathan felt the fear rise along his spine, an ache settling between his shoulder blades. He shuddered, and forced his fingers to unlock from around the book and reader to set them gently on the floor beside him. It was several seconds before he noticed someone standing beside the archway and looked up sharply.

Dhenuh leaned one shoulder against the arch, a hand placed delicately over her swollen belly, eight months pregnant. She wore no bead in her ear, no black transmitter clamped to her throat. Her eyes were indifferent. "I have been sent to see if you are hungry, Cousin," she said. "We may be here for some time."

He shook his head. "What's happening, please?" He kept his voice carefully flat, unassertive.

She smiled fleetingly, without warmth. "We are resisting an extremely hostile industrial takeover."

That she had not told him to be silent was a positive sign. He decided to push his luck. "Changriti?"

She grimaced, rubbing one hand against the child in her womb. "Of course. With the help of your people, it seems. They were conspicuously quick to take advantage of the problem."

"Problem." He repeated the word, careful not to make it a question.

She wasn't fooled. "You, little brother. You are the problem."

He glanced past her toward Yronae, the pratha h'máy still locked into her remote trance. She seemed either unaware or unconcerned that her kinswoman was standing talking to him. "How am I the problem, Cousin?"

She laughed, low and humorless. "You breathe. It's enough."

He went still. "That's easily changed," he said, his voice colorless.

"Easily," she agreed. "But it wouldn't solve anything. Not now."

He felt rather than heard the rumble through the earth, feeling the vibration in the pit of his stomach. Others felt it as well, multiple voices pausing. He knew what that sound meant, he remembered it well from Westcastle. He wondered if they knew as well. Dhenuh glanced up at nothing, staring vacantly, and grunted in her throat, her face blank with fear. Her head swiveled to glance at Yronae, as did several others'. Only the white-clad Dhikar security continued, unconcerned, their passionless murmuring oddly comforting in the muted room. Yronae had her head tilted back, staring at the vaulted ceiling, waiting. Whatever reports there were came in transmitted to each bead. Then with a collective shudder of relief, the hum of multiple voices resumed.

"Oh, dear Lady, protect us," Dhenuh whispered in disbelief.

"Where are the children?" Nathan asked sharply.

"Safe." She glanced down at her belly. "And the men, all safe enough." When she looked at him, he could see the fear in her eyes behind the brave smile. "As we are here, for now." She flinched again, her whimper of pain nearly inaudible in her throat.

He reached a hand toward her. "Your baby is hurting you, Cousin. Please, sit with me."

"It is normal," she said stiffly.

He nearly laughed. "Nothing is normal at the moment."

She remained standing. "I don't like you, Nathan Crewe Nga'esha," she snapped, her words uncharacteristically brusque for the normal Vanar manners. Rudeness seemed epidemic. "I never have, I never will."

He kept his hand extended. "Many people don't, Dhenuh dva Arjusana Nga'esha. I'm used to it. Please, for your child's sake sit down."

After a moment's hesitation, she lowered herself gingerly to the cushions, leaning on his arm and shoulder to lever her awkward weight. They sat without speaking, side by side, watching the activity resume. Yronae paced in a circle, reminding Nathan of a caged leopard, stopping only once to stare at them. Her expression was unfocused, like a dreamer caught up in a trance. He was unsure if she really saw them or not.

Dhenuh's breathing was ragged. She winced as her unborn baby kicked, and he could see the movement of the child in her womb, even under the silk sati. Wordless, he shifted position to sit behind her cross-legged. She made no protest as he placed one hand on her shoulder to hold her still and the other against the small of her back, massaging slowly, his fingers probing the strained muscles. She held herself rigidly erect, reluctant under his touch.

He said nothing, shutting his eyes as he let his hands work. Following the bones of her spine, he kneaded the tight muscles on either side, climbing the vertebrae one by one methodically. By the time he had reached her shoulders and neck, her tenseness had subsided, but he could feel the baby still moving, still agitated. He uncrossed his legs, stretching them one to either side of her. "Lean back against me, bahd'hyin," he said quietly.

She stiffened, trying to pull away. He held her by one shoulder, but not hard. "I don't like you," she repeated, her voice thick.

He chuckled. "And I don't like you," he said, pleased by her surprise. "But your baby doesn't know me well enough yet to hate me.

Perhaps you can teach her later. For now, put your legs out and lean back against me, my stubborn, cranky second cousin."

Unwillingly, she complied, and he adjusted her against his chest to let the heat of his body warm her back. Placing his hands firmly against her side, he spread his fingers and rubbed his palms in slow circles, feeling the outline of the child underneath his touch. "I learned how to do this for my wife when she was pregnant with my own child," he said, his head bent over her shoulder, mouth close to her ear. Her hair tickled his cheek, smelling of jasmine.

She started slightly, and he wondered why before she said, "Your daughter. She's Changriti."

"And part Hengeli, like me. A dangerous enemy." He meant it to be ironic.

Dhenuh snorted. "You might be the enemy. The Changriti are merely . . . competitors." She hesitated and added more kindly, "But I hope your daughter is safe."

His hands stopped their soothing movement. "Thank you. So do I." The baby kicked, as if annoyed he had interrupted his therapy. He resumed, feeling the child's agitation yielding under his touch. Even after the baby had subsided, he continued to massage Dhenuh's belly. She sighed, closed her eyes, and leaned her head back against him, nestling her cheek against the curve of his neck. He kept his own eyes open, alert. He was doing this as much for himself as for her, he knew, using her like a shield between him and the relentless activity he didn't understand going on around them outside the tiny alcove.

"I'm frightened," she whispered suddenly, barely audible.

"I know."

Yronae gestured as she spoke to someone who was not in the room with her: angry, jerking motions of her hand.

"They say you've been in war before," Dhenuh said, her voice kept low.

He stared at the pratha h'máy's profile, at the sharp, fine chin and nose, dark skin, trying to see Yaenida in the woman's face. "Yes," he said inattentively.

"What is war like?"

He glanced at Dhenuh. Her eyes were open, watching the muted commotion around them. He didn't know what to say. "It's bad." He didn't want to talk about it.

She sat up, pulling away from him without looking at him, and got to her feet. "Thank you," she said stiffly, and walked away. When he looked back at Yronae, she was staring directly at him, hostile. He froze, then forced himself to bow his head toward her, very humble and very correct. Her mouth twitched, and she spoke, her words directed into the transmitter at her throat.

As if on command, a Dhikar turned from the far end of the room and walked to stand guard outside the arch of the alcove, legs apart, hands clasped loosely behind her back. Yronae had already looked away, again focused on the world outside channeled into her ear and eye. He wondered if Dhenuh was in trouble. No one spoke to him again for several hours.

He settled his back against the wall and dozed off, the drone of voices monotonous. When he woke, his bladder was full.

"Excuse me," he finally said to the Dhikar standing outside the alcove. She turned her head to him indifferently. "I have a need . . . ?"

She nodded, touched one finger to the transmitter anchored to her throat, and spoke quietly. Within seconds, another Dhikar had joined her to escort him between them across the room. He passed Yronae by less than an arm's length, but the woman didn't appear to notice him, oblivious to his existence. The guards marched him down a short hall to a large bathing room, various fixtures obviously designed for the benefit of female anatomy rather than male. Behind him, the water in the long, shallow bathing pool was mirror smooth, reflecting the pinpoints of lights arranged in patterns of constellations above.

There was no possibility for privacy. He turned his back to his guards, reaching between the folds of his sati, and lifted the hem of the mati. It took several awkward moments before he could ignore the eyes behind him and relax his sphincter enough to piss. He shook himself and rearranged his clothing before he turned. The women watched him steadily, no expression on their flattened faces. He looked toward the pool, then back. "May I bathe?"

He was not so interested in hygiene as he was in the answer. The two women exchanged a glance. One shrugged, speaking quietly to someone far outside the room. Yronae? She listened, then nodded to him. His heart sank. It meant it would be some time before he saw the surface again. Things had to be very bad above them.

Without enthusiasm, he unwrapped his sati and drew the mati off over his head, folding them sloppily and dropping them onto the shelf. He stepped into the water, the reflected lights shivering in the circles radiating across the surface. As the first ripple reached the other end of the pool, he heard a hum as the recycler activated. Bubbles erupted from the far end. He ignored the two Dhikar, lowered himself into the warmth, and swam toward the other end.

It was hotter at the foaming end of the pool. Steam began to rise from the pool's surface. He swam aimlessly for a long time, back and forth across the length of the pool, having nothing better to do than allow his muscles to take over, letting his mind drift. Ducking his head underwater, he drew his knees in to sink to the shallow bottom. He listened to the muffled sound of the machinery in his ears, blotting out the world above him for as long as he had oxygen in his lungs. His chest burned, and he shot up again, gasping in a breath as he broke the surface. His eyes stung as he blinked, rubbed at them, and squinted through the steam at the stout shape of a woman sitting on a bathing stool at the other end, waiting for him.

Mahdupi.

Glancing behind him, he saw the two Dhikar still stood watch back-to-back, one facing him, the other out. Reluctantly, he swam to the other side and held on to the edge, wordless. The old woman smiled.

"When you are finished, you will need someone to braid your hair," she said calmly, and held up a comb. "As there are no other men here to help you, allow me the pleasure. I should like to satisfy my curiosity about how such fine, golden hair might feel."

She handed him a towel as he pulled himself out of the water, and didn't avert her eyes as he dried himself. He wrapped the towel around his waist and sat down on another of the bathing stools. Her fingers unraveled the braid and picked the banded string of beads from his hair before she toweled it until it was mostly dry, saying nothing. It hung to the middle of his back, thick reddish gold, curling even when wet, as she began to comb it out from the bottom.

"Why am I the only man here?" he risked asking. She paused for a beat, the comb through his hair pulling his head back on his neck. When she didn't answer, he added, "It's me, isn't it? They want me."

"Mm." He couldn't tell if the grunt was an assent or denial.

"The Changriti?"

He twisted to look at her. Her face pinched in distaste, but she didn't answer. She pushed his head back around and continued worrying the tangle of hair.

"Why? What have I done?"

"You needn't take it personally," she said thinly. "At least not this time. They are worried about what you know."

"What I know? *What* do I know?" He knew he shouldn't have persisted, but the mystery was more ominous than the possible consequences.

She exhaled in irritation. "Nothing. Only they haven't realized it yet. But they're frightened."

"Not of *me*."

"Of course, of you."

He said nothing for a long moment, letting her strong fingers divide his hair into thick strands. "Are you also afraid of me, l'amae Mahdupi?"

She chuckled. "I haven't decided yet, child. It has been most educational watching you over the years, like a fox set loose amongst the pigeons, but not always agreeable. Would you like me to work the beads back into your hair?"

"I don't care."

She left them out, the hair pulling his scalp as she wove the plait. When she had finished, he swiveled on the stool to face her. "Pratha Yaenida always respected your opinions greatly, *maetaemahi* Mahdupi."

She grimaced. "Please, don't call me a grandmother. It makes me feel ancient. And it gives you no advantage to exaggerate your relation to me. I know full well my kinship with you."

"I need to know what is happening."

She smiled, and he could see in the fine bones of her face how she must have once been quite attractive. "I wish someone would explain it to me, bah'chae."

He continued to gaze at her until she tilted her head questioningly. "Please don't call me a small boy. I am not."

Her chin lifted, and her smile widened. "Ah. *Now* I am afraid of you."

He looked away, frustrated. "It was not intended as a threat."

"I didn't take it as one. Get dressed," she said gently. He stood and retrieved his clothing, the gauzy silk dampened from the steam. Pulling the mati over his head, he kept his eyes averted from any of the watching women, his hands expertly pleating the sati around his waist, tying it off and looping the rest around his neck to let the end hang down his shoulder. He clipped it to the mati with the brooch Kallah had given him.

He followed his guards out passively, Mahdupi beside him, back to the circular room. Fewer people crowded into it now. Yronae sat before a low desk, three screens embedded in its surface. She looked up as he entered, unfocused, still locked into another world, although her eyes tracked him as he returned to the small alcove. Dhenuh was nowhere in sight. Mahdupi patted him gently on the shoulder. "When there is a need for you to know, I'll come for you."

As she left to speak with Yronae he settled back into the floor cushions. Someone had set up a small table, various covered dishes left on it. He lifted a lid to one, the sudden aroma of spice making his mouth water. He ate quickly, his hunger sharpened by his swim.

He fell asleep sometime later, waking only to notice that the table and empty dishes had been removed, and the light in the alcove turned down. He rolled over to look out into the circular room, not certain what had woken him. Yronae sat silently, staring up at the curved ceiling. Then he felt it: the low growl through the stone, too low to be audible but discernible enough to set his heart pounding.

He sat up, studying Yronae. He noted most of the others in the room also watched her intently. She sat as if carved in stone, listening to the bead whisper in her ear. Then she exhaled, her head lowered in relief, hands rubbing against her face. She nodded to whatever question had been asked from a distance, then spoke quietly. Even from the distance, Nathan could hear the words: alien, enigmatic, forbidden.

After several days, he had not lost his fear, but he was thoroughly bored. It had been like that during his childhood, endless periods of grinding monotony punctuated with brief terror. He worked on what he could on his reader, although he was uneasy when it wouldn't access his library. Nor would it receive any of the news services, broadcasts being actively censored out of men's readers. But his concentration was limited, much of his time spent watching the activity around him.

After the first few days, life had settled into a regular pattern, Yronae's lethal household guard cycling through in shifts, those women who seemed to be coordinating whatever action was happening on the surface above staking out their own territory in the domed room. In the alcoves around the circle, women napped, including Yronae, before returning to the ethereal world built up of earbeads and shimmering scanner lenses. Mahdupi had taken to sitting on the shelf-seat nearest his alcove, although she spoke very little, either to him or to the transmitter on her throat.

He'd been halfheartedly trying to finish his translation from the ancient book when the room fell eerily silent. Alarmed, he looked up at a tableau of women frozen in place, mesmerized, as they took one synchronized indrawn gasp, their eyes wide in blanched faces.

"Oh, sweet Lady Goddess," he heard Mahdupi murmur. Then she laughed quietly, a stricken sound.

Yronae stood slowly and removed the scanning lens from her eye, dropping it to the floor and cracking it under her foot. She picked the bead out of her ear and peeled off the throat transmitter, letting them fall carelessly from her hand. The earbead hit the floor, bouncing. *Tick. Tick tick. Ticktickikikikik.* It rolled under a table and vanished. No one spoke.

The pratha h'máy turned and stared at him unblinkingly. She strode toward him stiffly until she towered over him, glaring down with unfocused eyes that had nothing to do with her attention called elsewhere. His heart skipped.

"My mother, l'amae Yaenida dva Daharanan ek Qarshatha Nga'esha," she said finally, her voice deadly calm, "was an utter madwoman."

He stared back at her with uncertain fear. Without another word, she turned and walked out of the circular room, the steel doors hissing shut behind her. Mahdupi held her hands together, rubbing her knuckles as if they hurt from arthritis.

"L'amae Mahdupi," he said softly. She looked up, her expression vague. *"Please . . ."*

She took a deep, shaking breath. "The Worms." He stared at her. "The Pilots have closed the Worms."

"The Nga'esha?"

"Nga'esha, Changriti, Ushahayam, Hadatha . . . All of them, every single one."

XLII

THE MURMUR OF VOICES BEGAN AGAIN, BUT YRONAE DID NOT RETURN to the circular communications room. After a few hours, Mahdupi beckoned to him, and he followed her with his omnipresent guards through the same door through which Yronae had retreated.

"Be careful what you say, Cousin," she warned him quietly. "Our pratha h'máy is not in the best of moods." She glanced at him. "And nothing that is said leaves that room, understood?"

"Yes, l'amae."

A second set of double reinforced doors hissed and locked behind them before he found himself inside a small version of a woman's apartment. Silk lace curtains stirred in the faint briny breeze through a large window, the constant motion of the sea rolling onto a black sand beach in the distance, all artificial and impeccably realistic. Quiet music played a soothing ambience, meshing perfectly with the sound of surf.

Cushions of muted colors embroidered in patterns of maroon, dark blue, silver, had been aesthetically arranged on a sleeping dais, the four pillars twisting to join at its peak. On it, Yronae lay propped against a pillow, staring dully at the synthetic vista. She wore only a sheer tasmai around her body, her hair loose over her shoulders.

As they approached, she glanced first at him, then at the household Dhikar, jerking her head slightly. They bowed and left as Mahdupi sat on the edge of the dais, taking one of Yronae's hands as if she were a child. Yronae resumed watching the endless waves break over the ersatz sand.

Before he got halfway through his ritual bow and kneeling, she spoke without looking at him. "Come sit over here, Nathan." He hesitated with one foot still hooked around his sati, then crossed the small distance to sit on the other side of the dais, his back to the ocean view.

"My mother called you Nathan, didn't she?" She pronounced it Nay-teen, always and forever unable to say it correctly.

"Sometimes," he said. "It is my name." She stared at him, waiting. He smiled weakly. "And sometimes she called me other names less complimentary." She didn't respond to his feeble attempt at a joke, but Mahdupi winked at him, amused.

Yronae's attention drifted back to the ocean scene. "What did you talk about with my mother?"

"Everything and anything, pratha h'máy. History, art, religion, sex, science, everything. Pratha Yaenida had an insatiable curiosity, and I was starved for conversation in my native language." He faltered, glancing at Mahdupi before he added carefully, "Was there a specific subject we might have discussed that is of interest to you?"

She didn't answer, gazing off bleakly over his shoulder. Mahdupi patted her hand and stood up, crossing to a small coffee set to place the ornate kettle on the microburner. The smell of fresh coffee made him suddenly light-headed with hunger.

He kept his hands laced together, focusing his awareness on the sound of porcelain clinking, the distant rumble of the fake ocean and placid music. When Yronae finally spoke, he started.

"I don't know how to talk to you," she complained, her voice bitter. She still avoided his eyes, her own haggard. "Why should I know how to talk with you?"

He said nothing, not knowing what to say to this woman, either. Mahdupi returned with two steaming cups, handing one to him silently. He took it, surprised, and watched as Yronae refused the one offered to her with an impatient flick of her hand. Unconcerned, Mahdupi sat on the dais, one leg drawn up under herself, and sipped from the small cup judiciously, the coffee scalding hot.

"Hostilities have been suspended," Mahdupi told him. "Most of our people are unhurt, a handful of casualties, mostly Dhikar. We haven't been able to assess the total damage to the House yet, but our internal security precautions survived—all data is intact." She smiled with malicious scorn. "They seriously underestimated the Nga'esha. Vanar has no offensive capabilities, but we aren't quite as ignorant of military technology as your Hengeli compatriots imagined, our defenses far better than they expected. Pratha Yaenida's time spent serving in your absurd political conflicts came in handier than even we anticipated." She gestured vaguely at the room. "When she had this shelter built the first year she was pratha h'máy, we all thought she was crazy. Her crazy idea for Sukrah Station made us rich, and it seems yet another of her crazy ideas has saved our lives. She knew from experience just exactly the sort of destruction it had to withstand."

His skin prickled. "Hengeli?"

"Mm," Mahdupi affirmed mildly. "Blowing up houses any idiot can do. Blowing them up without destroying the valuables inside you want to loot? Not quite so easy."

The pratha h'máy was still preoccupied by the artificial seascape, ignoring them.

"But we were still very lucky, little brother. If the ambassador's aide had not tipped her hand, it might have been too late."

"I don't understand, l'amae. Why would either the Changriti or the Hengeli attack the Nga'esha?"

Mahdupi frowned at him disapprovingly, but shrugged. "Sukrah Station is a vital link between many of the Hengeli worlds and those accessible through the Changriti Worm. It's ours. We built it, we financed it, we maintain it. It gives us a monopoly the Changriti have long objected to. It has taken many decades of careful mediation with contracts and concessions to keep the balance as fair as possible between all the Families without significant loss of revenues to our own. I won't go into the details. Family business affairs are far more complicated than you would be capable of understanding."

Naturally, he thought sourly.

"However, one of the compromises reached was that while every Family maintains their own household Dhikar protection, all Station and Vanar security is overseen by the Changriti, and the Dhikar Qsay-ati appointed by Eraelin herself. Which is how the Hengeli knew about your daughter." Mahdupi smiled dryly. "Ruuspoelk inadvertently gave us that first thread. Pull on one and it all begins to unravel." Her smile vanished. "We haven't untangled everything yet, but it seems the Dhikar credibility has been severely tarnished."

"Dhikar?" Nathan said. He glanced around, remembering Yronae had dismissed them all. "I thought—"

"They were incorruptible?"

Yronae choked a bitter laugh, and muttered to herself, "*No one* is incorruptible anymore, it seems."

"But I have nothing to do with any of this. Why is anyone after me?"

"Because someone on Sukrah Station reported to Pratha Eraelin that you were a plant our late pratha h'máy had arranged to marry into the Changriti Family in order to pass on information about them to us and our so-called 'allies,' the Hengeli. When Pratha Yronae included you in the talks yesterday, that only served to confirm her suspicion."

Nathan's mind seemed to function too sluggishly. "Wait, wait . . ." he said in dawning anger. "They think I'm a spy? The Changriti believe I was *spying* for the Hengeli? But that's *impossible* . . ."

Mahdupi waved his outrage away nonchalantly. "A thousand inquiries to prove it otherwise would never change Eraelin Changriti's fear of the outside. The Changriti strategy to undermine our security in order to take over Sukrah Station was going much too slow for the Hengeli. When negotiations with the Nga'esha looked unfeasible, they were about to offer to expose the Changriti conspiracy. Fortunately, our intelligence, like our defenses, isn't that ineffectual." She grinned fleetingly, ruthless. "We figured it out before we had to pay for the information. That left the Hengeli only one option. Eraelin, or someone representing her, accepted the off-worlders' offer to help her cover her tracks and destroy any incriminating evidence. But I suspect the Changriti misunderstood the scale of violence your people are capable of. The damage to our property has been extensive. If it had not been for our Pilots, there might not be a House still standing above us. And we might not be here talking about it."

"Our liberators," Yronae growled under her breath.

"In any case, with the Worms closed, the Hengeli can't go on to Novapolita or back where they came from, and they certainly aren't going to be welcomed downside. So they're just as stuck as we are, waiting to see what happens, only their cages are less comfortable than our own."

"That's good . . . right?"

Yronae inhaled a deep, ragged breath. "They can outwait us," she said.

"Who, the Hengeli, l'amae?" he asked after a moment of silence.

She wrenched her gaze from the scene behind him, eyes dark with anger. "No. Your devoted friends, the Pilots."

He glanced helplessly at Mahdupi, gaining only raised eyebrows and a taciturn shrug in return. She sipped her coffee.

"What do they want?" he asked.

Yronae laughed softly. "Only the death of Vanar."

He blinked. Before he could speak, Mahdupi had frowned. "Yronae—"

She turned her baleful expression on Mahdupi. "What else would you call it, then?" she cut the older woman off sharply.

"An exaggeration," Mahdupi responded mildly.

Yronae snorted, and glared at him. "We must give you your freedom, allow you to leave Vanar."

"You offered that already. I refused. Surely they must know that, pratha h'máy."

"Not just you, Nathan. Anyone," she said thickly. "Including all our Pilot bloodline males, any who wish to leave Vanar."

His head reeled. *Anyone.*

"This will never happen," she said sharply. "We will destroy all the Pilot males before that happens, every last one of them. Without their males, it will not matter how long they wait, they'll eventually die. We can survive on Vanar for all the generations it takes to wait, and once the last of them are dead, we'll create new Pilots." He said nothing, staring at her in disbelief. She laughed harshly, almost hysterical. "We created them once, we can do so again."

Mahdupi cleared her throat, examining the back of her hands as if to read portents in the traces of veins under the sun-baked skin. "Unfortunately," she said, her tone casual, "the 'we' you are speaking about is not, at least at the moment, unanimous. Others of the Nine Families are displeased over the prospect of long-term lost revenues. And the Changriti are not alone in their claim that since Pratha Yaenida's irregular acquisition is at the root of this unhappy turn of events, the Nga'esha should be liable for any deficits."

"They had their voice at Council!" Yronae shouted at her, sitting upright, her rigid body trembling. "They voted with the rest, so are as much responsible for him being here as the Nga'esha." She thrust a finger at him.

"Your mother—" Mahdupi began.

"*Shut up!*" Yronae screamed, her hands balling into fists. "You will not say one more word, Mahdupi, not *one!*" Nathan flinched, certain she was about to strike either him or Mahdupi. The older woman remained unafraid, well within Yronae's reach.

Yronae was breathing hard, her nostrils flaring. "Be glad Yaenida is dead," she said, more quietly, "because if she were still alive, I think I would strangle her myself." Pulling the tasmai around her shoulders with angry jerks, she leapt from the dais, pacing the room like an enraged leopard.

"What could she have been thinking of? Not the Family, certainly not the honor and welfare of the Nga'esha. Willful, selfish, stupid, thoughtless *bitch.*"

Nathan's hand holding the coffee trembled hard enough to spill hot liquid onto his fingers. Quickly, he put down the cup and sucked the spilled coffee from his skin. He looked up, hand still in his mouth, meeting Yronae's spiteful glare.

"The instant she was dead, I should have had you stuffed back into a whitewomb and left you there to rot," she said softly, chilling him.

Mahdupi sighed dramatically, breaking the tension. "Are you finished with your tantrum yet, child?"

To his surprise, Yronae closed her eyes, her shoulders slumping. "Quite," she said softly.

"Feel better now?"

"Infinitely."

"Always healthy to have a good screaming temper once in a while, so long as it's kept private." Mahdupi glanced at Nathan, smiling tightly. "And now that you've indulged yourself with a delightfully gratifying sulk, Yronae, it's time to face the problem."

Yronae sat back down on the dais and swept the mass of loose hair back from her face, fingers raking her scalp. "The terms are totally unacceptable, as they well know," she said directly to Nathan, her voice calm, businesslike. "We will be expected, of course, to offer a counterproposal."

"What sort of proposal, pratha h'máy?" His own voice shook.

"First, allowing our male Pilots to leave Vanar is out of the question. They would have precious little opportunity to enjoy their so-called freedom before they were seized and exploited by potential off-world competitors." Her tone was brisk, pragmatic. "Second, I will not permit you to go anywhere outside the Family jurisdiction. You would be murdered inside an hour."

"What exactly, then, *would* you be offering them, Yronae?" Mahdupi asked wryly.

"We'll offer a share of the revenue income."

"Which they have little use for," Mahdupi said, earning a glare.

"More control over their own reproduction," Yronae continued.

"Another useless offer," the older woman said, pouring herself another cup of the strong, thick coffee. "They can't leave the Worm long enough, and the boys can't survive there."

"And his safety," she answered, ignoring Mahdupi as she studied him, her eyes narrowed. "He can't stay here, and we haven't had complete reports on how badly Dravyam has been hit. Have Calidris Station evacuated, and all personnel completely replaced with Nga'esha Dhikar."

"Calidris? That's just a freight depot, there's hardly anyone there."

"Exactly. It's small enough to ensure complete security. He'll be safe there. I want him removed to a Nga'esha station immediately."

Nathan started. "No," he objected. "I'm not leaving Vanar."

Yronae snarled in frustration, punching the dais beside her with one fist. "I am sick and tired of your pigheaded yepoqioh defiance, Nathan Nga'esha. You will leave if I say you leave!"

"It's not much of a difference either way: a hostage isolated on a station or a hostage down here, hiding like a mole in the dirt." He couldn't keep the anger out of his voice.

"The argument is moot," Madhupi interrupted evenly. "You would need Pilot cooperation to transfer him to a station in the first place, which they are unlikely to give. And while I'm sure most of Vanar would be pleased to see him gone, you don't defuse a bomb by putting it in a box and hiding it at the back of a storage cabinet."

Yronae swore, a remarkably vulgar curse he had rarely heard from a Vanar, and never from a woman. Even Mahdupi's eyebrows lifted. "Then instead of constantly naysaying me, *you* tell me what compromise they might find acceptable!" Yronae snapped.

Mahdupi smiled and sipped her coffee. "I haven't the vaguest idea, Pratha. I haven't spent all that much time in their company to know what Pilots might possibly want." Yronae, absorbing her meaning, turned on Nathan with narrowed eyes.

"But *you* have."

"Yes," he retorted hotly. "Mostly what they want is to be amused. I think they must be very amused right now, Pratha Yronae."

Mahdupi chuckled as Yronae glared. "Pratima was your lover," she said doggedly. "She would listen to you. Talk to her, reason with her. Surely she wouldn't wish any harm to come to you as a result of her reckless actions."

He glared at her, furious. "Willful, selfish, stupid, thoughtless bitch," he whispered.

Her jaw clenched, the muscles along smooth cheeks twitching. "You will not dare refuse, Nathan, not and jeopardize the entire Family. The contempt you show for the Nga'esha name would be severely penalized—"

"Don't threaten me," he said softly. "It's beneath you."

She flushed, calming herself by visible effort. "I will not—do you hear me?—will *not* permit the dismantling of seven centuries of Vanar culture on the caprice of lovesick Pilots. But whether I like it or not, you now wield considerable influence for which I need your cooperation. I have offered you your freedom, which you have foolishly turned down. I have offered you more wealth than most men could ever dream of, and that doesn't seem to interest you either. I somehow doubt offering you a more substantial role within the Family hierarchy will satisfy you. What you *do* want is as unreasonable as what our Pilots are demanding. It's impossible. I know you have no reason to feel any loyalty toward me, to the honor of the Nga'esha or to Vanar. But neither of us will leave this room until we have reached an agreement."

"No loyalty?" he said in disbelief. "Why do you think I chose not to leave Vanar, Yronae?" He used her name deliberately, watching her eyes widen, but she didn't protest. "I know you've despised me. You don't agree with my beliefs, but you haven't gone so far as to unlawfully silence me. Not because you were protecting Nga'esha interests, but because it was *right*. Your honor won't let you do otherwise.

"But your honor didn't keep you from using me to negotiate with my own people, just as you would use me again, and I have never refused you, *never*. What more do I have to do to prove to you I am as Vanar as you are, possibly even more so because I *chose* to be. I've paid ten times over to be given that right."

Yronae remained silent. He walked around the dais to stand in front of her, looking her straight in the eyes.

"Look at me," he said softly. "Open your eyes and see that I am not so different from you. Yes, I am angry, and yes, I want changes. But is what I want really so unreasonable? All I want is to walk down the streets of Vanar with my head held proudly, as you do. I want to be free to go where I want, on *Vanar*, as you do. I want the right to see my daughter, to help raise her to grow up to love and respect me. I want to choose what I do with my life, and not live in constant fear and submission. I want only what is just, and I want your help to do it. I *need* your help."

He paused, gauging her reaction. Her face had paled, but she was listening.

"We are both at fault, Yronae. I have never thought of you as my sister, family in name only, but not in my heart. You've never seen me as anything but *aeyaesah yepoqioh*, a bad practical joke your mother inflicted on your Family. But I *am* Nga'esha. I am proud to be Nga'esha. If now you need my help, just ask me for it. Say, 'help me, little brother.'"

Mahdupi put a hand over her mouth as if to hide a smile, but her eyes were somber.

"I promise you nothing—" Yronae began.

"I don't want promises. Say, 'help me, little brother,'" he repeated firmly.

"I will not beg!"

"It's not begging, Yronae. I'm your brother. All you have to do is ask for my help. As I've asked you for yours."

She stood with her lips pressed so tightly together they were bloodless, as if she had to keep them clamped shut to prevent the hated words from spilling out. Her chin trembled, her entire body shaking as she turned away from him, stalking across the room with aimless fury. Mahdupi moved to her side and placed a gentle hand on her arm, stopping the frenetic movement.

"Help me, little brother," Yronae said stonily, her back to him.

He exhaled, unaware until then he'd been holding his breath. "My pleasure, Pratha Yronae."

XLIII

ONCE IT WAS CLEAR THE HENGELI WERE NOT GOING TO CONTINUE their assault, the Nga'esha began to return to the House. Or what was left of it. The west half of the House had nearly been obliterated, many of the women's lavish rooms buried under rubble. One wall of the council room had fallen, the roof gone, leaving the once burnished parquet flooring exposed to the elements. The men's quarters had been relatively unscathed, and men were doing their best to make their women comfortable in unfamiliar surroundings, mingling freely for what might possibly have been the first time. But while repairs had begun almost immediately with the usual Vanar efficiency, many of both sexes still wandered the ruins aimlessly, dazed and tearful.

Push that button, pull that trigger. Nathan wondered how tiresome and dull Yaenida would have found this violence inflicted from a safe distance on a people with no experience of war. He watched as one of the dozens of taemorae sifting through the debris suddenly fell to her knees and vomited, still holding onto a severed hand—Dhikar, he noted distractedly, to judge by the silvery threads of implants dangling from the jagged stump. The two stoic Dhikar Yronae had assigned as his omnipresent bodyguards didn't so much as blink.

The attack had been conducted with impressive precision, demolition confined to the Nga'esha House, and even then only to areas the Hengeli thought most vulnerable or likely to yield results. Yronae's personal quarters and administrative offices had been targeted, but when whoever had ransacked her state-of-the-art equipment had realized they were only facades for the real machinery safe underground, the search was abandoned and the remains torched.

The damage to his library was impressive but mostly superficial. There was nothing in the old pratha's archives of value to their rivals, anything of a sensitive business nature long removed. Yronae had little interest in antiquated literature or obsolete cultural records. The shelving had been pulled down with savage force, books and papers scattered and trodden on. Although some of the ancient books had been irreparably destroyed, like Yronae's offices, the information within them was preserved in the data archives deep underground. The entire room could have been burnt to the ground without the loss of a single word. Still, the wanton vandalism saddened him.

The huge table of native wood had been methodically hacked to kindling. Whatever it was suspected of concealing, it had been nothing but a very antique, very beautiful slab of venerable timber, and its destruction made him angry.

Broken glass crunched underfoot, hidden under the scattered papers. He kicked torn pages aside to find the shattered remains of Yaenida's water pipe. He squatted in the wreckage, picking up fragments, then sighed. Any fleeting notion he had that somehow it could be put back together again evaporated. He let the broken pieces fall from his fingers.

"Qanistha bhraetae," he heard a voice say behind him. He stood and turned toward the door of his library. Four taemorae stood just outside the door, or at least what was left of a door hanging on twisted hinges after an explosion had ripped it to shreds. Even in the midst of the devastation, the women still rigidly adhered to the Family formalities. They would not, could not enter without his permission. He smiled bleakly, put his hands together, and bowed with almost ironic correctness.

"Qanisthaha bhaginae?"

"The pratha h'máy has sent us to ask if you require any assistance."

He looked around at the wreckage, then, unable to hold back, began laughing. Fortunately, they could see the black humor in the situation as well, and smiled.

"Please, cousins, be welcome."

They were happy enough to take instructions from him without undue offense, carting off the hopeless rubble while salvaging as much as they could from what was left. Once the remains of Yaenida's great table had been removed, the carpenters had plenty of room to work and swiftly repaired those shelves still standing or rebuilt those that had to be replaced. Even the two Dhikar grudgingly helped with some of the manual labor, while keeping one eye constantly on him.

Yronae visited briefly only once to examine the renovations, all of the Nga'esha House under refurbishment. He thanked her earnestly for the workers she'd allocated to him. She'd grunted, noncommittal, and left without a word.

He was pleased to find his small collection of music cubes, although many of them were still missing, scattered into the general mess after someone had stomped on the antique coffer to break it open. The machinery with the player was beyond hope, and one of the taemora graciously fetched her own personal system. He selected Mozart's Coronation Mass, and smiled when the taemorae glanced at each other, puzzled by the "Gloria" movement. The mix of men's and women's voices reverberated in the cavernous room, one of the very few choral works the Vanar Customs had reluctantly allowed him to keep once he had convinced them the language was far too ancient for him, or anyone else on Vanar, to decipher.

They hadn't understood, he thought as he watched Vanar women hammering and sawing and reconstructing his library to the exuberant voices of long-dead singers. He didn't need to understand the words to understand the music.

For their part, the taemorae endured it patiently before one of them asked him courteously if they might be allowed to listen to their own music. Mozart's ebullient chorus was replaced by the whining insipid melodies Vanar women preferred. But they were happy, and he was having his library repaired.

Once the shelves had been replaced came the more tedious task of trying to organize the old books back into some semblance of order. Two of the taemorae had been called away to more pressing work, while the remaining two helped him collect what books were still intact, sorting them into various woven wicker boxes, guessing at categories by titles. Any damaged books or loose pages were placed into other boxes for him to try to sift through later.

"I don't know what to do with these, Nathan Nga'esha," one of them said, interrupting his fruitless interpretation of a scrap of an obscure Vanar document, wondering if he'd ever find what it had been ripped out of. His eyes ached.

He looked up from where he sat cross-legged on the floor surrounded by a sea of orphan paper. She held several crudely bound portfolios. "What are they?" he asked.

"I don't know. It's not in Vanar."

He gestured to a pile next to him. "Leave it there, then. I'll get to them when I have time."

He finished sorting what he could and gave up on trying to decipher the Vanar text of those he couldn't, dumping them into a general box to file later, before he picked up the top portfolio with casual interest, opening it to find a carefully organized assortment of obsolete data chips with the oldest reader he'd ever seen in his life. He inserted the first chip and skimmed the first few pages. The hair on his arms prickled as he read, his breath shallow in wonder.

A couple hours later, the taemora had to repeat his name to get his attention. "What?" He blinked up at her, still dazed.

"We're going now," she said. "We'll come back tomorrow morning with new doors and windows."

"Oh, yes, of course. . . ." He held up the ancient portfolio. "Where did you find these?"

She shrugged. "In a pile of books under a smashed bookshelf, just like everything else." The young woman hesitated, then asked kindly, "Are you all right? You seem unwell."

"I'm fine, l'amae."

She left, unconvinced, as he returned to words written hundreds of years before in an archaic Hengeli script, reading well into the night.

XLIV

"READY?"

Standing outside Pratha Yronae's makeshift council hall, he felt as nervous as Namasi Sahmudrah looked. This hadn't exactly been the career-enhancing case she'd hoped for, he knew, but it certainly would be one to establish her reputation for the historical records. Margasir adjusted his sati pin, stood back, and nodded his approval.

"As I'll ever be," Nathan said.

Namasi Sahmudrah smiled wryly. "Last chance. No second thoughts?"

"Plenty."

She nodded. "Let's do it, then."

Over the past week, the young vaktay had become more than his speaker, she was as close to being a friend as he'd ever had with a Vanar woman. She had been the one to take his discoveries to the

Pratha Yronae. He'd been sent for many hours after, kneeling nervously as she examined Namasi's evidence. But all the pratha h'máy had demanded of him was clarification of a couple of Hengeli phrases. Otherwise, she'd said nothing, to Nathan's disquiet. She obviously did not like what she had read, but two days after, Namasi burst into his library without even knocking, to the consternation of his Dhikar bodyguards.

"She did it!" Namasi said excitedly. "She's demanded the Assembly grant us an immediate hearing, and we've got it!"

The Assembly might have dragged their feet forever, but hadn't dared to refuse a request by the Nga'esha pratha h'máy.

They had spent long hours in the privacy of his library breathing in the smell of new wood and fresh paint, books and papers still stacked in untidy piles as they debated this approach, argued heatedly over that, feverishly translating the archaic Hengeli with an electric urgency. Margasir had kept them supplied with food and tea, scuttling uneasily past Nathan's Dhikar bodyguards. Now, moments away from leaving for the Assembly, Nathan realized he knew almost nothing about Namasi's personal life, wondered what she did outside their time together, whether or not she had some kharvah at home waiting for her return. His curiosity got the better of him.

"Vaktay Namasi," he said. She paused inquiringly. "Are you married?"

Even Margasir gave him an odd glance.

"Yes. Why?"

"What does he . . . or they . . . think of all this?"

"He doesn't agree with you." She smiled. "He fears you threaten his security, that you would like to take away all the benefits without enough in return to justify it."

"He can save his breath. I've had exactly this argument myself with my eccentric práhsaedam," Margasir groused, "to no avail."

Nathan didn't point out that a few days ago the sahakharae would never have dreamed of addressing a High Family Vanar woman with as much familiarity as he did now Namasi Sahmudrah. They both obviously understood the change in their rapport.

"Right," he said. And took a breath before nodding at the Dhikar. But when the doors were pulled back to allow them in, his sister waited for him while pacing with barely contained impatience, not bothering with the observance of Family customs. A good many of his other female relatives had also assembled, the buzz of conversation dying away as he walked with diligent observance of the formalities, stopping exactly the proper distance from her and bowing with the precise amount of respect. She inspected his appearance critically. Pratha Yronae had involved herself in the discussions of their strategy, even down to his choice of attire. Nathan was Nga'esha, and he would do his best to behave in a manner befitting the Nga'esha.

"You'll do," was all she said. And that concluded the audience.

He had thought it more appropriate to use the men's public transportation to get to the Assembly of Families, but the pratha h'máy overruled that idea. The city of Sabtú might have fallen into an unnatural sense of subdued calm after the attack on the Nga'esha, but she still expected some opposition to be waiting for them at the Assembly. Private vehicles were rare, usually belonging to intercity freight handlers or those battered work floats common in the agricultural fields. Nathan hadn't even known Yronae owned her own hoverfloat, and he wondered what it was used for. Whatever it was used for, by the musty smell of the interior, it wasn't used very often.

He and Margasir climbed into the rear compartment, their backs to Namasi and Yronae in the front of the float. Fortunately, this part of the float was also enclosed, protecting him as much as the women from any dust or wind. A single Dhikar drove the small vehicle, and they sped off to leave the rest of the entourage following behind the best they could.

Nathan had expected to draw considerable attention, but the float wasn't even able to come anywhere near the Assembly. The immense crowd swelling through the streets numbered in the thousands, the entire city seemed at a standstill. Margasir twisted in his seat to stare past the women in astonishment. Nathan fixed his gaze on his clenched hands between his knees, unwilling to even look out the windows at the mass of people staring in at him. The crowd was mostly women, not unexpectedly, and although the mood was hostile, there was little show of aggression, no waving of signs or fists or chanting of angry slogans the way any other world might have displayed. Which made it all the more ominous, Nathan thought.

"Let's hope we manage to get close enough to the Assembly to make a run for it before they lynch us," the sahakharae said, the humor strained.

"Thanks, Margasir. I can always count on you to look on the bright side."

The float inched laboriously forward and stopped, inched forward and stopped. After nearly an hour at an impasse, he heard the hiss of the women's compartment opening, then Yronae opened his end. "We'll have to walk from here," she said dryly.

He stepped down out of the float and turned. His stomach lurched. Vasant Subah stood in the way of the float, her arms crossed belligerently, legs braced, a full armada of Vanar Security Dhikar arranged in her wake.

"I didn't expect anything like *this*," he heard Namasi murmur.

"I did," Yronae said shortly. She motioned at Nathan curtly, and without looking to see if he followed, began striding toward the security chief with imperial arrogance. Vasant Subah stepped forward to block her, the Dhikar behind her impassive but alert. Forced to a halt, Yronae glared at her opponent. "Get out of my way," she said. She spoke softly, but the hush of the crowd made every word seem loud and unmistakable.

The Dhikar chief shrugged eloquently. "It is my right as a citizen to stand in a public place. Would you threaten me with violence if I choose to assert my rights?"

Namasi Sahmudrah stood beside the Nga'esha pratha h'máy, and all Nathan could see was her back, but it was enough to tell him the young woman was frightened, her spine rigid as she tried to mask her trembling.

"I have come to hear my brother speak at the Assembly of Families, as is *his* right. I do not threaten anyone with violence, and your insulting suggestion that I or any member of my Family would stoop to such measures is deeply resented. But should you deny me access to the courts, Qsayati, I don't care whose protection you think you have, it will not be enough to prevent my taking vengeance on you. Personally."

The Qsayati blinked, her only sign of uncertainty. "With all respect, jah'nari pratha, surely you must have more pressing business to attend to? I would humbly recommend that you take your so-called 'brother' home and teach him some manners. He may wear the Nga'e-sha blue, but he is still only an ignorant, barbaric yepoqioh, and no one here is interested in anything he has to say."

She snapped her fingers, and the Dhikar behind her fanned out, a slight twitch of their fingers activating their implants, faces impassive. Namasi swayed, as if struggling with herself to keep from retreating, while Yronae remained unyielding. In the tense silence, Nathan's shoulders sagged in defeat. At least he'd tried, the gesture had been made, he thought. Then someone slipped a hand into his, squeezing it tightly. Daegal dva Pakaran stood beside him, looking as terrified as he felt.

"I am," she said in a near whisper. It carried like a trumpet.

Both Namasi and Yronae turned around to stare, Vasant Subah's face clouding with bewildered anger. He was gazing down at Daegal in wonder when someone took his other hand. This time his jaw dropped. The Dhikar he knew only as Two-Knock confronted Vasant Subah with dignified defiance.

"I am," she said.

Another woman, a total stranger this time, moved to stand with him. "I am." Another, this time a distant cousin. And another. And another. "I am," he heard a male voice say, as Yinanq dva Hadatha Nga'e-sha and his práhsaedam Jayati joined the small group confronting Qsayati Vasant Subah and her company of Dhikar police. Namasi and Yronae both twisted in amazement as the protective cluster around him grew, and Nathan knew this hadn't been planned, *knew* this was a groundswell of spontaneous support. The number of people joining their voices and their hands in his defense was far from the majority of the crowd, but impressive enough that even the usually imperturbable Dhikar police wavered in wariness.

Yronae grinned humorlessly, then leaned in toward Vasant Subah, her nose nearly touching the other woman's. *"Move,"* she hissed.

He couldn't help himself from staring, fascinated by Vasant Subah's entire face quivering with rage. She gestured brusquely at her Dhikar to fall back as his protective escort slowly pressed its way through the crowd with Nathan in its center like diligent workers surrounding a queen bee, until they reached steps leading up to the columned terrace of the Assembly of Families.

In the confusion, Daegal dva Pakaran lost her hold on Nathan, swallowed by the crowd while Two-Knock deftly but courteously plowed a path through the throng for Yronae, Namasi, and him. He wasn't sure how he'd gotten there, but before he'd managed to catch his breath, he found himself on the main floor of the Assembly reserved solely for the use of the High Families. Several women waited silently along the semicircular marble wall—his arbitrators for this case.

Namasi Sahmudrah caught him by the elbow. "They're all ancillary Family," she said in a low voice, "but don't let that fool you. You may not see them, but every pratha h'máy will be listening." She glanced at the spectators swarming into the Assembly behind them, jostling for room. The men's balcony above them was already packed with the curious of both sexes. Namasi's fear had been replaced with brisk excitement. "We'll take our place and confer, give the public time to settle."

And to give him as big an audience as possible, he understood, as he watched journalists scrimmage for a viable broadcast alignment. He followed Yronae as she strode toward the arbitrators and settled onto the emblem of the Nga'esha inlaid into the floor, one leg under her, resting her arm on the other knee. As it was a member of her Family who had brought the litigation, she would have no vote with the arbitrators judging his case. He didn't have to calculate the proper distance any longer as he stopped behind her right shoulder and started to kneel.

"No, in front of me," the pratha h'máy said without even glancing at him. "You and your speaker both."

Surprised, he hesitated, then took his place in front with Namasi Sahmudrah beside him. He hadn't realized before now how accustomed he'd become to Vanar hierarchical arrangements, and the sudden exposure made him feel oddly vulnerable.

"Are we ready to begin?" the arbitrator from the Daharanan Family asked. What little disorder and whispering there was ceased abruptly.

"We are ready, jah'narha l'amaée," Namasi Sahmudrah said. Then looked at him.

He unfolded his palm-sized reader to open his carefully prepared speech and took a steadying breath. "By tradition, Vaktay Namasi dva Ushahayam Sahmudrah should be presenting this case to you. I could not have hoped for a better advocate, no one has worked more tirelessly and conscientiously than she. According to law, however, I do have the right to speak for myself. My command of Vanar is not perfectly fluent, and I hope you will forgive the many grammatical errors I know I will make. But I have learned Vanar well enough by now to present my own case this one time."

The arbitrator glowered at him. "Irregular, but permissible." She folded her hands primly. "Be warned, however, that any errors you make will not be an excuse for us to tolerate the slightest infraction in the rules of law."

He bowed, meticulously polite, and glanced at his notes on the reader, not really seeing them. He set it down, knowing by heart the text he'd painstakingly drafted and rehearsed for weeks.

"Most of you here from the High Families know me, as I am related to at least half of you through my adoptive mother, the late Pratha Yaenida dva Daharanan ek Qarshatha Nga'esha. I am also aware that all of Vanar has seen enough about me in the media to know who I am. My story is widely known, and I will not waste the Assembly's time in repeating it. All I will emphasize is that I was trained as a research botanist before I came to Vanar. I love the science of living plants, botany is the only thing I've ever wanted to do. While my pratha h'máy has been tolerant, Vanar laws and customs have frustrated my studies. When I first asked l'amae Namasi to speak for me, I only intended to ask for the freedom to pursue my research work in any manner I like. But I knew even then that this would mean asking the court to consider changes in orthodox Vanar laws."

"The laws lain down by our Founders seven hundred years ago," the Daharanan arbitrator retorted, "established a peaceful and just society, and have worked well enough unchanged for generations."

Nathan kept his head lowered respectfully. "I most humbly beg to differ with you, jah'nari l'amae. With the help of my learned vaktay, I have researched Vanar legal history. There is precedence, which I ask this Assembly to allow me to present."

A muted consultation whispered briefly between the arbitrators, then ceased. "Continue," the Daharanan arbitrator said shortly.

He bowed, the silence in the vast hall unnerving. "I am not allowed admission to the best university libraries or laboratories because I am a man. I am forbidden to approach those scholars with whom I might share research, because I am a man. I cannot make field trips to collect specimens or so much as leave the Nga'esha House without permission, because I am a man. I cannot own property or handle my own finances or purchase anything without consent, because I am a man. I'm not even allowed to see my own child without consent, because I am a man. If the pratha h'máy Yronae dva Daharanan Qarshatha Ushahayam ek Nga'esha were not my sister, and were not as lenient with me as she is, I would never have been allowed to continue my personal interests at all."

He looked up at the arbitrators regarding him coldly. "And why should I be? I know there are those who say I am not even Vanar-born, why is it fair for me to expect privileges denied other men only because I am different? If I have chosen of my own free will to remain Vanar and Nga'esha, why should I not also accept the ancient traditions limiting the rights of men as established by the Founders?"

Nathan glanced at Namasi, who nodded and brushed her fingertips across her reader to activate it. He took a quick breath.

"Because I *am* different. Not because I wasn't Vanar-born, but because I have one thing no other man has ever had before: I own the archives of a pratha h'máy. The records and data are only those of the Nga'esha Family and stop with the death of Pratha Yaenida, but I have access to seven hundred years of detailed Vanar history. Including the original records written by the Nga'esha founders, written not in Vanar, because that language had yet to be established, but in Hengeli, my maternal language. Hundreds of official ship logs, thousands of requisitions from early pioneers to administrators back in Vanar's first capital, journals kept by ordinary people of everyday life, letters to their friends and relatives.

"I've translated many of these from Hengeli into Vanar. The life described in those records is nothing like the traditional history you are teaching your children, including my daughter. These were not wise women rebelling against patriarchal Hengeli rule who came here to construct their ideal society. They were the survivors of a wrecked seed ship who reached Vanar more by miracle than design, people desperate merely to stay alive. Most of the survivors were women, but not all, in contradiction to another of our sacred legends. These men were not subjugated because their women feared violence, but from biological necessity any farmer understands: a limited food supply and the need for every individual to survive in a hostile environment. One man's sperm could supply all that was necessary to reproduce another generation—"

"This is rubbish," one of the arbitrators snapped in irritation. She wore the Hadatha sati, but the trim underneath was burgundy. Nathan instantly adjusted his posture, at once respectful and silent. "Do you really expect us to trust that whatever records you've dredged up haven't been taken out of context and twisted to support some hoax? We have only your word that any translation you've made bears any resemblance whatsoever to the original—"

"And mine," he heard Pratha Yronae say from behind him. He didn't dare turn to look at her. The astonishment on the arbitrator's face was enough. "My little brother's command of Vanar is, as he's said, not perfect. I've assisted him myself with these translations, and I assure you, they are as faithful as possible to the originals. May I assume my word is good enough for you?"

The Hadatha woman leaned back silently, yielding to another arbitrator, this one Nathan recognized as a close cousin of the formidable Ushahayam pratha h'máy, as well as distantly related to Yronae. "Of course your word is good enough, jah'nari bahd'hyin. Does it not worry you, however, this sensitive information in the hands of such a subordinate member of your Family?"

"Yes, it worries me," Pratha Yronae said serenely, hiding it well. "As pratha h'máy, the honor of the Nga'esha House is my responsibility. I have only recently gained an appreciation of our history, an oversight I should have corrected long before now. I know what is in these records, and it is not pleasant. But while I may not like the truth, I will not conspire with those who would prefer to suppress it."

The Ushahayam woman sucked air through her front teeth and

exchanged glances with her counterparts. "Then perhaps you would be willing to allow us to examine these translations of yours before we continue any further with this proceeding?" she said to Nathan. He smiled without looking up.

"We have no objection, jah'nari l'amae," Namasi Sahmudrah said. "On behalf of my client, I requested and was granted permission by the pratha Yronae Nga'esha to release copies, in both Vanar and the original Hengeli for those who wish to verify the integrity of our translations, into the public domain. I have done so just now. Anyone who wishes may read them. We are willing to wait."

The subsequent uproar exploded around him, arbitrators on their feet shouting unheard as the crowd in the gallery above them scrambled for the nearest reader. While Namasi Sahmudrah leapt to her feet to brave the Hadatha arbitrator screaming in her face, Nathan remained frozen in his empty circle of isolation.

"You had no right to release that information without the express consent of this Assembly!" the arbitrator shouted angrily.

"You already gave it!" Namasi shouted back just as fiercely. "The court adjudicated the terms of Pratha Yaenida's will and ruled it was within the prescript of legal statutes. Nathan Crewe Nga'esha is within his rights to release any information he wishes contained in his mother's legacy to him."

The Ushahayam arbitrator and Pratha Yronae likewise stood confrontationally as they argued, only slightly less belligerently, as their status required. Almost unnoticed, Two-Knock had organized a Dhikar defensive buffer, half a dozen casually alert Nga'esha women standing around him, their implants squirming under the skin.

"Jah'nari Dhikar," he said, still not knowing her name, "I appreciate your concern, but please do not protect me."

Two-Knock looked down at him solemnly. "There are many here who wish you harm, including Dhikar."

"I am aware of that."

The Dhikar tilted her head curiously. "Are you not afraid?"

He allowed himself a small laugh and grinned up at her. "Shitless," he said, using a very un-Vanar expression. Behind her, he noticed one of the media jockeying for an angle, and knew that even through the clamor, his voice was being recorded. This wasn't part of his memorized script. "But I will defend myself only with words, as any civilized Vanar should do, never with violence. Please, stand away and harm no one."

Two-Knock grunted, unconvinced, but raised an eyebrow and shrugged. The Nga'esha Dhikar withdrew, pointedly sitting down and ignoring the small crowd of hostile litigants still standing. Yronae had noticed the exchange, and spoke briefly to the Ushahayam arbitrator, who nodded then pulled the Hadatha woman away from her dispute with Namasi. The pratha h'máy, following her Dhikar's example, gestured to Namasi as she crossed to retake her place on the floor behind him.

"Clever boy," she chided in a low voice as she passed him.

"Foolish boy," he replied without looking at her.

Her laugh was hushed. "Also true."

The arbitrators returned to their seating ledge, consulting one another in subdued murmurs as they waited for the hall to quiet. Again next to him, Namasi inhaled sharply, and Nathan looked up to see the Daharanan pratha h'máy and the dalhitri h'máy from the Arjusana Family shoulder their way into the hall. The Daharanan and Arjusana arbitrators stood, bowed, and relinquished their place to the higher-ranked women. "That's either a very good sign or a very bad one," she whispered to Nathan.

Most of the crowd, both litigants below and spectators above, had again settled, the Assembly Dhikar struggling to hold back those who could find no room in the galleries above packed three and four deep against the walls with no concern for sex or caste. He spotted Daegal dva Pakaran standing beside Margasir, the sahakharae's arm around her shoulders protectively. Nathan wondered where Amitu was. The shouting at last died down to whispers and the hum of hundreds of readers.

"May we continue?" Namasi asked, as dignified as she could manage.

As the most senior woman present, the Daharanan pratha h'máy said, "Are you or your client likely to subject us to any further of these annoying surprises, l'amae vaktay?"

"None that I'm aware of, jah'nari pratha."

The Daharanan pratha h'máy glanced at the reader handed to her, scanning it with a frown. "This Assembly has not had adequate opportunity to properly examine these documents. Does the petitioner realize that no decision can be reached before we can evaluate their relevance?"

"Under ordinary circumstances, we would be willing to accept a postponement until our translations had been thoroughly verified." An angry murmur rippled through the hall, the closure of the Worms already starting to bite into the reserves of many, not just those of High Family. "However," Namasi continued hurriedly, "these are not ordinary circumstances, as I'm sure I don't need to point out to this Assembly, or to any one of the High Families. Since my client is not requesting an immediate decision, we ask to be allowed to continue presenting our complete case at this time."

The Daharanan pratha h'máy raised an incredulous eyebrow. "And exactly when would you expect a decision?"

"That is entirely at the leisure of this Assembly, jah'nari pratha," Namasi said innocently.

When none of the arbitrators dissented, the Daharanan pratha h'máy scowled, but gestured gruffly at Nathan. "Then by all means, continue."

He picked up the small reader, skimming through his notes nervously. "As I've said, the survivors found life on this world difficult. Although Vanar is geologically an old planet, it is very young on the evolutionary scale: no animal life at all, only primordial plants, none of which are edible. The soil is sterile by human standards, as any agriculturalist here can tell you. Every inch of farmland has had to be enhanced with imported bacteria and worms, fertilizers and conditioners worked into the ground. The survivors of the original seed ship had only what was in their genetic banks, no new supplies would arrive on Vanar for another century. They had no animals, no milk, no eggs, no meat. The early settlers depended on a totally vegetarian diet. They came close to catastrophe many times. The Nga'esha Founders, as did the other founders of the High Families, chose to procreate only female children over several generations, until the supply of genetic stock had run dangerously low.

"Only then was it decided to reintroduce living male children, but solely as a means of replenishing their reserves. By that time, the original men who had arrived with the women had long died, and few of their descendants if any had ever seen an adult male. The fact that there were two sexes had nearly been forgotten. They didn't even have farm animals to make the correlation between males and females of any species. These women were not members of the Hengeli Territorial Convention. Before the Worms were discovered, the early greatships connecting the systems by perpetual rotation never reached here. Vanar had little contact of any kind with any other world.

"A farmer today caught treating her livestock with such brutality as these boys were raised in would be hospitalized for insanity. Once reaching sexual maturity, young men were used like milk cows, then slaughtered. The Founders, who Vanar children today are taught to worship as the wise engineers of an altruistic society, committed atrocities on their own children. I refer you in particular to a letter you will find referenced under T-N 176, written by one Tais Nga'esha of the Neku-Baou settlement, now known as the town of Naebokul, west of Dravyam."

The rustle of fingertips across hundreds of readers resonated in the huge hall. He paused a moment for the arbitrators and spectators alike to access the letter. Clearing his throat, he wished he had a glass of water, and furtively glanced around at the women packed into the hall poring over their readers avidly, those without readers straining to see over their neighbor's shoulders.

"At that time, Neku-Baou was a small farming community of about twenty-five families. The settlement's breeding stock had died during a fire. Tais Nga'esha authorized her daughter to travel to Sabtú to hire a particular woman who specialized in bearing male children for sale. She also instructed her in the standard method of removing the young boy's legs and arms at the knees and elbows so his body would better fit the extraction machine in which he would be permanently confined and force-fed until he either died or was butchered if production fell below acceptable quantities. This would be the standard practice for over two hundred years until the development of the first whitewomb system, originally designed for hygiene rather than for the welfare of the contents."

Muttered incredulity rumbled through the spectators. The arbitrators scanned the documents with expressions of suspicion and disgust, several already shaking their heads in denial.

"Instruments used then for such amputations were primitive, usually axes and hot irons for cauterization. Most male children were lobotomized to make handling them easier. Some were not, and were fully aware of what was being done to them. Even the modern Vanar word 'kharvah' originally meant 'mutilated.' These women made no effort to conceal their actions, nor did they consider what they were doing particularly horrendous."

"This must have been an isolated incident, some deviant custom in the Nga'esha provinces . . . ," the Daharanan pratha h'máy interjected.

"I'm sorry, jah'nari l'amae, but it was not. Quality control records kept by inspectors and breeders prove the treatment of men as depicted in the Tais Nga'esha letter was common practice not only in the provinces but in the capital, employed by all of the Families, not just the Nga'esha. From all other accounts, Tais Nga'esha was a loving mother and a respected member of her community. She wasn't a cruel woman. She simply regarded men as literally equivalent to human excrement: one necessary for the fertilization of the soil in order to raise crops, the other for the fertilization of women to raise daughters. There are enough cross-references in the Pratha Yaenida's archives to suggest all the Nine Families have similar histories. They have gone unnoticed over the centuries because your records would also be in Hengeli, not Vanar."

"Those which still exist," Pratha Yronae said from behind him.

The Daharanan pratha h'máy shot her a warning glare. "Are you accusing anyone of conspiracy, jah'nari tulyah?"

"Accusing?" Pratha Yronae's voice behind him sounded coldly amused. "Not anyone living, no."

The arbitrator scowled. "I think we've had enough of your historical exhibits, Nathan Crewe Nga'esha. But I fail to see what relevance this has to your suit. If anything, it shows how the spirit of the Founders' laws have been applied to defend men, rather than exploit them."

A small disturbance caught his attention. Two Changriti Dhikar cleared a path for Pratha Eraelin behind them. He faltered as she strode imperiously to the arbitrator's section, waving away the Changriti subordinate who rose to relinquish her position. Settling in her place, she carefully adjusted her sati before lacing her hands in her lap and glowering at him. She gave no hint that she was even aware of the notoriety she had earned by her schemes against the Nga'esha with the Hengeli warships still trapped in orbit around Vanar. In the uneasy quiet, someone coughed. Nathan looked back down at his reader, oblivious to the words.

"I've lost my place," he whispered to Namasi, his nerves jittery.

"Take your time, Nathan."

He took a deep breath, and found what he was looking for.

"These records show that, ah . . . the laws and traditions credited to the Founders were not made by them at all, but by their descendants many generations later—women made wealthy enough by the Worms to import luxuries their ancestors never dreamed of. Women with leisure time enough to create art and music and debate philosophy and create a new language to suit their new world. Women could now regard men as more than just a basic genetic resource; if not as individuals equal to themselves, at least as valued possessions that enriched their own lives. I've included in the translations several early letters from women expressing surprise to find men capable of a level of intelligent speech and emotion almost equal to their own. Men were granted the right to a basic education, allowed to learn to read and write, less than three hundred years ago. These were the women who reformed the Vanar legal system, not to repress men, but to protect them. To give rights to the people they acknowledged for the first time as their sons and brothers and fathers."

Eraelin Changriti's slow, deliberate applause interrupted him, the solitary clapping resonating through the hall.

"An eloquent speech," she said when she finally stopped. "And so convincingly delivered. One might be fooled into thinking you actually wrote it yourself."

Namasi flushed in anger. He heard her inhale for a retort, and stopped her with a small motion of his hand, not quite touching her. Deliberately, he closed his reader and left it in his lap as he put his palms on his thighs, his head bowed deferentially.

"I won't deny that I had help, jah'nari pratha," he said calmly.

"Vanar is a difficult language to learn, especially for someone already an adult." He thought of Yaenida, wishing the old woman could have lived to see what havoc she'd set loose. "Once it was thought I was too old and too yepoqioh to ever conform to Vanar life, even if I was intelligent enough to learn the language." He smiled wistfully and looked up at the arbitrators, aware of his hypercorrect demeanor. "Now I'm often accused of being more Vanar than the Vanar. I have never been able to please anyone."

The Arjusana dalhitri h'máy caught her upper lip with her teeth to bite back her laugh, and several of the other arbitrators looked fleetingly amused.

"I know I make many errors, and some find my accent unpleasant and hard to understand. But I respectfully suggest this is hardly proof I am stupid or ignorant. I am capable of continuing without the benefit of my notes, if my using them is offensive to anyone."

"What's the point either way?" Eraelin rasped dismissively. "It's ancient history, totally irrelevant." Even the other Changriti arbitrator on the sidelines squirmed in disapproval. Yronae's snarl behind him sounded like that of an irritable cat.

"The point, jah'nari l'amae," he said, aware that in the years he'd been married to her daughter he had never once used his mother-in-law's name, nor would he now, "is that Vanar law has never been inflexible. Those traditions we hold sacred as set down by the Founders are myths. Vanar women gave men rights not because they were forced to, not because men rebelled against them, but from compassion and decency and a moral sense of justice."

Eraelin Changriti's expression didn't change, but he sensed her seething hatred.

"Nonetheless, the jah'nari pratha h'máy does raise a valid objection," he said, once again addressing the Assembly. "Ancient history. Laws have changed over the centuries, and I do not dispute that life is easier now for men than it was seven hundred years ago. Vanar prides itself on being an enlightened, pacifist society. Theft, burglary, vandalism are all practically unheard of. The standard of living, for both women and men, is excellent. Education and health are superior to many other cultures in the settled systems. Why should laws that safeguard this be changed?

"But please consider a few statistics that are not only to be found in the Nga'esha archives, but are a matter of public record." He gestured to the little reader still in his lap. "If there is no objection, may I be allowed to refer to my notes?"

The Daharanan pratha h'máy flicked her hand dismissively, massive bracelets jingling. "Of course."

He bowed politely and unfolded the reader. "Thank you, l'amae." He quickly flipped forward to find his place. "In the year before Pratha Yaenida died, according to the official records kept by Family medical taemorae as well as the municipal hospitals in Sabtú, seven hundred and twelve men were treated for injuries inflicted on them by women. I've listed only cases where the person who caused the injury was known—most often wives or relatives. In many other cases, men treated for injuries refused to identify their assailant. You will find those statistics appended without comment or speculation.

"These injuries ranged from minor bruising to broken bones and severe stabbings or slashing, many directed at men's genitals. Sixty-five men died as a result. Only four cases were ever referred to the Dhikar for investigation. I know from personal experience that men who have been assaulted are discouraged from seeking assistance from the Dhikar, and inquiries are rare." He didn't look at Eraelin Changriti, knew he didn't have to.

He paused, his mouth dry. Although the interior of the Assembly was cool, he could feel the silk of his sati clinging to the sweat between his shoulder blades.

"In contrast, eighteen women were assaulted by men, none of them seriously injured or killed. In six cases, the assault was verbal only, no physical injury. Although rape is frequently cited as a justification for restricting men, there has not been a single reported case of rape or attempted rape in the past twenty years, and only one in the past fifty. All the accused men are now either naekulam wearing lajjae, or are permanently confined to a whitewomb.

"Three hundred and seventy-two men committed suicide that year compared to thirty-eight women. I doubt there has been any significant improvement in these statistics in the years that have followed Pratha Yaenida's death. I ask the Assembly to consider: do these statistics reflect a truly enlightened, nonviolent society?"

"And I would suggest," said the Daharanan pratha h'máy acting as the spokeswoman, "that the lack of women murdered and raped by men is confirmation that restricting men works, and is therefore a legitimate argument against change."

Nathan listened carefully to her tone. Although the words might have been hostile, her voice was not.

"Possibly, jah'nari pratha. Statistics are only numbers. How they are interpreted is subjective. My intention here is to challenge the validity of that argument, and ask you to at least listen to a different point of view."

She exchanged glances with other arbitrators, only Eraelin Changriti glowering darkly. "Continue," she said with a shrug.

"Traditional Vanar reasoning is that women are the glue of society, natural communicators, mediators, conciliators, all innate abilities that make them excellent business people. Men are driven by testosterone. It makes us aggressive, violent, and irrational. It's not our fault; we can't help ourselves. But the obvious conclusion of this hormonal impairment is that men cannot be trusted. Do you agree with this precis?"

The Daharanan pratha h'máy nodded guardedly. "Absolutely. The fact is, jah'nar bhraetae, men and women are biologically different, whether you like it or not. Far from it being a privilege, women accept the heavy responsibility of providing the necessary balance between the two genders for the safety of us all, including you."

Nathan nodded, as if agreeing. "Women make the rules; men obey them. Men can only be civilized when women can control them. If men do not behave as women think they should, they need and deserve to be disciplined, for their own good as well as the good of the community. So it follows that if a man is disciplined by his family or his wife, he must have done something to provoke it."

She frowned, wary. "Again, that is a logical assumption."

"May I refer to my notes again? In one case, a man had all his fingers broken after he won a game of qaellast played against his wife. Another was hit in the face so hard he required three teeth replaced because his sister found the way he laughed annoying. Another died from severe burns when his sati was set on fire by his wife because he had accidentally spilled tea on himself. You will find many more similar anecdotal reports. I ask you now: how did these men provoke such extreme punishment?"

Nathan read the facts and figures off his reader with very little emotion, having gone through them so many times he felt as if it had burnt all the anger away.

The Arjusana dalhitri h'máy scowled. "I don't question the accuracy of your research, as far as it goes. But as you've said, interpretation is subjective. These incidences taken in isolation may not give the complete picture, there could well be other factors you are not aware of."

Beside him, Namasi grunted softly to herself in satisfaction. She had spent hours speculating on every possible objection she could think might occur, drilling him on the responses. This was one they had anticipated, almost word for word.

"Then I strongly encourage you and the Dhikar to investigate each and every one of these cases thoroughly, jah'nari dalhitri, which would be more than anyone else has ever done."

"Surely this sort of thing isn't common in High Families," the Hadatha arbitrator protested.

"The numbers are in the public record. High, Middle, or Common makes no difference."

"But *you* have never been treated so harshly."

"Me personally, jab'nari l'amae?" He was all too aware of Pratha Yronae's presence behind him, with the familiar sensation of walking on eggs. "Not to such an extreme, no. It is well known that I've had difficulties with my Family and that of my wife's in the past. But I'm very fortunate that the Nga'esha is notably one of the more liberal of the Nine Families, as the fact that I'm even here speaking today with my sister's consent, if not her endorsement, proves."

Eraelin Changriti snorted. "You're speaking today only because you've managed to sway the sympathies of Vanar Pilots," she snarled. "It's always easier to persuade someone to listen to you when you hold a knife to her throat."

The assent in the mutters that swept the Assembly didn't disturb him. The scar along his ribs ached with the memory. "Again, jah'nari pratha, you raise a valid point. It's been my personal experience, however, that on Vanar knives are more often used to silence people."

Even Namasi gasped. Eraelin Changriti went as white as if she'd been slapped.

"Yes, well." The Daharanan pratha h'máy cleared her throat cautiously. "You've presented your case suitably enough. But I would ask *you* to consider a question: are you genuinely expecting this Assembly to believe that, were the reverse true, men would treat women with any more tolerance and equity?"

He smiled wryly. "Of course not, l'amae. You have several thousand years of human history on your side as proof enough of that. My point is a simple one and an ancient one: when one group of people, regardless of gender or race, hold power over another, it always leads to brutality and exploitation. Your gender, pratha h'máy, has not made you any wiser or more compassionate than mine."

The Daharanan pratha h'máy raised an eyebrow, but didn't respond to the murmur of indignation in the Assembly. "We have listened to your arguments patiently and with an open mind. Now, what is it, exactly, that you want?"

"Legal recognition of my rights as a human being equal to yours."

"Biological fact proves we are not equal people. That idealistic path has been tried before, and led only to anarchy. We will not allow it to happen on Vanar." The Daharanan pratha h'máy smiled sympathetically. "Try asking for something a little less ambitious, qanistha bbraetae. What do you want, *personally*?"

"The right to leave the Nga'esha estate whenever I choose without having to ask permission, and to travel anywhere on Vanar I wish."

"That is an internal Family matter, not one for this Assembly."

"I respectfully disagree. If I am denied permission by my Family, I should have legal recourse to the courts to enforce that right."

She frowned, then yielded. "We will consider the lawful basis for such a demand."

"Thank you. I further wish the right to divorce my wife."

Furious, Eraelin Changriti sprang to her feet, but before she could speak, the Daharanan pratha h'máy placed a restraining hand on her arm, persuading her to sit down again. That the Changriti pratha h'máy subsided so quickly surprised him.

"A moot point," the Daharanan pratha h'máy said. "Your wife has already dissolved your marriage."

"It's not the same thing. Men are still legally considered the property of their wives and have no right to ask for a dissolution of their marriage, for any reason. My wife repudiated me for 'unmanageable behavior,' the standard reason women cite for divorcing any kharvah. Evidence to support the allegation isn't even required."

"Marriage is a business transaction between Families, not an agreement between two people," the Daharanan pratha h'máy countered.

"So is divorce. Men are regularly repudiated because their wives have succeeded well enough to attract kharvah from more favorably positioned families. Divorced men can only return to families who pay an indemnity to the wife. The rest become naekulam because their families either can't or won't repay the marriage price, an unjust burden on both the men and their families. No one should have to suffer being made naekulam because their wives are greedy or because their families are too poor."

"Which is not what happened in your case, however," the subordinate Changriti arbitrator said.

"No," he admitted. "Neither my wife nor I wanted this divorce. I was repudiated because my wife's mother ordered her to do so." Eraelin Changnti glared at him stonily.

"As is her right as the head of her Family," the Changriti arbitrator retorted.

"Exactly." He returned her look steadily.

The Daharanan pratha h'máy studied him narrowly. "And were the dalhitri Kallah dva Ushahayam Changriti to agree, would you return to the marriage willingly?" She flicked a hand at Eraelin Changriti's surge of outrage without even looking at the woman. He glanced between them warily in the sudden realization of how much power the Changriti pratha h'máy had lost.

"I don't know," he said slowly. This hadn't been one of the possible responses Namasi had coached him through. "It might be . . . negotiable. But I request access to our child, my daughter Aenanda, and to have an active say in her future whether I am married or divorced."

"You share her fatherhood, Nathan Crewe Nga'esha. She is not yours alone."

"No, she isn't. She is blessed with two other decent, loving fathers.

Why should she be denied the benefit of any of us? I would insist she continue to see her other fathers as well."

The Daharanan pratha h'máy sighed. "We will consider your request," she said without enthusiasm. "Anything else?"

"I wish the right to control my own finances. Not just the interest, but the capital my Family profits from in my name."

"For what possible purpose? You are Nga'esha. You already earn more money on your Family interest alone than most Vanar women earn in a lifetime."

"I wish the right to buy and own property in my own name."

"Property?" The Arjusana arbitrator seemed utterly baffled by such an odd request. "What property?"

"I intend to use as much of my own funds as I can afford to buy as much land as I can between the southern coastal plain and up into the mountains north of Dravyam."

"To do what with?"

"Nothing."

"A rather extravagant way to make a point, isn't it?" the Daharanan pratha h'máy said dryly.

"It isn't to make a point, jah'nari pratha. I'm a botanist. Some of the most interesting and varied native Vanar plant life is to be found in that area. The transformation of land to human use has been slow on Vanar, but the methods are becoming more effective and the rate of destruction of native habitat has tripled in the last ten years alone. At this exponential rate, there will be little if any native Vanar habitat left inside a century. I'd like to establish reserves for scientific examination and encourage our people to study the unique assets this planet has to offer."

"Isn't that already Nga'esha land anyway?" Startled, Nathan glanced briefly at the woman who had spoken, a token representative of the Nga'esha Family whom Yronae had instructed to remain uninvolved. But the Nga'esha arbitrator seemed more puzzled than contentious.

"Most of it," he said. "But it belongs to the Family. Not to me. I have no voice in how it's used." He hesitated, having argued with Namasi over revealing too much of their strategy, then decided to risk it. "It would also establish a precedent, jah'nari l'amae. The business and fortunes of the Nga'esha operate in a universe of their own, far beyond the concern of most Vanar. But how many Middle and Common families here have daughters who are forced into professions they would never have chosen for themselves in order to preserve their family's economic interests, while their sons are excluded, the only future for boys in making a good marriage or becoming sahakharae? How many women marry men they don't like because they need the family connections? How much unhappiness do these unjust traditions cause *women*?"

He felt rather than heard the ripple through the crowd, knowing he'd struck a nerve.

The Daharanan pratha h'máy gauged the shifting mood of the crowd deftly. "We will consider the legal basis for such a demand," she said cautiously. "Are you finished?"

He deliberated a moment, weighing how far he could ignore Namasi's advice as well as annoy his pratha h'máy.

"Not quite," he said, which earned him a perplexed glance from Namasi. "I wish the right to sit on the board of the Nga'esha Corporation and have an equal vote in any and all business we transact off-world." He heard Yronae's gasp of disbelief behind him.

Namasi leaned toward him to whisper, "Are you out of your mind?"

A sentiment echoed a moment later by the Daharanan pratha h'máy. "You don't seriously expect us to consider such a ridiculous motion for one moment, do you?"

Actually, he did. Just not in his lifetime. "Of course not, jah'nari pratha. But is it not a practical strategy to make a few unreasonable demands you are willing to give up in order to gain those you truly want?"

The Daharanan pratha h'máy grunted disapprovingly. "Possibly. However, I strongly suggest that in future you leave such business tactics to those whose domain it is."

"Good advice," Yronae muttered behind him, "which I'd take if I were you."

"If that concludes your petition?"

"Yes, jah'nari l'amae—" Namasi said quickly.

"No."

"Nathan!" Namasi hissed at him.

He ignored her, his attention focused on the arbitrators. "I have one more request, this one a personal matter. I wish to adopt a child." From the corner of his eye, he saw Namasi's helpless gesture at Yronae, bewildered. The Daharanan pratha h'máy rubbed her forehead as if fighting a headache.

"You, a man, wish to adopt a child?"

"Yes, jah'nari pratha."

She exhaled impatiently. "What for?"

"Because if you grant me access to see my daughter, then I intend to extend my rights as a father to include someone with even less rights than myself. And more simply, because I love him."

"Him who?" Pratha Yronae grated out behind him.

He licked dry lips. "Raemik Nga'esha."

He saw the sudden understanding dawn on Namasi, and wondered if Yronae would be as quick to grasp the ramifications. Especially since he had yet to play their last trick card.

Clearly, they wanted nothing to do with it, however. "We are willing to examine the legal requisites for such an irregular request, but that is a private negotiation you must enter into with the boy's guardian, in this case, the Pratha Yronae Nga'esha," she said firmly. "Have you anything else to say to this Assembly?"

"No, jah'nari l'amae."

"Good." She leaned back, her eyes narrowed. Now that he had completed his case, he knew the crux would be addressed. "We have had the courtesy to listen to you, Nathan Crewe Nga'esha. But the circumstances surrounding your case are unusual, and our situation urgent. We would like to know what we can expect from you in return for any immediate agreement to some, if not all of your petition."

Namasi had walked him through this part of her mock trial again and again, acutely conscious of the media attention that would be concentrated on him. But what had seemed clever in the privacy of his library was terrifying in the midst of a crowded Assembly.

"Nothing."

The shock and dismay on the faces of the arbitrators echoed the rumble of anger in the crowd.

"This is totally unacceptable!" the Daharanan arbitrator retorted, incensed. "The economies of hundreds of worlds, not just the prosperity of the Vanar, rely on the Worms for shipping vital resources. Do you seriously intend to hold us and every inhabited system hostage until we meet your demands?"

Deliberately, Nathan stood. "I have been in contact with the Nga'esha Pilots with the consent of Pratha Yronae. I have asked them, and they have agreed, that regardless of any decision you eventually reach they will reopen the Worms the moment I leave this Assembly. Events happen at a slower pace for Pilots, but I doubt it will be much longer before the other Family Pilots follow suit. The Worms are back in your control, l'amae. Now I am going home."

He bowed politely and had turned before the Daharanan pratha h'máy called out, "Hold on a moment, qanisth bhraetae." He stopped, his eyes lowered. Beside him Namasi and Yronae had also stood, waiting. "Explain yourself, please."

"What is there to explain?" he said without turning.

"You are giving in without a single concession?"

"Yes."

"*Why?*"

He glanced at Yronae before facing the arbitrators. "I believe in the decency and generosity of most Vanar women. Your ancestors raised men literally out of the shit because it was the ethical thing to do. Any change must come from the heart. Because it is right, not because you were forced into it. Otherwise, it is meaningless and I don't want it."

Namasi and Yronae had considered this merely a tactical maneuver, but he meant it, every word of it.

"If I am wrong about Vanar women, I will live with the consequences." He dared to look the Daharanan pratha h'máy directly in the eyes. "And so will you." He turned slowly, his gaze sweeping across the several hundred women and men watching him.

"And so will you," he repeated quietly.

Epilogue

(Fourteen Years Later)

"THE NEW GRADUATE STUDENT IS HERE," RAEMIK SAID TERSELY.

Nathan leaned back with his hands on his hips to stretch his spin[e] and squinted up in the bright sunlight at the large greenhouse exten[sion] slowly taking shape. A dozen young men and women, dressed [in] casual shorts and mati that might have shocked their more conven[n]tional parents, clambered over the half-finished frame like agile mon[n]keys. Armed with laser drills and socket wrenches for the inch-thi[ck] bolts, a drone crane with another partition in its jaws waited patient[ly] for instructions. Another ten thousand feet above, snow dusted t[he] summits of the Dravyam Peaks, winter on its way.

"Fine," Nathan said without glancing away from his supervisi[on] "Show her where the women's dormitory is and tell the kitchen to s[et] another place for dinner." He winced as a young woman vaulted ov[er] the top of the greenhouse girder, doing a lazy handspring onto t[he] scaffolding catwalk. "Goddamn it, Aedwyn! You kill yourself and I[']m] docking the insurance increase from your pay chit, knock it off!"

The girl just laughed at him merrily, and darted along the sc[af]folding with no fear for the sheer drop below her.

"The new graduate student does not wish to take instructions fr[om]

383

a lowly male underling such as myself." Raemik's voice dripped sarcasm. "She wishes to speak only with Dr. N. C. Nga'esha."

"Ah." Raemik had used the feminine variation of his title, the error becoming obvious.

Nathan turned to Raemik, whose attention was fixed with naked longing on the young girl still turning cartwheels along the scaffolding. His interest being her reason for showing off, Nathan suspected, the pair in constant rivalry for who could perform the most dangerous gymnastics. "Well, let's not keep the young lady waiting."

They walked down the narrow hill path toward the untidy cluster of habitat domes nestled in the valley, sheltered from the raw wind by the lee side of the mountain and the thick stand of native forest. The largest served as both Nathan's private office and quarters, where an irritable young woman in an elegant Arjusana sati totally unsuited for the climate paced the small entrance foyer and kicked the small pile of luggage on the floor. She turned and scowled as they entered.

"I didn't instruct you to fetch yet another useless flunky," she snapped at Raemik. "I told you to inform Dr. Nga'esha that I had arrived."

Raemik shot a heated look at Nathan before crossing to a small window ledge to practically throw himself onto it with studied disdain. The younger man sported the latest off-world fashion with a Vanar twist; loose native kirtiya blouse tucked into skin-tight pants many Vanar considered indecent.

Nathan pressed his palms together and bowed to the woman politely. "He did, l'amae." He ignored Raemik's pleasure at her expression of disbelief, keeping his own gaze averted just over her shoulder.

"*You're* Dr. Nga'esha?"

"Hae'm, qanistha bhagini."

She stared at him pop-eyed, her mouth working before she blurted, "There must be some mistake. . . ."

"There is, and you're the one who made it," Raemik said sourly, then added, "jah'nari l'amae," with unmistakable disdain.

"I am Dr. Nathan Crewe Nga'esha, the director-in-chief of this research facility. And you must be Ulkar dva Daharanan Arjusana. I've been expecting you. We are honored you've chosen to accept a position with us. Please be welcome." He bowed even lower to her.

"No, no," she said, waving him off like an annoying insect. "I've been tricked, brought here under false pretenses. There's no way I could work here, certainly not. I insist you take me back to Dravyam immediately."

"Good," he heard Raemik mutter under his breath. He kept his own expression mild.

"I'm sorry to hear that, jah'nari bhagini. Yours was one of the best graduate papers I've read this year, and the recommendations from the university were impeccable. I had very much looked forward to having your talents applied here. But of course, I understand your objections completely. Unfortunately, the float that brought you here is already on its way back and won't return until tomorrow." He shot a quick glare at Raemik to keep his son's mouth shut, not wishing him to expose the lie. "It's a long journey, and you must be tired. The least I can do is offer you a meal and a place for the night before you return in the morning."

The girl glowered, annoyed. "Well, if I'm a prisoner here, I might as well make the best of it."

"Your understanding is most gracious, thank you." He bowed again then said to Raemik, "Would you ask Aedwyn dva Changriti if she would be willing to show our guest around the station?"

Raemik grinned, and vanished like a cat out the door.

"I don't need the grand tour," the girl was still complaining. "I won't be here long enough to appreciate it. Just a bed for the night is enough."

"Of course, l'amae."

Aedwyn sauntered into the habitat dome with Raemik following on her heels wistfully. With her shorts loose on her hips, her mati artfully tied to show off her impressive abdominal muscles, Aedwyn Changriti was a beautiful young woman who knew all too well the effect she was having on his male graduate students and enjoyed every moment of it. Her eyes lit up at the sight of the new arrival, seeming oblivious to the look of horror she garnered in return. "Fantastic! The new peasant for the salt mines is finally here!" she crowed. "Don't worry, he does allow us at least three hours' sleep a night. You'll get used to it in no time."

"I have no intention of staying!" the new girl gasped. "When the float returns in the morning, I'm going straight back to Dravyam!"

"The float . . ." Aedwyn exchanged a quick look with Nathan, and smiled, her white teeth sharp in her dark face. He appreciated her more for her quick wits than her young, lean body. "Right. Well, let's get you bunked in for the night then, and see if we can thin out the gruel with more swamp water."

The Changriti girl led her scandalized visitor out of the habitat dome still chattering away at top speed, her banter disguising a formidable intellect.

Raemik tossed his head irritably, making the artful fringe of beads across his forehead rattle, another innovative fashion statement Nathan didn't much care for.

"What a conceited imbecile!" he sneered. "As if anyone could *not* know who you are?"

"I haven't been Nathan Crewe Nga'esha the troublemaking social reformer in a long time, Raemik. There are people whose world only consists of their own narrow specialty; the only Dr. N. C. Nga'esha they know is a research botanist. Which isn't too far wrong."

"I don't understand you, Nathan. You, of all people! Why do you still let women like her treat you that way?"

Nathan sat down behind what passed for his desk—several packing crates cobbled together—and tapped his reader with his forefinger meaningfully. "Because while that particular woman may indeed be an arrogant shit, she is also the most talented botanical student I've read all year. This is the best research facility on Vanar, and she knows it. So we've got a day and Aedwyn Changriti to convince her to stay. Laws are easier to change than minds, and neither happens overnight. But once she's here, she'll adjust, just as everyone else has. If she's not too major a prig, she may even learn to like it.

"And *you* had better remember you're my son as well as Nga'esha—you represent this research facility as much as I do. That sort of rudeness is not acceptable. I can always send you back to your Aunt Yronae should you need a refresher course in manners. Understood?"

"Sorry," Raemik muttered, subdued but unrepentant. Nathan shook his head, bemused. The lanky teenaged boy had long disappeared, the years filling out his body with adult muscularity. But underneath, he was still very much a child, his cockiness merely a veneer hiding the vulnerable insecurity underneath.

When Pratima returned briefly to Vanar, her son had obediently done his duty. She conceived twin girls immediately, her body instinctively weeding out the male sperm. It would take a dozen more years before Pratima's children would be born to the Worm, her newest sisters and infant Pilots. But once he had fulfilled his obligation, Raemik had waited with stoic resignation for the blade to fall on his neck, his distrust of women still unswayable.

Nathan's own reunion with Pratima had been strangely genial, her love for him undiminished, but his own tempered by fifteen years in the wait. He had caught her up on the family gossip, bragged endlessly about both his children, teased her about the difference in their ages, and made love with her with a sad tenderness while studiously ignoring her reason for being on Vanar. She'd returned to the Worm several weeks later, Raemik's twin daughters safely embedded in her womb. Pratima would never come back to him again, he knew; she had lived forever and would die young, her time in the Worm was running out. And when the temple had come to claim Raemik, the Pratha Yronae had politely sent them on their way empty-handed, as Pratima had promised her son, before a very relieved Raemik was sent back with his father to the haven of the Dravyam mountains.

Nathan picked up the snapshot of Aenanda from his desk and cradled it in his hands, smiling. "Besides, I think that's the same thing you said about Aedwyn when she first came, almost word for word, isn't it?"

Raemik flushed, the red accentuated by his pale skin. "That's different," he protested. "She's not like other women, not at all."

"Mm-hm." Nathan twisted the snapshot to make the sequence begin. Aenanda perched on top of a camel, grinning and waving merrily with the Sphinx in the background. Behind her, her petrified kharvah clutched her around the waist with the same stunned expression he wore in nearly every picture taken during their honeymoon. *Hi, Dad!* he could hear her tiny voice say just before the camel harrumphed and spat disgustingly and the sequence cut off her peal of laughter. He reactivated it to run it through the little performance again.

"Well, she's not," Raemik insisted sulkily. His carefully nurtured hatred of the female sex had been under severe strain since his hormones had taken a lively interest in the Changriti girl. "Anyway, are you staying here over the term break?"

Nathan grinned, replacing the snapshot on his desk. Raemik's change-of-subject ploy was far too obvious. "No, I'm seeing Kallah for a couple days. She's taking another kharvah, and asked if I'd be willing to participate in checking him out with Ukul."

Since Raetha Avachi had divorced her and was happily living with an ex-sahakharae he'd known since boyhood on a remote community farm in the Praetah province, Kallah had been deliberating whether or not to replace him. Kallah had had an uphill struggle as the Changriti pratha h'máy to salvage the prestige her mother had blackened. Disgraced and censored by the Assembly of Families, Eraelin Changriti had accepted temple exile, where she kept herself content with terrorizing hapless disciples, by all accounts. Her agent, Vasant Subah, had long vanished, the latest Qsayati a Hadatha Dhikar of impeccable reputation.

The man Kallah had selected seemed delighted with the proposal. A modestly ranked member of the Qarshatha Family, he was neither young nor handsome. But he was known to be a perceptive and resourceful diplomat, and even Nathan thought it would be a sensible arrangement. He'd decided to try talking Ukul into dispensing with the usual dancing and singing routine and go instead for the more yepoqioh tradition of them all getting stinking drunk together. Now that Ukul's nine-year-old daughter, Ornas, had been named Kallah's dalhitri and heir, the senior kharvah's perpetual gloom had relaxed considerably, making him much more serene these days.

"Do you want to come with me? I'm staying with Margasir after. His wife has offered me tickets to a performance at the East Suvamam Theater to show off their new students."

Raemik grimaced. "Would you mind if I didn't?" Traditional Vanar dance wasn't high on his list of exciting entertainment, competing with too many off-world novelties.

"No, of course not. I take it you and the gang are planning another seek-and-destroy expedition into the wilds of Dravyam? Is the lovely Aedwyn going as well?"

The young man's flush deepened, his transparency painful. "Amaliel is planning a party for his birthday. It's a surprise for his mother."

Nathan chuckled. "I'll bet. Happy birthday to poor l'amae Uzzael dva Seonae. You pay for what you break this time and don't look to me for the money." The ancient Vanar tradition of honoring mothers on their children's birthdays had lately degenerated into an excuse for general revelry and mayhem amongst the younger members of society. Amaliel was from a cheerful Middle Family used to the Dravyam Mountain Botanical Research Facilitys staff's locustlike invasions of their tranquility every off-term. Nathan couldn't help feeling his students were taking advantage of the family's obvious pleasure over their son's companionship with famous Nga'esha members. All Nathan really wanted was for Raemik finally to have a taste of long-overdue normal life, and was grateful to the Seonae for that. Any damage caused he knew he'd pay for, willingly if covertly.

"Pratha Yronae is coming end of the month to see exactly what she's been wasting Family money on, so that extension had better be finished before you go. I suggest you get those beads out of your eyes so you can see what you're doing, and get back to work."

Raemik ignored him, his attention diverted by the girl leaning into the doorway of the habitat dome.

"Dinner's on, Dr. Nga'esha," Aedwyn said, diligently ignoring Raemik. "You'd better come before there's nothing left."

"Thank you, Aedwyn. Is our guest still foaming at the mouth?"

The girl laughed. "She'll change her mind before the day's out, you wait and see."

Nathan raised an ironic eyebrow. "Our cuisine has made that much of an impression?" The food at the Research Facility was nutritious but not notable for its excellence.

"Never underestimate the power of a properly aimed challenge," Aedwyn said, mocking one of his own slogans. "Tell someone they can't do something, and they'll kill themselves to prove you wrong."

"Oh?" Raemik said innocently. "Bet you can't do this." With the supreme grace the genes he shared with his sister gave him, he did a lazy handstand, then balanced on one hand, the other patting his mouth in a mock yawn. Provoked, the girl aimed a kick at the boy's ankles, knocking him over before they both sprinted down the hill, competing with extravagant somersaults. Nathan watched them go, then shivered in the chill of early evening.

From the kitchens, he heard laughter lifted in the thin breeze. The sky over the Dravyam mountains was tinged a pale rose. A few migrant martins trilled faintly, far from their roosts in the distant city below, riding thermals in search of winged dinners of their own. As he shrugged into a worn padded jacket, he breathed in the smells and sounds, and knew he had succeeded in finding on Vanar something he had never known anywhere else in his life, something even stronger than love, more powerful than family.

"Home," he whispered. And smiled.

Acknowledgments

WRITING IS A SOLITARY OCCUPATION. BEING ABLE TO WRITE NEEDS THE support and love of special people. I'm more grateful than I can ever express to those who made this novel possible: my friend, grammarian and polyglot extraordinaire, Andrew Plant; my "cousin" Sue Wood; my friends in the south of France, Martine de Roulhac and Eric Noye; my agent, John Silbersack; my editor, Jaime Levine; my "girls," Caroline and Lynsey Spruce, and their mother, Sarah; true Geordie knight in shining armor, Jon Barron; and even though he couldn't care less, my best mate, Robinson the cat.

Born in Hartford, Connecticut, and subsequently bounced all over the United States and Europe, **Lee Wood** has worked as a long-haul truck driver, a surgical nurse, an insurance company secretary, a graphic artist, and in sundry other jack-of-all-trade jobs. Easily bored, she devotes her meager spare time to such activities as patchwork quilting, archaeological digs, reading bad French novels, writing medieval history research papers, and tending her medicinal and poisonous plant garden. She is currently single and no wonder.